BATTLE OF THE NEW ORLEANS

Some stories are best told when started in the middle or, at the very least, where the teller enters the story. Later, as a means of explanation, the storyteller may relate facts going back to earlier events that put things into perspective. So it shall be with this story, for I shall relate it to you as it happened to me.

My name, as given to me on Earth by my parents, is Thibodaux James Renwalt, though while growing up everyone just called me Tibby or Tib for short. Today most people throughout the Galactic Federation know me as Tibby the Recoverer or First Citizen Tibby. I'm sure there are a few other names that I'm called by those less enamored with my existence; however, those names seldom reach my ears. But I digress. You've asked to hear my story and so you shall.

Earth is a remote planet on the other side of the galaxy in a region not fully explored or colonized by the Federation. The dominant species of this planet is an intelligent humanoid life form that has existed for only a few thousand years. When I lived there in my youth, humans had developed enough technology to achieve the very beginning stages of space exploration; but manned space flight had progressed only as far as the moon that circled the planet.

I lived in a coastal region of the northern hemisphere that was known for its swamps and marshes and for a rather unique city named New Orleans. I grew up in a smaller town about 95 kilometers, or 7.5 dragmas in galactic units, outside of New Orleans. If you're familiar with the Halovids of the planet Irribis and have seen how the villagers capture food from the water using poles and lines with hooks on the ends, you will understand what on Earth was called *fishing*, though this particular practice was more a form of recreation than a way of life in my community.

My story begins on a day when I decided to go fishing.

The morning was warm and very muggy when I started out navigating the small aluminum fishing boat through the bayou. A bayou is what the local residents called a slow-moving stream that meanders through the marshes of that part of the planet. The region had been plagued by a drought condition for the preceding five years, leaving water levels throughout the wetlands lower than normal. In some places channels had dried up completely. Still, the swamp remained forested, shading me with large bald cypress and overcup oaks, species similar to those found on the planet Golsax that thrive in shallow waters of its subtropical regions. The drought had left some of these groves protruding from banks of rich, moist land; so, using a long wooden pole, I propelled my small boat through a remaining deeper channel that led to a somewhat circular clearing in the swamp referred to by the locals as *Mound Island*.

Mound Island was small, as islands go, and was a strange feature in this lush landscape, as no trees would grow on it. Some shorter grasses had periodically thrived on its barren surface, but even these had mostly died out in the hot, dry conditions. When I was a boy, some friends and I tried camping on the island, but we were unable to drive tent stakes deep enough into the ground to hold the tent down. There seemed to be a huge rock under the shallow soil that covered the island, which was peculiar in itself, as a swamp is essentially a delta of accumulated mud laid down by an ancient river basin – not the kind of place that normally hosts boulders.

Nevertheless, Mound Island had been there as long as anyone could remember, so no one really questioned what lay beneath the mysterious surface. My grandfather often took me there to fish as a small boy; and as I approached the bank, I remembered him telling me how the ancient indigenous people of the area were superstitious about the island, refusing to set foot on it. He said that, since nothing grew or lived on this island other than the sparse grasses, the natives felt it was cursed. It was true. For reasons I never really pondered the animals and birds that flourished in every other part the wetlands were never seen on the island mound. There even seemed to be fewer bugs and biting insects around the island than elsewhere in the swamp.

Despite all the oddities of Mound Island, I always enjoyed fishing from it and usually had good luck catching some rather large bass and catfish (these fish are native to the area's bayous and are delicious to eat). I pulled the nose of the boat onto the island to prevent it from drifting off and collected my gear to prepare for my day of fishing.

I had only taken a few steps when my foot slipped into a small hole that caught me at the ankle, causing me to fall face down onto the dried island mud. Spitting dust as I cursed and checked my gear, I scanned the featureless ground to see what could possibly have escaped my view and cause me to fall. Through the settling cloud of dust I was surprised to see in the dirt what appeared to be an old bronze or tarnished brass bowl with some sort of bar or rod sticking through it. My foot had slipped into the depression of the bowl and under the recessed bar and had been the cause of my fall.

I must confess that my reaction was a bit on the irrational side; I was angry at this stupid object that had caused my fall. My impulse was to grab the piece of trash and hurl it out into the swamp. Without any real thought I grabbed the bar and gave it a yank, thinking I would easily dislodge this annoyance from the dirt; and though the bar seemed to give a little, the bowl didn't budge at all. Now even angrier, I bent over and took hold of the bar with both hands, braced both feet and, with a deep, grunting breath, heaved with all my might.

What happened next is still confusing to me. I suddenly felt myself being pitched into the air in an uncontrollable spin, landing on my back onto the hard, encrusted ground. Stunned and breathless, I nearly blacked out waiting for the pain to ebb. I don't really know how long I laid motionless before mentally checking myself for injuries and talking myself into getting up to confront this opponent.

I struggled to turn onto my side. My head throbbed and alternating waves of red fading into darkness, then back to light, passed through my vision. I was still fighting for breath; the hard landing had knocked the wind out of me. Yet my mind continued to race, trying to comprehend what had happened. When my head cleared and my eyes began to focus, I found myself looking at a large, dark object protruding from the ground at my feet that had not been there before. It was somewhat oval in shape with traces of soil and grass clinging to it; and where it was bare, I could see that same dark bronze or brass color that I had noticed earlier when examining the bowl. Before long, my eyes came to rest on a smooth depression in this slab and I recognized the rod passing through it. Obviously what I had assumed to be some small bit of junk was part of this larger monolith at my feet.

At this point, I was able to move, though still with a good deal of pain. I sat up to take a closer look at this mysterious object that had obviously been responsible for my unintentional excursion into the air. Slowly I got to my feet and began to walk around to the other side when, to my amazement, I saw a gaping hole in the ground where the object had previously been lying flat. Clearly, the slab was some type of door or closure over this large space. I peered inside but couldn't comprehend what I was seeing. There appeared be a floor about twice my height at a distance below me. Everything inside seemed to be spotlessly clean and the escaping air had a dry, sterile scent that reminded me of the smell of a newly built house. A dim glow came from someplace within the illuminated interior, but nothing I was seeing made sense. The surface below me slanted away at an angle and I could see an edge where the floor appeared to drop off into a deeper area that I couldn't see from my vantage point. I took a closer look at the door. It measured about as thick as the distance between the tip of my thumb and my little finger with my fingers spread as far apart as possible. "About 20 centimeters thick," I thought to myself. I could see a tapered edge around its circumference to fit a corresponding contour where it closed against the surface of whatever it was attached to below my feet. There was no sound emanating from inside the hole at all. Other than the wafting cool, dry air, all was still.

I wondered what lay further inside and whether I should go for assistance or stay and investigate more on my own. I had about ten meters of rope in the boat that I used for docking. Curiosity prevailed and I decided to lower myself inside to get a better look before reporting my find to others. I retrieved the rope, but the barren mound offered no anchor other than the strange door itself. I first thought of the bar I was gripping earlier when the door was activated. I didn't trust to use that, given my unfriendly encounter with it thus far. Instead, I settled on securing the rope around the single hinge mechanism at what I assumed was the base of the door. After a bit of tying and testing of the knot and looking about, hoping I would see someone mysteriously appear to help me, I lowered myself inside.

When I entered the chamber, the dim glow within began to brighten, as though some kind of sensor was detecting my presence and adjusting the light level accordingly. As I descended, it became clear that what I thought was a floor below me was actually a wall and what I had assumed was a wall adjacent to me was in fact the floor. Whatever this structure was, it was lying more or less on its side and was buried deeply in the mud of the swamp. Mound Island had been around all my life. I knew from the stories my grandfather told that it had also been there all his life and during the lives of the generations of natives preceding him. Suspended in the middle of this surreal space, I tried to interpret my surroundings as if it were positioned upright. My mind filled with questions, "What is this place? Who built it? What kind of energy source was lighting the interior? Why can't I see any light fixtures?

I noted a small rectangle on the surface of the interior wall by the door, a panel illuminated with several small lights and what I thought might be buttons. With my usual impulsive curiosity, I reached out to press on the panel; but common sense took hold and I figured it would be safer not to touch anything else until I had a better idea of what might be activated.

I continued to lower myself by the rope until I was standing on what I now knew to be a wall. I carefully moved in the direction of the edge that I had previously thought was a drop off, now recognizing it as the receding corner of the wall. Peering past the edge, I saw the same diffuse light illuminating a corridor that dropped for a distance longer than my rope would allow me to investigate, so I turned my attention in the other direction. The corridor where I was standing didn't extend far before terminating at what I thought might be an interior door. Another small rectangular panel adjacent to this door glowed with a faint, pale green jade color. Without thinking, I touched the panel, which responded immediately by retracting the door into the wall, starling me, as a large room that extended below me was revealed.   A series of three high-back chairs were mounted to the floor in front what I thought might be a control console of some sort.   Just behind those chairs and staggered between them were two more chairs.   The wall in front of the console seemed to be made of a different material than that of the other walls, though it was the same dark color as the rest of the room.   The console, however, was illuminated with numerous lights, two of which were flashing – one amber and one red.   Several smaller screens built in the console appeared to be displaying images; however, my vantage point and the distorted, sideways view prevented me from discerning what was displayed.

As I leaned inside and tried to contort myself to get an "upright" view of the nearest screen, I lost my grip on the doorframe and tumbled into the room.

In mid fall I managed to grab onto the back of one of the mounted chairs.   There I hung for a few moments, trying to ignore my aching ribs as I sorted out how to pull myself up and sit on the arm of the chair.   Once situated, I looked up at the entrance to assess what kind of challenge I was facing to climb my way back out, only to see the door silently slide shut.   I could almost feel my pupils flare with panic as I realized that, even if the door had *not* closed, I had no way of getting near enough to it to get back out. Now calling out for help in hopes of another fisherman hearing me was out of the question.

Cursing my stupidity, I looked about the room for some solution to my quandary.   Carefully, I climbed to a chair much closer to the console, where I could make out the details that were scrolling across the smaller monitors.   To my further amazement, *nothing* was recognizable.   Cryptic figures and shapes moved along some of the screens and on others the images were stationary. Not one of them was like anything I had ever seen before. Some of the symbols vaguely resembled Japanese characters, while others were more like hieroglyphics. On the screen next to the blinking red light, which I could now recognize as a button, figures flashed on and off like some kind of prompt. Adjacent to it was the blinking amber light and yet another screen, on which an equally obscure set of figures flashed. I deliberated for what seemed like an hour, trying to figure a way out of this mess – even moving back to the uppermost chair to reassess my distance from the door; but I could find no escape. For all practical purposes, I was trapped here until someone else happened upon my strange Mound Island discovery and investigated – hopefully, with more caution than I had. "That could be weeks, or even months," I thought, "By then I'll have died from starvation!"

Instinctually, moving about seemed an easier way to cope with the futility of the situation than sitting still; so I maneuvered back to the center chair and, with all the ignorance of a small child pushing buttons in an elevator to see what happens next, I braced against my precarious perch, reached out and pressed the flashing red button.

Other than the feeling of a slight pressure change that made my ears pop, I didn't notice any significant changes, though the red flashing light stopped and the display on the small screen beside it responded with a new set of characters. Thus emboldened (since nothing had exploded, nor had any poisonous gas flooded the room), I pressed the flashing amber button.

Immediately, lights throughout the room flickered into action and everything began to shake. At first I thought the place was falling apart and caving in; but as my bearings shifted, I understood that the room was in motion, slowly rotating and righting itself to position the floor beneath me.

I recognized that this might be my only chance for escape; so, as soon the floor reached an orientation where I could get a stable footing, I moved quickly toward the doorway, until I was stopped in my tracks by the commanding sound of a male voice that came out of nowhere in a language I didn't understand. Bewildered, I looked every direction within the shifting, rumbling room, searching for the source of this voice, which then repeated with the same tone and inflection whatever it had said moments earlier.

Suddenly the room seemed to lurch. After a brief pause, I was propelled at incredible speed toward the wall near the exit, and then all went black.

The next thing I remembered was feeling like my head was full of buzzing bees. Images of daily life seemed to whir randomly about me, until the realization of pain grounded me again in the moment. When I finally opened my eyes, I didn't know straightaway where I was or what had happened; but slowly my surroundings came into focus and I recalled my topple into the control room and everything that unfolded after pressing that *damned* flashing amber button. At first I thought the floor had again tilted into wall position, until I realized that it was *my* position that had changed – I was lying on the floor.

Once more, I raised myself up with a groan. This time the floor was the floor and the walls were walls. Everything seemed to be oriented correctly, except possibly me, as I was in a great deal of pain and quite unstable on my feet. While I tried to sort out the events that that occurred before I blacked out, my eye caught view of the wall behind the console. What had been a large dark panel that ran the full width of the room now appeared to be a viewing monitor lit up by what I *really hoped* were not passing stars. But the denial didn't last long; it quickly became clear that they most certainly were. Periodically, colored lines appeared on the screen that connected various stars in angular paths and geometric patterns, arguably forming navigational triangulations and calculations. After a short time, I had no choice but to accept that I was no longer on Earth, but in an inconceivably advanced spacecraft going someplace I could not fathom at speeds which I had been taught were impossible. From time to time, the male voice would speak, announcing what I could only assume were prompts or perhaps navigational details; but there was no one around to hear them other than me, at least to my knowledge.

I scanned the expanse of the control room and spotted a second door at the opposite end of the wall where I had entered. Supporting myself against the wall, I limped my way toward it and touched the green pad. As expected, the door glided open, revealing another long corridor similar to the ones I had seen when "boarding" what I now understood to be some sort of craft.

I passed through a short distance of the corridor and came to an intersection with the end of a narrower passageway that seemed to extend across the width of the ship's interior and connect with what I deduced would be the corridor where I had begun this adventure. Halfway across this passageway I noted a door on one side and a connecting corridor on the other that extended to the right.

The periodic announcements continued to be broadcast throughout the ship as I explored further, finding what I guessed to be a galley with a table and seating for about six people; two cabin spaces, obviously meant for one person each; and third cabin designed to provide four people with sleeping spaces and seating around a table, all of which were secured to the floor. Like those mounted in the control room, these were cushioned, high-back swivel chairs, though some appeared to be locked in position by a means I didn't yet understand. I sat in one, wondering what it was made of, as there were no visible seams in the covering. The material felt like soft leather and the cushions seemed to conform mechanically to my body's contours just enough to be comfortable, while still providing firm support. I noted that the armrests of each chair were equipped with the now familiar panels of colored lights and buttons. To be sure, I kept my hands clear of them, not wanting to repeat the consequences of my earlier curiosity where buttons were concerned. Past the quarters I found something I couldn't easily identify, but I had a hunch it might be a secured airlock, as there was a window installed in it that allowed me to see into the chamber. Inside were suits and helmets. "Space suits," I imagined.

Opposite the airlock was a small room that contained the biggest surprise so far since boarding the craft.

As I entered this room, I was greeted by a long, white surface that bore resemblance to an examination table – and a mummified body that was strapped to it.

The shock of this find wasn't terribly great and didn't last very long. It made sense, really, that since I had not yet encountered anyone aboard the ship and that given the length of time it apparently had been buried in the swamp, whoever had been on the ship originally would by now be dead.

As far as injuries were concerned, this individual didn't appear to have spent his last days feeling very well. There was a line of tubing extending from a compartment on the wall that connected to the mummy like an IV and other instruments attached to mechanical arms that projected out over the corpse. I was surprised that there was no smell of death in the room. While attending college I had worked part time at a museum, where my duties included cleaning the display cases that held mummified bodies. Though the odor of a mummified body is not as bad as that of a rotting corpse, there is still a definite smell of death that lingers even after centuries. These remains seemed to have none of that odor and, for a moment, I questioned whether it was a real body at all. Though the corpse was desiccated, it was not rotted away or decayed in any way and the skin maintained a flesh-like color. On one of his hands there appeared to be a mottled wound; other than that, the body appeared to be unharmed. Clearly, this room was an infirmary and the patient on the table had died before completion of a procedure of some kind. As I continued my self-guided tour, I wondered what had happened to him – and for that matter, what had happened to the rest of the crew.

Between the infirmary and the airlock there was another door leading to what I now guessed was the back of the ship. When I activated the door, it opened into the largest space I had seen so far. I was looking into an enormous cargo hold, but the only thing I saw stored in it was a container big enough to cram in perhaps eight people. The encasement looked like a ceramic-type material and the lid, made of the same material, was fitted with what appeared to be an electronic seal and locking mechanism. The whole assembly was loaded onto the front of a machine which, I gathered from its appearance, was used for moving cargo about the space. The rest of the hold was empty and featureless, with the exception of a large door or hatch on the far wall, obviously meant for loading and unloading cargo, and a smaller door on the opposite wall leading into what I could only guess from its configuration was the engine room. A second doorway at the forward end of the engine room (moving back in the direction of the front of the ship) opened into a storage area that contained a small variety of supplies. Again, at the front of that room was another doorway that brought me back into the corridor near the control room where I had first entered the ship.

Having explored what I was now relatively sure was the extent of the craft; I returned to the control room and plopped down in the center chair. It was obvious that, except for the mummified body in the infirmary, I was the only one on board. What had happened to the rest of the crew? Had they died? Abandoned ship? Where did the ship come from? How long had it been lodged the mud in the swamp, and why was it there to begin with? My mind was plagued with such questions, as I also pondered whether I was ever going to get back home or how would I accomplish that little challenge. The craft obviously originated from some place other than Earth and, if the display on the screen was correct, the ship was traveling in excess of light speed which, according to the best scientific understanding on Earth was impossible. But then, I thought to myself, many things that were believed in the past to be impossible turned out to be quite achievable, once science caught up enough to prove them so.

As I sat facing the giant display of passing starlight, probing my sore ribs and head, I found myself simultaneously surrendering to the unknowns that faced me and to the exhaustion that had overtaken the excitement of the day. "Day," I thought, "I wonder if that word is ever going to mean the same thing to me again."

I began to drift into sleep every few minutes, only to be roused by the intervals of broadcasts that I surmised were providing data and status reports. The male voice was also repeating a short phrase that started when I seated myself in this central chair, which I found myself thinking of as the captain's chair. This new phrase seemed to be expressed as a question. In my exhausted state the repetitive interruptions became agitating; and I eventually blurted out, "Will you please *shut up*!"

This outburst was met by a momentary silence; followed by, "Mar goomie deluzkie mebulea?"

I had no idea what the hell that meant; and I responded with further exasperation, "Yeah right! Just my luck, I'm gonna die listening to this crap."

The voice responded with something a bit longer that again sounded like a question. I replied, "I can't understand a damned thing you're saying and I'll bet you can't understand me either, so why don't you just *shut up*!"

A few more moments of silence followed before a portion of the star-filled screen before me opened up another display, within which a human figure appeared and began speaking! I leapt to my feet with a jolt of excitement at the welcome sight, because I first thought it was a real person on the other end of some kind of telecommunication system. When I tried to initiate a dialogue, however, it became obvious that I was seeing a recorded video message.

I sank back into the chair with disappointment, just more gibberish in some sort of instructional video that directed the proper positioning and activation of what looked like a headband-like apparatus. The video was of short duration, showing an ordinary-looking man who walked to an enclosure in a wall to retrieve the headband, place it on his head in a specific arrangement, and then press a sequence of buttons mounted on the side of the band. The instructor repeated a series of words for about a minute then took the headgear off and placed it back in the enclosure. He then seemed to turn directly toward me, as if speaking to me specifically, and said something, which, again, I didn't understand.

After a short pause, the recording began to replay from the beginning.

Largely ignoring the recording, I absent-mindedly pressed one of the armchair buttons, which triggered the chair to tilt back gently into a more relaxed position.   I allowed myself to recline, discovering that there were also small screens on the ceiling above each chair that I had not seen before. The few that weren't blank displayed more characters that I couldn't decipher. I pressed the button on the armrest again and the chair returned to its original position.

I kept wondering what all of these displays meant, where the ship was going and what was guiding it. Based on the movement I saw on the screen and the sequential appearance of lines connecting the stars, there was a definite course in mind, but who or what was navigating was unknown, at least to me. When I pressed that amber flashing button, I must have somehow activated an automatic pilot that was responsible for the ship's launch and my painful introduction to the back wall. No doubt, the voice had at that time tried to warn me to be securely seated.

If pressing that button had launched the ship into space, would pressing it again take me back? It was a long shot and I knew it, but I decided to try it anyway. Making sure this time that I was seated in the captain's chair, I extended my arm to the button I had pressed before, only now it was glowing a constant blue. I pressed... and I waited.

Nothing happened. The stars kept whizzing by at the same rate as before and the ship seemed to be going in the same direction. Meanwhile, the headgear instructional video in the smaller window had repeated for about the thirtieth time.

I was getting hungry and thought perhaps there was chance that something still edible might be stored in the galley and, for that matter, something to drink. Looking at my watch I realized that it had been seven and a half hours since I had entered the ship. I must have been unconscious for some time after smashing into the wall.

"I suppose it's better to get up and look for food and water than just sit here and wait to die," I said to myself. I returned to what I believed to be the galley and began to poke around. While most of the fixtures were unusual, I thought that I might figure out what they were if I exercised some imagination. A cubic opening was positioned in the wall near a column of buttons, each of which was accompanied by what looked like a description in the alien writing that I guessed might be food selections. Next to that was a similar but smaller opening with fewer buttons and descriptions, which I hoped might be beverage selections. I was at least going to give it a try.

I took a deep breath, stood clear of the opening, and pressed the first selection on the larger of the two fixtures. I heard a whirring sound, followed by a series of buzzing pitches, a moment of silence, and then another whirring sound, after which a small steaming container slid out of the side of the opening. I started to pick it up by the sides, but it was too hot. I found the two handle-like extensions at the top of the container to be room temperature, so I carefully moved the container to the table and focused next on what I was now somewhat more certain would be the drink dispenser. With a bit less caution, I pushed the first button. This time I watched what transpired. Almost instantly, a transparent, sealed container appeared that held what I expected to be water. I took it to the table and had a seat, wondering how I was going to get the liquid out, when I noticed a small nub like protrusion on the edge. I shook my head in disbelief; surely I was not expected to drink from a sippy cup...? "Oh, what the heck," I thought, and a placed edge to my mouth, not really expecting anything. To my surprise, water entered my mouth – and good tasting water, at that. I stared at the container a moment, trying to see where the water was exiting this strange glass, and then took another sip.

The food looked like mixture of something like rice and lentils with some larger pieces of what may have been vegetables or meat. I was fiercely hungry, so I didn't much care how it tasted; but it certainly smelled good. It was then that I realized I had no eating utensils. I glanced about but saw nothing resembling a spoon or fork. On one wall of the galley area I noted several outlines that resembled cabinet doors, but I had no idea how to open them. Tentatively, I pressed on one and it popped open, not unlike handleless latches and releases back on Earth. Inside I found a number of strange objects and containers, the functions of which I could not identify. I checked several more cabinets with the same results before thinking logically that eating utensils would likely be next to the food dispensers. Upon closer examination of the dispensing area, I located a much smaller, almost drawer-sized outline. The mechanism slowly opened a sliding panel, revealing several utensil-like items – some that looked like chopsticks, others that looked more like square spoons, and a two-tined spear-like object that resembled a fork. The last item was clearly a knife, though the handle was a bit odd.

I had always been a fan of eating with chopsticks, so without much thought I selected a pair from the drawer and returned to sample the food. I was surprised at the richness of flavor. I found the dish to be a bit spicy – not that it bothered me a lot, but I have never been that big a fan of spicy food. Aside from that, it wasn't a bad dish and it seemed to satisfy my need to eat.

Then I realized that I was sooner or later going to need a toilet facility – probably sooner, as I had now been traveling on this ship for several hours. I didn't recall seeing one on my earlier tour of the ship, so I thought I'd better not wait long to solve that particular problem. I had no idea what to do with the dishes and chopsticks, so I left them on the table.

Oddly, I found the facilities right between the control room and the quarters area on the other side of the wall where I stood when I first descended into the ship. I was rather surprised to find both the toilet area and what I assumed to be showers in a common location. One partial wall was a full-length mirror, which I found a bit unnerving. The two motion-activated lavatory basins operated a bit differently from what I expected. Unlike the basins on Earth that generally poured water onto the hands from a spout, these sprayed the water up onto the hands from a raised portion in the center of the bowl, and the dirty water ran down the perimeter and into a drain. A few seconds of soapy solution was automatically followed by clean water for rinsing. I wondered how I was supposed to brush my teeth, but that came much later. The toilet was something else altogether and it took me a few minutes to figure it out. It wasn't the conventional bowl arrangement that I recognized, nor was it the recessed in-the-floor contraption like those used by some societies on Earth. Instead, it was a sort of reclining contrivance that, frankly, I'm at a loss to describe. Fortunately though, I managed to figure it out and the waste disappeared afterward, so I assumed I did it right.

Upon leaving the facilities, I decided to take a closer look at the crew quarters and infirmary. The two cabins that appeared to be for single individuals were more or less the same; both were furnished with a single bed that was a bit larger than those in the four-person quarters. I was surprised that these rooms weren't equipped with private toilets and showers; apparently everyone was expected to use the one facility. I assumed these individual cabins were meant for officers. Similar to that in the galley, the walls of all the quarters contained cabinetry that opened to reveal shelves, this time containing clothing items in one area, blankets and bedding in another, and what I imagined to be personal items in yet another. All of the quarters were equipped with a viewing screen, all repeating the same headgear instructional video again and again. I hoped I was not going to have to listen to this thing until the ship got to wherever it was going – or until I died, whichever came first.

I stepped back into the infirmary and once again examined the mummified body. It looked like a typical human male with maybe a two to three-day beard growth on the shriveled, dry face. The body was covered in a one-piece jumpsuit or coveralls that appeared to be quite dirty and stained and not at all like the clothing I had discovered in the quarters. Even the cut and type of textile was different. Something about this individual lead me to believe that he had not actually been part of the crew; but if he wasn't, why was he here and where was the *real* crew?

I again scanned the walls for cabinetry when I recognized a unique compartment door with a keypad panel beside it. It seemed curiously familiar. Then, in a sudden moment of recognition, I crossed the hall back to quarters where the video was now playing for about the hundredth time. I watched intently as the instructor retrieved the headband from a similar wall compartment. With a sense that I had discovered something important, I returned to open the infirmary compartment and was not surprised to see a headband identical to the one in the video. Could it be that I was expected to place this object on my head? Was the message playing on the screen intended specifically for *me*? It seemed to be too much to believe, yet there had to be a purpose for the video. With some degree of apprehension, I retrieved the headband, placed it on my head and pressed the sequence of buttons, as I had seen on the video more times than I cared to count.

Within moments I became lightheaded. The sensation escalated until I felt as though the entire universe was speaking to me at once in different voices and languages. This sensation gave way to what seemed to be some fantastic dreams running in fast play. Everything sped along so rapidly that I couldn't focus or keep up with it all; and at some point I fell asleep.

When I awoke, I found myself reclined in the control room captain's chair, though I had no memory of leaving the infirmary. My head ached. Traces of voices still rang inside my head. Out of habit, I glanced at my watch and was shocked to find that several hours had passed since entering the infirmary. As I lifted my head and glanced at the control panel in front of me, I was amazed to discover that I now understood the figures and symbols flashing and scrolling across the small screens. These were status reports – details as to conditions inside and outside of the ship and information about the journey – speed, location and special coordinates. While I was absorbing the data and trying to adjust to this unexpected development, the male voice spoke to me.

"You should be able to understand me now. Please respond affirmatively in Federation galactic language."

For the briefest moment I thought, *"How am I to respond in a language I don't know,"* when it occurred to me that what I had just heard was not in English. Just as quickly, I realized that I *did* know what to respond; so, in the Federation galactic language I replied, "Yes, I understand you."

The voice continued. "This ship is equipped with a standard Federation educational headband which, upon proper application, has provided you with a thorough understanding of our language so that effective communication can occur henceforward."

"Who are you?" I asked.

"I am the ship." the voice responded.

"Are you sentient?"

"No. I am designed to perform extrapolations based on available and observable data, from which I make decisions and execute actions according to programmed command patterns."

I didn't have to think long before saying, "I command you to take me back to where you found me!" I said.

"I am unable to comply with your command."

"Why?" I asked with some angst.

"I am programmed to perform a principal command that supersedes all other commands until completed."

"What is this *principal command*?"

"That information is restricted."

I thought for a moment. "Can you tell me where we're going?" I pressed.

"That information is restricted."

"Can you tell me how long the journey will be?"

"Eight hundred, twenty-two hours and twenty-six minutes at our current speed," was the response.

The response was, of course, not actually in Earth hours and minutes, rather I understood this to be the equivalent duration. *How* I knew this I could only attribute to whatever this headband had done to my brain, thought I did have to do some mental calculations using my newly acquired information.   As I sat there contemplating the situation, I realized that I could perhaps get some information from the ship that might explain what was going on.

"How did you happen to be in the swamp back on Earth?"

"What is *Earth*?"

"Earth is the planet where I found you."

"This ship was taken illegally and flown to Earth, where it landed in the place you call *swamp*."

"How long have you been in the swamp?"

"This ship was located on Earth for 4,563,983 hours, 42 minutes and 38 seconds."

"Holy shit," I thought, making a rough calculation in my head, "that's over 500 years." In that amount of time the ship would certainly have sunk into the mud. It must have settled unevenly over time, which would account for the ship's sideways position.

"Is the corpse of the person in the infirmary one of the people who took you illegally?"

"The body is that of the man who illegally appropriated me."

"What happened to the others?"

"There were no others. He was the only one."

"Why did he take you?"

"He needed me to undertake his escape."

"Escape?! Escape from what?" I asked with confusion.

"That information is restricted."

"Can you tell me what happened to the man that stole you?"

"Yes. He died."

"Well, yes, *that* is rather obvious," I said with lost sarcasm. "Can you tell me what *caused* his death?"

"He died from a toxic substance injected into his bloodstream by way of a bite from a creature of your planet Earth."

"Really? Which creature?" I asked in a somewhat incredulous tone.

"I do not have that information. I was unable to observe the event. When he returned from his excursion he had already been bitten. My analysis of his blood indicated the bite was venomous and the poison was a variety of neurotoxin that did not exist in my database."

I remembered studying poisonous snakes in the coastal swamps of the United States (the region of Earth where I am from), and only one of those delivered a venom that was primarily classified as neurotoxin – the coral snake. The others were variations of protein digestive venoms that necrotize the tissues. But people didn't normally die from coral snakes bites if treated with the antivenin. For some reason, though, this man had not survived.

One thing bothered me, so I thought I would ask – though I didn't think I would get an answer.

"When you concluded that I didn't understand your language, you showed me the video, believing I would find the headband and use it, correct?"

"That is correct," replied the ship. "In the event the crew is incapacitated or killed, leaving no pilot, and I am discovered by someone unable to understand the Federation galactic language or any language in my database, I am programmed to repeat the instructional video on all available screens until the individual finds and applies the headband." Indeed, the instructional video had since disappeared from the screen.

"Why didn't you do that when I first entered the ship?"

"Communication functions had been disabled by the thief. Only the basic maintenance functions were still active. When you pressed the amber indicator on the console, communication capabilities and controls were restored, making it possible to not only communicate with you, but also to carry out my prime directive."

This last bit made me laugh, as it reminded me of an entertainment program that was performed on Earth television called Star Trek.

"Prime directive," I chuckled to myself, as I summarized these already inconceivable circumstances to myself out loud. "I'm talking to a ship by way of an electronic hippy headband as I fly through outer space to an unknown destination… and now I learn the ship has a *prime directive*."

"What is *hippy*?"

"Nevermind," I murmured, rubbing my head with exasperation. "So, this *prime directive* is the same as the *principal command* that prevents you from taking me home?"

"Essentially, yes. The principal command refers to the executed actions that result in fulfillment of the prime directive. Shall I explain further?"

"NO!"

This rather dry conversation was going nowhere. The ship had already said it would not tell me the *prime directive*, so I didn't bother pressing for details about the related *principal command*. I had little or no choice in any of what was unfolding, and wouldn't, until the ship completed its mission – whatever it was. Obviously it required going somewhere specific, but the *who*, *where* and *why* would remain unknown until the ship arrived. Mulling over all of this in my mind generated another question.

"So what happens if you are unable to complete your prime directive? What if your destination no longer exists?"

"There are contingencies. A secondary destination is programmed in case of an emergency."

"But all of that was over 500 years ago," I exclaimed. "Those who programmed you are long dead and the civilization that created you may not even exist anymore."

"Such a contingency has not been included in my program."

"Well," I waited for more clarification, "what happens in that case?"

"Under my prime directive I would be required to search for any remnant of the civilization that created me and report to their authorities."

"And what would happen to *me* in that case?" The ship did not reply.

This largely fruitless conversation had come to its natural end. At this point I was becoming rather tired, so I tilted the captain's chair into a more relaxed position and almost immediately fell into a deep sleep. I dreamed of finding the ship in the swamp, a flying saucer, and when I boarded, the body in the infirmary came to life and told me I was being held for ransom. In the dream I was imprisoned in a cage in the cargo hold, while the over the ship's communication system the song *Blue Moon* played repeatedly.

When I awoke, every moving part of my body was sore from the body slams and falls of what I assumed qualified as the "day" before. I decided that it was time for me to try out the shower. I asked my "host" if it was possible to display instructions on the use of the shower; and to my delight, it did so with no hesitation. The instructions included explanations of functions for all other items in the bath area as well, including a bladeless depilatory device for shaving that was rather amazing and effective, though I hadn't a clue how it removed the hair or where it went afterward. I also asked for instructions regarding toiletries –

specifically, deodorant – but the ship didn't seem to understand the request and only commented that perspiration odor was not an issue while onboard. While I did not understand it, I had noticed that I didn't seem to be producing any perspiration odor, in spite of not having showered for some time. As far as cleaning ones teeth, in place of a toothbrush was a device similar to the *Water Pik* used on Earth. This small handheld device was attached to the wall and dispensed fine stream of water containing antiseptic to spray across the teeth and gums. When finished with the device, it was to be placed into a small recess in the wall, where it was sanitized for the next user.

The shower itself was rather unusual. I anticipated that it would perhaps be something like the lavatory sinks, dispensing a soapy wash first, followed by a rinse. Even my host found this to be a logical extrapolation from my earlier investigations. However, the spouts first emitted something like a thick fog that coated my body and head with a film scented somewhat like a floral and mint combination. After the fog, there were a few moments of mild tingling, described in the video as being something akin to ultrasonic cleaning; only there was some other element involved that I didn't understand. Finally, I was rinsed with a fine mist of pure water. The entire process only lasted about three minutes, after which streams of warm, dry air played over my body, drying it in seconds. I was surprised that such a short process left me feeling cleaner than any bath I'd ever taken at home. The ultrasonic treatment seemed to relax and soothe my sore muscles as well.

I had asked the ship earlier how I would go about cleaning my clothing; so, as instructed, I placed everything, including my shoes, inside a small compartment in one of the crew quarters before showering. I was told to wait until the light on the door changed from orange to green before removing them. By the time I was finished with my quick shower, the green indicator was already lit and the laundry was finished. The clothes and shoes were spotless, without any scent of detergent or cleaning agent – not a stain, smudge, or odor to be found, surprisingly (and pleasantly so), not even on my shoes.

Feeling fresh and revived, I went to the galley for some breakfast. Though I could now read the labels adjacent to the food and drink dispensers, I still didn't understand what any of the items were. There was nothing equivalent to "bacon and eggs" or "hamburger" and the only drink labeled on the drink dispenser that I could understand was "water" which, luckily, was the first button, the one I had selected the day before.

I realized that the only way I would ever come to understand what dishes were would be to try them; so I moved to the next selection on each machine and was rewarded with a beverage that reminded me of a light mango or kiwi juice and another variation of noodle dish containing a something like a vegetable or meat mixture. Whatever it was, it tasted incredibly good and I was tempted to have a second bowl.

While I ate, I asked the ship to clarify other functions in the galley. I was instructed as to the use of a recycling repository for dishes, utensils and any remaining waste food. Apparently the ship recycled *everything*. Even dishes and utensils were broken down to base components and reformed to make new bowls and utensils after each meal. Protein and organic materials gathered from throughout the ship were processed with some sort of molecular converter and reshaped into the food selections in the dispensary. I wasn't too keen on the idea of investigating what those organic material sources might be; but I resolved to think of it as being no different from Earth practices where organic materials are processed to manufacture fertilizer for crops or feed for livestock. So I simply pushed the thought from my mind and was satisfied to understand that everything on the ship was recycled – water, waste, organic and inorganic materials – and that the ship was essentially self-sufficient and equipped to perform practically indefinitely in this way.

I was a bit more curious and, to be honest, somewhat worried while out in that expanse of space, as to whether the ship's source of power was sufficient to get the ship to its destination. Perhaps it was even degraded after the long hiatus in the swamp. This nagging concern prompted me to inquire about the ship's fuel and the rate of power consumption. I gave the question some thought before asking, hoping that some careful wording and a commanding air in my voice might solicit an answer that would give me further clues as to the nature of the prime directive.

"Is there any risk that your power source may have become depleted or contaminated during the long period of inactivity in the swamp? I haven't seen any fuel stores anywhere on the ship. Perhaps you should tell me where to find them so I can complete a visual inspection."

I received the standard reply. "That information is restricted."

I was starting to feel rather troubled about the ship and its mission. At one point I asked about its ownership and was told that it belonged to the Galactic Federation; but when I asked the names of the captain and crew, I was again told, "That information is restricted." I began to wonder just what sort of classified mission was underway when the ship was stolen. When I asked whether the ship was armed with defensive weapons, the response was "Yes," but when I asked what *type* of defenses, I was again told, "That information is restricted." My inquiries regarding offensive weapons were met with like answers.

I was curious about the devices on the console in the control room, which I now thought of as the bridge instead, so I asked the ship about them. The ship was most cooperative in explaining all of the displays and controls, except for those relating to the weapons system; but when I boldly tried to manipulate some of the controls, I discovered that they were inoperative. When I asked this about this, I was told that all functions were locked, until such time when the ship had completed its prime directive.

"Then how was the ship stolen by the man in the infirmary?" I wondered out loud, only to be told "That information is restricted." The ship did, however, agree to set up simulations for flying the ship, teaching me the basics of control and course plotting. For all the busy displays and buttons on the console, the ship was actually very easy to maneuver; however, from what I could tell it was rarely flown manually. Primary navigation was by verbal instructions given to the ship's computer, and it essentially flew itself.

I thought to ask the ship what should be done with the body in the infirmary, since I didn't think it appropriate for the remains to just lay there. I was told that the body would be taken care of when its primary directive had been completed and that it should be left as it was "for evidentiary purposes;" but the ship would not elaborate further when probed.

It occurred to me that, since I had re-activated the ship's communication and operating systems, the ship should be able to attempt contact with the government that it claimed was its owner. I expressed this to the ship, asking if it had done so. Apparently, though faster-than-light travel had been developed, a faster-than-light communication system had not.   Communication over distances was achieved by way of drones deployed to carry messages to a general location and then broadcast them to the intended recipient until acknowledgement was received.   Even with this technology, weeks could pass before getting a message to more distant locations.   The ship said that, while it was able to pick up communication signals from the Federation's nearest planets during its time on Earth, the messages had originated hundreds of years earlier.   Until the ship came within the solar system of a given planet, any meaningful two-way communication was impractical.   I found this to be a strange obstacle.   In all the science fiction books or movies I had known, communication never seemed to be problematic.   I suppose it was somehow assumed that, if faster-than-light drives or warp drives were invented, then the space-time problem would automatically resolve itself as far as communication was concerned.

I found the ship to be very helpful and cooperative with anything I asked, as long as it didn't conflict with its prime directive (whatever that was).   Eventually, though I had my wristwatch for reference, I lost my sense of time.   I realized at one point that I didn't know if it was 2:36 in the afternoon or 2:36 in the morning.   My watch was an old analogue timepiece with a self-winding mechanism that had belonged to my grandfather.   It didn't have any of the fancy features of the newer watches of my generation.   I had always expressed my fondness for that watch and, when my grandfather died, my grandmother insisted that I have it.   Now, however, the concept of a watch seemed rather silly, since it was highly unlikely that any planet I encountered would have exactly the same 24-hour days and 365-day years.   I had no real sense as to how long I had been on the ship or even how long I had been unconscious or sleeping.   What had seemed a few passing minutes to me may actually have been hours or even a day or more.   So I asked the ship how long I had been onboard, only to get an insane answer in minutes and seconds as defined by the Galactic Federation. While it was possible for me to translate these numbers into units of Earth time using the information implanted in my brain from the headband, I found it frustrating to have to do so. I was able to instruct the ship to automatically translate the time into Earth units, after first explaining these units as they related to Galactic time. From then on I was able to ask the ship exactly how much time had elapsed since I had come aboard. I must say that I was surprised to discover on my initial inquiry that I had been aboard the ship 14 days, 13 hours, 45 minutes and 12 seconds Earth time, according to my host.

It was two days later when the ship announced that it had contacted a nearby Galactic Federation military airship and that I would shortly be receiving company from its representatives.

I'm not sure who or what I expected for an introduction, but it certainly did not turn out to be a scenario that I could have anticipated. The first thing I saw looked like a swarm of wasps approaching the screen – maybe 30 to 50 of them – smaller vessels that surrounded the ship in seconds on all sides. A few minutes later, three additional groups of ships, equal in size and quantity, joined in a similar configuration, after which all moved en masse into a tight formation around my position. Upon closer view, I could see these craft were not wasp-like at all; rather their shapes more closely resembled the first generation stealth bombers of Earth, only with blended curves.

I was starting to get very nervous about all of this, when suddenly a second viewing window opened on the ships screen, inside of which the image of a man wearing a Kelly green uniform appeared. From the expression on his face I assumed that he could see me and my surroundings inside the bridge, as well.

"Congratulations on your recovery of the *TRITYTE*," he began. "I trust the cargo it still intact?"

This initial communication did not match what was beginning to feel like a military interception. I was still processing *Congratulations* and *TRITYTE* (probably with my mouth agape), when he cleared his throat and collected himself. "My deepest apologies for my lack of courtesy, sir. I'm Captain Maxette of the Federation starship *DUSTEN*. And who might you be?"

In my insolent nature I wanted to say, "I might be the Easter Bunny," but on second thought, I figured this was not the time to be funny – besides the fact that the reference would surely have been lost. "I'm Thibodaux Renwalt, but you can just call me Tibby. Everyone else does."

"Well congratulations again, Tibby! But, uhh, the cargo *is* intact, yes?" he asked again with some trepidation.

"Sir," I began, "to be honest, I am not really sure, as I have no idea what *the cargo* might be. My discovery of this ship was quite accidental; and, actually I have more or less been a captive on this craft. I seem to have unintentionally activated some primary directive program that has taken over navigation and I have been trapped in the ship ever since."

There was a momentary pause as the captain hesitated, looking dumbfounded by my comment. He turned to a man standing at a console behind him (I presumed another officer), who looked equally befuddled. The captain turned back to face me. "You are from what planet?"

"Earth."

Again, the confusion was apparent on his face. He turned to the officer, who now seemed to be looking manically through data on a screen. After a brief pause, the officer announced to the captain, "Sir, the data banks have no reference for a planet by that name. Tibby, please allow us a few moments to access *TRITYTE*'s guidance program to ascertain the origin of your journey."

Several moments passed as a number of lights on the console flashed and blinked and several of the smaller screens on the console displayed bits of data that scrolled across the screens so rapidly that I could not follow any of it. After a brief period, the displays stopped and the officer spoke to the captain. "Sir, apparently Earth is a planet quite some distance outside the Federation territory in one of the unexplored areas."

Captain Maxette's confusion appeared to give way to something more like curiosity. "Tibby, how much of the ship have you explored?"

"I think all of it, sir, though I really didn't spend much time in what I think may be the engine room or what I assume is the storage room. The really large room in the rear of the ship that has the big door or hatch looks like a cargo hold, but the only thing in there is a piece of equipment and a big box."

"A big box, you say? Please describe it," he said anxiously.

"Well, Captain Maxette, sir, it's about as tall as I am and big enough to fit about eight people inside..." The captain appeared to be waiting for me to continue with more information, perhaps something to indicate that the container was still secure, so I offered, "...and it has some sort of sealed locking device on it, so I don't know what's in it. But that's all that I see in that space."

The captain suddenly relaxed and a smile appeared on his face. Until that moment, I hadn't been fully aware of how tense he'd been.

"Tibby," he began, with a tone in his voice that made him seem like a different person than the one who greeted me, "if what I hope is in that box is there, and I have every reason to believe it is, you have just become the luckiest and the richest man in the universe – without a doubt *the richest*. We will arrive at your location in a few moments to retrieve you, the *TRITYTE* and the solbidyum. This is a day that shall go down in history." He turned briefly to the side and announced with resounding command, as though dictating an order to someone out of view, "All ships under this command are to remain on restricted communication with the *DUSTEN* only. All communications from the *DUSTEN* and its flight wings are hereby restricted to communication with the High Command at the capital only. Such communications shall be encrypted for delivery only by me or my successor, should I be unable to perform my duties. From now until we reach Megelleon all ships are to be at the ready and on full alert. Word of this development must not be disclosed to anyone before we arrive. Anyone attempting to communicate outside these parameters will be subject to court martial, punishable by death under Section 14589-QR-4."

He then turned back to me, again with a huge, genuine smile and said, "Tibby, I look forward to meeting you very soon. You have no idea just how glorious a moment this is for you and for the galaxy."

As I waited for their arrival, I hoped that all of this was going to be as good for me as it sounded; but the commands to his ship and crew left me with a great deal of apprehension. While it was fairly clear that the *TRITYTE* was name of the ship, I wondered what in the hell *solbidyum* was and what made this ship and this solbidyum so damn important.

As the captain finished speaking, I saw a larger ship appear on screen. Since my points of reference were rather skewed in the vacuum of space, I could not clearly understand the size of this massive craft moving toward me. I had expected to see a larger vessel approach after speaking with the captain, but nothing I had ever experienced or heard of prepared me for staggering height and breadth of this ship. I couldn't help exclaiming my astonishment out loud. "That thing has to be the size of a small city! It's close to a half a kilometer in height and at least kilometer and a half in length! There must be *thousands* of personnel aboard a ship of that size!" I was nearly in shock at the spectacle I was seeing on the screen.

The console lights and displays became active again and things were obviously taking place to move matters forward. I assumed that either the larger ship had somehow taken control over the *TRITYTE* or that orders had been given to the ship's computer for docking with the *DUSTEN*. Whichever it was, I was approaching a section of the *DUSTEN* where there appeared to be a rather large opening. Some of the squadrons of smaller craft that were surrounding me broke off from their positions, forming a corridor through which my ship slowly passed. I wondered whether this was for my protection (from what I had no idea) or to prevent me from escaping (as if I knew how). In any case, it didn't matter; I was pretty sure I wasn't going anywhere but into that bigger ship. During this period, it suddenly occurred that I had not mentioned the body of the man in the infirmary. The communication link with the *DUSTEN* was still active; so I felt it was better that I say something about the corpse before the *TRITYTE* was boarded.

"Ah, Captain…" I began, "there is a mummified body onboard this ship that I think you should know about."

The captain had been sitting in his chair facing away from me to finish giving orders to someone. He turned rapidly to look at me through the screen. "A mummified body? Do you know anything about it or how the person died?"

"Well, sir, I asked the ship about it. Apparently this man was the thief who had originally taken the ship. He died after being injected with some sort of poisonous venom from a creature on my planet. I suspect it was a coral snake, but I can't be sure."

"Interesting…" replied the captain while considering this information. "It's quite possible that he perished as you have stated. We are currently accessing and downloading all of the ship's records for analysis to find what has been happening since the *TRITYTE* was taken centuries ago. Stories will be told about this event and its history for many generations to come."

"Uhhh… about that, sir, could you enlighten me on just what *did* happen and what is happening now? I'm afraid that I'm at a total loss as to what this is all about."

The captain laughed a bit. "I think we both have lots of questions. You will soon be aboard the *DUSTEN*. Once you are and we have confirmed that everything is secure, you will be provided with accommodations and an opportunity to refresh. Thereafter, we will gather for a debriefing and an explanation, in its entirety, of the significance of your find. You and I can exchange questions at that time…and I will certainly do my best to answer your questions. I think you are in for the surprise of your life," the captain chuckled. "Yes, indeed... the surprise of your life!"

By this time, the *TRITYTE* had moved much closer to the *DUSTEN*. I was in awe. The receiving hatch on the *DUSTEN* now appeared big enough to pass an aircraft carrier from Earth through it. I was equally overwhelmed by the scale of things inside as the *TRITYTE* entered. The hold itself was immense. To the right and left I saw levels, likes shelves, filled with what had to be *hundreds* of spacecraft of all sizes. This was not a ship – this was a MOTHER SHIP... or *the* mother of *all* ships! I couldn't begin to comprehend the man-hours it must have taken to construct this monstrosity. The small craft in the squadrons that had surrounded the *TRITYTE* were like fleas on an elephant next to this behemoth. As the ship entered this "hangar bay" (I didn't know what else to call it, though it seemed to be much more than a hangar bay), I noted smaller hangars arranged around the perimeter of the interior. It was to one of these bays that the *TRITYTE* was maneuvered.

The ship was barely inside and landed before the door to this smaller hangar was closed. Just moments later, I could hear hissing sounds. It was clear from the displays on the console that the *TRITYTE*'s airlock had been activated. I had barely turned away from the console when an armed man, wearing a uniform and what I suspected was some sort of body armor, entered and politely greeted me, "Thibodaux Renwalt, I'm Lieutenant Reidecor. Please come with me. I am here to escort you off the *TRITYTE* and assume guard over it... and may I say, sir; it is a real honor to meet you."

We headed down the corridor to the main airlock and then turned to exit down a ramp that extended away from the ship. On both sides of the ramp stood troops at the ready, looking in all directions, fully armed and prepared for action.   I was a bit distressed by all the security and expressed my concern to the lieutenant.

"Why all the security, Lieutenant Reidecor?"

"I'm afraid, sir, for the moment that information is restricted. Perhaps the captain will explain it to you, but I am not authorized to comment at this time."

I was beginning to wonder if "*That information is restricted*" was the standard answer to every question in the Federation.

As we reached the end of the ramp, I turned to look back at the *TRITYTE. U*ntil this moment, I had no *real* idea what the outside of the ship looked like. All I had ever seen of the outside was a hatch and a hint of a contour that shaped Mound Island. Now that I was able to see it in its entirety, I was a bit surprised, as it looking nothing like what I expected. What I saw before me was a mass of smooth lines and blended curves. Other than the hatch opening in the side where we exited, I saw no indication of any doors or windows, save for a small bowl-shaped indentation in the hull further aft on the ship that I recognized as being similar to the one that tripped me in the mud and started this whole expedition. Overall, the *TRITYTE* resembled some sort of symmetrical blob and not much more.

While aboard the *TRITYTE*, I perceived the ship as being quite large; but now, seeing it in this hangar inside the *DUSTEN* made it seem quite small and almost insignificant. Stepping away from it, I could see that the entire shell had a dark, tarnished brass finish. If the ship were sitting in a field of dead grass, one might think from a distance that it was little more than a grass-covered hill. Compared to the magnitude and quantity of ships I saw lining the main hangar, I could see nothing in the stature of the *TRITYTE* that justified all the fuss being made about it.

Once removed from the immediate vicinity of the *TRITYTE*, I could see another person approaching, flanked by four fully armed and ready troopers. There was no mistaking, even from a distance, that this person was female... and the closer she got the more attractive she became. It was not that she was outstandingly beautiful in her physical features, though she certainly could have held her own in any beauty competition; rather her greater beauty was in the way she carried herself. She emitted an air confidence and relaxed composure that gave me the feeling she was at home in any situation and was better prepared than anyone to deal with the unexpected. My first thought upon seeing her was that of a cheetah; something in the way she moved indicated both grace and speed. She was about 1.7 m tall by Earth measurements, which put the top of her head at about my eye height. She had a light olive complexion, long black hair that cascaded past her shoulders and the most beautiful eyes I had ever seen. She could have been Hispanic, Native American, Italian, Middle Eastern, or any number of other Earth races or nationalities; yet there was something about her that told me she was none of these. It took me a minute to realize that her eyes were light blue-grey, an unnatural color for anyone on Earth. Even if they had been a common shade of Earth blue, they would still have appeared unusual, as darker complexioned persons on Earth seldom have black hair and blue eyes.

The woman and her entourage stopped several steps from us. Lieutenant Reidecor also stopped, beckoning me to do the same with an almost indiscernible, but clearly understood gesture. He stiffened into a posture that I assumed to be a position of attention and acknowledgement that this society used when encountering a higher-ranking officer. He then stepped forward to make a brief and formal introduction.

"Major, I present you with Thibodaux Renwalt, as ordered." Then he turned to me and said, "This is Major Kalana, she will see to you from here." He then returned to the *TRITYTE* to resume his guard with the troops.

"Tibby, it's a great pleasure to meet you," began Major Kalana. "I understand you prefer to be called Tibby, is that correct?"

"Yes ma'am," I replied. "Either that or Tib. Both are fine with me. Most of my closer friends just call me Tib."

"Well in that case, if you do not object, I will just call you Tib and you may call me Kala. I hate being called *Major*," she said with a smile. "Do you have any personal possessions onboard the *TRITYTE* that you require?"

"No ma'am, uh, I mean Kala," I stuttered. "I'm afraid I was not able to bring any personal possessions with me, other than the clothes I'm wearing."

"Ahhh... interesting," she said, giving me a quick appraisal. "You must forgive me, Tib, if I seem overly curious at times. My specialties are those of a cultural attaché. I am the advisor to Federation diplomatic representatives for the many planets, cultures and local governments throughout the Federation and outlying areas and I often serve directly as the first point of contact – just as I am, essentially, with you. You, of course, present me with a new learning opportunity, as we have no historical indications of ever having had contact with the peoples of your planet before now. So again, please excuse me if I say or do something that is offensive.

"While you are traveling on the *DUSTEN*, I will be available to inform and guide you as to the conventions of society and matters of protocol. I will also serve in a similar capacity later, when we arrive at the capital. I suspect that things may seem a bit strange to you; but rest assured that, on the whole, most of the planets and cultures within the Federation are very forgiving of social missteps and indiscretions of protocol.

"Now…let me show you to your accommodations and allow you to get settled." During this orientation, she led me to the back of the hangar area. We were preceded by two of the troopers and two fell in at our rear.

My mounting anxiety about the heavy military presence prompted me to ask a rather direct question, "Excuse me, Kala, but…am I a prisoner or being held for some crime or something?"

Kala stopped abruptly and looked at me strangely. Then, in a moment of realization, she responded, "Ah…you mean the guards and the ship escorts. I forget that you don't yet know the significance of the ship that brought you here, nor do you understand the complications it creates for you and for the *TRITYTE*, as far as safe transportation to the capital is concerned. To answer your question, no, you are not a prisoner, nor are you in any legal trouble. The escort ships and these troopers are for your protection, just as the troopers surrounding the *TRITYTE* are there to protect the ship."

Kala's demeanor became a bit more serious as she continued. "Until we reach the capital and are able to make your status regarding the *TRITYTE* official, you and the *TRITYTE* and all who are aboard the *DUSTEN* are in potential danger. I must ask that, other than for the few officers that the captain or I may introduce to you, you do not speak of your origins or mention the *TRITYTE* in any way. This restriction is of critical importance for the time being; and we will very shortly explain it to you in full.

"In the meantime, please be assured you are not in any trouble with our government, nor are you a prisoner. It is simply necessary that we protect you and that you to keep secret the existence of the *TRITYTE*, especially its cargo. I cannot express strongly enough the importance of this mandate. Let it suffice to say that anyone possessing knowledge of your arrival with the *TRITYTE* or the nature of its cargo who discloses *any* information outside official channels could face a penalty of death. The situation is *that* critical and, hence, our protective posture must be maintained. Again, all of this will be explained to you very shortly. I apologize that I cannot tell you more right now."

Her explanation did little to relieve my anxiety.

By this time Kala and I had reached the far wall of the *TRITYTE*'s hangar. At a nod from Kala, one of the two guards standing by the doorway in front of us turned to open the door, which led to a small compartment equipped with several seats. Kala took a seat and indicated that I do the same. Two of the attending troopers also took seats in front of us, while the other two attached themselves to lines and eyelets installed in opposing walls. They positioned themselves to face the exit from both ends of the room with weapons pointed at the door. Again, the heavy guard left me feeling rather uneasy. I wondered whether the *DUSTEN* was safe. Perhaps there were mutineers running about... or maybe the ship was being attacked.

My anxiety must have been visible. Kala smiled and said, "No, Tib, the ship is not under siege of any kind, but if knowledge leaks of the matters at hand, we could be. These guards are here to protect you, the *TRITYTE*, and its cargo at all costs. Their orders give priority to the cargo first, the ship second, and you third. All the rest of us are expendable until issues regarding you, the *TRITYTE* and the cargo are resolved at the capital."

Kala then said with a somewhat different sense of importance, "Oh…and one more thing, Tib. If no one has told you yet, you are the luckiest man in the entire universe; though at the moment you do not understand what that means." A knowing smile took over her beautiful face, "But soon you will. I envy you, Tib, and so will every other person in the galaxy, once news of all this is released." As she spoke, I detected that the room had started to move. I noticed a familiar small console in front of one of the seated troopers and realized that we were in some sort of transport pod.

It took a few minutes for our transport to reach its destination. I had no idea where we were – whether we were in the middle of the *DUSTEN,* the top or the bottom of it. For all I knew, we might have left the *DUSTEN* altogether. However, when the door opened and we disembarked into what seemed to be a very well-decorated and furnished lobby area where people were streaming about, I felt we were still on the ship. Above the lobby area was a skylight that showed the dark sky. Just below the skylight were numerous fixtures that emitted diffuse light at a daylight level. With the troopers configured around us we moved a short way through a broad corridor, stopping at a door on one side. Kala walked to a small panel by the doorframe, placed the palm of her hand against a plate, and muttered some phrase I didn't understand. As the door opened, she stepped back, waiting for the forward guards to enter first. Once we passed, the door closed behind us and I found we were inside yet another corridor – this one smaller and, for the most part, empty of people. There appeared to be a receptionist sitting at a desk in a small alcove to the side.

Kala approached the woman and spoke to her briefly. The woman glanced at me, then nodded as Kala spoke. Kala then turned to me and asked me to approach the desk. I was instructed to press my right hand on a plate by the desk and to say my name and follow the subsequent instructions. Both Kala and the receptionist stepped away from the desk during this process. I was then prompted to provide a password that only I would know, followed by a "distress" word to use in case of an emergency or compromised situation where I might be forced to use my password under duress. In both cases I used words in English, an Earth language that would most certainly not be known here. My password was *catfish* (my favorite food) and the distress word was *alligator*. Both of these words represent creatures I would have found in the swamp back home, and both words I would easily associate and remember.

After this process was completed, the four troopers resumed their positions around Kala and me. I was starting to think of these ominous figures as the Four Horsemen of the Apocalypse, the four mythical characters in a religious writing who bring about the end of the Earth. Kala and I were escorted further down the hall to another entry flanked by two armed sentries in enclosed guard stations. We were each required to present our palm prints at the guard station before the door was opened. We passed through a series of more lavishly decorated corridors to a large set of double doors guarded by yet two more sentries. Again, we presented our palm prints for identification before we were allowed to pass.

On the other side of the door was a huge space that I can only describe as opulent, nearly to the point of decadence. It was obvious that great wealth had been spent and no luxury spared in its decoration. It seemed to be both a living and socializing area. I was amazed by the height of the ceiling, as it must have extended a good 15 meters. The furnishings of the room were excellently crafted. Elegant pictures adored the walls and sculptures and large potted plants decorated the entire space. We were barely inside the room when a small group of individuals assembled before us.

Kala spoke first, "Tibby, the areas you are about to see will serve as your accommodations while you are with us on the *DUSTEN*. This is the diplomatic section of the ship. These accommodations are provided for ambassadors and other visiting dignitaries who require a personal staff and various living spaces. You are to be treated as a top dignitary while you are with us and, since you have no personal staff of your own, one has been provided for you by the Federation. It is their duty to see to your wishes and needs. All of them hold the highest levels of security and training; but even so, it is advised that you do not discuss with or in front of them any details relating to your visit. This is the main or common room. All areas inside the doors we just entered are secure, so you can move about freely. All of the attending staff, your four bodyguards and I also have quarters within this section.

"This is Piesew Mecarta, house majordomo. Any needs, requests or services you require should be directed to him, so it will not be necessary for you to actually make requests of the other staff, unless there is an immediate or pressing need."

After greetings were exchanged, Piesew Mecarta stepped forward and presented me with a wide wristband that had a rectangular piece on one side. This item resembled a watch so much that I thought for a moment that it was, until Piesew explained. "Sir, this is a communication device that puts you directly in touch with me at any time. To activate it simply press these two buttons, like this, between your fingers to speak to me your wishes and I will immediately see that they are carried out. For instance, if you require a beverage or a snack or require assistance with an item of clothing, all you need do is ask and I will see that it is addressed immediately. Likewise, if any aspect of the accommodations is not to your liking, we can make changes for you." I replaced my wristwatch with the communication device. Piesew then proceeded to introduce me to the staff and explain the functions of each member. When he finished, Kala continued with her orientation.

"My personal quarters are located right next to yours. Two bodyguards will always be stationed outside your door while the other two are off duty. Even when off duty, the guards are quartered here within the dignitary area and near your accommodations.

"All of the staff will have access to your personal quarters, but they will be admitted only while in the presence of at least one guard. This protocol applies to everyone, with the exception of Captain Maxette and me, as well as two additional officers of the *DUSTEN*, whom you will meet later. Again, no one else will be permitted to enter your quarters when you are there without at least one armed bodyguard present."

I was becoming a bit overwhelmed with all the security, even more so by the level of opulence around me.

Now followed by only two guards, Kala, Piesew and I proceeded across the room and down yet another corridor that was finished with wood paneling and trim and decorated with paintings and tapestries at varying locations. Along the wall of this rather long corridor only four doors could be seen – two on one side and two on the other, spaced at about 30 meters apart. It was to one of these doors that I was directed. Once again, I was told to present my palm to the door, which immediately opened to allow me entrance. One of my guards stationed himself outside my door and one entered with Kala, Piesew and me.

What I saw next was nothing that I could have anticipated. My personal quarters consisted of an enormous suite of rooms.   There was a personal dining area, a luxurious bath facility, a private office and study, the bedchamber, which had to be at least 112 sq meters, and screens throughout the perimeter that mimicked windows with simulated moving scenes of beautiful country vistas. The detail was so clear and real that I felt I could have stepped through it into the open air. Piesew explained that, should I desire, the views could be changed to display any location on any planet or space itself and that he would be most happy to assist in altering the view.

The bed itself was large enough to accommodate five people, which made me wonder what sorts of activities went on with ambassadors and dignitaries that required such a bed. I mentioned to Piesew that I thought the bed was a bit large.   He replied that he would have it replaced immediately, if I could please provide him with an idea of the bed size I required. I noticed Kala looking at me as though she was curious to hear my reply. I responded simply by saying that the bed would be fine for the time being and that I would let him know later if I wished it to be changed.

Piesew also related to me that my quarters were equipped with a "safe room," only it was called a "safe *pod*." He showed me the hidden door to access it. I was told that, in the event of an emergency or situation where my life may be in danger, I was to immediately enter the *pod* until all was safe.   Also, if the pod should be discovered while I was inside, there was a special *eject button* that would launch the pod into space, where I would later be rescued. All of this was becoming too much. The security around me seemed to be excessive even for a president. What was making me so damn important anyway? Piesew and the guard left the room but Kala remained. She informed me that the captain would be meeting me in about two hours and that this would be an appropriate time to freshen up and perhaps have a bite of food. All of this sounded pretty good to me. I said that I could use a nice shower and a chance to clean my clothing.

"You *do* know that you need not continue wearing the same clothing, don't you?" she asked. "There is a complete wardrobe here for you that consists of a full selection of current fashions and styles from all across the galaxy. I would be happy to assist you in selecting something for your meeting with the captain, if you like."

"Yes, thank you, if there is something here that fits me."

Kala laughed, "Every item here will fit you. You were scanned for measurements when entering your quarters and your wardrobe was assembled before we entered this room. I assure you everything will fit you quite well."

"Gee…and I thought I was doing well when I was able to be fitted for a suit and have alterations completed in a day back on Earth."

Kala just looked at me as though I had to be kidding, then turned to look through the large room-size closet lined with hundreds of outfits.

"While you're looking, I'll shower." Kala didn't respond. I went into the bath, undressed and got into a shower large enough to accommodate four or five people, and started the fog mist that I had experienced in the *TRITYTE*'s bath. The process had barely begun when I was aware of Kala entering the shower behind me. I turned to see her standing next to me, nude, not really looking at me as she began to shower also.

"I decided to get cleaned up here to save time," she said, as she vanished in the foggy mist. "I hope you don't mind."

"Ahhh… no… it's quite alright," I said somewhat awkwardly as I pondered her actions. The situation seemed just like one of those scenes in an Earth movie, where one person follows another into the shower and they end up making love. The only difference was I didn't get the sense that Kala had any intentions other than bathing. I tried not to display any surprise or outward sign of confusion or discomfort, as the fog and ultrasonic cleaning gave way to the water rinse and then the drying process. I glanced at Kala as her shower entered the rinse mode. I couldn't help but admire her body, which had all the loveliness of a goddess… please forgive the cliché, but she truly did. I stepped out of the shower and looked about the bath for one of the depilatory shavers and found one conveniently laid out by the mirror. As I was shaving, I took a good look at myself for the first time since I started this journey. It was obvious that before too long I would need a haircut, as my red hair was getting a bit long. Other than that, I didn't look too bad. My tall frame was moderately muscled and trim and, while I was not a handsome head-turner for most women, I did manage to catch a few female eyes from time to time.

As I contemplated my appearance in the mirror, I noticed behind me that Kala had entered the room. She proceeded to a small compartment where she retrieve a device reminiscent of a hot curling iron that many women on Earth use to style their hair, though this device had no power cord. She moved it around her head and long hair with an artistic grace that had me mesmerized. With each pass, her hair dried more, and she was able to style it in different configurations that seemed to hold just as she wanted. I know this would sound strange to my fellows back on Earth; but we both stood there – quite naked – this lovely woman and I – focusing on her hair and the way she was styling it with apparent ease using this strange stick contraption.

She noticed me staring and, without interrupting her work, asked me, "Have you not seen a style stick before?"

"Ahhh no...I haven't. We have something that looks similar on Earth called a curling iron, but it works nothing like that." By now I realized how strange I must look, standing there naked, staring at her with my mouth open as she styled her hair. I closed my mouth and focused on finishing my shaving.

"Does that device also trim hair? " I asked while I finished my shaving.

"Yes, actually, it does," Kala said as she made one last adjustment to her hair, "Do you need a trim? I'll show you how to do it, if you like."

"Ahhh...yeah, sure," I muttered. "If you don't mind." Kala approached me – still nude – and began waving the wand through my hair while explaining which button to push and how to adjust the length of the cut by rotating a ring at the base of the rod. As she moved the wand through my hair, her body brushed against mine in a most pleasurable way, yet I could see by her expression and her actions that she had no intentions other than to demonstrate this device.

I decided to speak up.

"Kala," I began, "you said you were here to help me understand the cultures in the Federation and help me to not make a mistake in dealing with the peoples of the Federation, is that correct?"

"Yes," she answered, as she finished the final touch to my hair and then added, "Is that your question? Oh, and by the way, when you used this device in the trim modes, only make one pass through your hair or it will take off too much or leave you with uneven results. Or you can simply have one of the ships stylist come in and do it for you." She stepped back to look at my hair, checking to see that it looked okay.

"Well, I was wondering if it's customary for men and women to bathe together in your culture when they are not romantically involved or bonded." *Bonded* sort of came out as I searched for the word for marriage in the Federation language, but failed to find one that matched the concept.

"Why, yes, it's fairly common. Is it not so on your planet?" she said as she drew back from me with a look of amazement on her face.

I chuckled and said, "Well, yes and no. That's kind of difficult to answer. The general moral voice on Earth would say no, but it's not uncommon for un-bonded men and women to bathe together as a pair...and generally, it's as a precursor to a sexual relationship or may occur after one."

"And sex on your planet is a romantic relationship function and not simply a general thing men and women do together for pleasure?" she said with a concerned look on her face.

"That's more or less the way the majority of cultures on my planet think and act, but many do not follow those tenets. Some do have sex with multiple partners simply for the physical enjoyment, though it is frowned upon by Earth societies as a whole."

"Oh," Kala said drawing back even further, "I'm so sorry. I didn't mean to offend you. I never stopped to think nudity might be a taboo to you. I sincerely apologize, it won't happen again. Please forgive me. I had no idea that our showering together or being naked together might have a sexual implication to you."

"No, no! I said, perhaps a bit too eagerly. "You have not offended me in the least, and our being nude here is not bothering me or creating any sexual desires in me," which was a lie, as she was really very beautiful and I couldn't imagine any heterosexual human male not being attracted to her, "but it was unexpected and I thought I should get clarification, lest I make some mistake later on."

"Oh," she began relaxing a bit. "I'm glad you were neither offended nor bothered by this event. While many accommodations and cabins on ship have their own baths and toilet facilities, many do not, so common facilities are routinely used by both men and women simultaneously. The same holds true on most planets and cities throughout the Federation. There are a few settlements, however, with regions and religious cultures that have differing views and practices. On Reyes for instance, men are not allowed to see a woman's nude body until they marry – and then only that of the woman they marry. On Ceirector men are not allowed to see another man nude, nor a woman to see another woman nude; however, they may see members of the opposite sex nude and it's perfectly acceptable."

"Wow," I exclaimed, "I wonder how *that* tradition evolved."

"We can discuss this more later, if you like, but right now we need to dress and get something to eat before the captain arrives. I laid out some clothing for you on the bed. I hope you approve." While she spoke, I saw her retrieve her uniform from the cleaning unit in my closet and begin donning it.

I could not help admiring her physical form – a well-toned body, smooth, enticing curves and the shape of her breasts as she pulled on the uniform and adjusted it. Fortunately, she didn't notice my stare or the physical reaction my body was beginning to have by the scene. Suddenly I realized what was happening and turned my back to her to dress in the outfit she left for me. So much for my speech about how her nudity was not having any sexual effect on me. Secretly I was hoping we would have other opportunities to shower together.

The outfit Kala chose for me consisted of a pair of black pants, a black short-sleeved shirt – much like a T-shirt, only with a mock turtleneck – and a black jacket that reminded me of the old Nehru jackets of the 1960s that I had seen in pictures. The black boots, which extended only to the top of the ankle, were made of a leather-type material that appeared to be synthetic on closer examination. After dressing, I looked at myself in the mirror and, I must admit, I was impressed with the image I saw there. The black suit seemed to accent the red of my hair. Though uncommon for most redheads on Earth, I did not have the typical lack of melanin in my skin that resulted in a perpetually fair complexion. My mother had once told me that my grandfather on her side the family was a Redbone, a term used in my home region for a person of mixed race – usually meaning part black, part indigenous and part white. My grandmother was Irish (one of only a few groups on Earth known for their red hair) and others in my family tree were from all over the Earth, so I had a menagerie of genetic material that was expressed as a rather unusual physical appearance. I tended to be thin in the waist and broad in the shoulders, built more like a basketball player, but not quite as tall. A relatively brief exposure to sun would always transform my skin to a golden bronze; however, the sunless travel over the past few weeks had left me a bit on the pale side.

I glanced over at Kala in her gray military uniform that had black stripes around the chest. The air of command presence seemed to come so easily for her – and most certainly not at the cost of her femininity or stunning beauty.

Kala explained that the meeting with the captain would take place in a conference room within my general accommodation area and emphasized that the captain was trying to keep the recovery of the *TRITYTE and* its cargo a secret as long as possible. All of the troops and pilots involved in the retrieval and sequestering of the *TRITYTE* had been isolated from the rest of the *DUSTEN*'s crews and several thousands of passengers, solely in an effort to contain dissemination of these developments beyond the current scope.

Kala had apparently sent some sort of signal to Piesew, letting him know that we wanted a meal to be prepared and served in my quarters, because we had barely finished dressing when the front door opened and the guard escorted in Piesew, one of the service staff, and a cartful of assorted dishes. They proceeded to the dining area, where they arranged the dishes on the table. Two glasses of beverage were poured by Piesew from a strange-looking bottle. Then, offering their best wishes for enjoyment of the food, Piesew and the other staffer left the quarters, but the guard remained. From a pouch on his belt he produced a device that he passed over the food and drink before announcing that everything was poison-free and safe for consumption. Then he also left, returning to his station outside the door.

The dining room in my quarters had a glass wall with a view that looked into a small atrium garden consisting of tall, fern-like plants and a small waterfall. We were seated at a small table, ideally sized for two, though four could have crammed around it with some effort. Regarding the table, I commented to Kala, "I guess I won't be holding any dinner parties here."

"Why not?" she inquired between bites of food.

"Well, for one thing, this room and table are too small."

Kala gazed at me for a moment with one of those looks that said, "Is he kidding?" and then she got up from her seat to push a few buttons on a nearby wall panel. Suddenly the walls began to move and the room expanded. "This room can be adjusted to accommodate more people. There is a larger table under the floor that can be brought up that is suitable for seating up to 24 persons at a time, if you wish." She then pressed another button, shrinking the room back down to its more intimate size.

"Wow," I exclaimed, "I had no idea. We have nothing like this on Earth, at least not that I know of... I mean, we could have... we certainly have the technology to make something similar, but I've never seen it done."

"How do you like the food?" Kala asked.

"It's very good. It reminds me very much of a dish we have on Earth called *spaghetti and meatballs*. It tastes much the same, only the sauce on spaghetti is red instead of green. We even have a similar beverage that we drink with the meal. On Earth we call it wine. It has a mild alcohol content to it."

"So then your people on Earth do consume alcoholic beverages. I had ordered our meal through Piesew before we showered; and when you mentioned your planet's attitudes about nudity, I became concerned, as most of the cultures of the Federated planets that have nudity issues and taboos also seem to have alcohol restrictions."

"It's the same on Earth," I replied. "We have numerous cultures and religions there that ban the consumption of alcoholic beverages as an evil practice, while others use them as a part of their religious ceremonies."

"That interesting," Kala said intently. "When we have the time, I really want to hear and learn as much as possible about your planet and its cultures."

"Any time, madam," I replied with a playful formality and a smile. Her words gave me the impression that I would be spending a lot of time with her in the future, which made me smile, indeed.

Before I realized it, we had finished our meal and Kala indicated it was the appointed time for our meeting with the captain. I was not sure how she knew this, as I saw no timepieces about that were recognizable. We went to the door, where we were immediately joined by the bodyguards. Kala led us through the large common room and to the right where there was a door about mid wall. We entered what turned out to be an elevator that went up about eight meters or so to a second level that looked out over the common room. The conference room itself was somewhat recessed and had a balcony that extended out so its edge was flush with the wall of the common room. We arrived before the others, so I took the opportunity to investigate the conference room closely. In the center was a large table sufficient for seating at least 18 people. At one end of the room was a podium and I assumed that behind the three sections of wood paneling were probably numerous viewing screens. The wall separating the balcony from the conference room was glass, including the door positioned in the middle that didn't seem to have any visible hinges. Yet, when I pushed on the door, it swung open easily to allow access to the balcony. One of the stewards assigned to my accommodations was preparing the conference table and asked whether we would care for a beverage.

Before replying Kala explained, "While is it not exactly a ritual, people who are gathering at meetings traditionally share a beverage we call foccee. It's made from a plant that originated in the jungles of the planet Epur, but today it is grown commercially on many worlds. It has a mild non-addictive stimulant in it that increases alertness, reduces fatigue and seems to enhance mental acuity. Would you like to try some?"

"Sure, I'll give it a try."

My first thought was that the people of the Federation had found and cultivated coffee; however, when I was handed a cup of purple liquid that looked more like burgundy wine, this thought was quickly dispelled. I was surprised to find with the first sip that it tasted much like a Coke from back on Earth, with an added twist of mint. I savored the cool flavor and I could feel a relaxed sensation spreading over my body.

"Hmmm... I think I like it, "I offered. "It's very refreshing."

"Just don't drink any within a few hours of going to bed or you will be tossing and turning for hours. It has a tendency to keep one awake."

"We have a beverage on Earth that is used in much the same fashion, but it is a dark brown or black in color and served hot. It, too, can keep one awake. I think I like this foccee much better though; has a nicer aftertaste to it."

Just as I finished my comments, Captain Maxette and two other officers entered the room. Both Major Kalana and the trooper guard assumed a stiff posture and placed their right hand on their left shoulder. The captain and the other two officers repeated the same gesture, but from a more relaxed posture.

"Captain," Kala said in acknowledgement of his presence.

The captain responded with "Major," as he averted his eyes from her to me. There was no verbal acknowledgement between any of the others, and I had the impression that when two military parties met, only the senior ranking members of each group acknowledged each other verbally as a sign of recognition of leadership for each group.

"So, Tibby, we get to meet face to face at last," the captain began with a warm smile. "I'm sure you're eager to get some answers from us, just as we are from you. Please, sit down. Everyone please sit."

Everyone took a chair at the table except for the guard, who remained stationary inside the room by the door, and the steward, who was busy placing beverages in front of everyone before leaving the room. Captain Maxette took the chair at the head of the table and his two officers sat to the right of him. Kala immediately sat next to him on his left and motioned for me to take the seat next to her, as Captain Maxette began the formalities of the gathering.

"Before we begin, I would like to introduce you to Commander Thimas," Thimas nodded in my direction, "and Lieutenant Commander Wanoll." Wanoll also nodded.

I acknowledged them with "Gentlemen," all the while wondering about the structure of their military ranking system. First of all, the ranks that were announced by Captain Maxette were translated in my brain from Federation language to their English equivalents or closest equals. But in my homeland the military rankings from one branch of the service to another are not necessarily the same across all branches of service. For instance, the Navy has no Major, but the Army and Air Force do; and an Air Force rank of Major is higher than that of a Captain. In the Federation, however, it seemed that the rank of Captain is higher than that of a Major, so I was somewhat confused by the system. I had worked out, though, that the greater the number of stripes that ran around the trunk of the uniform jacket, the lower the rank of the officer. Captain Maxette's uniform had the least of those in the room, followed by Commander Thimas and Lieutenant Commander Wanoll. Major Kalana's uniform had the same number of stripes as the Lieutenant Commander; however, where Kala's stripes were all one color, the bottom stripe of the Lieutenant Commander was gold. It was all a bit confusing at that moment, so I tried to put the distraction out of my mind and make mental note to get an explanation from Kala later.

Captain Maxette continued, "I'm sure that, by now, Major Kalana has explained to you her role as a military attaché in our diplomatic service and described an overview of her functions. She is on full assignment to you, at the moment, to help you integrate with the Federation and also to help us learn more about you and your culture. Commander Thimas is my second in command and is here to learn as much of this event as possible so that, in the event something should happen to me, he will be fully apprised of the situation. Lieutenant Commander Wanoll represents the defense and security elements of this operation and is responsible for assessing any dangers to you, the *TRITYTE* and its cargo and, of course, the *DUSTEN*. As part of his duties, Lieutenant Commander Wanoll will direct all security provisions and advise me as to any situational safeguards and procedures. "With that, let me begin the debriefing with a bit of history that sets the stage for where we are today.

"A little over 700 years ago *(this is translated from Federation time to Earth years)* our scientists discovered an asteroid cluster on the edge of the galaxy that was believed to have been ejected from a black hole trillions of years ago. The scientists were interested in looking for new elements that might have been created in the black hole and, indeed, they found several.   One unique and extremely dense element, which accounted for only a minute percentage of the recovered materials, showed remarkable properties. During the course of their analysis, the Federation astrophysicists and metallurgists discovered that, when this element was brought into proximity of a second, very common element under certain conditions, a *tremendous* amount of energy was produced. Oddly, neither of these elements seemed to be altered or measurably depleted by the interaction in any way; and precisely *how* this energy was (and is) generated is still a mystery. To give you a hint as to the energy potential for this new element, which is now known as *solbidyum*, a quantity that measures the size of a single grain of salt placed in proximity to the second element and situated within a low-grade magnetic field produces enough energy to meet the needs of a large industrially developed planet with a population of several billion for a nearly infinite period of time.

"In the beginning, after the solbidyum and its tremendous potential were discovered, three planets quickly engineered and commissioned power plants to transform this new energy source into electrical power for planet-wide distribution using some of the original samples.   This enormous leap in energy technology gave the people of these planets huge advantages, in terms of industry and resources. Everything that required a power source was converted to electrical systems and the need for fossil fuels, nuclear plants and fusion reactors was eliminated. In addition, there was no requirement for hazardous waste or safety management systems related to processing or storing of radioactive byproducts from these new processes, because the energy was produced (as I have described) by an *interaction*, not a *reaction*, and hence yielded nothing but clean, non-polluting energy. The power facilities proved to be highly sustainable and required minimal space and personnel to maintain efficient operation.

"At first, the planetary governments rejoiced. At the time, the Federation was in its infancy - newly formed and dedicated to the principal of universal and unbiased opportunity for all peoples and planets to access the same resources for life and energy. The discovery of solbidyum meant that peoples of numerous planets, which had heretofore been struggling to survive as a result of limited energy resources, would now be able to flourish.

"Before long, however, the scientists came forward with news that was received with less enthusiasm. Solbidyum existed only in one very remote part of the galaxy, so far as anyone knew. The known quantity of solbidyum was finite and, while only the smallest particle of it was required to generate ample power, it was estimated to be so rare that each of the planets in the Federation would be able to possess only one, maybe two grains of it. Furthermore, several years would be required to locate, mine and process all the deposits of this resource for distribution.

"Immediately upon receipt of this information, representatives from every planet vied for priority consideration in the distribution of the first available solbidyum. Many heated debates took place in public arenas on the topic, creating a great deal of dissention between special interest groups and industrialists of the Federation planets. A consensus was finally reached that all solbidyum would be collected, refined and distributed at one time, so that no planet gained an economic, social, or political advantage over another as a result of earlier access to this resource. Each planet would be responsible for paying for their solbidyum at a rate to be set by the Federation. Planets that were not financially capable of paying in full upon receipt could obtain credit from the Federation, so that every planet would have equal opportunity to take advantage of this endless and unlimited energy source.

"Lastly, mining solbidyum was extremely dangerous, as the gravimetric site in which the solbidyum was found was extremely active. The asteroids of interest were known to be orbiting around a dense mass, also believed to have been ejected from the black hole. This environment produced frequent asteroid collisions and subsequent dense meteoritic debris which, in turn compounded the impacts and ultimately shrouded the entire site in a dense dust cloud. Our scientists had been observing this cluster for centuries, believing that, after a few million years, all the orbiting material would be pulled into the dense core particle and eventually become a new star – that is, if there were enough core and debris to do so, but there wasn't. After identifying the extraordinary properties of the solbidyum, they tried harvesting the meteoritic debris robotically to extract the element; however, the process proved very slow, resulting in the recovery of little or no solbidyum from most deployments and repeated delays due to continual equipment damage from meteoric impacts. Mining the solbidyum ore required manned equipment navigating the debris field with harvesters; but this, too, was very expensive – not just in terms of equipment, but in lives as well. A person volunteering to work in the harvesting area could earn a lifetime's worth of income in one three-month deployment period. However, few who signed up actually survived to collect their wages. The handful that *did* never signed up for a second deployment.

"Eventually, the pool of volunteers diminished below the minimum manpower requirements and operations were slated for termination…until several of the worst criminals that the universe had ever seen volunteered to work in the debris field in exchange for full pardons from their death sentences, if they completed (and survived) one year of service. At first, the citizens of the Federation were against the idea of letting these unreformable, psychopathic offenders – individuals convicted of the worst crimes that can be imagined – go free. Nevertheless, negotiations eventually resulted in an arrangement where such volunteers would be pardoned and, upon completion of service, relocated to a prison planet on the outer fringes of the galaxy, far removed from other habitable planets. The uninhabited planet chosen to become this penal colony was actually a very lovely world; however it was not close enough to any other inhabited planets to be of any real use to the Federation. Thus, upon completion of one year served without committing any new crimes, these individuals would be transferred to this exile planet with limited provisions and resources, where they would be allowed to prevail or die, based on their own skills. Surprisingly, numerous death row criminals submitted petitions for these assignments, even knowing that the chance of surviving just the first three months was about 1 in 50. To the amazement of the Federation, several of the prisoners actually exceeded the three-month period, but none ever made it the full year. Yet they never stopped trying.

"In the meantime, years of mining and harvesting operations produced only a small supply of solbidyum. Desperate for energy resources, many of the planets became suspicious, believing there was a plot to keep their worlds repressed and that a coalition had been formed to distribute solbidyum to certain planets in advance of others. Extremist groups and, eventually, organized mercenary and pirate ships developed to intercept solbidyum ore transports before they could reach the Federation's processing facility for refinement. Many lives were lost and ore destroyed in the attacks, leaving the Federation to search for more viable processing and storage solutions. It was decided that all solbidyum ore would remain stockpiled near the site, where it would be refined and stored on one of the larger asteroids at the outer edge of the cluster. The security of this location was nearly guaranteed – primarily because few people knew of its precise location at any given time and, secondly, because the normally vacant expanse of space between the site and the Federation's main territories made for easy detection and interception of any pirate ships or war vessels. The objective was to accumulate and successfully transport enough refined solbidyum in one shipment to meet the needs of all the planets in the Federation.

"Nearly 100 years passed before enough of the resource was collected and contained for shipment. The Federation recognized the terrible potential that existed, should all the solbidyum fall into the hands of one planet or group. Even though the solbidyum was to be transported in one large shipment under the protection of an armada of armed escort vessels when passing through inhabited territories, the Federation feared that a possible mutiny or coup within the fleet could result in the loss or theft of the entire supply. For this reason, a covert plan was established to move the solbidyum from the asteroid outpost to the Federation capital planet of Megelleon without anyone's knowledge with the exception of a few of the highest officials.

"The ship, *TRITYTE*, was built under the tightest measures of secrecy to serve as secure transport for the cargo. The hull was designed to mimic that of a typical patrol ship and to carry only a crew of six. Few people in the Federation really had any concept of just how little space the entire supply of solbidyum would require, most thinking it would take a major cargo carrier to transport the shipment.

"Though the Federation designed the *TRITYTE* to resemble a patrol ship, it was nothing like its lookalikes. The hull was made of a much stronger metallic ceramic alloy that could take just about anything the weapons of the day could launch at it. The ship was fitted with the most sophisticated guidance system ever produced and a top-secret prototype gravity wave propulsion system that facilitated greater speeds than any other known propulsion technology.

"One other thing regarding the unique design... the only energy source that could provide enough power to operate the *TRITYTE* was...solbidyum.

"The newly built and tested *TRITYTE* and its crew were transported to the asteroid production facility in the cargo ship that was to be used as the decoy solbidyum transport. One grain of the solbidyum was to be placed in the reactor on the *TRITYTE* to power the ship and the rest was to be placed in a single small container stored in the *TRITYTE*'s cargo hold. Meanwhile, the cargo ship would be filled with containers of disguised mine waste material and the inconspicuous *TRITYTE* was to take a place in the armada that supposedly protected the cargo ship while returning to Federation territory.

"If nothing happened and the ships all arrived safely at the capital, no one would ever know it was the *TRITYTE* that carried the solbidyum. Upon completion of the mission, the grain in the reactor of the *TRITYTE* would be removed and added to the supply. However, in the event that the fleet was attacked or a secretly planned revolt took place in an attempt to take over the cargo ship, the small *TRITYTE* could easily slip away from the armada. With its unequaled speed and super protective hull, the *TRITYTE* would be able to get the cargo safely to the capital, where it would then be distributed to all the worlds as intended. The crew members selected for this mission were carefully handpicked and tested psychologically for loyalty. This entire mission in all its detail was known to only a handful.

"No one could have anticipated what happened next.

"There was one prisoner at the processing facility named Roiax, a brilliant super-criminal, if ever there was one. He was the first to survive the one year of harvesting deployment and had only a few days more of processing protocols before he would receive his freedom on the prison planet…as its *only* human inhabitant. No one is exactly sure how he happened to get into the hangar where the *TRITYTE* was located. It had just been fueled and loaded with the priceless cargo that very day in preparation for the clandestine transport to the capital. What we do know is that an unlikely asteroid collision occurred on the periphery of the cluster, setting off a chain reaction within the vicinity of the hangar and cargo. Part of the prison facility was hit by meteor fragments. At the time, Roiax would have just been finishing his last shift and was probably still suited up, so he would not have been killed in the decompression of the prison building when it was struck. In all the chaos that ensued he somehow managed to get into the hangar, where he killed one crewman who was finalizing preparations for departure. He then entered the *TRITYTE* and either managed to deactivate the ships autopilot and Federation control system or the system had perhaps not yet be activated after the solbidyum power source was engaged. I don't think we will ever know those particular details. Immediately after taking control of the *TRITYTE*, Roiax blasted the side out of the hangar and fled. In all the confusion, it was nearly an hour before the remaining crew found their dead crewmate and discovered that Roiax, the *TRITYTE* and the solbidyum were missing.

"What followed was the biggest manhunt in the history of the universe.

"We do not believe that Roiax ever knew that he carried the greatest treasure in the universe on his escape transportation. He was driven solely by the desire to end his confinement and avoid a solitary exile. He did not turn on the ship's communication system and he changed directions and speed many times in an effort to throw off any pursuers, though there actually were none anywhere close to him. Millions of ships took to space looking for him, all going in the wrong direction. Roiax had skimmed the outer arm of the galaxy, not moving in toward the center for many days. All of the searchers expected him to head toward one of the planets in the Federation territories with the intent of using the solbidyum to bargain for his freedom…and more. The truth is he could have gotten anything he wanted, if he had tried. There were planets that would have provided anything his sick, perverted mind wanted. He could have bought armies, planets and governments with the precious resource he unwittingly carried in the hold of the *TRITYTE*.

"As years passed and no trace of Roiax or the *TRITYTE* was found, rumors grew that the three planets which had previously received grains of solbidyum had confiscated the entire supply and fabricated a story of the criminal's escape. Other planets that seemed to be prospering more than average were also suspected of have secretly obtained solbidyum. As a result of these suspicions and rumors, a cascade of diplomatic problems began to disrupt normally congenial inter-planet relations. Some of the planets withdrew from the Federation in protest of what they believed to be a plot to keep them impoverished and under Federation constraints. Groups of planets banded together in an attempt to get the solbidyum they believed to be stashed away on the three planets that had obtained the original three grains.

"The resulting attacks were swift and brutal; billions of people died in the battles that ensued. The Federation rushed warships to the scene as fast as they could. In the meantime, the rebels warned that, if the stores of solbidyum they believed to be on the three planets were not turned over immediately, they would destroy the planets. Of course, there was no solbidyum to be surrendered…and the rebels lived up to the threat, literally turning all three planets into small blazing stars of total annihilation. Everyone was horrified at the destruction; and now even the three grains of solbidyum that did exist on these planets were gone as well. Many of the Federation ships and crews in the area were destroyed during decimation of the planets. One of these planets was Caldon, capital planet of the Federation at the time. Luckily, most of the top government officials managed to escape when the first attack took place. However, much of the Federation control over the galactic community was still severely weakened. Wars broke out between individual planets. These wars and raids persisted for years across *all* the Federation territories.

"Megelleon was established as the new capital planet as quickly as possible and the reinstated government struggled to hold together as much of the Federation as possible. Nearly 200 years passed before restoration of peace was in sight and the Federation was able to lay new foundations for reestablishing the unified leadership over this segment of space.

"Over the years, prospectors have searched the outer fringes for the lost asteroid mining area in hopes of finding even just one grain of solbidyum. Federation star maps show the location of the original asteroid field, but searches in the region have been fruitless. Not a single grain of solbidyum has been found since the accident and Roiax's escape.

"Over time, the story of solbidyum and the *TRITYTE* grew to be a legend and, as such, billions of people have searched for them over the last several hundred years. Many today believe the entire story to be a myth. Only a handful of people in the government know the entire truth of what happened and, until now, no one had a clue as to where the *TRITYTE*, the solbidyum, and Roiax had vanished."

Captain Maxette paused for a sip of his foccee. While he was doing so, I glanced at the faces in the room. I could tell by their expressions that much of this was new to them also. The captain cleared his throat and continued.

"Unusual measures were taken in an effort to recover the solbidyum cargo intact, so that it could be equitably distributed among the Federation planets and prevent an imbalance in power or another outbreak of wars. Huge rewards were offered that would hopefully encourage anyone finding the ship to turn it over to the Federation, rather than sell it to one planet or a specific group. Originally, the reward consisted of about 1% of the value of the solbidyum which, by any standard, would have made the discoverer wealthier than anyone in the universe. As time progressed and the solbidyum was not found and concerns grew of one planet gaining control of the entire supply, it was decided that the discoverer would be rewarded 20% of the value of the solbidyum. Later it was increased again to 50% and eventually to 80%.

"Then, a few years ago, one man claimed he had found the ship and demanded 85% plus the *TRITYTE*, unaltered and with any remaining fuel and other features intact. There was a lot of discussion and shouting in the Capitol over these demands; few senators were willing to go to 85% of the value of the solbidyum. However, none of the political leaders knew of the solbidyum reactor in the *TRITYTE* and were ultimately willing to give up the ship as part of the compensation. In the end, it was agreed and written into law that anyone finding and turning over the solbidyum to the Federation would be paid 80% of the value of the solbidyum and would keep the *TRITYTE* unaltered, which meant the reactor would still be intact.

"As it turned out, the ship this man had found was a luxury yacht that had been stolen years earlier and parked in a remote asteroid cluster after it had largely been gutted. The man had spotted the craft from outside the cluster and was afraid to go near enough to retrieve it, so he didn't really know what it was when he made his claims and demands. The story made big headlines for a few days but then eventually died out. However, the laws passed at that time for recovery compensation remained in effect and still exist in the records today…and you, Tibby, are about to receive the reward of a lifetime. The total value of your find can't even be calculated at this time and will only be known once the last grain of solbidyum is counted. You could literally buy yourself several solar systems and all the planets therein and barely scratch the surface of your wealth."

I was starting to sweat and get light-headed as the impact of what he was saying took hold.

The captain went on, "So you see, Tibby, why all the security is necessary and your protection is so critical. Your worth is literally equal to 80% of the value of the solbidyum. Hence, there will be many a kidnapper out there looking to snatch you just for a ransom. You may soon become the richest man in the universe, but you will also become the largest target for the criminal elements that exist in Federation territories. Until your claims on the ship and the solbidyum have been resolved at the Capitol, you are the responsibility of the Federation. After that... well, time will tell."

Suddenly I saw myself spending the rest of my life being surrounded by two dozen armed bodyguards, preceding and following me wherever I went. It was not a pretty picture. On the other hand, I envisioned huge estates with every luxury ever imagined by man and, in my fantasy, I saw Kala there as well. Then the bubble burst and I found myself back in the moment, looking at Captain Maxette and asking, "But what about Roiax and the ship... how did it get on Earth and what happened to him?"

"We're not exactly sure but we have a good idea," he began. "Like I stated earlier, many of the *TRITYTE*'s computer functions and communication interfaces were turned off during the time he was on the ship. Since your arrival we have been able to trace from the ship's navigation logs the evasive actions he took to avoid discovery and capture. He changed directions and speeds many times, going from gravity wave warp speeds to faster than light (FTL) speeds and, a few times, dropping to slower speeds. Your return trip was a retracing of that route, until the *TRITYTE* managed to pick up the signal of a Federation vessel and send communication, as it was programmed to do, if out of touch with the Federation for an extended period. I think 600 plus years qualify as that." He chuckled and then continued, "Once communication had been established, the

TRITYTE headed toward us and we toward it until we met. At that point, the ships prime directive had been met and the computer relinquished navigational controls over to the Federation. It's really a bit more complicated than that, but it suffices to describe what took place.

"As for Roiax… from what we can tell, he continued taking evasive actions, removing himself further and further from Federation territories, never once stopping or leaving the ship. After about five weeks of traveling, he began to feel safely insulated from chances of capture…and I think he just wanted to set foot on a planet and take in a deep breath of freedom. Obviously, he didn't make a very good choice, from what understand of the information in the ships logs. Had the computer been in control, it never would have allowed the ship to land where it did. As it was, I don't think Roiax planned to stay there long. The ships records indicate he left the ship briefly, returning about 20 minutes later, agitated and complaining of pain. The recording in the log indicates he was cussing and mumbling about some red, yellow and black creature he thought was a strange stick, which ended up biting him when he tried to pick it up. Shortly thereafter, he developed breathing problems and his hand began to swell. He went into the infirmary and hooked up to the med unit for diagnostics and treatment... and minutes later he was dead. With the *TRITYTE*'s automated navigational system turned off, the ship was stranded, slowly sinking into the mud, until you arrived and turned it back on. With the infinite power of the solbidyum reactor at its disposal, the ship was able to maintain itself, but could do nothing more until you arrived."

The captain paused, took another sip of his foccee and said, "And now we would like to ask you a few questions, if you don't mind. First, could you tell us a bit about yourself? What do you do? Your profession?"

"Well I recently left the military – the Navy, actually. I worked as part the flight deck crew on an aircraft carrier. I'm not sure if you have those or not... but I guess you must, since Federation language seems to have a word for them. Since leaving the Navy, I have been helping to redesign the water drainage system for New Orleans, a city on Earth that is partially below sea level."

"Why did you leave the Navy?" asked Lieutenant Commander Wanoll.

"I had completed my tour of duty and didn't care to re-enlist," I responded.

"What was your rank when you finished your tour?" Lieutenant Commander Wanoll asked.

"Lieutenant."

Captain Maxette asked, "You said parts of this city you call New Orleans are below sea level. Are many inhabited cities on Earth below sea level?"

"I'm not entirely sure, I know there are several in Holland, but outside of that I don't know.

"Holland?" Commander Thimas asked curiously, "Is that another planet?"

"No, sir, Holland, or the Netherlands, is a country...a territory...on Earth. Earth is divided into countries, each with its own governmental and political systems. Each country is divided into smaller regions and those into still smaller regions."

Kala asked, "What about your family?"

"There's nothing much to say there. My dad was killed in a military operation in the Middle East. He was a Marine. I was a teenager when that happened. My mother died shortly after that from lung cancer and I went to live with my grandparents. My grandfather died just before I went into the Navy and my grandmother died two years later. I have no siblings. I did have an uncle, but he drank himself to death."

"Drank himself to death?" Kala questioned. "He kept drinking liquids until it killed him?"

"The liquids he was drinking were alcohol-based. He developed a disease called sclerosis of the liver, which is a condition on our planet commonly suffered by people who consume too much alcohol."

"You had no mate?" asked Commander Thimas.

"No, sir, I haven't found the right woman," I responded.

I noticed the captain seemed a bit relieved when I answered the last question. He said, "Tibby, I'm sorry to have to tell you this, but there is one thing more you need to know. As I told you, Roiax alternated mostly between gravity wave drive and FLT drive during his journey; and your journey back with the *TRITYTE* mimicked the original trip, which means you, too, traveled at these speeds. When using a gravity wave, you traveled in time with the rest of the universe; but when traveling at FTL speeds, you travelled in *relative time*. I don't know if this is yet part of your science knowledge or understanding on Earth."

"Well, sir," I replied, "I do understand the concept of time dilation, which occurs as something – or someone – approaches the speed of light; and that the passage of time experienced by the traveler as only seconds, minutes or days is experienced as a much longer period for those who are, for instance, on Earth...or some other place... traveling at a different speed. Gravity waves are new to me, though."

"Well, Tibby, it suffices to say for our purposes here that, if you were to travel four days on a gravity wave *only*, an equal four days would pass at your origin and destination as well. But when traveling at FTL speeds for four days, the corresponding passage of time at your origin or destination could be a week or even more, depending on just how fast you are traveling. What I am trying to tell you, Tibby, is that since you left Earth, even though to you it was only a little over two weeks, nearly 20 years have passed on your Earth. The ship was duplicating the path and speeds used by Roiax, only in reverse, to get back into Federation territory." The captain sat back and gazed at me along with the other officers, waiting for my reaction.

Up until this point during the debriefing, I hadn't really thought about Earth; I never really stopped to wonder what people were thinking when I didn't show up for work and I simply disappeared. Perhaps they found my boat in the swamp. Mound Island would have disappeared, but few, if any, would really have taken notice of that. Besides, the murky water would have filled in the deep hole. If they *had* found my boat, no doubt it was believed that I had fallen overboard and been eaten by an alligator. Otherwise, I was just documented as a missing person.

"Well, Captain," I began after pondering for a moment, "I don't think they recognize Federation currency back on Earth; so if I am going to be rich, I think I will need to stay in the Federation's territories, if they will have me."

A huge smile appeared on the captain's face and from the corner of my eye I noticed Kala also turning toward me with a smile. The captain spoke through his broad grin,

"I have a feeling you won't have any problems gaining citizenship in the Federation, Tibby. None at all!"

The rest of the debriefing went forward with my account of events leading up to my inadvertent discovery of the ship, how I got onboard and the weeks that followed. Occasionally, one of the officers would ask me a question relating to information in the ships records, in order to clarify some point in my testimony. Eventually, the captain interrupted the interview.

"Tibby, I apologize...when was the last time you slept?"

I had been engrossed enough in the interviews to be oblivious to my exhaustion up to that point, but the captain's question made me immediately aware that I was starting to droop with fatigue and that I had no idea how much time had transpired since leaving the *TRITYTE*. "Well, sir, I had been awake about six or seven hours before you contacted me on the ship, and I've not slept since then."

"That was over 12 hours ago, so you've been awake at least 18 to 19 hours. You must be exhausted."

"To be honest, Captain, I can feel myself starting to fade," I replied.

"Major Kalana," the captain ordered, "would you see Tibby back to his quarters. We can resume tomorrow afternoon, once Tibby has had a good rest."

"Yes, sir," Kala replied, as she rose to her feet and turned to watch me slowly push away from the table.

As we headed for the door, the captain said, "We are approximately three weeks out from the capital now, Tibby. Though you are not a Federation military officer under my command, I respectfully order you, as well as my officers, that outside of the persons in this room, you shall not discuss any of the details of what was spoken here for the security and safety of all. I think you understand why now."

"Yes, sir," I replied with equal respect and earnest. "I understand the gravity of the situation and you need not worry. I have no intention of telling anyone."

Once Kala and the bodyguards returned me to my room and the guards stationed themselves outside my door, Kala asked if I had any questions before she left for the evening. Even as tired as I was, I didn't want her to leave, but could think of nothing to say that would justify keeping her there longer – at least none that would not come across as an obvious move on her. So I simply said, no, that I could not think of anything. Kala then walked to a panel in the far wall and touched the framed edge, which slid the panel aside to reveal a door. "Our separate quarters are connected by this door. You can lock it from this side if you desire privacy for some reason, but it is preferred that you leave it unlocked so I can reach you if needed."

She then proceeded to show me how to open, close, and operate the lock. She said that if I should need anything that Piesew Mecarta or the staff could not provide, she would be available at all times to assist me. As she stepped into her own quarters and closed the panel from her side, I fought the thoughts trying to enter my mind as to just what she *could* do to assist me. Wearily, I stumbled into my oversized bedroom and stared for a moment at the bed that was large enough to sleep everyone that had been in the conference room...with room to spare. I scarcely had removed my clothes, which I let fall to the floor, and crawled onto the bed before falling into a sound sleep. That night I dreamed of Kala and me floating naked down a wide river on my bed, as though it were a boat. In the dream Kala was running her fingers through my hair and reciting a poem about a ship carrying a stolen cargo, while overhead the *TRITYTE* was flying by with millions of dollars blowing out the open hatch.

I awoke in the morning to the sound of Piesew's voice. "Greetings, Sir Renwalt, I am most sorry to wake you, but it has been 10 hours since your meeting of yesterday with Captain Maxette and Major Kala, and I thought perhaps it best if I see to your personal needs before you meet with the captain again today."

I rolled over on the bed to see Piesew moving about the room as he spoke, picking up the clothing I had dropped there the night before. Just inside the doorway to my room stood one of my bodyguards. Neither he nor Piesew seemed the least bit concerned that I was lying naked on the bed. At that moment I realized that I had not even bothered to get under the covers. I shook off the deep sleep with a yawn. "Thank you, Piesew. I guess I should eat something before I meet with the captain again. Could you get me something? I'm not familiar with your foods yet. So perhaps you can just bring me something that is considered appropriate for this time of day."

"Major Kala asked that I tell you that you are invited to join her in her quarters to dine once you have fully awakened," Piesew related. "Of course, if you do not wish to do so, I shall tell the Major and bring your food here, as you request."

While Piesew was talking, I watched the guard inside the door. He reminded me of the guards at Buckingham Palace in England, standing rigid, eyes never moving nor face showing expression or even a small indication that he was aware of our conversation.

"Oh, tell the Major I gladly accept and as soon as I have showered and dressed I will be most pleased to dine with her.   Oh and Piesew, could you choose something appropriate for me to wear for today?"

"Indeed I can, Sir Renwalt. I shall lay out the items on your bed while you shower."

"One more thing Piesew. You need not call me Sir Renwalt. Tibby or Tib will be fine."

"That would be most inappropriate for my position and frowned upon by most people – and by the staff in general, sir. If you do not mind, I will continue to call you Sir Renwalt, but I am most flattered by the honor you show me with your request."

While the shower I took after shuffling my way into the bathroom was refreshing, it wasn't nearly as enjoyable as when Kala was there. I found myself staring at the spot where she bathed the day before with a sense of longing that surprised me.

After bathing, I returned to the bedroom to find the room immaculately cleaned and restored to order after my night of disrobing and sleep. Piesew selected a deep blue outfit identical to the black one Kala had picked out for me the night before and I wondered if there was some significance to the cut of the garments. Walking into the closet I found that a large percentage of the outfits, though available in different colors, were similar in cut. I hadn't seen many occupants of the ship so far, having passed through only one large common area on my way to quarters with Kala. Of those I did see, I couldn't recall anyone else dressed in this style. I made a mental note to add this to my list of things to ask Kala.

Piesew indicated that I should just go to Kala's suite after getting dressed, so after a quick glance in the mirror to admire how great I looked in the Federation styles, I walked to the doorway that separated Kala's suite from mine. I found both the panel and door already open, so I proceeded into the room and called Kala's name to announce my arrival. Kala's accommodations were similar to my own – perhaps a bit smaller, but equally as lavish. I noted, though, that where my suite had a definite masculine feel to it, Kala's held a more feminine sense. Many items I noticed around the suite seemed to have a quality that reminded me specifically of her.

"Hello, Tib. I trust you rested well." At the sound of Kala's sweet voice I turned to my left to see her standing there in her typical gray uniform, stripes and all. "You look quite handsome in that blue outfit. Did you choose it yourself?"

"Thank you, but I can't take credit for the selection. Piesew laid it out for me as I showered. But while we are on the topic, I noted many of the outfits in my closet are of a similar cut and design; yet on my brief trip to this secured area I saw no one wearing anything similar. Is there some significance to this uniform that I should understand?"

"Yes there is." Kala led me to her dining room adjacent to a small glass atrium, similar to the one in my own suite. In fact, after looking at it for a moment, I realized it was the same atrium, only seen from a different perspective and situated so that there was no direct view through the space into one suite from the other. "For now, moving you about the ship with armed guards could provoke unwanted questions and curiosity, if you were to dress otherwise. The particular attributes of this outfit are identical to those worn by most government dignitaries or ambassadors, who are generally known to be accompanied by bodyguards as they move about the ship. Distinguishing you as a dignitary by way of your attire allows us to maintain heightened security, while making your presence appear to be part of the normal execution of operations within the organization. Few people will pay you much attention and will acknowledge you simply as another leader or representative from one of the many planets in the Federation."

"But what if we should run into another visiting official? Won't they expect to recognize me and become suspicious that I am not actually an ambassador or dignitary?"

"First of all, you *are* a dignitary, Tib, whether you realize it or not. Your significance to the Federation is greater than any individual from any planet, so you are a dignitary in the full definition. As for being recognized by other visiting envoys, you must understand that there are millions of planets in the Federation; no one knows or recognizes all of the representatives. The only thing that may seem odd to other visitors is that you have four bodyguards – two more than normal protocols require, which is extremely rare for any dignitary. So, again, some may wonder who you are to be of such importance. This is yet another reason why we wish to minimize your contact with the rest of the ship's occupants as much as possible for now."

"*Millions*." I knew I had been told before what the size of the Federation membership was. Perhaps now that I was rested and more accustomed to my environment, the facts were just beginning to gel in my mind as to what was happening to my life. Just as Kala began to explain that visiting dignitaries to not expect to recognize each other because there are millions of planets in the Federation, I suddenly felt weak, finally comprehending the magnitude of wealth that was involved when Captain Maxette and Kala repeatedly emphasized the value of the solbidyum.   Each grain was worth the equivalent of billions, perhaps trillions of Earth dollars; and there were enough of these precious grains on the *TRITYTE*, which was now *my* ship… *MY* ship, to supply every member in this coalition of *millions* of planets.   I *alone* was to get 80% of the value of this supremely rare commodity as a reward – a reward for stumbling onto a mud-covered ship while fishing in the bayou. My head began to spin and I felt myself falling as Kala caught my arm and helped me to my chair.

"Are you ok? I saw her reach for my wrist and press the two buttons. "Piesew, send a medic right away."   Then she hovered over me with a look of extreme alarm and concern, and all I could think of was how lovely her eyes were, as blackness waved over me.

"He's coming around now," I heard a male voice say. "You say he was fine one minute and then just went pale and dropped?"

"Yes," replied Kala.   "He looked fine, and then suddenly got a sick look on his face before he blacked out."

"Sir Renwalt," said the man, "are you aware of what just happened? Do you know where you are?"

I was actually coming around very rapidly.   My sense of humor was the first thing to recover fully. "Yes, I'm in heaven.   Please send back the angel I was with earlier."

The medic was looking at an instrument in his hand and Kala was kneeling beside me.   She said to the medic with genuine concern, "He sounds delusional. Do you think he has suffered some damage to his mind?"

I could see the medic smile. "No, Major, the monitor indicates that he is attempting humor. His mental and physical functions are all returning to normal." He looked at me and asked, "Can you tell me what happened?"

"I'm embarrassed to say this, but it suddenly hit me when the Major was talking about the millions of planets in the Federation just how much… " I trailed off as I noticed a change in Kala's expression. She shook her head slightly with shock and panic etched across her face, making me realize I was about to say something I shouldn't, so I said instead, "…I mean, just how beautiful the Major is…and I simply swooned at her beauty." Kala's look of alarm gave way to relief and momentary embarrassment. I winked at her while the medic looked over his instruments. The uncharacteristic blush in her cheeks made her even more beautiful.

"Well, Major, I can see no indications of anything physically wrong. I performed a rapid diagnostic; the prick of blood from his finger reveals nothing to account for his passing out, so his statement of your beauty must be it." He grinned as he helped me to my feet, adding quietly, "…and I cannot disagree with your appraisal." He summarized his findings as he packed up his gear. "You appear to be in good health, though you are mildly dehydrated. I would suggest you drink plenty of liquids, eat something light and don't do anything too strenuous today. If you should feel ill or suspect the onset of another episode, don't hesitate to call me." With a last acknowledgement to the Major he turned and left the room, leaving Kala, the guard and Piesew standing in the dining area near the food cart, which must have arrived during the medic's assessment of my condition.

"I hope that's our meal. I'm so hungry that I could just faint." Kala started laughing so hard at my comment that tears started to flow from her eyes.   Even Piesew struggled to hold back a grin as he placed dishes on the table.

Once Piesew and the guard left the room and Kala and I were seated at the table, she said with a still fresh look of relief on her face, "I nearly panicked there for a moment when I realized you were about to say something about the solbidyum. That was quick thinking on your part. You have quite a sense of humor, by the way." She paused for a sip of foccee. "Exactly what did happen that caused you to pass out?   I realize, of course, that it was not actually my overwhelming beauty." She looked at me over her cup with a sort of twisted smile."

"No, but it came close," I replied with a bit of flirtation.   "Really, it was the realization of how much wealth you and the captain have been talking about when it comes to the recovery of the solbidyum. Until that moment, I hadn't really grasped the concept of the size of the Federation. There are millions of planets, and each one is paying me." My head started spinning again and I had to steady myself. "Well, let's just say that it overwhelmed me."

I could see the relief and amusement on Kala's face as she replied, "Gee, and just when I thought that some guy had actually swooned over me, it turned out to be money."

We both laughed at the joke and looked down at the food on our plates. It appeared to be some green salad with fruits arranged on top.

"Is this a typical first meal of the day in the Federation?"

Kala gave me another of those looks that made me feel like she was thinking, "Good grief, where does this bumpkin come from?" But instead she said, "There is no typical menu for any meal. Basically the same foods are available for any meal. Selection varies substantially from person to person, as far as which foods are preferred for the first meal or other meals, if they have a preference at all. Do you have traditional first meal foods on Earth? If so, I can have Piesew see to it that you have a proper meal prepared immediately in accordance with your tradition."

"Kala," I began, "I feel rather foolish at the moment. There are, actually, many variations of foods that people eat on Earth for their first meal of the day; but first meal, or breakfast foods as we call them, are generally different from those eaten at midday and evening meals. To be honest I don't know why, they just are. Some people eat fruits or cereal grains. Others prefer small pieces of meat they call bacon or sausage, which are served with cooked eggs. I understand in the Asian countries on Earth they eat noodle dishes. When I think about it now, it does seem rather silly to have certain foods reserved for a particular time of day. I never really gave it any thought before. Tell me, what *is* this we're eating?"

Kala started to speak as I used the chopsticks to raise some of the green leafy salad to my lips. "The greens are a mixture of plants grown here on the ship's greenhouse gardens. The brown items are eggs from the giant gormonts on Nidell Four. Gormonts are a form of flying mollusks found only on Nidell."

I have to confess the meal was very good and I told Kala so. After we finished dining, Kala led me into her stylishly decorated living room, where we relaxed for some time in rather large and comfortable chairs that faced each other. I commented to Kala on her accommodations. "Are these your normal accommodations? I mean, I know you are an attaché and your diplomatic functions require you to stay near your assigned dignitaries, but I guess what I am trying to ask is, do you stay in this secured area all the time and they assign dignitaries to these suites with you already here? I feel like much of what I see is tailored to your tastes."

Kala laughed. "No, my personal quarters are much smaller and far less opulent than these, though a few of my personal items have been brought here temporarily. I frequently have quarters assigned to me in the general area of the dignitaries. My personal tastes are recorded in the ship's system and when I am on assignment, as I am now, my suite is tailored to my tastes to a limited degree and some of my personal items are brought in. But enough about me. When you were regaining consciousness, you mentioned *heaven*. Is the belief in a place where people go after death common on your world?"

"Well, it's not a universal belief, but yes, it's very common. Not everyone's concept of an afterlife is the same, though. I'm guessing that such beliefs must exist among some of the peoples of the Federation as well, otherwise a word would not exist in your language for it."

"Yes, a large percentage of people throughout the Federation do, even those without organized religions. It's something I've often thought was rather odd," Kala responded. "How about you? Do you believe in an afterlife?"

"I did at one time," I responded, "now I sort of hope there isn't one." I said with a sad smile.

"Tibby, I'm not even going to ask," Kala said, "but I have a feeling you and I think alike on that one."

In an effort to change the tone of the conversation, Kala shifted to a more innocuous topic. "I'm guessing, but I imagine that people on your planet swim. From what you've said about swamps and sea levels I gather there is quite a bit of water on your planet."

"As a matter of fact, water makes up almost two thirds of the Earth, but there are also vast deserts in some places and giant mountains in others; and though many people do swim, many others do not. A large number of them have a fear of water. Why do you ask?"

"Sounds like an interesting planet," Kala said. "Normally I like to swim for exercise every day and, since we still have several hours before we meet with the captain, I thought perhaps you might like to join me. I don't imagine that you've had much of a chance to exercise since you left Earth."

"I would enjoy that," I replied. "Let me go back to my room and check to see if I've been provided a swim suit."

"Swim suit?" Kala said in a shocked tone. "People dress to swim on your planet?"

"Uhh, yes, actually most do," I said awkwardly. "What do you normally wear here in the Federation when swimming?"

"Why, the same thing we wear when we shower," Kala said with a smile. I knew then that I really wanted to take a dip.

I wondered where we were going to swim on the ship. I expected that there was a giant community pool somewhere onboard, so I was surprised to learn that one was provided as a part of my accommodations. It wasn't quite the size of an Olympic pool, but it was certainly large enough to swim laps. When we arrived in the pool area, Kala immediately slipped out of her uniform and dove into the water. I followed, finding the water to be at a perfect temperature. I noticed that my eyes didn't sting and that there was no scent of chlorine in the water, though it did have a slightly salty taste on my lips.

"Ionization? Salt water pool? "I asked when Kala's head popped above the water.

"Why, yes, what else would you use?" she asked.

"On Earth most people chlorinate their pools heavily to treat the water," I replied.

Kala reacted with a look of horror. "Chlorine?! But that stuff is deadly!"

"I agree," I said, "but that's what most of them use."

"Remind me not to swim in an Earth pool if I ever go there," she said as she began her laps.

I had always been a naturally strong swimmer and performed well enough on the college swim team to earn a partial scholarship. I was even able to pass the Navy's swimming requirements with ease. I was enjoying the movement of the cool water across my skin while I fell into the familiar rhythm of strokes and breaths, when suddenly I found myself next to Kala. When she was aware of my approach, she immediately picked up her pace. I correspondingly increased my speed to match hers. We both hit the end wall at the same time, then turned in unison and raced back. Kala kept increasing her speed, as did I; but I was beginning to wonder whether I was going to be able to keep pace with her much longer. We hit the other end wall simultaneously, turning again to race to the far end. I could see that Kala was giving it all she had, and I had reached my limit as well. We matched pace the entire length of the pool, no matter how hard either of us tried to break ahead. Even as I struggled to keep up with her, I was admiring how smoothly her body cut through the water and how efficiently she used her strokes. She amazed me in so many ways. I gave it one last push hoping to beat her, but we both touched the end of pool at the same time. We got out of the water, both visibly spent and breathless, and sat on the edge of the pool.

"You swim very well, Tib. It's been a long time since anyone has been able to tie me in a race."

"You're not so bad yourself," I panted, all the while admiring the rise and fall of her breasts with each deep breath. "But if it helps you feel any better, I swam competitively in school."

"Ha," she said, splashing me with a handful of water. "Good thing I didn't make a wager with you."

"Ha," I said, splashing her back. "Good thing I'm not up to form and out of shape."

We both laughed and Kala slipped into the water, pushing off into a graceful backstroke down the length of the pool. "I'll give you a little time to get into shape and then I want a rematch," she said with a mischievous grin.

"You're on," I replied, matching her playful taunt. "What's the wager?"

"I'll think of something," and with that she turned at the wall, swimming the full length of the pool without surfacing.

When she arrived at the wall by my feet, she drew in a long breath and said that the hour was drawing near when we were to meet with the captain, so we should get ready.

We showered and dressed at the facilities by the pool, then returned to the suite so that Kala could style her hair.

I stood by, watching Kala turn curls in her hair, as we chatted briefly about swimming and how similar the strokes were here to those on Earth. When Kala finished with the wand, she looked at me and laughed. My hair was its usual mess, sticking up randomly in typical male non-fashion. I never paid much attention to my hair. Kala then moved toward me with the wand, fixing my hair as she had done before, teasing me as she fashioned a smooth, loose style. "You know something, I'm not sure if I am an attaché for you or a hairdresser!"

"I didn't know there was a difference," I volleyed back with a feigned innocence. She laughed, and then got a strange look in her eyes as she stared into mine. For a minute I thought we were going to kiss, but after a few moments the spell was broken and she said, "We had better go. The captain will be waiting."

The second debriefing was delayed. Kala and I sat alone in the conference room for some time before Captain Maxette and Lieutenant Commander Wanoll arrived. It was obvious from the scowl on the captain's face that something was not right. The steward poured drinks for everyone and departed before the captain spoke. He addressed me first.

"Tibby, are you feeling alright? I heard you had an incident earlier today."

"Yes, sir, I'm feeling okay now. I was simply overwhelmed at the sudden realization of the size of the Federation and the vast wealth you have been talking about. I've never had anything like this happen before, of course."

The captain smiled briefly and said, "Actually, I was shocked that you didn't pass out when we first told you. I can see where it might have taken a while to sink in." The captain's countenance returned to its former severity. "But now, I fear I have some disturbing news. Just a few hours ago several of our own troopers – carefully selected and briefed troopers that were supposed to be guarding the *TRITYTE* – attempted to take the ship and its cargo by force. There were only three of them, but they managed to kill several other guards and gain entry into the *TRITYTE*. Fortunately, we still have a lockout on the controls from the bridge of the *DUSTEN* and the rebels were not able to successfully override it; nor did they have the code to open the lock on the container in the hold. We lost several more men when actions were taken to reclaim the *TRITYTE*; but in the end we were successful. The problem now is that we believe these individuals may have been able to get word out to others on the *DUSTEN* and to at least one scout ship. One of the patrol ships returned without one of its gravity wave message pods. The crew tried to act as though they had no idea what happened to it; however, using mental probes and other detection methods, we were able to discover that the pod was sent to the Bunem System at about the same time that the *TRITYTE* was captured by the rebels. The Bunem System is the one major planetary system that has resisted rejoining the Federation and has spent the greatest amount of time and resources trying to find the *TRITYTE*. The Bunemnites are also the original aggressors responsible for the destruction of the three planets that once had solbidyum power capabilities.

We are now left with the terrible probability that the pod will deliver its message successfully and, since the Bunem System is between us and the capital, the Bunemnites will be able to mobilize their forces against the *DUSTEN* before the Federation even knows we have the *TRITYTE* and the solbidyum. I have dispatched a gravity wave message pod with a coded memorandum apprising those at the Capitol and the High Command of our situation and of the discovery of *TRITYTE* and its cargo. I know they will immediately send every ship in the Federation to assist us; but the question at this point is to what degree the Federation leadership and military may be compromised by rebels and mutineers and on which ships. While this ship is equipped and staffed to present a formidable force, we do not know who or how many others there are here who might turn against the Federation to get a share of the wealth and power represented by the solbidyum. This area of the ship is the safest, Tibby, but we are increasing the guards in the area just the same.   We are rigorously testing troopers using mental probes to determine where their loyalties lie before we assign them here.   We have about a week to prepare before the Bunem forces arrive; but honestly, I don't know what we will do if they attack us in full force. Tibby, you mentioned that you were in your Earth's Navy. I assume that you were trained in the use of hand weapons in both offensive and defensive situations?"

"Yes, sir, and I've also achieved a master black belt in mixed martial arts and served as an instructor while in the Navy," I replied.

"Martial arts?" the captain asked. "What sort of training is this? I'm not familiar with the term."

"*Martial arts* is a term that refers collectively to the codified systems and traditions of hand to hand combat practices that use the opponent's movements to an advantage and uses one's own body as a weapon against the opponent." I explained this as best I could, but from the look on everyone's faces, I may as well have said it in an Earth language.

"I still don't understand," said the captain. "Can you demonstrate this skill?"

I looked about, making a quick assessment of the room; it was large enough for a demonstration without risking damage to anything. The problem was how to do it without hurting someone. "Yes, sir, I think I can, but without padding on the floor I'm afraid someone might be injured in the process."

"The body armor worn by our troopers provides cushioning that protects them from hard falls," assured the captain. "Can you demonstrate using this trooper here?" He pointed at the trooper standing guard inside the briefing room."

"Yes, sir, but I won't demonstrate any techniques that could be lethal or that could break any bones. I would hate to injure him."

The captain and his officers laughed. "No offense, Tibby, but I doubt anything you could do with your body could break the bones of a trooper in body armor, so give it your all."

"Okay, sir, but I will still limit the demonstration to non-lethal moves."

"Trooper, do whatever he tells you to do. Just don't kill him. We need him," the captain said with a grin.

"Yes, sir," the trooper said.

This trooper was a brute of a fellow – the perfect type for this sort of demonstration. He was well muscled and at least a head taller than me. Basically, he was built like an ox. The first thing I told him to do was to try and place me in restraints. I had noticed that all the Federation guards carry them in their tactical belts. The trooper approached me with a grin on his face, expecting to easily subdue and restrain me using nothing more than strength and physical intimidation.   As he grabbed my arm to pull it behind my back, I responded with the speed of practiced reflex to reverse the hold on his arms while at the same time twisting under his massive trunk. Simultaneously, I used my body as a lever to I lift him and then sent him flying across the room where he crashed into the wall. Both Commander Thimas and Lieutenant Commander Wanoll jumped to their feet in amazement.   The captain simply sat with his jaw agape.   Kala also reacted with shock, but I was sure I detected a hint of a smile at the corner of her mouth. The trooper slowly got to his feet, visibly shaken, but unharmed.

"Okay," I said.   Clearly these people had no knowledge of any martial arts at all.   With the next demonstration I needed to show them the true value of these skills in combat. "Now I want you to take your knife and attack me with it. Don't hold back, I want you to seriously try to hurt me."

"Wait a minute," the captain said.   "We can't risk you getting hurt. Trooper, leave the scabbard on your knife, but attack in full as though it were unsheathed."

I smiled and the trooper did as the captain ordered. He came at me swinging and stabbing with his knife. I evaded, baiting him into a direct thrust, which I countered with one disciplined fluid movement, body-slamming the trooper on his back and immobilizing him between his now contorted arm and my foot, which was instantly leveraged against his shoulder. I had restrained and disarmed him, holding his own knife to his exposed throat, all before anyone in the room had taken their next breath.

Holding this posture, I heard the captain exclaim, "Unbelievable! You were a blur of motion. It all happened so fast! Wanoll, have you ever seen anything like this?! We need to have all our military personnel trained in these techniques as soon as possible. Okay, Tibby, you have me convinced. I would like to see more of these martial arts, as you call them, but right now we have more pressing matters. Trooper, I trust you're okay to resume you post here?"

"Yes, sir," the rattled trooper responded, as I helped him to his feet and returned his knife. "I'm just a bit shaken." Before resuming his post by the door, he addressed me. "Sir, I would consider it a great privilege, if you could teach me some of those techniques."

"Regarding my original question about hand weapons – well, after seeing your demonstration, I'm wondering if you need one," the captain chuckled. "In any case, we believe it might be in your (and our) best interest if we armed you with a weapon, in addition to maintaining your current squad of bodyguards. This goes for you as well, Major Kalana. As long as you're assigned to Tibby, my orders are that you remain armed at all times. I know that an attaché doesn't normally carry a weapon in diplomatic service; however, this situation is unique and I know you're well qualified. I would suggest the weapon be something small and concealable – for both of you."

"Yes, sir," Kala said, "I'll see to it."

"For now," the captain continued, "our primary focus is still much the same – to protect the solbidyum, the *TRITYTE,* and Tibby. Unfortunately, we now have the added task of avoiding the Bunem fleet while expediting our course to Megelleon. We don't know yet how much information has leaked out to the *DUSTEN's* crews and passengers. Word has already circulated about the quarantined area in the hangar that a portion of the flight crew is under lockdown. We've released a statement, advising that there is cause for concern that the crew of one of the patrol ships has returned with symptoms indicating a possible outbreak of Distalarian Fever and that they are being held for treatment on their ship until the contagious periods have passed, which is generally around five weeks. We've also announced that everyone who has been in contact with them during the past few days has also been quarantined as a safety precaution.   Unfortunately, this approach hasn't been working too well.   Friends and family are pressing for answers as to why they can't at least speak with them.   To keep the situation from escalating into a panic or media frenzy, we are allowing video conferencing with an officer present, out of camera range. The officer will activate a video kill switch, in the event the traitor deviates from permitted topics of conversation. Let us all hope and pray that our fears are for nothing and that we get through this alright.   In the meantime, we need everyone to be as vigilant as possible."

With that, the captain adjourned the meeting, confirming that we would meet again the following day at the same time.   He and Commander Thimas left together. Lieutenant Commander Wanoll remained behind, clearly wishing to speak with me.   "Tibby, that was quite the demonstration you gave us. Just how many of these martial arts maneuvers are there?"

"That's some question," I responded, thinking heavily on the matter. "On Earth we have many forms of martial arts – Karate, Jiujitsu, Bok Fu, Taekwondo and dozens of others. Each tradition likely has several hundreds of moves that apply to various scenarios. What I practice is a hybrid of several techniques, all of which are highly effective for hand-to-hand combat in military and non-military situations."

"That sounds terribly complicated and time-consuming to learn," responded Lieutenant Commander Wanoll, his thoughts clearly visible on his face.

"It is a disciplined art that takes a lifetime to master. It took me eight Earth years to achieve my current level of skill."

"Hmm. We don't have years for you to train the troopers and security forces." Wanoll's disappointment was as great as his former excitement.

"What about using a teaching device like the headband that was on the *TRITYTE*? Is there some way we can use that to teach them more quickly?" This was the only avenue I could think of for accelerating the training.

"I only wish that were possible," replied Lieutenant Commander Wanoll. "Unfortunately, while the device is good for passing on information such as language, math or history, it doesn't work for physical skills, which the body must learn as well as the brain. The headband could perhaps impart the knowledge behind each technique, but the students would still have to physically practice and get the feel of each move and then, if I understand what you've demonstrated, perform the moves in context repeatedly until each situational response becomes automatic. The headband would certainly improve the timeline, but I'm not confident that it would work fast enough to help us in this situation. However, if you would be willing to give it a try, the ship's medical experts and scientists may be able to locate the parts of your brain where your martial arts skills reside. If so, they can perhaps translate and download these synaptic memories into the headband units. If that much is successful, we could certainly attempt to pass on your skills in tandem with direct training to see if learning is enhanced. Let me talk to our science team and get back to you."

As Wanoll left the room, I turned to see Kala standing slightly behind me with her arms crossed, looking at me appraisingly. "That was quite the demonstration. I would love it if you would show me a few of your moves."

Okay, so we all know the first thought that crossed my mind. *A few of my moves.* I know damn well that's not what she meant, but it sure was what I was thinking. Nevertheless, I replied like a gentleman. "Anytime you like. I'm at your disposal. I would be most pleased to teach you a few moves."

"Great," she said. "Let's eat quickly and then go to the gym. I don't want to waste any time. If learning even a few of these skills will prevent the loss of more life and protect the *TRITYTE* and solbidyum, we need to take advantage of the opportunity immediately."

I used my wrist com to advise Piesew that Kala and I were heading back to my quarters to eat. Kala interjected with a suggestion for an appropriate meal. As we walked back, Kala voiced her concerns over the development that the captain had related to us. She thought the captain should turn the ship around, head deeper into space and ultimately approach the capital from a different direction. I pointed out that this strategy would consume precious time – time that would only facilitate a broader leak of information about the recovery of the solbidyum. This could, without a doubt, result in even more power-hungry groups and governments dispatching their own ships in attempts to intercept the *DUSTEN,* regardless of its direction of approach.

I could see the captain's reasons for wanting to get us to get to Megelleon as quickly as possible. Chaos and war were almost a certainty and thousands, maybe millions of lives were at risk. The decimation of the original three solbidyum-powered planets was only a small example of what could happen. The fewer people that knew of the recovery of the lost solbidyum in advance of the DUSTEN's arrival at the capital the better. Once there and properly secured, official announcements of the solbidyum recovery would assure governments that ample supply was available for all of the Federation membership, which would alleviate at least some of the motives for attack. Kala said half-jokingly that maybe I should just hop in the *TRITYTE* and fly it straight to Megelleon, since it was a faster ship and would pass Bunem before anyone expected; besides the fact that they would be looking for the *DUSTEN*. While it was a long shot, Kala's though it did have some merit. It gave me another idea that I didn't mention to her; I needed time to put it together in my mind.

I was surprised when the meal arrived, because of its resemblance to cold soba noodles and hot tea; just as it is served on Earth. The similarity of the dishes was uncanny – light tan colored noodles, a rich, soy-flavored sauce and some chopped greens that looked much like scallions. For a moment I believed the dishes were identical, but there was a subtle difference in the noodles, which had more of a woodsy, fresh mushroom flavor. The greens not only tasted like onion, but also had a cucumber-like taste as well. When I commented to Kala about the similarities, she explained the origin of the dish.

"The planet where this dish originated is called Pinop, which is mostly covered with water. The peoples of Pinop live on the planet's many islands, which are of volcanic origin. These islanders make their living from the sea. The noodles are made from the nodules of seaweed that washes up on the beaches and is collected by the inhabitants. The nodules are cut open to harvest the seeds, which the villagers dry in the sun and grind into flour that becomes the main ingredient in these noodles. They are prized all over the Federation for their flavor. The sauce is from an aquatic creature on the same planet that dispels clouds of this fluid into the water to confuse its enemies as it flees."

"We have two similar creatures on Earth that have a similar defense mechanism," I said, "octopus and squid. Squid ink is edible, but as far as Earth's version of this dish, the sauce is made from a bean, though the taste is similar."

I noticed as we dined that Kala kept looking at me in a contemplative way, so I asked her if there was something on her mind. She looked down at her plate a minute and then met my eyes.

"Tib," Kala began, "You have surprised me, first with your swimming skill and then with your display of martial arts. You possess physical skill and agility that I didn't expect and now I find myself wondering what other surprises you may hold for me. When you were coming around after blacking out this morning, your mind still reeling from the event, you managed to immediately interpret my signal to you and quickly correct yourself before making a serious mistake by mentioning the solbidyum. You did it with so much skill that, even knowing the truth behind what you almost said, I found it easy to believe what you were saying."

"What? That I simply swooned at your beauty?" I grinned and Kala's head dipped as bit of color touched her cheek. "If it makes you feel any better, it is true. I do swoon at your beauty, Kala, and I find you to be most pleasurable company. I also value your assistance highly. I would be totally lost without your guidance."

"Thank you, Tib. I'm not sure what to make of what you've said, but I appreciate that you value my support. As far as what the Captain said today about us being armed, I want you to know that I am fully combat-certified and an expert with small arms, as well as heavier arms. I am as capable as any trooper."

"Kala, I have the utmost trust in your abilities. Now let's go get our side arms issued, as the captain ordered, and then I will show you some martial arts techniques. Are there suitable gym clothes in my wardrobe, or will we be doing that naked also?"

Kala laughed as she shook her head. "Special gear is available at the gym. Sizing is not an issue; the suits are form-fitted and stretch to the proper size. Our side arms can be issued to us via Piesew. I will familiarize you with their features and practice with you at the range here in our quarters."

I thought to myself, "The suite has its own swimming pool, gym and firing range? No wonder this ship is so damn big!"   I wondered whether all dignitary accommodations were this extensive and how many of these suites existed on the *DUSTEN*.

The gym turned out to be right across the hall from the pool. Kala led me to some small lockers by an open shower. Inside the locker was a small compartment, from which she withdrew a package. She said to hang my clothing in the locker and put on the suit contained in the package. She then opened the locker next to mine, removed a similar package and began undressing. The outfits reminded me of two-piece dance leotards. I felt a bit conspicuous with the bulge between my legs, but Kala didn't seem to notice or, at least, pay any obvious attention to it. After we were changed, Kala directed me to a large room fitted with a padded floor mat.

"So, what do I need to do?" Kala asked.

"We'll, let's start with the basics. First watch as I go through a series of coordinated stances, blocks and strikes that form the foundation of all sparring techniques. Then I will teach them to you."

"Wow," Kala exclaimed, as I performed the choreographed fundamentals. "It's almost like a dance… a ballet. No wonder you said it took you years to learn."

After introducing and practicing these basics, I showed Kala some simple, yet effective techniques for dealing with attackers. She was amazed at how one could use an aggressor's physical momentum and weight to a defensive advantage and how straightforward these initial moves were to execute. I was likewise amazed at how quickly she learned and impressed at strength that her slim body seemed to disguise.

We became so engrossed in the lesson that we didn't hear Piesew until he cleared his throat to get our attention. He stood in his usual proper posture near the gym entrance holding a box. "Major, I have obtained the weapons, as you requested. Would you like me to leave them here or place them in the target range?"

"Leave them here, if you will, Piesew," Kala said. "Thank you."

Kala examined the assortment of weapons as I watched. "The target range is right next door," she said. "We can go dressed as we are. I'll explain and demonstrate each weapon, after which we can practice firing at various targets. We'll come back here to shower and dress."

The target range was nothing like traditional target ranges on Earth, nor was the selection of weapons. The targets consisted of animated holographic projections of attackers and enemy combatants in all sorts of changeable environments and settings. The weapons themselves were just as strange. None of the weapons fired projectiles; rather each of them directed some sort of energy beam. There was no noise or recoil when the weapon discharged and, other than for the light indicators on the target that confirmed a hit, there was no clear way to identify whether the weapon discharged at all. Some had the typical customary shape that is used on Earth, while others were appropriately called flat guns. Other varieties were worn on the wrist with a band attached to a ring that extended past the knuckle where the ring was worn on the index finger. This weapon fired by squeezing the hand to make a fist. I shot well with the familiar pistol-shaped weapons, but not quite as well with the flat guns. I did, however, shoot superbly with the wrist weapon for some reason. For the most part, my scores with the hand guns averaged 97%, which surprised Kala. With the flat guns I averaged 90% hits, also acceptable. But with the wrist guns I consistently achieved 100% accuracy, surprising both myself and Kala.

Some of the weapons were designed only to incapacitate the attacker by causing temporary paralysis, while others would seriously wound or killed, depending on the setting. What amazed me was that all but one of them affected only living organisms, causing no damage to walls or other objects. Kala explained that hand weapons were generally intended for use inside a ship, as it was too dangerous to use anything that might breach the hull or damage a life support system that sustained the ship's occupants. Ship-to-ship weapons were designed to cause structural damage, but small personal weapons were designed to immobilize only people and aggressive creatures.

After observing me practice, Kala said the best choices for me would be the wrist gun, as it would essentially be hidden by my coat sleeve, and the small flat gun, which would also conceal well in any pocket. Even though I didn't do as well with this weapon, concealment was important. Anyone carrying a weapon tended to draw unwanted attention, except perhaps for the troopers, who were always armed. I had to agree with her; but I vowed to myself to practice every day until I could achieve perfect scores with it as well.

The whole time we practiced I was mulling over a plan to protect the solbidyum and get it to Megelleon safely. While Kala and I were showering and dressing, I decided to solicit Kala's assistance in making arrangements to present my idea to the captain.

"Kala, would it be out of place for me to invite the captain to my quarters for a meal?"

Kala turned to me with a surprised look. "There is nothing in protocol that would make it out of line, but unless you are inviting other officers to attend with him, it's not normally done. Do you have a special reason in mind?"

"Yes, I do, actually," I replied with a tone of caution, "but other than for you and the captain, I would prefer at this time to not include anyone else. I have an idea I wish to put before the captain and I would prefer that he decide who else to include in additional discussions after he's heard it."

"I think that can be arranged," Kala replied, "but I recommend you have the dinner meeting in my quarters. The captain and I often dine together to discuss diplomatic issues, so it would not appear out of the norm for him to come to my cabin. You could join us through the door between our suites to prevent anyone from knowing you were in attendance, other than for Piesew and the staff, of course. Does that suit you needs?"

"Yes, I think that will work. How soon can you arrange it?"

"It's not uncommon for me to request to see the captain on short notice, so I can try to reach him now and possibly arrange to meet in an hour or so, depending on his schedule. Let me contact him and see."

Kala pulled a small device from the pocket of her uniform that looked at first glance like a card, but then I noticed that it was more like an ultra-thin version of the cellular telephones on Earth.   I heard her say "Captain Maxette," followed a few moments later by the captain's voice. "Major, I hope everything is okay with our guest."

"Indeed, Captain, all is well. We just left the target range. There is no need to be concerned about his skills with hand weapons. He beat or matched me with every weapon except the flat gun and with a bit of practice I think he will beat me with that one as well."

"That's great to hear, but I'm guessing that's not what you are contacting me about…?" the captain probed.

Kala laughed, "You are right ,Captain. Actually, I am calling because our guest would like to meet with you in private to discuss a sensitive matter. I thought it might be a good idea to gather in my suite, so as to draw less attention and minimize curiosity among the ship's inhabitants."

"Hmm, I'm intrigued," the captain replied. "It just so happens that I was about to have a meal delivered to my quarters, but I would enjoy dining with you instead. Why don't we meet in about forty minutes? Or is that too soon?"

"Forty minutes would be perfect, sir," Kala said looking at me. I nodded my approval. Kala next contacted Piesew. "Piesew, the captain and one other will be dining with me in my suite. Could you have the chef prepare some Canip'lurb with Tagirian sweet sauce and some of those delicious caramelized Nibulan fruits. Oh, and also some green salad. Tell the chef to add appropriate beverages and anything else that he thinks will complement the dishes."

"Yes, Major," Piesew replied. "Meals for three, you say?"

"That is correct Piesew. The captain should arrive in about forty minutes. Hopefully that will provide the chef enough time to prepare everything properly. I know this is very short notice."

"I do not think it will be any problem. As we were speaking, I verified that all of the necessary ingredients are readily available. Will that be all?"

"Yes, Piesew. Thank you."

"Now, I don't suppose you're willing to tell me what this is all about, since you haven't brought it up until now…?" Kala prodded inquisitively.

"I think it's best to present this idea only once," I said, "so if you don't mind waiting until the captain arrives, I would prefer that. It's no reflection on you in any way. Actually, I will be most interested in your thoughts and comments."

The next forty minutes didn't go as quickly as I would have liked and I found my stomach knotting up in anticipation of the meeting. Kala tried to keep up small conversation about the martial arts training that was scheduled for the next morning while practicing the sequences in front of her reflection in the atrium glass. I found myself admiring how quickly she seemed to comprehend and remember the execution of each move. There was a unique grace about her fluid movements that was almost hypnotic.

"Kala, what will happen, assuming we make it to Megelleon with the solbidyum... I mean, with you and me? Will you still be assigned to me as an attaché?"

Kala stopped practicing and looked at me with a brief pause. "For a while probably, though I am sure a more high-ranking attaché will be assigned over me to assist with the negotiations and transfer of the solbidyum, your funds and the *TRITYTE*. After that I will no doubt be reassigned to the ship, as this is my base of operation. You will be given a more senior attaché to assist you in the future." I thought I detected just the slightest note of sadness in her voice.

"And what if I don't want you to go? What if I were to request that you to be permanently assigned to me? Would they do that? And how would you feel about it?" I asked.

Kala raised an eyebrow. "I must confess that, until now, I had not given any of this a thought. To answer your first question, as to whether they would permanently appoint me to you upon your request, they might, if I agreed to take the assignment. Your desires, coupled with the tremendous power you will have, are going to make the Federation want to have an official delegate close to you at all times. They will do almost anything to cultivate your personal favor. As to your second question," she said as she resumed her martial arts practice, "I think I would like that. Yes, I think I might like that very much." She interrupted her practice again, turning to me with her hands on her hips, "Why do you ask?"

"Well, first, I feel very comfortable with you and that's important in my situation. Second, I trust in your abilities. Third, we get along well, or at least I think so. And last, to quote the words from an old song on Earth, I've grown accustomed to your face!"

Kala smiled broadly, "That's about the nicest thing anyone has ever said to me. Thank you."

Just then there was a signal at the door. Kala opened it and invited the captain to enter.

"Major, Tibby, good to see you both smiling. I hope that whatever it is you wish to discuss with me will have me smiling as well. However, I fear I have more bad news." Kala poured the captain a cup of foccee." Earlier today I was approached by Ambassador Rifnan from the Kandurian System. He wanted to know whether rumors of the discovery of the *TRITYTE* and the solbidyum are true. According to him, word is that the ship has been recovered by a tall Pakarian. I'm assuming that someone must have seen Tib and, because of his red hair, assumed he was Pakarian. He also heard that there was an attempt to steal the *TRITYTE* and repeatedly assured me that no one from his planet was involved. Of course, I denied it all and told him that, to my knowledge, there had not been any Pakarians onboard, nor had any Pakarians recently arrived in a ship carrying the legendary solbidyum. Not exactly a lie, as Tibby is *not* Pakarian. Nevertheless, we have a problem; if Ambassador Rifnan has heard it, you know everyone else will very soon. He loves to spread rumors."

Just as he finished sharing this information, the door chime sounded again. Kala suggested I move to another room so that Piesew would not know I was the other guest. I slipped back over into my own suite until the table was set and Kala indicated it was okay to return.

"What's going on?" the captain asked. "You don't trust Piesew?"

"Actually, I trust Piesew very much," I said, though I really didn't know him well yet. "But I want this meeting to be known to as few as possible. I have a plan that I think may help to get us off the hook with the Bunem System and Ambassador Rifnan, as well as everyone else on the ship. We can discuss it as we dine. I don't know what we're having, but it sure smells good."

As we seated ourselves at the table, I began to lay out my plan.

"It appears that word has spread about the *TRITYTE*, the solbidyum and me. We know that an attempt was made to steal the *TRITYTE* and the solbidyum and that this mission failed. We are also aware that one patrol crew sent a message pod to the Bunem System telling them of the discovery. By the time we get close to their system, it is safe to assume that the Bunemnites will already be deployed and standing ready for us. We also know that there is no way we can get any of the fleet here to assist us before then. Am I correct so far?" I asked the captain.

"That pretty much sums it up, yes," the captain said heavily.

"Okay. Now what would happen if another attempt is made to steal the *TRITYTE* and the solbidyum, and it succeeds?" I continued cautiously, "and let's just say the story of its escape triggers a huge hunt to recover it, using almost every available ship on the *DUSTEN*. Then let's assume that the *DUSTEN* maintains its station here, while the search for the *TRITYTE* is conducted. How long do you think it would be before some other loyal Bunem spies would send a second message pod to inform the Bunemnites of these developments so they could immediately attempt to intercept the *TRITYTE*?"

"I think I see where you're going with this," the captain said with a smile. "But please continue; I want to hear your entire plan." I glanced at Kala. She was looking at me with a look of pride and amazement as I continued.

"This operation would need to proceed with the fewest possible number of people knowing what is really unfolding. We would have to be assured, without a trace of doubt, that each team member is loyal and trustworthy. You said that, outwardly, the *TRITYTE*'s construction is just like that of any other patrol ship, correct?"

"Yes," the captain said, "Only the interiors are different and, of course, the power systems. Oh, and there is a Federation symbol on our patrol ships that is not present on the *TRITYTE*."

"Is there anything unique, like perhaps the power signature, that can be detected or that would otherwise differentiate the *TRITYTE* from other patrol craft?"

"No," the captain said leaning forward in his chair, his food forgotten and a huge smile spreading across his face.

"Then I suggest that we switch the *TRITYTE* with one of the other patrol ships, hide the Federation symbol on this decoy with something that can later be removed in space, and then assign a trusted crew to steal this fake *TRITYTE*. Meanwhile, we install a temporary Federation symbol on the real *TRITYTE* and move it to a common patrol ship bay. After moving the decoy into the secured bay, the hangar can be made to look disheveled and damaged, as though a fight took place. Notify the next of kin and broadcast the story of the first attempt and the subsequent 'successful' theft over the ship's newscast, perhaps even showing the bodies of the troopers killed in the first attempt. Then immediately deploy every available ship to look for the *TRITYTE*, including the real, disguised *TRITYTE*. Since so little is known about the ship and the solbidyum, you could fabricate some information about it, perhaps announcing that the *TRITYTE* can be detected by a specific energy signature. This will add plausibility to the theft scenario. We would have to conjure up something that emits an easily detected signal, which we will install in a message pod on the decoy ship. The crew can program the pod to travel on some kind of erratic route, activate the transmitter to emit the signal *intermittently*, and launch the pod prior to uncovering the hidden Federation logo. Then the decoy *TRITYTE* will again look like a Federation patrol ship, which will join the hunt for the stolen *TRITYTE*. Everyone will be following and chasing after the signature emitted from message drone for light years." I exhaled, my stomach slowly becoming unknotted. My plan was falling favorably on the captain's ears.

I continued, "Perhaps choose one of the uninhabited planets, maybe the original prison exile planet, and send the pod in that general direction. The ploy should at the very least divide the Bunem fleet. Then, if the Bunemnites do come to the *DUSTEN*, act as though you think they are coming to help. Perhaps even invite their leadership aboard the *DUSTEN* and let them have access to the entire ship. They will most certainly be looking to see if the solbidyum is here but, of course, it won't be. It will be on the real *TRITYTE*, deployed on an unconventional route to the capital with Kala and me and four of your most trusted crewmen."

"Tibby, that is brilliant!" the captain said, "I think it might even work. I have an idea to make it even more plausible. Before the fake *TRITYTE* leaves the *DUSTEN*, we can plant another patrol ship at a rendezvous point. Using one of their weapons, that patrol ship can fire a non-lethal shot on the fake *TRITYTE* that will damage its propulsion system and make it look as though it encountered the real *TRITYTE* in a conflict. The decoy will then uncover the

Federation logo and be towed back to the *DUSTEN* as a regular patrol ship. When we have it towed back, we can broadcast a follow-up story that will convince any remaining skeptics that the hoax is real. Brilliant, Tibby, brilliant! Just one thing, why you and Major Kala on the real *TRITYTE* for this mission? Why not just leave the transport to one of my loyal crews?"

"Well, first of all, it gets me off the *DUSTEN*, so I can't be questioned or interrogated by the Bunemnites if they do come aboard. If you like you can make up a story that I was abducted by the traitors and that I'm being held as a hostage with them on the ship. Secondly, once I reach Megelleon I will need Major Kalana to assist me with protocols and communicate with the leadership there to convince them that I am not a pirate, so that we are allowed passage. I want a full crew, because we are in a combat situation and this calls for a combat-ready crew. I was lucky to have the computerized navigation after I launched from Earth; however, the craft is designed to operate with a crew of six people who have a skilled understanding of all the systems and weapons. Lastly, I have nothing to gain by taking the ship anyplace but the capital, and I have everything to gain by getting it there safely. Overall, I think the plan greatly increases the probability of getting the *TRITYTE* and solbidyum to Megelleon safely."

"I agree with these points," said Captain Maxette. "Shrewd thinking. I think I have a crew in mind that will increase probability even more. Damn, Tibby, the plan is brilliant! Absolutely brilliant! Now, if we can only keep it under wraps and pull it off. Tell me, why didn't you have Commander Thimas and Lieutenant Commander Wanoll here for this discussion as well?"

"Because, Captain, I don't know who you can trust on your staff and who you cannot. I leave that to you. The fewer people who know about this, the better our chance of pulling it off."

"I agree, Tib," the captain replied thoughtfully." I believe I can trust Commander Thimas and Lieutenant Commander Wanoll to carry out this plan with us. However, neither of them can go with you on the *TRITYTE*. I need to find four competent crewmembers that I can trust. You'll need an engineer, a navigator, a seasoned pilot and a gunner."

"Captain, I think I know an experienced engineer you can trust that would fit into the crew nicely," offered Kala.

The captain grinned. "I think I know exactly the engineer you have in mind and I could not agree more." Kala smiled back at the captain; and I wondered who this engineer was and what made him so special.

The next two days were dedicated to training Kala and two of the guards in the fundamentals of martial arts and practicing some key combat sequences. Between sessions Kala and I burned off some anxious energy by swimming laps. As time passed and no word came from the captain, I became worried. We were only a few days away from our imminent encounter with the Bunem fleet.

Kala and I were together at all times, other than when we were sleeping. We shared many details of life and customs both on Earth and on the Federation planets. The more time I spent with her, the more I found myself drawn to her. Her competitive nature compelled me to push my abilities to the limit to keep up with her in the pool and on the target range. I finally got the hang of the flat gun and was matching her scores with all weapons by the end of our training period.

We had just finished eating breakfast on the fifth day after our meeting with the captain, when Kala finally received word from him to get to the hangar. Kala was told to see to it that I was dressed in something that would not differentiate me from others passing through the hangar area. Kala made a quick call and Piesew appeared shortly after with a package he said had just arrived for me, along with a set of orders for Major Kala.

Kala read the message and handed it to me. After reading it twice, I handed it back to her. "Well, I guess this is it." Kala placed the message in the recycler per the instructions written in the communication. I opened the package to find a flight mechanic's outfit complete with shoes. While I was dressing, Kala packed two duffel bags for us that contained pertinent items from our wardrobes. She suggested that we make our way to the hangar with two of the guards walking ahead of us as though they were on a casual stroll, followed by me and another guard walking together. She and the forth guard would follow approximately ten paces behind, appearing to chat as though they were friends leaving their shift. This informal profile would be inconspicuous in the high traffic of the main corridor. I must confess I was rather nervous, but I was glad to be paired up with the same trooper who had participated in my first martial arts demonstration and who had been practicing with Kala and me the past few days. This association gave us something to talk about naturally so our conversation would not appear forced or fabricated. In addition to wearing an ordinary mechanic's uniform to detract attention from our movements, Kala also darkened my hair to a more commonly seen brown shade using the styling wand.

We strolled casually through the corridor to a different hangar entrance than the one where the *TRITYTE* and I were originally received. The two guards who preceded us through the corridor took up positions outside the hangar door and the guard who walked with me entered the hangar first.   We were immediately challenged by a trooper inside the door who required us to place our hands on a scanner that confirmed identification and clearance. Once cleared to enter, we moved directly toward a patrol ship bay that housed what looked like a standard patrol craft with a Federation emblem displayed on the hull. The hatch was closed. Kala instructed me to grasp the handle and then step back. I did so with some apprehension, recalling my first encounter with this door handle on Mound Island. There was a momentary delay while a small light (which I clearly had not seen through the crusted mud the first time) blinked at one end of the handle, after which the door swung open – much more gently than it had in the swamp. As soon as we entered and closed the hatch behind us, I recognized that were in the airlock of the *TRITYTE* looking through the open inner airlock door toward the wall where I had originally rappelled into the craft. Back on Earth I didn't notice the inner airlock door, but I suppose everything looked foreign when the ship was lying on its side.

Once inside, we proceeded to the galley where Kala said the others would be waiting. We arrived to find two other men and a very lovely woman standing there, all in military uniforms. All of them snapped to attention and saluted; right arm across the chest and hand on the shoulder. Kala returned the salute and greeted the next in command; "Lieutenant," to which the Lieutenant returned, "Major." It was Lieutenant Reidecor, the first officer to enter the *TRITYTE* on my arrival and escort me off the ship.

Kala spoke deliberately and quickly, knowing there was little time for a full briefing.   "Crew, I would like present to you Thibodaux James Renwalt. He prefers to be called Tibby or Tib. Tib, this is Lieutenant Reidecor, whom I believe you have met once before. He will be our pilot.

This is Corporal Lexmal, our navigator. You know Sergeant Marranalis, who has been guarding you for nearly a week now. He's our gunner. And this is Corporal Luinella, our engineer... and my sister. She prefers that you call her Lunnie." Lunnie smiled in acknowledgment. "Now, per the captain's orders for this mission, Tibby is in charge. You all will report to him directly. Although you've all been briefed on this mission, I will let Tibby summarize the plan, since he was the one who conceived it."

"Thank you, Major." I began. "First of all, I'm sure you all have a clear sense of what this mission means – both if we succeed and if we fail – so I won't belabor that issue. You have been handpicked by the captain because of your skills and your loyalty to the Federation. If this mission succeeds, you will all be remembered in the history of the Federation for getting the ship and its cargo to Megelleon. If we fail... well, if we fail, we may not be remembered at all. Anytime now a battle will ensue in the secured bay where the *TRITYTE* was originally stored and the *decoy TRITYTE* will make its escape from that bay into space in the hands of "traitors" desiring to capitalize on the wealth its holds. Shortly thereafter, a general alarm will be issued and this place will be buzzing with ships leaving in pursuit of the *decoy TRITYTE*. When approximately two thirds of the ships have left, I will receive a signal from the captain and we will depart like all the patrol ships in the general direction of the pursuit. However, we will at one point slowly veer off in a direction away from the Bunem System. Once we are out of detection range of the pursuit ships, we will make a u-turn around and in front of the *DUSTEN* out of their sensor range and follow a course that is forty five degrees off the usual direct path to Megelleon at maximum speed. This will cause us to pass outside the range of the Bunem System and the fleet of pursuers, after which we will correct our course to head directly for Megelleon. We will not make contact with anyone until we are well within the capital's perimeter fleet protection, at which time Major Kalana will broadcast a coded message briefing leadership of our presence. At that point we hope for prompt landing instructions and protection. Any questions?"

"Sir," Lieutenant Reidecor stepped forward. "What if the Bunemnites don't buy the ruse and we run into their fleet?"

"We have every reason to believe the Bunemnites will suspect some sort of trick, but they must equally consider that the situation may be real. We believe they will split up their forces, sending one contingent out after the decoy ship and another to the *DUSTEN* in the belief that the solbidyum may have been secretly stored onboard. Before the Bunemnites can attack, the *DUSTEN* will contact them, thanking them for coming to aid in searching for the *TRITYTE* and its cargo. The captain will then invite the officers from their flagship to join him on the *DUSTEN* and allow them to roam about the ship, knowing full well that they will be searching for the solbidyum. They will even be shown a patrol ship that supposedly was damaged when fired upon by the escaping decoy *TRITYTE*. Even if it doesn't convince them, it will slow them down tremendously. They will not want to start a war, unless they are securely in possession of the solbidyum; and when it can't be located on the *DUSTEN*, they will know that it's got to either be on the *TRITYTE* or stowed in some other ship on a clandestine route to Megelleon. In either case, their ships will be divided up with the bulk of them between the *DUSTEN* and the Bunem System, or between the Bunem System and the decoy. We, on the other hand, will be on the opposite side of the Bunem System and headed for Megelleon by then. At the very most, they might spare two or three ships to monitor activity on that side the system, in the remote chance that a ship, meaning our ship, escapes detection and passes Bunem surveillance. If this is the case and we are discovered, we will either have to outrun them or fight them." I tried to read the intense faces of the crew. "Any other questions?"

No one raised their hand. "Just one more thing, even though this ship appears to be the same as all the other patrol ships, it isn't. The power distribution system is much more advanced. It's faster than anything else in the fleet and it is better armored." I hoped this information would raise their confidence in the mission. "The ship's computer should be programmed to respond to all of us and our commands according to rank. Though I hold no official rank in your Federation military service, the ship will recognize my orders as priority one commands, overriding any and all conflicting commands. If all goes well, we should make it to Megelleon in three weeks. The prolonged travel time is a result of the indirect route we must take."

I turned to Kala, "Major, does everyone know where they are to be quartered?"

"Yes. You will have the captain's cabin, I will have the first officer's cabin and the rest of the crew will be bunking in the main crew quarters."

"We will be departing shortly. I'd like to change out of this mechanics uniform before we do. In the meantime, make sure all gear is secured and support items are stowed and that you're at your stations, ready for take-off." I went to my cabin and opened my duffel bag; inside I found several suits of the dignitary cut and two that looked like they would be something one might wear on a spaceship. Both were solid black, a color that didn't seem to be of any military significance. I put on one of the plain uniforms, noting that the top had two breast pockets with flaps and the pants had two pouch-like pockets on the outside, also with flaps. When I glanced in the mirror to see what it looked like, I was shocked to see my now brown hair. I had forgotten about the color change and the sudden sight of it startled me. Kala had assured me she could restore the natural color with a style stick. I was contemplating having it changed before leaving the hangar; but I recognized that it might be best if I didn't have red hair, in the event that I needed to be seen on a view screen before we completed the mission.

When I arrived in the control room, everyone was seated at the console stations, with the exception of Lunnie, who was at her station in the engine room. The center chair was reserved for me and Lieutenant Reidecor was positioned at my right in the pilot's seat. Corporal Lexmal was on my left in the navigator's chair; Kala was behind me to the right and Sergeant Marranalis was behind me to the left. I noted that Marranalis was wearing a helmet equipped with a view screen that simulated a view of the area outside the ship in whatever direction he turned his head. On the armrest was a series of buttons that I surmised were weapons controls.

Kala was smiling at me. "Is there some significance to this uniform?" I asked.

"It's a typical uniform worn by mercenaries who are affiliated with the Federation and deployed for special operations." Kala answered. "It suits you well."

Sergeant Marranalis glanced at me and added, "I agree. You look like you belong in that uniform."

Just then a slight tremor shook the ship.

"Looks like the action is starting," said Lieutenant Reidecor. "It won't be long now." A second, larger tremor shook the ship. "That would be them blasting out the hangar door. Any moment now we should hear –" He was cut off by a general alarm signal coming through the speakers on the *TRITYTE*.

"Attention all ships and military personnel: An attack has taken place in the hangar.   A patrol ship containing an extremely valuable cargo has been commandeered.   It is imperative that this ship be captured at all costs.   All flight crews are ordered to report to their ships immediately.   The ship you are seeking is the TRITYTE.   I repeat, the objective is the TRITYTE.   This craft can be identified by a specific signature detectable on frequency Delta95446.   I repeat, frequency Delta95446!!   Also, this ship does not bear the Federation logo on its hull.   If encountered, DO NOT DESTROY.   It is imperative that this ship be taken intact with its cargo.   All flight crews are ordered to report to their ships IMMEDIATELY!"   The voice overhead boomed out its orders through the alarm system.

The *TRITYTE's* crew grinned, fully aware that, as soon as people on the *DUSTEN* heard the name *TRITYTE* in the broadcast, pandemonium would erupt.   Teams raced to their ships, knowing full well that any crew capturing the *TRITYTE* would be well-rewarded.   This craft was the ship of history – the golden egg.   At that moment I envisioned every ambassador and diplomat on the *DUSTEN* launching GW message pods to their home worlds with news of the ship, hoping that the *TRITYTE* would somehow be heading near enough for their troops to intercept.   Most of those message pods wouldn't arrive at their destinations until the real TRITYTE was already on or very near Megelleon.   Since the Bunem System was nearby, the pods sent earlier by the crew of Bunem loyalists were already being received and preparations for deployment were most certainly in progress.   By the time the Bunem fleet assembled and moved to intercept the *DUSTEN,* the *TRITYTE* would be well out of reach of their ships.   Everything was falling into place so far.

Lieutenant Reidecor activated the screen so we could view the flurry of activity in the main hangar.   It reminded me of a nest of angry hornets.   One ship after the other zoomed out the main hangar access. Several ships nearly collided in their haste to join the chase after the decoy *TRITYTE* and the unfathomable fortune held in its cargo. Crewmen were racing all over the place, while we stood by watching the commotion.

The number of ships leaving the *DUSTEN* began to slow down, when a beacon lit up on the console. "That's our signal, Lieutenant," I said. "Move us out of here and let's get this ship on the way."

Lieutenant Reidecor activated a few controls on the console. Silently the *TRITYTE* rose and headed out into the launch area. We lined up with other exiting ships. Then, on the signal from the *DUSTEN* bridge, the last battalions of airships launched into space and away from the *DUSTEN*. Slowly Lieutenant Reidecor navigated to the outer edge of the fleet and away from the Bunem System, until the last remaining indicator signaling the position of a Federation ship disappeared from the *TRITYTE's* monitoring systems. Everyone relaxed and exhaled a breath of air.

At that point we turned ninety degrees, heading even farther away from the pursuit ships. After an hour we turned back on a course that would bring us in front of the *DUSTEN* but out of range of its sensors. Once we had traveled a roughly equal distance to the other side of the *DUSTEN*, we began a course toward Megelleon, but on a route that would take us farther away from the Bunem System until such time that we were safely past their colony. The crew was on full alert, remaining focused and pretty much silent in their own contemplations as we headed away from the *DUSTEN* and the Bunemnites.

The first two days of the journey were fairly uneventful. Two of the crew members were always on the bridge, monitoring the surrounding area for ships and the air waves for transmissions. Most of this was actually being done by the ship's computer system with human eyes scanning the screens out of habit.   Kala, Sergeant Marranalis, Lieutenant Reidecor, Lunnie and I practiced martial arts techniques in the cargo hold. Originally it was just Kala, Sergeant Marranalis and I; but after seeing our practice sessions, Lunnie and Lieutenant Reidecor joined in. Corporal Lexmal watched, but showed no interest in joining our activities and either spent his time on the bridge or in the crew lounge watching vids. While he talked with the crew and occasionally joked, he didn't appear very interested in socializing with the team.

It was on the third day of travel after one of our more strenuous training sessions that I was showering as Lunnie arrived. Sergeant Marranalis had just stepped out and Lunnie took his place at the second shower. Without her clothing there was more of a resemblance to her sister than I had noticed when she was in uniform and I couldn't help admiring her form.

My shower was just going into the drying mode and hers into the rinse mode when she looked me and said, "Hey, Tib, how about I stop by your room and we can enjoy some sex? I've not had any for several days now and I'm rather on the horny side."

I froze at Lunnie's direct and candid approach. "Wow, Lunnie, I am deeply flattered, and you definitely have an attractive body," I stumbled, trying to gracefully get out of this situation with no wounded feelings. "I must decline though, for, ahh well, because I care, um, uhh…." I continued stumbling.

Lunnie was looking at me with a very strange and analytic gaze, eyes slightly squinted, until suddenly, a huge smile spread across her face. "Oh, I can't believe it! You're in love with my Kala! Oh my, this is too funny, and she…" Lunnie was almost doubling over with laughter unable to finish her sentence, "…she doesn't know, does she?"   I could see that, far from feeling rejected, Lunnie was finding this all very funny.

"I never said that!" I blurted. "I mean I wasn't going to say that. It's just…." I trailed off, unable to finish my sentence.

"Look," Lunnie said, "your little secret is safe with me. I won't tell a soul," she giggled. "This is too much." She was cracking up at this point. Just then Kala came in to take her shower.

"What's so funny," she asked Lunnie. "I've not seen you laugh this hard in years."

"Sorry, sis, but you're going to have to get Tibby to tell you, because I'm sure not going to," and with that she burst out laughing again.

I was trying to get out of the shower, as it only was big enough for two and my shower was over; but Kala blocked the exit.

"Tib?"   Kala looked at me with eyebrows raised questioningly.

"Don't ask," I said while blushing brightly and looking down, trying to conceal my face. "I have no idea what she is talking about."

That only made Lunnie laugh all the harder. She leaned against the wall for support as I slipped past Kala out of the shower and into the dressing area. As I dressed hastily in my uniform, I could hear Kala saying, "All right Lunnie, what's this all about?   You didn't go and say or do something offensive toward Tibby, did you? You do realize he is considered of the highest importance to the Federation and is my responsibility? If you have offended him in any way, I will, well, I'll...." Lunnie was now sitting on the floor laughing so hard that the tears were rolling down her face and she was gasping for air.

It's funny how sometimes it takes someone else to point out something that has been under your nose all the time. That's what happened to me. Since I was first picked up by the Federation I had been experiencing a range of feelings for Kala. I was very aware that I found her attractive and liked her company and certainly aware that I found her sexually appealing. But until Lunnie said it out loud, I hadn't realized the full truth of it; I really was in love with Kala. But how did Lunnie know? How did she figure it out in mere seconds when I couldn't? And why did Lunnie find it all so funny?

I quickly headed into the control room to take my shift, all the while wondering what I was going to do about my feelings for Kala. How would she react when she found out? I feared that she might want to leave and not be my attaché, as it would most likely be professionally inappropriate to stay. I feared that if she did leave, I might even lose the friendship I had with her. I also didn't know her relationship status. Maybe she was already seeing someone. Or perhaps she was a lesbian, which would certainly explain Lunnie's reaction.

Kala and Lunnie were very different from each other, aside from their physical resemblance. Kala was methodical and cool. She wasn't cold, but she certainly wasn't overly outgoing. She was competitive and wanted to be the very best at everything she did. She tended to be more formal which, I knew, was required in her profession. Lunnie, on the other hand, was very outgoing and often showed physical affection towards the crew members; which Kala seldom did.   It wasn't that Kala avoided physical contact, but she never went out of her way to initiate it. Lunnie was always touching people when she talked to them – always joking, laughing, touching their arm or hand, putting her arm around someone as she walked down the corridor – nothing overtly sexual, though Lunnie did radiate sexual energy that boosted a man's libido. The men knew, though, that it mostly amounted to teasing and play with Lunnie; it was just part of her nature.   Despite these differences, Lunnie and Kala seemed to be very close, talking and sharing things often.

Kala and I were together often on the *TRITYTE*. When I was in the control room she was usually there as well.   We also spent a lot of time practicing martial arts together, after which we regularly talked in my cabin about issues of protocol and various cultures in the Federation.

I would also meet with Kala in my quarters after finishing my duty in the control room with the intention of learning more about the workings of the Federation government. Through these informal meetings I had come to understand that the Federation governmental and political systems were structured in a fashion somewhat similar to the American system of government, in that they elected senators who served to represent the Federation citizens. But because there were more than one million planets in the Federation, electing a separate senator to represent each individual planet would create too many voices to effectively be heard in government proceedings; so groups of planets collected into "systems" that elected a single representative. Even with this arrangement nearly one thousand senators were required to fully represent the Federation membership.

One significant difference in this governmental structure was that a single individual was not elected as president over the entire Federation. They instead had three of what they called "*leaders*," who performed this function collectively. The implementation of any executive decision or action required at least two of the three leaders to be in agreement.

There were some other differences that stood out. For instance, this government didn't consist of only two relatively equal political parties; rather, five principal parties were represented at all times. Major elections were held every eight years instead of every four. Each leader held the office for sixteen years as one term. Though a leader could not serve consecutive terms, he or she could be re-elected eight years later. The three leader elections were staggered, which meant that at least two of the three were already in office at various stages of their terms when a new leader was elected into office. This helped to eliminate partisan politics and force the senators and leaders to compromise and work together, rather than try to dictate politics by gaining and holding a majority of representation in a two-party system. Due to the vastness of space occupied by the Federation and the reliance on the relatively slow gravity wave pods for interplanetary communication, it was necessary for each planet to have a number of ambassadors and embassies in key worlds and locations. Larger and more powerful systems could afford to maintain more ambassadorships; in fact, many of them had ambassadors who were permanently assigned to residency on various Federation starships, so as to facilitate quick resolution to situations that may arise and impact their particular system.

During one of these governmental tutorial sessions, when we had pretty much exhausted the subject matter, I decided to change the topic. "Kala, I hope you don't mind, but I have a personal question. If you don't want to talk about personal things, I understand… but I'm curious."

"Go ahead and ask," Kala responded.

"You and Lunnie seem to be very close, yet you have completely different personalities," I started.

"Yes we do," Kala said, "but what's your question?"

I laughed nervously. "Well actually, I guess I'm just curious as to why the two of you are so different and yet so close."

Kala began thoughtfully, "I'm not really sure I can give you an exact reason. I am the eldest of us by three years. I enjoyed keeping to myself growing up, staying interested in almost everything but content to entertain myself. We lived in a remote area on Gosney back then and the community where we lived didn't have many children, or they were too far away to play with often. So we didn't have a lot of friends. As we grew older, Lunnie looked up to me. I was her *big sister*. When I was about twelve, we moved to a new settlement on Gosney that was larger and more populated.

"Lunnie was very outgoing, whereas I was more reserved. She quickly became very popular in our new community, as she was always very self-confident. On the other hand, I always felt I needed to prove myself, I guess. I was always involved in competitive activities, whereas Lunnie was more into social gatherings. When I was gaining recognition for my competitive skills in athletic and academic events, Lunnie was being elected president of social clubs and winning popularity contests. I think everyone was later surprised that, despite Lunnie's social skills and my more physical interests, she became an engineer and I became the attaché. I'm sure it was always predicted that the outcome would be the opposite."

"How did that happen?" I asked.

"For me the choice came about after I signed up for the military," Kala began. "Originally, I wanted to be a trooper and did quite well in training. Our unit was on its first active mission on the planet Maitag, trying to end a war between the original settlers and a local warlord. The warlord was in the process of committing genocide of the original settlers. It was a really bloody ordeal, until a military attaché from the Federation showed up to act as a negotiator, serving an instrumental role in bringing the war to an end. I was immensely impressed that the professional diplomacy of one person could bring about the end to a war more effectively than hundreds of troops. The experience made me think that perhaps I could be of more service to the Federation as an attaché than as a trooper trying to force people into submission by way of physical might. After we were relieved of duty on Maitag, I asked for a transfer and trained to become an attaché.

"Lunnie joined the service during the period that I was on Maitag trying to quell the conflict. I think her intents were to follow in my footsteps. She had no idea what she wanted to do upon entering the service; but when they tested her, she showed a great aptitude for mechanical and engineering skills, so they made her an offer to train as ship engineer. At the time, I'm sure her decision was also swayed by an attraction she had for a guy who also happened to be an engineer," Kala added with a nonchalant hand gesture and a shrug. "We were surprised to find out that we had both been assigned to the *DUSTEN* two years ago.

"Now," she continued, "perhaps you will answer a personal question for me…?"

"Sure," I said. "It's only fair that if I ask you a question, you should be able to ask me one in return."

"Earlier today, when you and Lunnie were showering and I showed up, Lunnie was laughing," she began. "I asked what was so funny and she wouldn't say… and you looked, well, distraught. So I asked Lunnie about it again later and she still wouldn't tell me anything more; but she did relate that she invited you to have sex and that you declined. I have never known anyone who didn't want to have sex with Lunnie. In fact, I'm not sure she's ever been turned down before, though she didn't seem to be upset by it. I'm curious as why you turned her down."

"I'm not sure I can explain it so that it fits into your culture, but I'll try," I began. "Your sister is attractive and certainly sexually appealing; but for me personally, engaging in a sexual relationship with someone without a meaningful emotional attachment is not something I want. It's not that I haven't done so in the past, because I have. But it's just so meaningless… and I've come to recognize that it leaves me feeling emotionally empty. I really prefer sharing a sexual relationship when it includes a mutual emotional attachment."

"Hmm," Kala was thinking over my statement. "That still doesn't quite explain Lunnie's reaction. I got the feeling there was something else. She didn't say anything more?"

"No, not really," I lied. "That was pretty much it." There was a strange look of sadness in Kala's eyes that made me want to ask her what was bothering her, but I decided against it. I felt that whatever may have been on her mind was probably personal and I had no right to intrude.

Kala got up to leave my compartment after our discussion. As she opened the door, we both heard music coming from somewhere down the corridor.

"Shall we investigate?" Kala asked. A lighthearted smiled spread across her face and into her eyes, replacing the previously sullen expression. We decided to follow the music. We proceeded down the corridor together toward the crew lounge and galley. The music sounded much like the disco-era tunes heard on Earth in the late 1970s or early 1980s. Inside the lounge we found Lunnie and Lieutenant Reidecor doing a dance not unlike some of the dances I'd seen on Earth.

Lunnie spied us lingering at the door. "Come on in and join the party. Tibby, I'm assuming that people on your planet dance?"

"Yeah," I grinned. "Where I come from people love to dance – not unlike the dance you are doing now, actually."

"Well, come on in! Grab old *Stiff Ass* there beside you and show her a few of your moves," Lunnie said with a grin and a wink.

"Hey! "Kala retorted with a smile. "Watch who you call *Stiff Ass*, Corporal, or I'll report you!" They both laughed at that comment.

I was a fairly good dancer. My mother was a part time dance instructor at a community studio and taught me all the popular dance steps when I was growing up. She instilled in me a love for dancing that continued even after she died. I remembered a step that seemed to fit the music Lunnie was playing and I instinctively began gyrating to the rhythm. I motioned to Kala, holding out my hand as an invitation to join me. Both reluctance and temptation showed in the crooked grin on her face. From across the room Lunnie called out, "Come on *Stiff Ass*, you need to get them hips into motion before they lock up for good!" Kala shot her sister a dirty look and then took my hand.

I demonstrated a few steps and told Kala to repeat them. Just as in martial arts training, she recalled the steps so excellently that I gave her a few more, which she added to the original sequence in a completely choreographed dance. It seemed that Kala had an especially good memory for execution of progressive movements; she never forgot a step once she saw and performed it. In no time at all we were completely absorbed in the dance and the music, our eyes locked on each other's as we moved through the room. I don't think I could have taken my eyes off her if I tried. Suddenly the music ended and was replaced by the sound of applause. Kala and I turned to find that Sergeant Marranalis had come in. He was standing against the wall with Lunnie and Lieutenant Reidecor, where the three of them had been watching Kala and me.

"Now that was some dancing, Tibby," Lunnie said in amazement. "You even managed to coax the stiffness out of Kala. Quite an accomplishment, I must say. You two dance very well together."

Both Kala and I blushed when I realized I was still holding her hand. I could feel it was damp from one or both of us perspiring. I released it quickly and said admiringly, "You do indeed dance well, Kala. I haven't had this much fun in a long time. We should do this more often."

"Perhaps, if circumstances permit," Kala responded professionally. "I did enjoy it. You seem to be a man of many talents, Tibby."

"Hey, Kala," Lunnie called in a teasing voice, "Maybe you can convince Tibby to teach you some moves beneath the sheets. With the way he moves his hips, I'll bet he could teach you a lot," she taunted while twisting her body around playfully.

Kala's face went dark red as she turned to Lunnie. "That will be quite enough, *Corporal*." she said with stern emphasis. "I think your *engines* need checking. Report to your station *at once*."

Lunnie's huge grin exploded into a laugh as she walked out the door and headed toward the engine room. She glanced at me over her shoulder as she continued out the door, winking as she turned into the corridor toward the engine room and hips swinging like she had just accomplished a great feat.

I glanced back at Kala. Her anxious approach made it clear that she was quite upset over the exchange. "Tib, I apologize for my sister's actions and comments. Please excuse her behavior. Her sexual comments are a result of her ignorance of your customs on Earth."

"I'm not offended, Kala," I laughed in reply, hoping to lighten the situation. "Similar teasing and comments are also common on Earth, so I didn't find it insulting or impolite. Please don't be hard on your sister. Really, she has in no way offended me."

"I'm glad, Tib. I would be mortified if my sister offended you. She means well and she loves to tease, especially me... but sometimes she goes too far," Kala explained.

The next day everyone but Corporal Lexmal joined in the cargo hold to practice martial arts skills. Lexmal seemed to prefer spending most of his time in the control room and, in fact, rarely left it. The arrangement worked out well. Though the *TRITYTE*'s computer would alert us to any approaching ships long before we came into their range of detection, it was always good to have at least one person monitoring things in the control room at all times.

We had just completed an exercise, when suddenly I saw Lunnie slump and drop to the floor, followed by Sergeant Marranalis and Lieutenant Reidecor. Kala quickly moved toward Lunnie and suddenly crumbled to the deck as well. Everything then started spinning into darkness as I, too, felt myself collapsing to the floor. It seemed like I was falling forever into infinite darkness. After some unknown period of time, my ears began to buzz and light slowly returned to my vision.

Upon opening my eyes I had trouble focusing on the dim, blurry surroundings. With some effort and concentration my vision seemed to return to normal, only to find myself looking at my crewmates seated against the wall with restraining cuffs on their wrists. My own wrists were bound as well. As my awareness broadened, I quickly looked around and noted two armed guards brandishing rifle-type weapons and then, to my horror, I recognized that we were no longer on the *TRITYTE*. Corporal Lexmal was not bound with the rest of us... and I had a sinking feeling that I knew why.

I appeared to have been the first one to come around, as the others seemed to still be unresponsive. One by one, they slowly regained consciousness, though no one spoke for awhile. As the rest of the crew finally came to terms with their surroundings, I broke the silence in a hushed tone. "By the look of things, I'm assuming that we have been captured and that Corporal Lexmal had a hand in it...?"

"We must have been gassed in the cargo hold," said Lieutenant Reidecor in a quiet tone of disgust. "I never even stopped to think of the possibility."

"It's not your fault, Lieutenant," Kala said. "Typically the cargo hold of a patrol ships isn't equipped with gas neutralization defenses, as they never carry cargo of any value. On this point we failed to remember that the *TRITYTE* is not your standard patrol unit." Shaking off the last of the stupor she asked, "Anyone have an idea where we are?"

"My guess," said Sergeant Marranalis, "is that we are in one of the smaller holds in a Bunem cargo ship. I suspect that they have the *TRITYTE* in one of the larger holds."

At this, one of the guards chuckled arrogantly. He had been listening without our notice. "Pretty smart for a Feddie. But don't worry, you won't be harmed. We've got orders to just keep you restrained until we get back to Bunem.   Then you'll be sent back to your precious Federation, if they still want you after losing their prize of all prizes." He and the other guard both laughed. Just then the hold door slid open and Corporal Lexmal sauntered in, wearing a smug smile.

"Well, my friends," he began, "I want to thank you for making me a VERY wealthy man – maybe not as wealthy as the Federation would have made you, *Thibodaux James Renwalt*," he said with a sarcastic twist, "but then I could never spend such wealth in a lifetime anyway. What the Bunemnites will give me shall be quite satisfactory. Once they have taken the solbidyum they need for their own purposes, they will sell the rest to the highest bidders, from which I will enjoy a handsome share. Unfortunately for you, *Federation loyalists*, I will not be sharing any of my good fortune with you."

"Lexmal," Lunnie spat. "You're scum! I hope the Bunemnites treat you with the same disloyalty and lack of fairness that they have everyone else."

A venomous look that revealed his true nature replaced the smug smile on his face. For a moment I thought Lexmal was going to hit her; but instead he turned to the guards. "It would be better for you to stand guard outside the compartment to monitor them from there, rather than remain in here with them." The two guards looked at each other, nodded and moved outside the door to take up their stations.

"Tell me one thing," Kala said. "How did you pull it off?"

"Well, that was the tricky part," Lexmal offered arrogantly. "It was some time before I could get a message off to the Bunemnites relating my plans. Unfortunately, it seems that by the time my message arrived, they had already deployed their entire fleet – half headed to the *DUSTEN* and the other half in pursuit of the fake *TRITYTE*, just as Tibby had anticipated. I was ultimately able to instruct a confederate on the *DUSTEN* to dispatch a gravity wave pod carrying a message to the Bunemnites that included the rendezvous coordinates and time when I planned to have the *TRITYTE* waiting for them." The narcissism returned in his voice as he continued. "I wasn't sure how I would get control of the ship, but you all made it terribly easy by holding your *silly exercises* in the hold. When the time came, I was able to disable all of you in one fell swoop with the press of a button. Unfortunately, the Bunemnites had sent out all their warships to chase after your *decoy*, Tibby, but a freighter had just come in to unload a cargo from Kalax; so they emptied it quickly and staffed the ship with a few remaining guards before dispatching it to the coordinates I provided. They arrived there about the same time we did and, luckily, you were all in the cargo hold together, practicing your ridiculous exercises, completely oblivious to the situation when they came into range. I can't thank you *enough* for making it *so effortless* for me." He clapped his hands together and bowed his head slightly towards us in sarcastic appreciation.

Lexmal laughed. "Enjoy the rest of your trip. We should arrive at Bunem in four days. Now, if you don't mind, I think I will return to my own accommodations, which are a bit more – shall I say – luxurious. Besides you all seem to be *tied up* at the moment." He laughed again, reveling in his own twisted amusement as he left the compartment.

"Eat some Dragonian glow worms and die, Lexmal," Kala shouted after him in a moment of unleashed fury that was uncharacteristic of Kala.

After the door closed behind Lexmal I asked quietly, "Do you think they have this compartment bugged?"

"I doubt it," said Lieutenant Reidecor after a quick visual assessment of the chamber. "This is a lesser cargo storage area. There wouldn't be a need for monitoring sound in here."

"Good, because I think we have a fair chance of getting out of here and this ship could play right into our plans for getting the solbidyum to Megelleon safely. Lexmal sorely underestimates what we can accomplish using martial arts. Only our hands are restrained. We can still use our feet and even to some degree our hands, if used in unison. Though you have very little training, these people have *no* idea what even a novice is capable of performing. Most of you will have to think deliberately about what you are doing, because you're not practiced enough for much of it to be executed as an automatic response. That'll slow you down some and maybe feel a bit awkward, but it won't matter much. They'll be so unprepared for what happens that they'll pretty much be stunned into submission. Before we do *anything*, though, we need to know how many of them there are."

"I think I can help you out there," Lunnie offered. "During engineering school we used one of these old freighters as a training ship. I recognize many of the engineered components in this hold and in the door design. It's the same model used by the Federation for the past two hundred years. It's designed with space for a crew of only eight, so it's unlikely they have more than that onboard – unless they set up extra quarters in the main cargo hold, where they now must have the *TRITYTE.*"

Lieutenant Reidecor said, "I doubt they have more than nine people at the most, counting Corporal Lexmal. Two to four of them are likely guarding the *TRITYTE* in the cargo hold. So that would leave five in the rest of the ship… and we know two of them are guarding this door. Of the remaining three, two are likely to be on the bridge, and the last would be Corporal Lexmal, probably reclined in his *luxury suite*. We should be able to disarm and subdue them, arm ourselves, and take the cargo hold by surprise."

"Precisely," I said. "Kala, you're the ranking officer here, what are your thoughts?" Up to this point Kala had remained quiet, listening intently to our plans."

"Tibby, you're in charge. The captain made that clear at the start of this mission. Even though you hold no rank you're still in charge."

"I know," I said. "But I asked for your judgment as the senior ranking officer."

Kala looked at me for a moment and smiled. "I think we should kick some Bunemnite ass and take the solbidyum to Megelleon."

"Okay. Now all we need is a way to get both guards in here at one time." I paused for a moment to devise a scheme. "Wait for me to make the first move before any of you do anything," I said.

Fortunately we didn't have to wait long.

It was obvious that the crew manning the Bunem freighter did not consist of the elite soldiers of the fleet. The fact that they were even able to get into space and find preset coordinates only attested to the capabilities of the freighter's computer and the skills of those who built it – not to those currently managing its functions. In all likelihood, the best fighters and crews were immediately deployed on the hunt for the *TRITYTE* and solbidyum. Most certainly every available ship and body that could fly one had taken to space when Corporal Lexmal's message drone arrived at Bunem. There was probably still wailing, gnashing of teeth, and a good deal of finger pointing and fist shaking among Bunem's high government officials when they realized that there was nothing and no one to send to the rendezvous point to pick up the *TRITYTE*. No doubt that it was with much relief and celebration that they welcomed this lone freighter's return. Only the most critical civilian members of the original freighter crew were retained to fly the ship, while others were replaced with whatever remaining bottom-rung military men that Bunem could scrape together.

It came as no surprise when the door to our holding space opened and *both* guards entered, carrying trays of food. Both of them, grinning like the fools they were, carried their trays to the ladies first, as though they believed that this act would be smiled upon. As they simultaneously bent down to hand the trays to the ladies, I rocked onto by back and then whipped forward, bringing me off the floor to land on my feet. Each guard reeled around clumsily to face me, just in time for one and then the other to have a jaw introduced to my foot. The action lasted only a second before the two guards laid insensible on the floor.

Kala quickly sprung forward, grasping the electronic locking mechanism from one fallen guards. She removed the restraining devices from our hands in seconds, while Lieutenant Reidecor quickly relieved the guards of their side arms and tossed one to Sergeant Marranalis. Marranalis had already finished restraining the guards and quickly ducked outside the compartment, only to reappear seconds later with the two rifles conveniently left behind in the corridor when the guards came in to serve the food. Marranalis gave a rifle to Lunnie and a pistol to Kala, keeping a rifle for himself.

I crept into the corridor, where I heard someone moving about in what I expected to be the galley. I took a quick peek into the entry to find only one person with his back to me as he loaded another food tray. As I stepped into the galley, he said without turning, "Back for another tray so soon?" Before he had a chance to move, I rendered him unconscious with a quick karate blow. Marranalis followed directly with another pair of restraints that he used to secure the man's hands behind his back, rather than in front as they had done with us. He then tossed the unconscious guard across his shoulder and carried him back to the cargo space. Lieutenant Reidecor moved cautiously down the corridor, stopping briefly by a closed door to listen for a moment and then motion to me while quietly mouthing the word "Lexmal," before moving on toward the bridge. Lexmal could wait. He was most likely unarmed and basking in his daydream of fame, glory and wealth in the Bunem System. Reidecor slipped into the bridge area and placed his gun against the head of the sole individual in the control room. Other than emitting a small whimper of fear, the man made no sound, as Marranalis arrived to cuff and gag him and carry him off to the holding cell. By our count this left four or five of the crew still free.

We returned to Corporal Lexmal's quarters. Lexmal was too easy. All it took was a knock on his door, which he answered without calling out to see who was there. No sooner did the door slide open than he rendered a shocked expression as Marranalis's huge fist slammed into his face. Lexmal dropped like a sack of bricks. Marranalis whispered, "Man, I really enjoyed that," and then broke into a huge grin.

Trying to figure out how we were going to get into the cargo hold and overcome the guards there was another matter. We could wait for one of them to come out. There was no telling what arrangement they had for being relieved, fed or whatever. We still didn't know with certainty how many guards were in the cargo bay, nor their location or whether any were *onboard* the *TRITYTE*.

By now Lunnie and Kala had taken over controls on the bridge and were bringing the ship around on a course to Megelleon, but the men guarding in the cargo hold had no way of knowing that. As we were contemplating the situation, Kala came out of the control room and whispered, "Good news. There's a monitoring camera in the main cargo bay. Lunnie has been able to activate it and she says she can only see one guard stationed outside the *TRITYTE*... and he appears to be sleeping on a cargo bale. There doesn't seem to be any other activity out there; but the main hatch on the *TRITYTE* is open and I suspect someone is inside."

One problem we anticipated when opening the door from the main part of the ship to the cargo hold was that the cargo hold door was pressurized; it was going to make a noticeable noise when it opened and closed. Unless the guard was in a really deep sleep, he would surely be roused by the noise of the opening door. Of course, we could shoot him from where we entered as soon as the hatch opened, but the ruckus would most likely be heard inside the *TRITYTE*, alerting anyone inside and causing them to take defensive action. I went into the control room with Kala to review the situation on the monitor and discuss a strategy, leaving Sergeant Marranalis and Lieutenant Reidecor standing ready inside the door to the cargo hold.

As we debated how we were going to approach the situation and get onto the *TRITYTE*, one of the guards inside the *TRITYTE* called out to the guard sleeping on the bale. Lunnie reached over and turned on the sound so we could hear what he was saying.

"...n't look like they remembered to bring us grub, but the galley in here has a good synthesizer. The captain said we shouldn't leave our post at this ship for anything, but he *didn't* say anything about us going into it or eating food from it. It's more comfortable in here too."

"I don't know," said the guard who had been sleeping on the bale. "I think one of us should be out here, don't you?"

"Yeah... like the captain wouldn't be all over your ass for sleeping right now. Shit, he could have you shot for that. The least he could do to punish you for guarding from inside the *TRITYTE* is chew your ass out really good," replied the guard in the ship.

"Good point. What the hell. I'm hungry and I gotta take a piss." With that the guard got off the bale, stretched and yawned as he walked up the ramp into the *TRITYTE*.

"Great..." I said when he went inside. "Now, if there were just some way to open the pressure door between the accommodation area and the cargo hold without making noise."

"You can hand-crank it!" Lunnie said.

"Hand-crank it?"

"Yeah.   In case of total power failure, the pressure doors all have emergency hand cranks.   They're slow, but much quieter – enough so that it's very unlikely that they would hear it from inside the *TRITYTE*.   Kala, if you can watch the controls, I'll take this handsome dancing machine to the back and show him the ropes…how to open the doors, that is."   She tossed her head at me with her usual wink. Kala dropped into a chair and stared at the screen with a sour look on her face, but said nothing.

On the way back to the cargo door I asked Lunnie, "What's the deal with all the digs that you toss to Kala? They seem to upset her.   You two seem close, but it's like you enjoy hurting her with some private joke."   Lunnie stopped and turned toward me, placing one hand on my shoulder.   "Loverboy, if you haven't figured it out yet, I *for sure* am NOT going to tell you."   Then, with one of her famous chuckles and hip swings, she preceded me down the corridor, humming a tune.

Lunnie said that cranking the door open would be slow and she was right.   First a panel had to be removed beside the door to reveal a sort of jacking mechanism that had to be levered back and forth.   Each crank opened the door about a half inch, so creating a wide enough opening for a person to fit through took several minutes.   Fortunately, no one in the *TRITYTE* emerged while we worked this mechanism.   Once the door was opened far enough, Lieutenant Reidecor, Sergeant Marranalis and I slipped into the cargo hold and carefully worked our way to the *TRITYTE*'s cargo ramp.   From the open door we could hear the voices of the two guards, but heard no indication that there were any others inside.

"Do you think there are only two?" Lieutenant Reidecor whispered.

I shrugged my shoulders and shook my head. "I've no idea. We need to assume there are more." I motioned for Reidecor to follow me and for Marranalis to guard the door. Reidecor and I slipped aboard the *TRITYTE and* moved toward the galley.

From inside we could hear the guards talking. We were about to pass the crew quarters on the way to the galley, when Lieutenant Reidecor motioned for me to stop. He carefully looked inside and motioned that someone was in there. I crept over and peeked in to see a man sleeping on one of the bunks. He was laying on his side with his back to us. Lieutenant Reidecor whispered to me, "I'll take care of this." He quietly slipped inside, and a few seconds later just as quietly marched the man out the door with a gun to his head. He moved down the corridor away from the galley and out of sight, only to return within seconds.

"Where is he?" I asked.

"Taking another nap," Reidecor said with a grin.

Ahead of us we heard the two guards talking from the galley. "Do you think we'll be heroes when we get back?" one guard asked.

"Probably, but the captain and that Corporal Lexmal traitor fellow from the Federation will probably get all the glory. I suspect we'll get a nice promotion and some sort of recognition, though. Plus, I'm sure there will be lots of women wanting to be with us," the second guard said with a hint of excitement in his voice.

"Yeah," said the first guard dreamily. "Having the women is almost as good as having the money."

"Sure would be nice if we could open that container back there in the hold and take just one grain of that solbidyum stuff. They would never miss it...millions of grains in there and all."

"It would never work. I heard them say back on Bunem that the container is rigged. If you try to open it wrong, it's booby trapped and would kill you. There are alarms and poison gases and other protections. There's no way to break into it."

"Then how'r the officials going to get into it?" one guard asked emphatically.

"Because they got the codes, dummy... got'em back when we was still part of the Federation. They know how that thing is put together," the first guard said in an insulting tone.

"Don't you be gettin' high and mighty on me; you're not any smarter than I am. You're always acting like you're so much better than me, but I know that you never would have passed the qualification tests if you hadn't cheated. At least I didn't cheat!" retorted the second of the two.

"Yeah and you only passed by one point. At least I was smart enough to cheat...and got a lot better grade than you did too!"

Suddenly there was a sound of fighting in the galley and I motioned to Lieutenant Reidecor that it was time for him and me to make our move. We simultaneously burst into the galley, guns at the ready, confronting the two buffoons in mid tussle. It took a second or two for the guards to realize what was happening and to raise their hands. Guard number one looked at guard number two and said, "If you was so smart, we wouldn't be staring at these guns right now." Reidecor and I couldn't help laughing.

With all the crew and guards restrained and locked in the very same hold where we had been earlier, I met with my crew in the cargo ship's galley. We had the ship on autopilot and I felt it would be safe long enough for us to have a brief meeting.

"It's highly unlikely that Bunem has received communication yet that confirms the *TRITYTE* was captured at the meet point. If we keep the *TRITYTE* aboard this freighter, we can fly pretty much undetected all the way to Megelleon. Even though *we* are aware that the Bunemnites were prepared to attack the *DUSTEN*, peace is still generally believed to exist between the Bunem System and the Federation, at least as far as we know; so a cargo ship traveling to Megelleon will not be perceived as strange. Since the Bunemnites have deployed all their military craft to either chase after the decoy or remain stationed by the *DUSTEN*, it's unlikely that we'll encounter a Bunem ship enroute to the capital. Even if we do, they will simply assume we are either completing a cargo mission or hunting for the *TRITYTE* ourselves and, as such, pay us no mind. If we encounter any Federation ships, they will basically assume the same thing and, again, ignore us, as would any mercenaries trying to acquire the solbidyum by means fair or foul.   Unknowingly, the Bunemnites have given us the perfect disguise to get to Megelleon without detection. By my calculations we are still about a week and a half outside of Megelleon."

I looked around the table at everyone. All of them were beaming. Kala was looking at me with a broad smile. "We never would have gotten this far without you, Tib," she said with admiration.

I laughed and said, "Well, I guess it's a good thing I actually fell into the *TRITYTE* then."

Kala looked at me with a more appraising look. "That's not what I meant, Tib. You seem to be way ahead of us in thinking, planning, and in action; and I think everyone else here agrees." Everyone was nodding their heads in my direction. "If it hadn't been for your plan, the *DUSTEN* would be in a battle right now with the Bunem fleet and the solbidyum would most likely be within their grasp, if not their hands. Without your deliberations and your mind for action we would still be back there and the Bunemnites would surely have prevailed. We simply could not have done it without you and your leadership."

I think what impressed me most about her speech were the tears of gratitude that ran down her cheeks. At that moment I loved her more than I have loved anything or anyone in my life and I reached out my hand and took hers. "Come with me to my cabin... we need to talk." As I was leading her out the room I heard Lunnie exclaim, "It's about time!"

Kala seemed surprised that I took her hand. Except during our recent dance together, we hadn't really held hands or showed any other signs of affection at any time. Yes, we had touched during many of our activities, like martial arts training and other occasions, but not like this. I didn't release her hand, nor did she try and pull away; but I could tell she was confused by my actions. We no sooner entered my cabin than she began talking – doing her best to address the situation with a professional approach.

"Tibby, if I have done something wrong, I apologize. It was not intentional and I..." I didn't let her finish. I pulled her to me and kissed her lips. She broke the kiss and started to draw back, looking at me in surprise. "Tibby I'm not sure this...." I interrupted her with another kiss. For a moment I could feel her yield as her inhibitions surrendered to the moment, then suddenly resist as she stiffened and tried to pull away again. But I pulled her tightly against me, unrelenting, kissing her more passionately, opening my lips and tracing hers with my tongue as she remained still and seemingly breathless. Finally, casting off the last of her reserve, she threw her arms around my neck and returned my kisses as passionately as I kissed her. I opened my eyes to see tears streaming down her face. I drew my head back to see all of her and then kissed them off her cheeks. I looked again; and the smile on her face told me all I needed to know. I pressed her against the wall, as she wrapped her legs around me, kissing me and tasting the warm sweat that was beginning to form on my neck. I lifted her away from me and carried her to the bed, letting us both fall into it. I fixed my gaze on her shining blue-gray eyes and the most beautiful smile I have ever seen, as I quietly asked, "Kala, do you love me?"

"I can't answer that. I'm not supposed to…." I stopped her.

"I don't care what you're *supposed* to do or feel. I want to know… Do you love me?"

"Love is not typically part of our…," she started, but again I cut in.

"Kala, I am not asking you about your culture or your society or Federation practices or policies. I am asking you… Do you love me?"

Kala looked at me, her glowing face inches from mine, her eyes moving over me, looking at every feature of my face. Softly she said, "Yes, I love you. I love you."

Her kisses were as ardent as my own. Our hands moved of their own volition and clothing fell away until, at last, her bare flesh was pressed against mine in the most pleasurable of ways. We held each other for the next several hours, never leaving my cabin, taking small naps between the affections of love and holding each other quietly after, kissing gently and often.

Finally there was a knock at my door and Lunnie's voice calling out, "This is a life check to make sure no one is dead in there!" Kala laughed and shouted, "Go away, brat!" Lunnie's laugh was broken by a "Just checking!" and all was silent again. I propped myself up on one arm and looked at Kala. "That's what she's been riding you about isn't it? Now I get it. She's known since she came aboard that you and I were in love, even before I – we – realized it. All this time she's been laughing as we stumbled around each other. Before she said it out loud, I knew I was attracted to you. But it was her words that day in the shower that made me realize I loved you."

Kala was smiling and tears were in her eyes again. "Yeah, that's Lunnie. She always has a way of knowing such things… and taking great pleasure in watching others struggle to pull it together."

"But how does she…." Kala raised a finger and pressed it to my lips.

"There are some things Lunnie will never tell you – or me, for that matter – and this is one of them," she laughed and shrugged. "I'm not sure we would understand even if she did tell us." She rolled onto her back and drew in a long breath. "Make love to me one more time and then let's get back to work. We have a cargo to deliver." When a Major gives an order, especially a very attractive and naked one, one should always obey.

We entered the bridge about an hour later. Lieutenant Reidecor and Lunnie were the only ones there and, other than for a normal greeting, neither paid any particular attention to us nor acted as though anything was different. Sergeant Marranalis had taken up a station outside the small hold where the prisoners were being held. Over the past several hours Lunnie had rigged up a slot in the door that was large enough to exchange food items, but not large enough for a person to pass through. The prisoners were required to turn their backs to the door to have their restraints removed during meals. She had managed to find and install components for a portable shower and a toilet, so there was no need for the prisoners to be removed from their cell to use the facilities. From the bruises on Corporal Lexmal face and the way he isolated himself to one corner of the cell, it was clear that he was no longer favored by the Bunemnites.

After arriving at Megelleon, Kala and the crew and I expected that the other prisoners would likely be released as a gesture of peace toward the peoples of the Bunem System. They would regroup for a period after the defeat and quickly thereafter nurture hopes and earnest efforts to rejoin the Federation and restore their good standing, so they too could eventually obtain a share of the solbidyum to help their planet prosper. Otherwise, they would suffer economically, and deeply so, as a consequence of their acts of aggression and piracy.

But the fates of others did not hold so much hope of forgiveness. Corporal Lexmal faced a court-martial and subsequent death penalty, as did the crew that sent the initially message pod to Bunem about the recovery of the *TRITYTE* and the priceless solbidyum.

Time seemed to pass quickly after overcoming our captors. Everyone continued to practice martial arts every day in the cargo hold of the *TRITYTE*, which was still parked in the cargo hold of the Bunem ship; only now we staggered our schedules so there were always two people on duty in the control room.   For the most part we didn't have any problems with the prisoners, other than complaints. Corporal Lexmal didn't seem to be faring too well; but after we threatened to put everyone into restraints for the rest of the voyage if they kept beating him, they stopped.   It seemed, though, that he was not getting his full portions of food and had lost some weight.   He stayed in his corner curled up in a fetal position and said nothing to anyone. Personally, I didn't feel sorry for him.

For the rest of the trip Kala spent every night in my compartment with me.   We talked of many things.   One day, shortly before we reached Megelleon, she asked me "Tib, what's going to happen to us after we land?"

"What do you mean what's going to happen," I asked.

"I mean, it's highly unlikely they will let me continue as attaché with you, if we are romantically involved."

"I see," I said thoughtfully.   This hadn't fully occurred to me yet for some unknown reason. "What would you like to do?"

"Tib, I don't want to leave you.   Ever.   I know that sounds strange for our culture.   Here in the Federation relationships seldom last a lifetime, but I don't want any other relationships.   The reason Lunnie gives me such a hard time is because I haven't had many relationships.   I just never felt I wanted to be with anyone.   Then you came along... and now you're the *only* one I want to be with."

"I understand.   That's how I feel, too.   But what about your career?   How do you feel about that part of it?" I asked.

"Well, I've always felt it was important; but up until you came along, I never felt that I did anything of significance.   You have changed that; and now I and everyone in this crew is going to be a major part of the history of the Federation.   That makes me feel – well – good... and excited.   But that will have to end when we get to Megelleon."

"Why does it have to end?" I asked again.

"Because I can't be your attaché!" she exclaimed. "Our romance violates all the rules."

"Who says you have to stay my attaché?   What if I get the military to make you my personal assistant?   Then you could be on leave to work for me."

Kala rolled over and looked at me.   "What makes you think that they will buy that idea?"

"If I'm going to be as rich and powerful as everyone keeps telling me, I think the Federation will be bending over backwards to see that I am kept happy.   If I express that I want you to be my personal assistant on loan from the Federation, and if you are willing of course, I think they will see to it that it happens."

"I must admit I like that idea.   I just hope they buy into it," she said.   "But just what do you plan to do that you requires an assistant?"

"Lots of things, my dear," I said, as I leaned over and kissed her forehead.   "From what you have told me, there are a lot of planets in the Federation where things are still pretty primitive and rough.   I would like to see to it that they have a good foundation for the future by building hospitals where they need them... and schools...and help some of the planets establish agricultural programs to provide food for the settlers. There is a lot I can do much more quickly than the Federation, simply because I wouldn't have to operate within the bureaucratic votes and committees and miles of red tape. These kinds of facilities could be constructed in modules on one of the industrial planets, shipped where needed, and then set up in days instead of years. To accomplish such things I will need someone working with me who understands the system in the Federation and someone who is trained in dealing with the broad range of cultures, dignitaries and politicians. For *that* kind of position, a romantic involvement is *not* a conflict of interest."

Kala looked at me in amazement and said, "You're serious… you would do that? You don't even know these people. You barely know the Federation and you want to do this for the people… with your own money?"

"Yeah, why not?" I asked. "Near as I can tell, I will have so much money that I could build a hospital a day for the rest of my life and not even put a dent in my wealth. I want to do much more than just that, Kala. I can build theaters and arenas for events that otherwise would be years in the coming. I can create avenues of education and jobs for people to jumpstart their economies and help them thrive."

Kala rolled over and threw her arms around me and gave me a huge kiss. "No wonder I love you so much!" She exclaimed. "When did you think up all this stuff?"

"Actually back on the *DUSTEN*… the day I blacked out realizing just how much wealth everyone has been talking about."

The next day we entered the Megelleon system. There were lots of ships coming and going about us, especially Federation patrol ships, fighters and frigates; but none of them paid attention to an old Bunem freighter. We knew that Captain Maxette's GW message pod would have reached the Capitol before we got here, so they knew the situation and expected us – or at least hoped that we'd make it. Captain Maxette had given us a special frequency and code that would allow us to contact the High Command directly at the Federation base for top secret landing orders. As ranking officer, and also because of her attaché skills, Major Kalana was selected by Captain Maxette to make the contact when the time came.

I sat watching as Kala gave the orders for Lieutenant Reidecor to transmit the code. Moments later, a man appeared on the monitor, wearing a dark green uniform similar to Captain Maxette's, only with one gold band running around the chest. I heard both Lieutenant Reidecor and Kala give slight gasp.

"Greetings, *TRITYTE*, Admiral Regeny here," announced the man on the screen. "I *assume* that I am addressing the *TRITYTE*, though we don't seem to have you on our screen."

"Greetings, Admiral, Major Kalana here. The reason we are not visible on your screen is because Thibodaux Renwalt thought it might be safer and easier to deliver us in the belly of a Bunem freighter. On our way here there was a coup attempt to take us back to the Bunem System. It's a long story, one I am sure you would rather hear after we have securely landed. We also have some prisoners to deliver, as well as a traitor, I regret to say. But all is well at this time. We hope to be able to touch down as soon as coordinates are received."

"Traitor you say?" the admiral began.   "Most unfortunate. But you all are safe and the cargo is intact? Correct?"

"Yes, Admiral, the cargo is intact," Kala repeated.

"Excellent! Coordinates are being sent to you now. We are alerting our security forces to be expecting a Bunem freighter instead of a Federation patrol ship. Please proceed to these coordinates and follow the docking instructions precisely. Also, Major, we request that you and the crew stay onboard your ship and that you keep it sealed until we give you an all clear. Then you may open the hatch, but stay in the ship until our troopers have secured your craft and the surrounding area. I look forward to meeting this *Thibodaux Renwalt*. Captain Maxette has sent me some most amazing information about him."

"Admiral, no disrespect to Captain Maxette; but I after you hear about our journey and the events that unfolded on the way here, the captain's report will seem pale by comparison," Kala replied with a huge smile as she turned to look at me.

After the admiral signed off, Lieutenant Reidecor exclaimed, "That was *the admiral himself*, the top man! He was talking *to us!*" I could tell he was a bit shaken by the experience.

Kala turned to me and said, "You have just enough time to shower and remove that dye from your hair, I would suggest you wear the black dignitary outfit when we leave the ship."

The landing went smoothly and we were boarded shortly thereafter by a team of very professional troopers. We were escorted off the ship to a waiting bus-type conveyance and asked to board. The officer in charge said to

Major Kalana, "The admiral wishes to meet with you all personally after debriefings have been completed. Until then, you and your crew will be provided with appropriate accommodations. Someone will pick you up at the appointed time. For the time being, all of you will be accommodated in the same area."

The *TRITYTE* was moved into an underground hangar that Kala told me was designed and built hundreds of years earlier for the day when the *TRITYTE* would hopefully be found and returned. It was heavily protected and fortified to withstand almost anything. This highly secret facility was believed to be the most secure place in the universe.

We were taken to a very lavish set of quarters in a section of the underground base that reminded me of my accommodations on the *DUSTEN*, though Kala's adjacent suite did not have a connecting door, or at least none that I was aware of. Kala suggested that, until we had been debriefed and had a better idea what was happening, it might be best that we not sleep together; and though we both hated the idea, I had to agree with her. The debriefings didn't take as long as I suspected. Each of use was called in before a panel of three investigators and asked separately to relate the events between the time of our departing the *DUSTEN* and our arrival at Megelleon. I was surprised to discover that Captain Maxette had sent videos of every conversation that I had with him, other than the one in Kala's suite, which was not shared, but for which he *did* have an audio copy. Apparently he had a personal recording device on his person – a possibility I hadn't thought of, not that it really mattered to me. The debriefing was performed in a very casual and relaxed atmosphere in a lavishly furnished appointed room. Refreshments were provided and the whole process seemed more like a casual discussion than an interrogation. The interviewers were calm and polite. After about four hours, the interview ended and I was taken back to my quarters.

Sergeant Marranalis had already returned and had just gotten a drink from what I could only guess was an automated bar.

"Would you care for something, Tibby?" he asked, holding out his glass.

I laughed and said, "I would… if I knew what to order. I doubt that thing has tequila in it."

"I doubt it too. What's tequila?"

"It's a drink made out of a plant found in the deserts of my world."

"Hmmm," said Sergeant Marranalis. "Is the plant large or small?

"It's a fairly large plant," I answered.

Sergeant Marranalis punched up an automated order and handed me a glass of something. "Here, try this."

I took a sip. It didn't taste anything like tequila, but it did remind me of another drink.

"Well it's not tequila, but it's damn good, whatever you call it. Reminds me of a drink back on Earth called *Long Island Ice Tea*." I took another drink and started to relax.

"We call it a *Brown Bojo*," Sergeant Marranalis replied heartily, then added, "I have no idea why."

He paused a minute. "I don't know what happens after today. I'll probably be reassigned to other duty and eventually get back to the *DUSTEN*. I want you to know that guarding you, learning martial arts and serving with you on the *TRITYTE* has been the highlight of my career. It's been a great pleasure, sir."

Before I could reply, I heard, "That goes for me also!" I turned to find Lieutenant Reidecor returning as well.

"Make it three of us!" I looked to my left to see Lunnie draped across sofa-like piece of furniture. Either she had been there all along or she sneaked in while Marranalis and I were chatting.

"Well, I would like to let you all know that I have *very much* enjoyed my time with you all as well. I will definitely miss you after all this is over," I said. "I would like to stay in communication with all of you. I hope you will all look me up when you leave the service. In fact, if the Federation lives up to the agreement and gives me all they say they are going to, I'll make you all rich enough that you will never have to work another day of your life, if you don't wish too."

"I'm just hoping you will be here a while to continue teaching us martial arts – at least as long as I'm stationed here," said Marranalis.

"You can count me in on that," chimed in Lunnie with her usual sense of comedic humor. "I love contorting physically with muscular men."

"Say," interjected Lieutenant Reidecor. "Were any of your debriefings as strange as mine? I felt like I was being interviewed on one of those video documentaries and not really debriefed."

"Yeah, well don't kid yourself," Lunnie said. "I've heard about this new technique, and from what I've heard they can get a lot more from you this way. Besides, you're being monitored with vids and voice analyzers and all sorts of other stuff the entire time you're there. Did you drink any of the foccee or snack on anything during the debriefing? Those were all laced with truth inducing drugs. You couldn't lie about your own name if you tried right now. Those drugs last about nine hours, I hear."

"Damn," Marranalis said, "I thought the fruit didn't taste quite right."

"I thought it strange that I felt like all the investigators were my best friends," added Reidecor.

There was a moment of stillness in the room. "Have any of you seen Kala?" I asked suddenly.

"Nope," said Lunnie. "Maybe she didn't drink the foccee and they are torturing her slowly until she spills her guts about our trip here. She should be back soon. I understand we're supposed to be dining with none other than Admiral Regeny himself in about an hour."

"WHAT!?" exclaimed Lieutenant Reidecor. "I don't have a dress uniform with me, and not enough time to requisition one!"

"Don't worry," said Lunnie with a smile on her face. "Dress uniforms hanging inside the door – all tagged with our names. They must have been delivered while we were being interviewed."

For the first time since I met him I saw Marranalis nervous. His hands were shaking as he raised his drink to his lips and muttered, "The admiral himself, now that's one for me to tell my kids someday, if I ever have any," to which Lunnie replied, "Any time you want to practice making some, just knock on my door."

As the hour neared when we were supposed to meet with the admiral, I began getting nervous too, but it was because Kala still hadn't returned. I showered and picked up the uniform that had my name attached to the exterior of its packaging. The suit was of the familiar dignitary cut with one difference. It was white – shirt, pants, jacket and shoes; even the socks were white. On the rim of the collar and the very ends of the sleeves was a thin edging of gold. I put it on, feeling very strange and somewhat giddy inside. I wondered if it was my nerves or if it was the effect of the truth drugs in the foccee wearing off – if, in fact, there were any. Knowing Lunnie, she might just have made that up as one of her jokes. I walked from my suite and out to the common room to see Lunnie in a military-style uniform, also in white, displaying her chest rank stripes in a light gray. Sergeant Marranalis and Lieutenant Reidecor were attired similarly, also displaying rank stripes in gray.

Lunnie looked at me and said, "WOW! Did they ever give *you* a promotion!"

All three of them approached, looking me up and down. "I've never actually seen anyone wearing one of these uniforms in person before." said Lieutenant Reidecor.

"I doubt any of us have," said Lunnie.

"Why, what's the deal with this uniform?" I asked.

"*That*, my friend," began Lieutenant Reidecor, "is the highest ranking dignitary uniform there is. It's reserved for planetary leaders of the singular highest standings in the Federation. You won't find but one person from each planet wearing this uniform, if that."

"Hell, from what I hear, that means there are about a million of 'em out there," I said with a chuckle, trying to downplay their awe of the uniform.

"Maybe, but I doubt there are that many. You never see them, except on the vids or the news." Sergeant Marranalis said.

Just then a smartly dressed woman in a gray military uniform appeared at the door informing us that she was to escort us to the dining hall. I said that Major Kalana had not returned yet, and that we would need to wait a minute. However, our escort insisted that we go immediately and that she was sure the Major would be escorted to the dining hall in time for the meal.

I didn't like this at all. Kala was supposed to be my attaché, making certain that I didn't flub up in my interactions with the Federation – and now, on my first and *biggest* meeting with the Federation officials, she was absent. I wondered where she could possibly be and what was causing the delay. We were chauffeured down a long underground corridor in a vehicle similar to the one that had transported us from the hangar where the *TRITYTE* was kept. We arrived in front of a large underground entrance that looked like the receiving area outside a luxury hotel. All around us were polished marble floorings, marble columns and walls of differing hues all aglow with accent lighting. We exited the conveyance to find two guards standing at attention on both sides of the vehicle door. A carpet was laid out before us that lead to large double doors also flanked by armed guards standing at attention.

Our escort indicated that we should follow her. Each guard stepped forward to open one of the pair of doors. On the other side was a large room, also all in marble, which appeared to be some sort of ante room where people would gather before an event before admission into a grand hall. The carpet led across the room to another set of double doors, also protected by a pair of guards. As we approached this time, neither of them stepped forward to open the door. We were instructed to wait as our escort opened one door just wide enough to slip inside. A few moments later she returned saying, "Thibodaux James Renwalt and Lieutenant Reidecor will walk together and follow me. Corporal

Luinella and Sergeant Marranalis, you will walk together behind Thibodaux James Renwalt and Lieutenant Reidecor, if you please." As we lined up in the fashion she had instructed, she nodded to the two guards, who then stepped forward and opened the doors. As we entered, we saw a giant hall filled with thousands of officers and dignitaries seated about a sea of tables. All at once, everyone stood from their seats and remained there at attention in complete silence, until we were fully in the room and our escort announced, "It is my honor to present Thibodaux James Renwalt, recoverer of the *TRITYTE* and its lost cargo of solbidyum." Suddenly I was enveloped in a beam of light. "It is with honor that I also present those who helped him to safely deliver the *TRITYTE* and solbidyum to the capital. Against overwhelming odds and despite the actions of a traitor, who aided in the capture of the *TRITYTE* and solbidyum, they managed to escape the dangers of this remarkable mission and restore to the Federation a priceless resource that our histories had nearly written off as lost forever. Major Kalana." A flood light suddenly illuminated her in her white formal uniform where she stood next to Admiral Regeny. "Lieutenant Reidecor, Corporal Luinella, and Sergeant Marranalis." Flood lights enveloped them as well. "Citizens of the Federation, I present to you our heroes."

With that, cheers and applause exploded throughout the hall. The roar was deafening. I saw Admiral Regeny lean over and say something in Kala's ear. She nodded and then removed herself from the table to walk toward us, a huge smile beaming across her face. At that moment, it seemed we only had eyes for each other. As she approached, Lieutenant Reidecor stepped aside so Kala could stand beside me. Then, as the crowd continued to cheer and applaud, we were escorted to the admiral's table where aides stepped forward to hold out our chairs. I was escorted to the chair that Kala had previously occupied to the right of the admiral, followed by Kala, Lieutenant Reidecor, Corporal Luinella and Sergeant Marranalis. Once we were seated, the tumult of applause and cheering slowly calmed and the guests began to take their seats.

I leaned over to Kala. "I was in a near panic when you didn't show up back at the suites. I had no idea what was happening and I was afraid I would really do something stupid."

"I know," Kala said. "I tried everything to get back to you or at least get word to you, but the admiral and the other officers kept me right up until last minute. I had to shower and dress in a dressing room here and only arrived moments before you did. I wanted to enter with you all, but the admiral insisted I enter with him... and you don't deny an admiral."

From the other side of me I heard, "Tibby, I understand you prefer to be called Tibby," the admiral began. "I cannot begin to tell you how extremely pleased I am to meet you. Not just for recovering the solbidyum, but for your remarkable plan and execution to safely get it here. When the GW pod from the *DUSTEN* arrived with the message from Captain Maxette that the *TRITYTE* and solbidyum had been found and confirmed, we were elated here at the Capitol. Then when we learned of the traitors on the *DUSTEN* and that word about the recovery had reached the Bunem System, we were in a panic. We've been at peace with the Bunemnites, more or less, for the past two hundred years; but it's been a tentative one. Knowing their desires and past actions to obtain more than their share of solbidyum – at any cost, I might add – we were sure they would attack the *DUSTEN* before we could get any reinforcements there.   We feared for the loss of the solbidyum, the *DUSTEN* and the thousands aboard it. Then we received another message days later alerting us to your brilliant plan; and all we could do was wait. Your mission and the means by which you planned to arrive at Megelleon was our biggest secret. Only a very small handful of people knew the details. Even so, word of the solbidyum discovery leaked out. Ambassadors and senators were clamoring to learn where it was. They were prodding anxiously, asking when they would be getting their share. If you had not shown up with it, Tib, I fear the Great Wars would have broken out all over again." I listened to the admiral and actually saw tears in his eyes as he tried to relate the significance of the situation and the pain that had scarred the history of the Federation for too long.

"Well, sir, "I began, "I'm happy it turned out well also. Had it turned out otherwise, I'm not sure I would be here at all."

The admiral laughed. While we talked, food was being served. I felt Kala's hand move under the table to lightly rest upon my leg... and it made me feel wonderful.

"When we received Captain Maxette's report of your plan, we were impressed with you. Then, when we heard the rest of Maxette's report about you and some of your other talents with this form of fighting – this *martial arts* – we started thinking that perhaps Maxette had been hitting the liquor bottle. Fortunately, he sent along vid footage from the conference room when you disarmed Sergeant Marranalis in a demonstration. My officers and I were left with our mouths hanging open. And *now* we learn that you disabled two guards on the Bunem freighter while your hands were in restraints. Within hours of the capture of the *TRITYTE* you pretty much took out and captured the entire Bunem crew single handedly!"

"Sir I can't take credit for that. If it had not been for my crew here…," I gestured toward Kala and the rest to my right.

"Nonsense," the admiral interrupted me. "We have the testimony of your entire crew, as well as that of the Bunem crew you captured." The admiral laughed, as did several of the other officers seated to his left. "You're a one-man battalion."

"I wouldn't say that sir," I replied, feeling a bit self-conscious.

Kala squeezed my leg under the table and interjected. "Tibby is overly modest, Admiral. I can personally attest to his skills." From further down the table I heard Lunnie choking on a sip of water.

The rest of the meal went well. The admiral and the other officers at the table spoke to each of the *TRITYTE* crew. I asked the Admiral if the crew would receive medals for their action and service. He reacted with a look of confusion.

"Medals? He asked, "I don't understand."

I explained that military personnel on Earth were recognized for various acts of courage, bravery or sacrifice with medals that were worn on their dress uniforms. The admiral said he'd never heard of any such thing being done and was not sure he saw the merit of it. He dismissed this topic and asked me if I would do him a personal favor – would I be willing to put on a small impromptu demonstration of martial arts for the others to witness.

I was about to decline, when it occurred to me that I was being presented with an opportunity. "I will, sir, under one condition. When I was picked up by the *DUSTEN*,

Major Kalana was assigned as an attaché to assist me. She has done remarkably well. But now that we have successfully returned the solbidyum to the Federation, I am concerned that there may be plans to have her returned to duty on the *DUSTEN*. It would be a grave disappointment to me if this were to happen. What I would like is to have the Major continue to assist me further. I request that, if she is willing, she be assigned to do so for however long I need."

The admiral sat back in his chair and looked at me with a slight squint in his eyes, obviously analyzing my request. He scratched his chin and then said, "It appears that you're as shrewd as you are resourceful. Is that all you want?"

"Well, sir," I said, "as I understand it, I will be receiving the *TRITYTE* intact as my own personal ship, per Federation laws; and such a ship will require a crew. So here's my proposal. I'll do your demonstration here and now before these guests and, if it impresses you the way I think it will, I will consent to train fifty others to also become trainers for your Federation troops. In return, I request that Major Kalana, Lieutenant Reidecor, Corporal Luinella and Sergeant Marranalis, assuming they are willing, of course, be permanently attached to me for as long as I – or they – wish. Once rewards for finding the *TRITYTE* have been transferred to me, I will assume responsibility for all pay and compensation for their services. Until then, however, those responsibilities are yours. They will maintain their military commissions and be eligible for advancements while in service to me, as the Federation sees fit."

The admiral tented his fingers under his chin and smiled saying, "I don't know Tibby, having witnessed what you've done so far with this crew, I would be afraid you might conquer the entire Federation." He chuckled and smiled.   "What you are asking is unprecedented, you realize?"

"I'm sure asking a guest, while attending a dinner in his honor, to perform pugilistic self-defense moves as a demonstration while wearing formal attire is also unprecedented." I responded with a smile.

"Good point," the admiral noted. "Okay. I agree with your terms – providing your crew members also agree." I turned toward them to see if they had been following the conversation. All of them were looking at me intently with smiles on their faces, each one nodding, "I'm in." Kala had the biggest smile of all and was squeezing my leg with delight.

Admiral Regeny stood from the dining table and called for everyone's attention. Though I could not see any microphones, I concluded that there were some sort of directional microphones, because anyone who spoke to address the room was clearly heard by all.

"Attention everyone," he began. "I know many of you have heard tales of Tibby's skills in hand-to-hand combat. With some negotiating I have convinced him to demonstrate some of these skills for us tonight." This evoked a small applause from some of the military staff in the room. "Tibby seemed concerned about messing up his suit, but I think we can forgive a wrinkle or two, agreed? Another muted applause followed. Do we have any volunteers?"

All was silent, as the admiral looked about the room. "Looks like I shall have to pick a volunteer." He pointed to one of the guards by the door. "Congratulations, Sergeant you just volunteered." Everyone in the room laughed at this; slightly relieved, I'm sure – everyone but the "volunteer," that is. I stood up and walked to the carpeted area in front of the stage as the trooper approached. He was quite a bit larger in stature than me, standing well over 1.9 meters and certainly weighting more than me.

"What should I do?" He asked as he approached me.

"Grab me and try and put me in restraints," I suggested.

He moved forward, quickly grabbing me by the arm, which was precisely what I had hoped he would do. Instead of pulling away I move into him, catching him off balance, and placed one of my feet on top of his, causing him to fall backward. As he fell, I was able to take the restraints from his other hand and snap one ring to the arm I was grasping, while spinning him so he met with the floor on his side with his free hand up. With one quick move I attached the restraint to his other arm and he was left helpless on the floor with hands restrained behind his back. The entire demonstration took place in the blink of an eye and was followed by gasps all around the room. I removed the restraints and helped him to his feet. He was red faced and a bit shaken.

"Now, Sergeant, please take your knife and attack me," the sergeant looked at the admiral with a questioning look. The Admiral gave an approving nod towards the sergeant. Unlike the first demonstration on the *DUSTEN* with Marranalis, the sergeant pulled his knife out of its scabbard.

"I want you to really try and hurt me any way that you can," I said confidently.

It was almost a repeat performance of the demonstration on the *DUSTEN*. In just seconds the poor sergeant was lying on the floor with his own knife at his throat.   On the platform I could hear Sergeant Marranalis chuckle as he said, "Now I don't feel so bad." All around the room people were on their feet gasping in amazement. Applause broke out, as I helped the defeated man back to his feet and thanked him while we walked back towards the table. Kala beamed as the admiral said to me, "Looks like you got yourself a crew and I'm going to get a team of fighters. I wonder who is getting the better deal," to which Kala replied, "I think all of us, Admiral!"

Admiral Regeny looked me over from head to foot and then announced to the room, "Not a single scuff or wrinkle – amazing, simply amazing!" Once again applause rang out.

Later that night, reclining in my room with Kala in my arms, she asked teasingly, "Is there anything you cannot do?"

"Yes." I said, "I can't stop loving you."

The next morning we were awaken by the chime and feverish pounding at the door. Kala activated the door and Lunnie came bouncing in, clearly excited. "Come quickly, you guys, you've got to see this! Hurry, hurry or you'll miss it! No, no, don't waste time getting dressed. Just get out here!" Naked as a couple of Kobolian Binbaers, Kala and I followed her into the common room where Lieutenant Reidecor and Sergeant Marranalis were seated in front of a giant vid screen.

On the screen was a broadcast that displayed scenes of the previous night's dinner event, showing the crew as we were escorted into the great hall. A commentator said, "Members of the crew of the *DUSTEN* participated in the execution of the daring plan devised by Thibodaux James Renwalt, the recoverer of the *TRITYTE*. Here you can see the honored crew – Tibby, as he prefers to be called, Lieutenant Reidecor,   Corporal   Luinella   and Sergeant Marranalis. Now, coming down from the admiral's table to join them is Major Kalana, the attaché assigned to Tibby and member of the crew that brought the *TRITYTE* and the solbidyum back to Megelleon.

"It has been revealed that, during the dramatic journey from the *DUSTEN*, one of the crew, identified as Corporal Lexmal, gassed his fellow crewmates and hijacked the *TRITYTE* and its precious cargo. Corporal Lexmal then met up with a Bunem freighter at a pre-determined rendezvous location where the *TRITYTE* was taken aboard. We are told the crew of the *TRITYTE* were restrained and held captive on the Bunem freighter, guarded by two armed guards. Despite being restrained, Tibby managed to subdue both armed guards and free his crewmates by means of a hand-to-hand combat system he calls *martial arts*. He then led a daring counterraid, recapturing the *TRITYTE* within just a few hours of its hijacking. I believe we have a segment of Tibby's post-dinner demonstration of some of these skills, which was performed at the request of Admiral Regeny. Ahh yes, here it is. You can see a Federation trooper approaching Tibby in an attempt to subdue and restrain him. Now watch… Ahh! Did you see it? Here it is again in slow motion… AMAZING! Now watch, as the trooper attacks Tibby again, this time with a drawn knife. UNBELIEVABLE! Again in slow motion. Truly amazing! We interviewed the trooper after the event. He said that nothing was faked; he gave it his best effort, but was quickly and completely overpowered by Tibby.

"We have been told that later today the Federation Senate is to bestow on Tibby a status of Honorary Citizenship in the Federation and that he is to be considered a dignitary of the highest level within the Federation's realm. In addition, and in accordance to the finder's reward that has existed in Federation legislation for centuries, Tibby will receive full title to the *TRITYTE*, as well as a down payment toward the reward for recovery of the solbidyum.   After today, Tibby will officially be the wealthiest man in the universe.

"In related news, word of the discovery of the *TRITYTE* and solbidyum has created celebration in the streets on Megelleon as people of the Federation rejoice. We anticipate that, as each Federation planet receives word of these events, celebrations will abound there as well."

Lieutenant Reidecor turned to me and said, "Well Tibby, I think it's pretty much official. You are now top dog in the universe. I guess officially you are now also our boss, so what do you want us to do?"

I was completely taken off guard by the question. Kala put her arm around my naked waist and looked up into my eyes and said, "Yeah, boss, what do you want us to do."

I smiled and said, "Well, *you* can get back in the bedroom and I will show you. As for the rest of you, take the remainder of the morning off. I'll see you all at lunch. Oh yeah, somebody order lunch for us all!" Then I followed Kala back in the bedroom, closing the door behind us.

Later on, when enjoying a delicious brunch with my team that Lunnie ordered for us, I brought up a topic that elicited an unexpected reaction.   "Ok, crew, we've been together for several weeks now and I just realized that I only know you by your last names – or in the case of Kala and Lunnie, their nicknames. I would like to know your full names."   Everyone stopped eating and looked at me with their mouths still full of food – quite a comical picture really.

Kala swallowed and began, "Tibby, I never thought to explain it to you. Only on a very few Federation planets do people have more than one name. Unlike your planet, where you apparently have family names, middle names and maybe even other names, people here simply have one name or nickname. It's not that it's unheard of to us, but it seldom happens."

"But how?" I asked. "How can others be certain when directing communications to you? How do they refer specifically to you so others don't confuse you with someone else? Surely there are other Kalanas and other Marranalises in the Federation. How do you differentiate? Suppose I wanted to send a message to you on the *DUSTEN* and there was another Major Kalana onboard; how does anyone know with certainty which one is to receive the message?"

"You would simply direct it to Major Kalana, Attaché, Federation Starship *DUSTEN,*" she said in a matter-of-fact tone. "Well, I should add that we each have personal ID numbers that you can attach to our names; for instance, I am Kalana9549403956-GOS."

"What does the GOS" signify I asked?

"Gosney, my birth planet, of course."

"Ahh, ok. I understand now… or sort of anyway."

"Why do you have more than one name on your planet?" Marranalis asked.

"I think it was originally a way of differentiating one individual from another. It seems that in the earlier history of my planet many people named their children with the same names. For example, James has been one of the most popular names for centuries, probably because it has an affiliation with the stories and histories of a widely practiced religion that is more than 2,000 Earth years old. But across the hill there might live another family who also names their son James. The first James' father may have been named Thom and the second James' father may have been a blacksmith by profession. Over time, the duplicated names became differentiated according to their parentage; so, one would be identified as *James, Thom's son* and the second *James the smith's son*. Eventually, these references evolved into *James Thomson* and *James Smith* and the second name was carried on from generation to generation; so all of the decedents of James Thomson carried the surname *Thomson* and all the decendants of James Smith carried the surname of *Smith*. So I would say this probably accounts for at least one avenue of name development. Some cultures used a two-surname structure to track genealogy. Middle names are tricky and I have no idea how they came about, but quite often the middle name is that of relative or person that was of some significance or fondness to the parents. In my case, James was my grandfather on my father's side of the family and Thibodaux was actually my mother's maiden name before she bonded with my father."

"Maiden name," Lunnie asked curiously. "What's a maiden name?"

"Typically on my planet, at least in the some of the major religious cultures, a female child has the surname of her father until she bonds (meaning, for as long as she is a "maiden" – hence, the phrase "maiden name.") Once she is formally bonded in a practice called *marriage*, she takes the last name of her husband as her own last name. It's a little more involved than that when the two-surname structure is used, but we won't go into that."

"Sounds terribly complicated to me," Marranalis said.

"So if your mother decides she wants to bond with another man, what happens then?" Lunnie asked.

This was becoming way more complicated than I intended.

"Well, first off, bonding or being married on Earth is not exactly like bonding here. As I understand it, bonding here simply means that two persons cohabitate and may or may not have children together. If one of them decides that they no longer wish to be bonded to that person, they simply move out and the parental responsibility for any children is determined by the government.   If neither parent is considered responsible, the child is a ward to the government and placed in a foster family. Both parents are taxed by the government for each child, regardless of whether they are together; and the costs of care, clothing and food are funded out of those taxes, is that not right?"

"Yeah, pretty much so," Lunnie said.   I took particular notice that she was looking at Kala while she spoke to me.

"Well, on Earth when a couple marries, it's an official bond recorded by the government. In fact, you have to obtain a license to get married. A rite is performed where the couple and their witnesses stand before person who is legally authorized to conduct marriage ceremonies.   This person and the witnesses hear the couple profess their vows to love, honor and protect each other for the rest of their lives – at least that's how is used to be, but in the past 80 years much of that has changed. Now many couples only stay together a few years and then get a legal nullification of the agreement in what's called a divorce.   If they have children, they often share custody, meaning the children spend part of the time with one parent and then with the other.   Generally, the cost of rearing the child falls on the father until the child reaches the age of 18 years old."

"So, if I understand you correctly," Lunnie said getting one of the peevish looks in her eyes, "back on Earth if you were to bond with or, as you say, marry Kala, she would then be called Kalana Renwalt, right?"

"Ahh, yeah," I said. Out of the corner of my eye I could see a tight-lipped Kala squinting hard at Lunnie, who sat there with a huge grin on her face.

"But to get back to my original point," I said, hoping to get things back onto a different line of thought, "unless you feel otherwise, I would rather not have to go around referring to all of you by your rank." Without exception, every member of the crew granted me permission to address them by name.

After successfully redirecting the conversation, I enjoyed a relaxed lunch with my crew and laid out the assignment of duties and accountability. "During our dinner discussions the Admiral emphasized to me that the *TRITYTE*'s solbidyum reactor will most certainly be an object of envy and temptation for thieves and pirates. So he would prefer that we park the *TRITYTE* on Federation military bases or dock within Federation starships or space stations where sufficient troops are available for protection. It will be your responsibility, Reidecor, to make arrangements and file flight plans and the like, so these Federation facilities are provided with ample time to make the necessary preparations to receive us. Marranalis will take care of security matters. Also, we will need a navigator to join our crew, one we can trust. I would like for all of you to take part in finding one. Kala and I will have the final say on who is selected. Lunnie, you will still serve as Chief Engineer of all my ships – I plan to have a few. You will be responsible for maintaining supplies on all the ships and seeing to the operation and repair of all equipment and components.   Each of you may be given additional responsibilities later, but that's it for now.

"Kala, you have been my right hand since I arrived here and I want you to continue to be so. You will be making a lot of decisions for me and I want it understood by the entire crew that I fully trust your judgment. All of you will be answering to me through Kala. Any instructions she gives you carry my full authority and I expect them to be followed as if I gave them directly. Everyone clear on that?" Everyone replied with a "yes."

"Lastly," I continued, "Marranalis will hire and train no less than one hundred persons as a private security force, more if you think necessary. I'll assist in the martial arts training. Look for ex-military, if you can get them, both men and women. I want them to be highly skilled in a broad range of fields. Whenever we are outside of our personal compound, I expect each of you to be accompanied by at least one bodyguard. Kala will have no less than two at all times when outside our ships or compounds and, since the Federation thinks I need them, I will have four. All of our personal transportation will be served by our own trained drivers, who will also be sufficiently trained to act in an emergency as bodyguards. Marranalis, it will be your responsibility to find a pool of candidates; it will be Kala's and my job to filter them out. I want to make sure we have a highly efficient team that works like a well-lubricated machine." With this last statement I cleared my throat and gave Lunnie a stern look. She grinned and saluted me.

"I understand our meeting with the senators takes place this evening. Kala, if you can find out all the details and prepare us beforehand as much as possible, I will be greatly in your debt. I don't want the surprise that we had last night. I would prefer to not have too many surprises in the future. One more thing, I don't expect any of you to perform your duties by yourselves; you will need assistants and helpers. Give the matter some thought. If you know a qualified candidate that you trust, submit their name to Kala for consideration. Any questions?"

Lunnie, with her usual peevish smile raised her hand. I said to her, "If this has anything to do with Kala and last names, forget it and lower your hand. Otherwise, what's your question?" Lunnie's hand lowered as she stuck out her lower lip in a pout, but she winked at me just the same.

"Okay. Well, you have a lot to think about. The next few days and weeks will be a wild ride for us, I'm sure. Until we move out of here and into our own estate compound, we will be training instructors in martial arts for the admiral. Even after settling in we will no doubt have to continue the training for some time to come. None of you are even close to being proficient enough to truly train, but I will nevertheless need your assistance in doing so. I have a plan that will hopefully speed up the process, but I don't know yet whether it will work. Thanks for your attention, and… thanks, every one of you, for sticking with me. I will do my very best to make it well worth your while. Kala, could you meet with me after you find out the details of this evening? I have a few other matters I wish to discuss with you." As we were leaving the table, I heard Reidecor say to someone, he's going to have four bodyguards and he'll most likely be the one saving *them*. I heard chuckles all around as everyone dispersed.

As I waited for Kala to return from her fact-finding mission, I roamed around my accommodations, thinking about the enormity of my new life – the glory, which I would *never* get used to; the responsibility, which felt manageable only when Kala was by my side; and certainly the risks and dangers, which extended far beyond myself. The quarters we occupied were obviously meant to host dignitaries who traveled with an entourage. Each was set up much like my previous lodging on the *DUSTEN*. There was a gym, a shooting range, and a pool about the same size as the one on the *DUSTEN*. As was typical for me, I was immediately attracted to the pool area. While contemplating the multitude of things that would need to be done in the coming days and weeks, I absentmindedly stripped off my clothing and began swimming laps. Suddenly, my feet were grabbed and I was yanked backward under the surface. I had no doubt in my mind as to who the attacker was; by this time I knew the feel of those hands very well. I quickly tucked at the waist and saw Kala standing on the pool bottom in the chest-high water holding my feet. From this position it was easy to counter the assault by reaching for her ankles and dislodging her stance. A moment later we were spinning around each other in the water, holding on to each other's feet until we simultaneously let go and popped to the surface, gasping for air and laughing. She swam to me, throwing her arms around my neck and kissing me. I marveled at how her mouth always tasted like the sweetest of fruits. We broke free and began swimming in tandem, matching each other's strokes. Unlike our swims in the past, there didn't seem to be any competition between us as we swam. After several laps we both pulled ourselves out of the water and reclined on the lounge pads situated under a row of light fixtures that may have been tanning lights or heat lamps. The radiating warmth felt remarkably similar to natural sunlight. I reached toward Kala and she held my hand. We lay there calmly for a few moments before I spoke.

"Do you think you will regret your decision to stay with me as my assistant?"

"Well, I don't know," she taunted. "I don't seem to be getting as much sleep as I'm accustomed to now that I'm working with you, even though I *do* seem to be spending more time in bed!" We both laughed.

"Seriously though, you're going to be very busy in the near future, so I want you to hire a lead assistant team and begin training them as soon as possible. I will want you with me at all times, so you will need someone centrally located who will anticipate your thoughts and understand your style of working. The assistants can handle administrative duties and manage everyday affairs of our soon-to-be empire.

"One of the first things I will need you to do is to get ahold of the personnel files of everyone working for me, yours included." Kala looked at me strangely. "Don't worry dear; it's not what you think. I just want to have a comprehensive understanding of all your capabilities. I have great faith and trust in you and the rest of the crew, but I know that you all have multiple capabilities and talents and unique experiences documented in your personal folders that are important to me; and unfortunately I don't have the luxury of waiting to learn them gradually. I may need to draw on everyone's talents much sooner than I know; and as a leader, it's my responsibility to be well informed. But do me a favor. Don't tell the others, I don't want them to get the wrong idea."

"What makes you think the Federation will share military personnel records?" Kala asked.

"I suspect your request will be met with no problems whatsoever, because when you request them, you will do so through Admiral Regeny's office." I said with a thinly veiled grin.

"Oh, I see, and you and the admiral are great friends now, I take it!" she teased.

"Something like that," I said smugly.

She laughed and turned over and stretched herself out on top of me and kissed my lips gently. With a deep sigh she laid her head on my chest. "Tibby," she said, "I feel like all of this is a dream and I'm afraid I'm going to wake up."

"Well, think what it must be like for me," I said.

"I have another job for you to take care of – not this minute – but when you have an opportunity in the next day or so." She raised her head and looked at my face inquisitively as I continued. "We're going to need a place – I mean a really big place – an estate with lots room and preferably one that already includes lots of accommodations for staff. I need you to find us an agent who can locate some potential properties for us to consider. Of course, cost is not a factor. Oh, that reminds me – and this is important – we'll need someone to manage our finances, preferably a major banker and team of advisors who are accustomed to handling large and frequent transactions and expenses for businesses, governments, and the like. The sooner we get everything set up, the sooner we can start having fun."

"Wow," Kala exclaimed, "I feel like I need that staff right now!"

As we showered and dressed, Kala reviewed with me what she had learned about that evening's meeting with the Senate. The event would be similar to the previous night's dinner and would include a few of the senators who were also present the night before. Kala warned me that, unlike the first event, where the admiral dominated my time and presided with a very subtle control over the interactions with other guests, I should expect many senators to be vying aggressively for my attention. She told me that she would scratch her wrist if the individual was someone I should try to avoid and rub behind her ear if it was someone I should converse with at length.   Basically, she told me to acknowledge everyone, not to snub anyone, and to be careful not to let anyone talk me into anything. She also told me I should expect to see a few alien (non-humanoid) species in attendance, something I had not experienced thus far.

Alien species brought up another question for me; as we began to walk back to the common room, I asked, "Kala, I noticed some time ago that everyone I have seen so far is human – or at least physically speaking, similar to you and me. It seems odd to me that so many planets across a vast galaxy would have humans evolve in the same way; yet the evolution of plants and animals on the same planets differs widely. Why is this?"

"That's a question that has perplexed our scientists for centuries," replied Kala. "The current belief is that, at some point in time, a major portion of the galaxy was seeded with a pre-engineered but adaptable DNA and, though that DNA may have evolved and mutated to align with the various environments, ultimately most of the life-sustaining planets have developed humans like us."

"I've heard a similar theory on Earth," I said, "I think the idea was known as *star seeding*. How would that account for other sentient life forms?"

"I'm not sure," Kala answered. "I suppose those life forms could have evolved separately or, perhaps because of environmental factors, evolution took a radically different course. For instance, I know that Irribis is inhabited by sentient aquatic creatures that live under water and humans that live on the islands. Both are believed to have originally evolved there; and yet they have totally unrelated DNA. In fact, the DNA helix is completely reversed, strongly supporting the idea of two independent origins for life.

Perhaps with all your newly found wealth you can fund your own team of scientists to investigate the question."

Kala flashed me one of her priceless smiles and I thought to myself, "I just might do that."

A few hours later a military escort arrived to take us to the Senate dinner. This time the mode of transportation was quite different. I can only describe it as a luxury motor coach, similar to those found back on Earth, only larger. Inside was an arrangement of plush furniture and lavish tapestries, a wet bar adjacent to a buffet set with hors d'oeuvres, two vid screens, a toilet and shower facility, and a small galley. Unlike the Earth motor coaches, however, the driver's compartment was separated from the passenger area. Long windows along the sides of the coach appeared from the outside to be opaque and indistinguishable from the rest of the exterior, but they provided a perfectly clear view from the inside. As we boarded, I noted several military vehicles preceding and following us, all packed with troopers. There were also troopers stationed throughout the interior of our vehicle.

The trip was a bit longer than that of the previous day. At some point we emerged from the underground complex and moved along the planet's surface. For the first time I was actually getting to see the surface of an alien world. For the most part, what I saw didn't seem all that different from Earth. The sky was a familiar blue and animated with a parade of fluffy clouds; and I could recognize outcroppings of plants and trees that didn't seem all that different from the ones on Earth, at least from a distance. The manmade structures, however, were quite distinctive in appearance. Homes and smaller buildings of one or two stories were consistently designed with dome-style roofs instead of peaked roofs. Many of these homes had dome-like greenhouses attached to them as well. This feature intrigued me, so I asked Kala about it.

"Here on Megelleon the residents are very fond of fresh vegetables and fruits – so much so that most grow their own. Megelleon has two winters per year. During those seasons, temperatures are cool enough to prohibit outdoor gardening, so they keep greenhouses. They also use the warmth generated by the greenhouses to heat their homes."

As Kala explained more about the various kinds of produce and gardens, we moved rapidly into a more metropolitan area. Ahead I could see taller buildings, much like the skyscrapers of the larger cities on Earth. More and more people gathered along the road as we continued, many of whom were accompanied by small children. As we progressed further, the growing masses began to cheer and wave colorful banners.

"It looks like your fans have gathered to greet you," Kala said quietly.

"*Our* fans," I insisted, as we gazed out the window together. "All of you were instrumental in getting the *TRITYTE* and solbidyum here to Megelleon. It was *not* a one man operation."

"All we did was fly the ship and keep you company," Reidecor said warmly. "You were the one with the plan and you were the one who overpowered our captors – pretty much all on your own. We just tried to stay out of the way."

We were now getting into the heart of the city. The crowd was as thick as any I have ever seen. Even inside the conveyance the sound of cheers and the growing roar of the crowd could be heard. Eventually we pulled up to an enormous and rather intimidating gateway in front of a staggering fortress-like building that reached into the sky. On both sides of the gate stood heavily fortified guardhouses. As we passed into the confines of this citadel, we were greeted by numerous battalions and an array of military equipment stationed within the perimeter grounds.

"I thought we were going to a dinner, not a prison," I said to Kala, once again feeling overwhelmed by my surroundings.

She looked out the windows with a thoughtful expression and replied, "This is the Capitol building. Centuries ago, during the Great Wars that broke out over the loss of the solbidyum, assassination attempts and kidnappings of senators and leaders became a constant danger. Planetary governments were feuding and posturing constantly, exchanging accusations and threats on a daily basis. These tensions ultimately led to the withdrawal of the Bunem System from the Federation; and on that same day the Bunemnites carried out an organized raid on the Capitol that resulted in thousands of wounded and dead, including civilians, and total destruction of the Capitol complex. After quelling the violent outbreaks, the Capitol facility you see now was designed and built with unprecedented levels of security and protection. Even so, attacks on the Capitol remained common up until about two hundred years ago, which explains the protocols for high security that are maintained to this day."

Our coach stopped in front of the building entrance. Guards in dress uniforms lined the walkway into the Capitol building. We were met by our escort and led past the saluting guards into the building's lobby. From the outside the buildings was immense, but inside it seemed even larger. The height between floor and ceiling in most spaces seemed to be at least three to four stories tall. Like the underground hall, where we met with the Admiral and military officers, this building's decor had an art deco like style and feeling.

We were halted by security guards just inside the entrance and told that we would have to surrender all weapons before proceeding further. I hadn't even thought of taking a weapon with me and I was taken aback when Kala and the rest of the crew began placing their guns on a table as a guard carefully inventoried each one. I was even more shocked at the number each of them carried. Marranalis quickly and systematically laid out five, Lunnie had four, and Reidecor and Kala each had three. After completing his account of the crew's wares, the guard then turned to me. I advised him that I was unarmed and had nothing to surrender, to which Marranalis added, "...unless you want him to chop off his *hands* and leave them here." The crew exchanged glances and grins as we moved forward through the secured entry.

We were each required to walk through a scanner designed to detect any hidden weapons, after which our escort led us to an internal transit pod. We were soon moving through the maze of the Capitol building at great speed. Before long we arrived at a station where many other transit pods and people moved about. As we stepped out of the pod, eight troopers took up positions in front of and behind us as our escort led the way. People in the station cheered as we proceeded through a corridor to the receiving area outside the Senate Planetary Event dining room. Our grand entrance followed the same format as the night before, except this time Kala entered beside me.

The dining hall was larger than the largest coliseums back on Earth. Successive amphitheater-style levels surrounded a central arena area and extended to the inside of the domed interior, each decked with elaborate dining tables. There were too many tables and levels to count and thousands of people inside the place. Applause and cheering broke out as we made our entrance and proceeded to a central table in the middle of the arena where four other people were already waiting.

Our escort presented us to the four, introducing them as Leader Rieam and his bonded mate Risha and Leader Turaine and her bonded mate Nimatan. Leader Rieam was a tall, thin man with graying hair and a pale complexion. He stood at least 20 cm taller than me and presented himself with a gentle manner and slow grace of movement. There were lines in his face that suggested he was a man who bore great responsibility – an onus that was perhaps aging him before his time. He nodded in my direction when we were introduced. I had learned from Kala early on that there was no equivalent for the shaking of hands when being introduced, and that if any recognition was given, it was usually conveyed as an exchanged nod of heads. Leader Turaine also had gray hair. Hers was long and straight and hung down to the middle of her back. Unlike Leader Rieam, she was darker skinned, a complexion that I found reminiscent of the people from a nation on Earth called India. She appeared to be younger than Leader Rieam. If I were to guess their ages, I would place Leader Turaine in her mid-forties (in Earth years) and Leader Rieam in his late fifties. Kala had explained that the Federation's three leaders were never in the same place at one time; so I was not surprised at the absence of the third leader.

Leader Turaine motioned for us to be seated. After a few minutes the cheering and noise began to die down, during which time both Leader Turaine and Leader Rieam expressed how glorious it was that the *TRITYTE* and the solbidyum had been found and returned. Our dinner soon arrived and I could see food being served all around the coliseum by hundreds of attendants. I found it hard to believe that all these people were senators, some who were with and some without bonded mates. I could only guess what it must be like when they were in session. The meal was served in three courses. While the second course was served, Leader Rieam stood to address the room. He briefly related the history of solbidyum; its value and use; and the centuries of search and warfare brought about by its loss. Then he sat down to eat his second course, which the rest of us had finished by that time. As he sat, Leader Turaine stood and began relating the events that occurred between the time of my rendezvous with the *DUSTEN* and our ultimate arrival with the *TRITYTE* and cargo at Megelleon. Our third course was served and nearly finished before she sat down again. Leader Rieam rose to resume the presentation; and this time Kala subtly indicated that I should also stand. He turned in my direction and addressed me on behalf of the entire assembly, while images of the crew were displayed on giant screens situated around the dome.

"Tibby, we, the governing body of the Galactic Federation, cannot fully express to you the tremendous gratitude we feel for all that you have done. While we realize that you did not bring to pass the events leading to this historic moment all on your own, we recognize that you were not only responsible for finding the *TRITYTE* and the solbidyum, but also integral to its safe recovery and return to Megelleon. The value of the role you have played in the unfolding of these events and the feats you have accomplished are immeasurable. It is with our utmost gratitude that we present to you here this evening a portion of the rewards to which you are so duly entitled." Polite applause followed the leader's speech.

By now Leader Turaine had risen to her feet and an aide had come to her side, bearing several documents.

Leader Rieam continued, "First, allow me to present you with Full Citizenship in the Galactic Federation, and with it the honorable title of RECOVERER, which carries all the respect and benefits of a Federation dignitary of the highest level. From this day forward you will be known to the citizens of the Federation as *Tibby the Recoverer*.

"Second, in accordance with the reward agreement of the Federation Senate, we present you with the full title of ownership to the ship, *TRITYTE*, fully intact as discovered by you, save for the solbidyum cargo that was carried in its hold.

"Third, we present you with the first installment of the monetary value of the solbidyum. Due to the extraordinary amount of the reward, the Federation treasury will compensate you in five installments as the money arrives from the other planets for their shares of the solbidyum. It is estimated that full receipt of funds will require nearly fifty years, hence installments will be made to you in 10-year intervals."

As Leader Rieam made each announcement, Leader Turaine stepped forward and handed me a leather-bound folder containing each corresponding proclamation or legal transfer papers. With the third and last announcement, another man came forward with Leader Turaine. As she presented me with the leather binder, Leader Rieam continued, "Now, Tibby, Federation Treasurer Lionlim will complete and witness the first official transfer of funds."

Treasurer Lionlim approached me directly and produced a device that looked similar to a laptop computer. He asked me to press my hand to the bottom screen while staring into a retinal scanner located above the hand reader and state my name. I did as he instructed and noted a strange tingling sensation when I placed my hand on the

screen.   Upon completion of the procedure, Treasurer
Lionlim concluded with, "Congratulations, Tibby the
Recoverer, may this reward bless you as much as you have
blessed the Federation."

I was about to sit down when Leader Rieam stepped
forward and, bending down, kissed me on my forehead.
Leader Turaine then came forward and likewise, while
standing on her tip toes, kissed me on the forehead. With
that, the entire assembly of senators broke into a roar of
cheers and applause.   As I backed away from Leader
Turaine, I noted a huge smile on her face and tears running
down her cheeks. I glanced at Leader Rieam, who also was
smiling and applauding, his eyes brimming with tears.

I turned to my crewmates and motioned for all of
them to stand with me. Though reluctant to do so at first, I
motioned insistently. The roar and applause increased in
volume until they all stood with me in front of the assembly.
After a few moments in this posture, I approached each of
my crew in order of rank, as if taking cue from the leaders,
and kissed them each on the forehead. The roar of the
assembly became deafening. When I stepped back and stood
at attention as a formal gesture of respect to my crew, I saw
the glistening of tears on each of their faces.

When the roar finally died down, I addressed the
assembly, "I want to thank everyone in the Federation for
this wondrous praise and recognition; but in reality, I do not
feel I am deserving of it. Without the skilled assistance *and
friendship* of these four people here beside me, I would not
be here today and you would not be celebrating the return of
the solbidyum. These remarkable servants of the Galactic
Federation will not go without their rewards; I plan to
personally see to this. I paused to allow the crowd an
applause of thanks to my crew members.

"As for the unbelievable wealth you have bestowed on me, I plan to spend a great portion of it to benefit the greater citizenship of the Federation, to which I can now proudly call myself a member.   In the form of various programs and infrastructure, it will be among my primary goals to assist in meeting the needs of each individual planet and its people. It may be awhile before all of this is in place, but I hope to see in my lifetime that everyone benefits from the wealth that has come to me as a result of the solbidyum – this tremendous resource – which has always belonged to you and your citizens, and which has been returned to you after these many centuries of great cost." I paused again for the emotional torrent of applause and cries that filled the arena.

"While I realize that, with all that you have showered on me tonight, I should not be asking for anything more, but I am. For years your peoples have suffered from wars, death and destruction resulting from the loss of the solbidyum. Three worlds were destroyed, billions of lives were lost, and the Federation was nearly irretrievably broken and divided. Over the past centuries, as I understand it, the Federation has slowly been restored and today is almost whole. There are still a few systems that have not restored their membership, due to a belief that the solbidyum had been deliberately withheld from them.

Now the solbidyum is back. Unfortunately, anger, jealousy and despair still plague some systems today. I would ask that you extend to them the hope of reconciliation and restoration into the Federation to bring an end to the suspicion and rejection that they have perceived for so long. Hopefully, in this reconciliation, a fair share of the solbidyum can one day be distributed to them, as with all planets in the Federation."

My last statements were met with mixed reactions. Some *boo*ing and stamping of feet were heard from some senators in rejection of my words, while others cheered and applauded. The Senate was clearly divided on this issue. I didn't have a good feeling about how this was going to play out in the future. Just the same, I had made my feelings known.

When I took my seat Kala leaned over to me and whispered, "Do you have any idea what the significance of the kiss on the forehead in public means to the people of the Federation?"

"Not really," I said uncomfortably. "But I have the feeling that it's pretty damn significant."

"To kiss one on the forehead in a public setting is the highest form of respect you can show to another individual. This gesture is reserved for heroes and persons who have done great deeds. To kiss a person on the forehead means you would give your life for them. When a leader from the Federation kisses you on the forehead, it means that the government itself stands behind you and pledges to protect you. In the entire history of the Federation this gesture has been received only four times before you. When you immediately kissed us after you had been honored, you in turn brought us under the umbrella of the Federation's pledge to you." She seemed concerned about what I had done. I could see her lips quivering, as though she feared I would have to recant my previous actions.

"It's okay," I quietly reassured her. "I meant every bit of it, regardless of what it means to the Federation," and with that – right there in front of the entire Senate – Kala threw her arms around my neck and gave me the best reward of the entire night – an electrifying kiss that left my ears ringing. In spite of the roar in my head, I could still hear my crew, led by Lunnie no doubt, applauding and cheering.

I had hoped that the event would be over in about the same amount of time as the dinner the night before, but that was not so. Most of the thousands of senators in attendance felt it necessary to meet and greet me personally. As a result, the event lasted well into the early hours of the morning. Thankfully, Kala stayed by my side to assist me with the unending stream of introductions and discussions. Kala knew many of them personally, having worked with them before in her capacity as an attaché. While all who approached me seemed friendly and grateful for my contributions, few praised my comments on offering a chance for the rebel systems to rejoin the Federation. Some even told me flatly that they believed that the rebel systems should be annihilated upon the return of the solbidyum.

I saw Kala motion to Reidecor. She briefly spoke to him, after which he quickly left, returning immediately with our escort. The escort announced that our conveyance was awaiting our return to the compound. Suddenly our eight-trooper guard detail materialized to escort us out of the hall. Once onboard the coach I was able to relax and I promptly fell asleep for the duration of our trip back to the underground facility.

The next day everyone slept in late, exhausted from the events that had taken place the night before. It was midday before most of us awoke. There was a message waiting for me when I shook of the heavy sleep – a voice memo of sorts from the admiral, reminding me of the martial arts training that I promised to his tactical troops. He suggested that I could perhaps start in about four weeks. The Federal treasury also had left a message for me regarding the previous night's deposit. I had never seen so many zeros in a row in my life. Unlike Earth, the Federation did not utilize private banking systems. Instead, there was one Federal depository supported by all Federation membership and operated by way of multiple branches located throughout the Federation territories; and I was now their single largest account holder.

Kala was with me when I viewed the electronic receipt for my new account balance. I thought for a moment that she was going to pass out. I asked her how difficult it would be for me to transfer money to other accounts. She explained that it was very easy, once I had the account codes.

Kala checked her own messages and was shocked to see that she had received every last one of the requested personnel files. "I never thought that I would get them so easily," she said, "or that I would even get them at all. I expected it to take weeks."

"Did you talk to Admiral Regeny's office?" I asked.

"Yes, but still... I didn't think it would happen this fast."

"Kala, is all your pay from the Federation deposited directly in your personal account?"

"Yes," she confirmed.

"Good. Then it's safe to assume that your and the others' account numbers are in the personnel records...?" I continued.

"Well, yes. Oh, I see. You want to set up an automatic payment system for our compensation," she said.

"Yes, I want it set up so that each of you is being paid at ten times the rate of your current military pay. I also want to give you each one million credits right now. Call it a signing bonus."   I laughed to myself, knowing she probably didn't quite understand.

Awestruck, Kala turned pale and exclaimed, "Tibby, you can't – well, I guess you can, but – well, are you sure?!"

"Kala, I have more than I can ever spend. The least I can do is share it with the people closest to me – really, the people I owe my life to," I said.

Kala sat on my lap and helped me transfer funds to each of my crew's accounts. When it came time to transfer into her account, I transferred five million credits instead of one million. Kala looked at me and shrieked, "No!"

"What's' the matter, it's not enough?" I said teasingly.

"No, it's too much! I don't feel I deserve it."

"Good. Then you know how I feel millions of times over for what I have been given," I replied.

It was just before noon when messages were simultaneously delivered to each of my crew. The messages came to them in the form of official orders and to me in the form of a request regarding our formal depositions as witnesses in the court martial trial of Corporal Lexmal.

News, both good and bad, travels quickly. Not long after completing the transfers into each bank account, we were invited to join the rest of the crew for a special dinner hosted by none other than Lieutenant Reidecor, who had already checked his bank account and discovered that he was suddenly a rich man.   As it turned out, Reidecor had exquisite – and expensive – gourmet tastes, but heretofore did not have the budget to match. Now he was celebrating with a banquet of his favorite foods and we were all benefitting from it. Upon learning of his newfound wealth, he apparently contacted many of best restaurants in the capital city and had their chefs prepare and deliver their best dishes. He made sure the experience was complete by including white linen tablecloths, fine china and the most professional wait staff employed at the compound.

While we dined, Reidecor told us about each of the dishes – where they were from, their exotic ingredients and even more exotic preparation. I won't say it made the food taste any better, but it was interesting to learn and the food was delicious. Throughout dinner Lunnie and Marranalis kept thanking me over and over again "for everything." Kala sat by my side and seemed somewhat lost in thought, but from time to time I would see her smile and I would feel her hand reach over to rest on my leg. Finally I asked her what was wrong.

"I keep thinking about Corporal Lexmal and how he turned traitor for the sake of gaining wealth. And now here we are – every one of us wealthy. He could have been, too, had he not been so greedy and narcissistic. Now he will probably die for what he did."

"Probably so," Lunnie replied, "but had he gotten away with it, possibly millions or even billons more people would have died and a resurgence of the Great Wars would have been certain. I don't feel sorry for him. He made his choice and now he must pay the consequences."

"Oh!" Kala exclaimed, in a sudden change of topic. "With all that's been going on this morning I forgot to tell you. I may have a lead on an estate. It's in the mountains not too far from the city and it includes its own lake as part of the property. The estate belonged to an industrialist from Astamagota who wanted a place near the Capitol to entertain senators and other dignitaries. Recently his company went broke when the sun in Astamagota's solar system spewed out a flare, searing everything on the planet and destroying all life and property there. Shortly thereafter he committed suicide and now the Federation is selling off his properties to cover his debts. The estate is so huge that almost no one can afford to even consider placing a bid on it. The grounds include numerous cottages that he used for guests, as well as barracks for guards who were stationed on the premises. There's also a large landing pad, as well as a huge hangar built into the mountainside."

"It certainly sounds promising. When can we look at it?"

"Day after tomorrow, but let me confirm that," Kala said.

"Lunnie, tomorrow you and Reidecor check out the *TRITYTE* and its supplies. I want the ship ready to go when we're ready to go. Reidecor, check into flight plans; I would like to visit the estate in the *TRITYTE* to see how it fits in the hangar there."

I'm not sure when they had time to arrange appointments, but the next day brought a steady stream of candidates to Kala and Marranalis for interviews. Later in the day Lunnie and Reidecor returned from the *TRITYTE* with confirmation that everything was ready for the next day. While going about their business, Lunnie and Reidecor thought they may have found the replacement member for our crew. Lunnie ran into someone at the hangar that she had met when she first enlisted in the service and it turned out that Reidecor had known him also. Both were fond of the possible new crewmate; now it was just a matter of seeing if they could get this individual to join us. Marranalis also met with a number of candidates but insisted that he needed to conduct more interviews before decisions could be made. In the meantime, Admiral Regeny had promised us Federation security resources until we could acquire our own. As far as my obligation to the Admiral, I planned tentatively to combine the martial arts training sessions of the troopers with that of our own security force.

Kala came to me, primarily overwhelmed with the sudden realization of just how many more personnel and crewmen were needed, but also astounded by the unforeseen volume of applicants applying for positions. It quickly became clear why she needed a personal assistant and finding this assistant was going to have to be a top priority. To make matters worse, nearly 300 requests had arrived in two days from various senators, dignitaries and persons of other import wanting the five of us to attend functions to be held in our honor. Just handling these requests was going to be a full time task for one person.

"Kala, do they have temporary employment services or agencies here? Maybe we can use those kinds of resources on an interim basis; and maybe those individuals who seem to be a good fit can eventually be hired full time."

"Yes," she said excitedly. "Why didn't I think of that?"

"You've been too busy with too many things to give full attention to any one of them. I suggest you contact some hiring agencies and get yourself a temporary staff, at least until you can find the people you want full time. I would focus my search on individuals with military background and training; I think they will be more focused in their roles and easily cross-trained. But that's your decision."

"I remember about a year ago hearing of an agency that specialized in placing ex-military personnel in both government and civilian jobs. I could start there," Kala said.

"Great, I would also suggest that you narrow the candidate pool by prioritizing individuals that held high-level security clearances and maintained them during their career. It may save us time when completing background checks and trying to identify who we can trust," I rationalized.

Kala shook her head as she began sorting through something on her vid pad. "You amaze me at times. You just seem to pick ideas out of the air as you go along without having to think about it."

"One more thing, Kala. Find out when Piesew Mecarta's tour of duty is up and see if he would be interested in serving as house majordomo after we settle on an estate. Agree to whatever he wants for a salary and then double it... and let me know when he will be available."

Kala said with a smile, "You never forget anyone who serves you well, do you?"

Due to all the activity of the day, it wasn't until early evening that all of us had time to assemble in the gym for martial arts training. Everyone seemed off in their form, distracted by other thoughts and pressing deadlines; and I was probably a bit rougher on them than usual. They needed to remain focused with every fiber of their beings on what their bodies were doing; there was no allowance for momentary diversion of attention to things like wondering whom they were going to see tomorrow or whether someone that interviewed that day was right for the job. Full convergence of mind and body had to stay in the moment. In a way, the situation served as a kind of lesson in the dangers of distraction.   After the workout everyone showered. The shower in the gym was large enough to accommodate everyone; and it was quite noisy with conversation for the few minutes that we were in the shower and locker room together, each person wanting to talk about some aspect of a candidate they were trying to hire. The dialogues continued all the way to the dining room, until it suddenly dawned on everyone that, with all on the havoc of the day, no one had made arrangements for dinner. We broke into laughter as we all traipsed into the galley to line up at the food synthesizer and punch in our favorite concoction from the thousands the synthesizer could produce. Minutes later, we were all seated about the dining table, some slurping down noodles and others spooning up stew-like dishes, and all still very animated about the activities of the day.

There finally came a break in the conversation, as the crew all munched on a bite of food. I took the opportunity to speak. "I really want to thank all of you for working as hard as you do. The next several months or so are going to be very hectic, I know; but once we have things in place and everything calms down a bit, I promise you things will become easier and we will have some fun."

Marranalis said, "I don't know about anyone else, but I'm already having more fun than I have in my entire life. I never realized just how dull and routine my life was until you came along, Tibby. Since then, every day has been filled with excitement, adventure and fun." Marranalis's statement was followed by like comments and agreements. This warmed me to see and hear the affect I had made on this new group.

I sighed as I sorted out what I wanted to say. "So…tomorrow we are headed out to look at an estate that we may acquire. I want each one of you to be looking at it from several perspectives. First, how well does it work for your respective assignments? Think about where you may want to locate your staff's quarters and your own office. I also want you to think about it from an overall operations perspective. If you see any features that are not suitable, think of possible modifications or additions that will align with our needs. We can certainly make changes if needed; my understanding is that the estate is a one thousand square kilometer spread, so we have plenty of room to expand the infrastructure.

"Lunnie and Reidecor, the two of you may want to stay on the ship tonight so you can have it ready for an early departure in the morning."

"Woohoo," chimed Lunnie, "I finally get a chance to have Reidecor for a night without interruptions. Mind if we use your cabin, Tib?" Reidecor just hung and shook his head, while everyone else in the room moaned.

The flight to the estate lasted only about twenty minutes, most of which was spent arranging the takeoff with traffic control. It actually took more time to drive to the Capitol from the Federation base than it did to fly to the estate in the *TRITYTE*. As we navigated through the rolling terrain, I instructed Reidecor to make a pass around the property, displaying it on the view screen so we could get an idea of its size. A mountain range ran along the western border and sloped down to a sizeable lake situated on the eastern half of the estate. Most of the land seemed to be covered in forests, but there were also sections of fields and some meadows or pastures where large animals grazed at the southeast corner near an agricultural development. The main compound itself was centered at the south end of the lake and included a nearby landing pad situated to the southwest and adjacent to the mountainside.

Once we landed, a large conveyance similar to the one that had driven us to the Senate dinner pulled up adjacent to the landing pad. We disembarked from the *TRITYTE* and were greeted by a short woman with curly brown hair and cute dimples. She introduced herself as Mar'dana, the sales representative for the property. While she was talking, I noted several troopers quietly materializing around us, though I have no idea where from. They silently took up formation around the perimeter of the ship and around us.

"I see the Federation isn't taking any chances with the security of your ship," commented Mar'dana in an overly chipper tone.

"Just don't forget to close and lock the door," Reidecor said. I thought he was speaking to the troopers, when I noticed that he was turned toward me and gesturing towards the ship.

"You're joking, right?" I asked in confusion.

"No, I'm not. The ship is now coded to your DNA. Only you can lock and unlock it at the moment. As long as it's not locked, anyone can access it; and once you *do* lock it, *no one* is going to get in. Didn't anyone explain that to you?"

"No," I responded. "Are you sure this was done? I don't remember anything about it."

Reidecor laughed, "It was coded before we left the *DUSTEN*. Don't you remember having to open the door in the main hangar when you arrived at the ship in a mechanic's uniform... before we left to come to Megelleon?"

"I remember grasping a lighted rod before everyone could enter the ship," I trailed off thoughtfully, as I turned to walk back to toward the hatch. Could I have really missed such an important key step to our security?

"Well, that was you activating the security code to unlock the ship.   At that point my DNA was already imprinted into the ship's systems, so I could open and close the door; but I don't have permission to lock it. Only you can do that," Reidecor explained.

"But when was all this programmed into the ship?" I asked. "I don't remember doing anything on the ship that would give me this kind of control."

"It was done as part of the initial protocols. When you first entered the *DUSTEN* with Kala, your handprint, your voice print and your DNA were all collected. That information was programmed into the *TRITYTE*'s computer by Captain Maxette as a safety measure to prevent its theft. He felt that, since the ship was going to be yours anyway, he would complete this protocol in advance of your *formal* receipt of title to the ship."

"I see," I said. "And just how do I lock it?"

"It's simple. Just press this button here inside the hull and step out. The door closes and seals and then all you have to do is grasp the rod in the door recess, slide your hand to the left, say your name and a red light will come on. After that no one but you can unlock it and no one can get inside the ship."

"Interesting," I said thoughtfully as I followed the instructions and watched the red light come on. "Can more than one person be given locking and unlocking privileges at a time?"

"Yes, you can have as many persons authorized as you wish."

"Remind me before we return to the compound to assign authorization to each of you."

"Mar'dana," I said, returning to the purpose for our visit, "I apologize; I didn't mean to ignore you just now. There was just a small security detail that required my attention."

I took a closer look at Mar'dana as we began our tour of the property. I had expected a person who would be volunteering superfluous information about the attractive features of the property, as opposed to telling me what I needed to hear. On Earth most women in real estate tended to dress fashionably, yet conservatively; and Mar'dana tended to follow that same mold. Her demeanor, however, was more, like that of an accountant or banker than my idea of a real estate agent. Instead of employing hard sell tactics, she let the property sell itself and simply provided pertinent and informative answers to questions as they were asked.

I must confess that I was very impressed by the estate. There were at least 400 bedroom suites in the main building and nearly as many independent guest bedrooms. Twenty cottages of varying sizes were situated near the main building and at least 30 more were scattered around the grounds. There was also a small 80-room guest lodge at the opposite end of the estate and several nearby buildings that served as workshops and accommodations for the lodge staff. A short walk from the lodge was a natural hot spring that was landscaped and developed for bathing and soaking.

On the southeast corner of the estate were several large buildings that had once been used for farming this part of the property. It had been more productive in the past,

Mar'dana said, but most of the space was now unused. Marranalis saw this area as having strong potential for being converted into a training complex and barracks for the security forces. Marranalis didn't believe that the guards' accommodations by the main house would be sufficient to accommodate the entire security force we would eventually have in place, though there were housing units on the grounds that could be possibly used for lodging some of the more specialized security personnel.

Reidecor was impressed with both the landing pad and the hangars, especially the one that was recessed into the mountain.   The landing area was large enough to accommodate eight to ten ships the size of the *TRITYTE*. The external hangar could accommodate three ships of the same size. At the northern end of the property was a smaller landing pad that could accommodate two ships the size of the *TRITYTE*.   A dual purpose mechanic's shop and maintenance building was also located on the site that included ample office space.

By far the most interesting structure on the estate was the main house, which sat on a parcel of land approximately one square kilometer. It was several stories tall and contained thousands of rooms, according to Mar'dana, as well as fifteen indoor pools and three outdoor pools. The exact number of rooms was not known. One area consisted almost entirely of banquet halls, which could also be used as ballrooms. Adjacent to many of the indoor pools were large gymnasiums; smaller gyms and workout areas were situated in various locations throughout the shared and private areas of the house. Overall, the main house was more like a small city than a home. Around the perimeter were gardens and streams and broad areas of well-manicured foliage attractively distributed around patios and recreational areas.

Both Reidecor and Marranalis were especially interested in investigating the underground tunnel that ran between the hangar and the main house as well as the guard's quarters that were situated adjacent to the main complex. Kala was impressed with the overall layout of the house, especially the private office and administrative areas. I wished Piesew had been present to provide his input. There was ample storage space in the basement, which was lined with vaults where months of food could be stored to sustain the entire compound. There were several enormous kitchens and a huge greenhouse for cultivating just about every vegetable, fruit and flower known to the Federation territories. Just as the main house was more like a small city, the vast expanse of the property was more like a small country than an actual estate. I could tell that everyone was in awe of the place. Statuaries, paintings, and lavish furnishings surrounded us in every room of the house, all of which Mar'dana said were eligible for purchase with the property, if so desired.

Kala took me aside, "Tib, this is perfect. It could be years before another property of this size becomes available with all the appurtenances in place. If we built an estate like this from scratch, it would take us years just to *furnish* it; this one we can practically move into immediately."

I had to agree with her. The configuration and setup of the complex would require only minimal changes to make it fully functional in a short time. The biggest problem I saw was finding the right people to staff the place – and doing it quickly enough.

"Mar'dana, what is the current status of the staffing here? Obviously there must be staff maintained here just to see to the daily upkeep."

"When the place went into foreclosure, staffing was reduced to essential personnel only. All of the current staff were employed by the previous owner."

"If I were to purchase the place do you think that the current staff would be willing to stay on with a possible raise in income?" I asked.

"I believe there is a high probability of that. Would you like me to check into it for you?"

"Yes, please. Could you let me know by end of the day tomorrow? Would you also be able to confirm how much the Federation wants for the property?"

A huge smile spread across Mar'dana's face. I was sure she was envisioning the huge commission or bonus she would get when she closed the sale.

On the way back to the *TRITYTE* I told Kala that, when the call came in from Mar'dana with the asking price of the property, she was to offer them 75% of what they asked. Also, any of the existing staff that accepted my offer was to receive a boost their current pay by 50%.

Kala looked at me in shock. "Why would you offer them only 75% of what they are asking?!"

"I am infinitely wealthy. They will assume that they can ask whatever they want and I will pay it. They will most likely inflate the price accordingly. I also suspect that they have no other prospective buyers and it could be some time before they see another one. I'm going to assume that the cost of maintaining that property is biting heavily into their funds, so they will be willing to come down quite a bit on their price. In the end, it's important that I don't develop the impression that am willing to just throw money around or, worse, that I can be manipulated."

"Then why are you willing to pay more money to the employees at the estate? You're saving their jobs; they should be happy about that," Kala responded.

"True. But by offering them an increase at a time when they see we are hiring lots of *new* employees, it will inspire them to work harder and more diligently as the senior staff. If I pay them the same as the new-hires, their feeling toward us could be indifferent."

We had barely gotten aboard the *TRITYTE* and into the air when an emergency message came in from the Federation base. "Hey, Tibby," Reidecor called," you need to hear this."

The message from the base was instructing us to delay our landing. A surprise attack had just occurred at the base in an attempt to steal the solbidyum. The attack was unsuccessful; however, our accommodations had been damaged in the assault. During the time that we were on hold, Reidecor helped me to get everyone's security authorizations in place for the ship's lock. By the time we received communication confirming that the base was fully secured, the crew's DNA and ID prints were validated and uploaded to the computer database. It was nearly two hours before we were finally cleared to approach the base. When we received permission to land, we were directed to a new location and told to stand by inside the *TRITYTE*. It wasn't long before a major came aboard to tell us the situation.

Apparently, when the facility was designed and constructed centuries ago, a storage area was created for the eventual return of the solbidyum. At the time, an adjacent tunnel was secretly built by an organized band of individuals who worked on one of the construction crews, in hopes of returning through this passage to steal the solbidyum after it was found. They had stopped the tunnel development just shy of the solbidyum vault, believing that the remaining gap could be bridged with a quick and stealthy breakthrough after the eventual return of the solbidyum. This information was apparently imparted to the succeeding members of a surviving secret society that was formed around this purpose.

It was after the attack when the military was able to determine that the tunnel had been in place for several hundred years – hidden and unused, but waiting. The tunnel was several kilometers long and would obviously have taken years to dig, even with modern equipment. Upon further inspection it became clear that whoever built it did so with the expectation of leaving it dormant until some future time. Where their plan went wrong was that, in the time between the construction of the originally planned complex and the current utilization of the facilities, the military decided to repurpose this particular underground area as an emergency command center, complete with special dignitary quarters and accommodations, while a different location within the complex was selected for the eventual storage of the solbidyum.   Apparently, the breakthrough point for the raiders breached the side of an indoor pool, causing the water to gush into the tunnel. In spite of this unexpected result, they were able to continue their raid into complex, until they met heavy opposition and retreated back through the tunnel. Though troops chased after them, the tunnel had been constructed with a high speed rail system for rapid evacuation. By the time the troops followed into the tunnel, the invaders had escaped and blasted several segments to collapse the tunnel and eliminate the possibility of pursuit. The other end of the tunnel was discovered by troops several hours later; however, by then there were no signs of the invaders and no remaining evidence to identify who they were.

Since our quarters had been pretty badly damaged in the attack, we decided to spend the night on the *TRITYTE*.

We used the cargo hold for martial arts practice and we prepared the evening meal in the galley. That night the crew introduced me to a card game commonly played across the Federation territories. The game and bets were played much like *poker* on Earth; though the actual cards were different, consisting of a deck of sixty round-shaped cards in five suits instead of four. The crew was "*taking me to the cleaners*," as we say on Earth, before I finally got the hang of the game. Once I did, I started to recover my losses quickly. By the game's end, I had even made some small gains. Lunnie was the big winner and thanked us all profusely for the new outfit she was going to buy next time she was off duty.

Kala and I slept in each other arms. Kala fell asleep quickly, whereas I laid there enjoying the feel of her body against mine and the sensation of her steady breathing as it passed over my flesh. That night I dreamed of being lost in the huge estate house, while outside lurked some mysterious enemy who was trying to break in.

Early the next morning we were awakened by a call from Base Security informing us that several people were at the gate asking to see Kala. Kala jumped out of bed in a panic, exclaiming that she had forgotten about the appointments with job candidates and now she had no idea where she could conduct the interviews. Security also advised us that, due to the attack on the base, the court martial hearing for Corporal Lexmal was postponed until the following week.

Fortunately for Kala, the base provided a small conference room where Kala could interview for assistants and other staff. It was just after midday when we received a call from Mar'dana with good news; the existing staff agreed to stay on at the estate and the Federation had provided her with a price as well. Kala obtained the asking price from her and returned with the 75% offer. Though doubtful about the strength of the offer, Mar'dana said she would relay it to her bosses.

After she finished talking with Mar'dana, I asked Kala to place a call to Admiral Regeny. She was skeptical that she would be connected and surprised when the call was immediately answered by the admiral. "Tibby," I heard, as Admiral Regeny appeared on the vid screen. "I hope all is well! I heard about the shake-up there at the base yesterday. You and your crew didn't have to stay on your ship; other accommodations could have easily been arranged."

"Yes, sir, we were aware of that option," I explained," but it was rather late when we returned and it was just easier for us to stay onboard."

"Well I'm glad you're ok. I was especially concerned when I heard that the attack occurred at your quarters. The base commanding officer informed me that you and your crew were not on the premises at the time. He mentioned you were looking at an estate. How did you make out with that venture? Did you find something you like?"

"Actually, we did, sir, but the selling price is more than I am willing to pay. I'm trying to get them to come down 25% on the price. It's a great piece of property – the house is more than ample for my needs… lots of great areas are already developed for various purposes and would be immediately functional," I said, baiting a train of thought from the admiral that would work in my favor. "It has its own landing pads and even a hangar recessed into the mountain. There is also a perfect area that can quickly be adapted to accommodate your special troops for martial arts training, sir. We could easily instruct up to fifty trainees at a time. However, the Federation Bank seems reluctant to accept my offer. I just wanted to let you know that I've not forgotten our deal; and as soon as I find an estate large enough, we can get training underway. However, if my offer for this property falls through, it could be several months before we find another suitable location."

"Well I appreciate you letting me know that you are working on this matter and planning to get started as soon as you can. I have compiled a list of potential people for you to train, which I will forward to you soon. In the meantime, I would be very pleased if you kept me informed on your progress in finding a place."

"Thank you, Admiral, I will do that. Have a good day, sir."

"You also, Tibby."

"What was that all about, Tib?" Kala asked after the admiral disappeared from the vid screen.

"Wait and see, Kala. I think you will be receiving a phone call within the hour from the Federation Bank saying they have accepted our offer."

The call came twenty-two minutes later.

It's amazing how fast the wheels of progress can spin when a high-ranking government official gets involved. It only took the bank one day to have all the paperwork arranged and the property transferred to me. The following day we moved the *TRITYTE* and the crew to our new home.

Two patrol ships accompanied us to the estate, carrying dozens of troopers in their holds. Marranalis directed them to the main security accommodations until other arrangements could be made and our own security forces put into place. Some problems occurred due to the initial lack of understanding on the part of senior ranking personnel in these troops as to their roles in relation to those of my crew. There were times that orders were not followed strictly, due to a difference in the usual protocols related to uniforms and ranks. Higher ranking officers often tried to override the direction of my staff, despite the fact they were deployed to the estate premises to follow *my crew's* orders. I was becoming increasingly frustrated by the delays and conflicts. After making some calls to key individuals, I brought my crew together.

"As you all know, we've been having problems getting the Federation troops to adhere to orders because they're confusing the accountability within their own ranks with the authority you each have over their movements. All of this confusion is causing delays in completing the critical tasks that are before us. I looked into possible solutions to the situation, hoping that I might be able to provide you with different uniforms; however, the Federation High Command won't allow it. As a compromise, I've come up with a solution that *is* acceptable to the High Command. I have here a pair of small gold stars that you will wear at all times on the collars of your uniforms, one on each side. These insignia will identify you as senior members of my staff who are exempt from orders issued internally by leadership of the Federations troops stationed here. In addition, those troops and their leadership will adhere strictly to your orders and answer to you, regardless of rank. Of course, your authority is only effective while they are here at the estate. I've already discussed it with Admiral Regeny. He is issuing a directive as we speak. By the time you leave this meeting, all troops and their leadership will have been briefed and you will be henceforth provided any protection and cooperation you need." I passed out the gold stars and watched as everyone added them to their uniforms.

With the rank issue straightened out, things started moving more efficiently and, over the next few days, we organized every major operation within the estate. Kala was able to hire a staff of people to direct the administrative functions of the estate and manage my personal holdings. She even succeeded in finding a very capable assistant to take over the bulk of her daily responsibilities. Marranalis recruited a number of ex-military troopers and began assembling our private security force. Before long, the Federation guards were moved to the newly converted buildings at the farm that now served as their quarters. Reidecor and Lunnie hired mechanics and acquired supplies for the ship as they continued to conduct interviews to fill the role of the newest member of our crew – a navigator.

One of my primary concerns was getting the martial arts instructors trained for Admiral Regeny, but I was working on an idea. I instructed Kala to get her staff looking into the company that manufactured the learning headbands like the one on the *TRITYTE*. I had an idea that, though this tool might not actually be able to imbue on the user the actual physically coordinated execution of martial arts, it might speed up the rate at which the students learn the concepts and skills.

I was exploring the endless recesses of the house, when I discovered a room that I found especially intriguing. The room had a tangible familiar feeling about it that I liked. One wall was solid glass that looked into a giant aquarium, alive with all kinds of colorful fish and aquatic plants. The room must have been at least 215 square meters with a ceiling height of at around 3.5 meters. Dark, rich wood panels covered the walls, which were decorated with unique and beautifully framed paintings. In a number of areas were glass-enclosed shelves recessed into the wall to display various objects of artistic and scientific interest. One wall consisted almost entirely of bookshelves, something that surprised me. Up to this point I had not seen any books and had grown to believe that all books in the Federation were stored electronically, but I was wrong. Kala later explained that many of the worlds in the Federation lacked the electrical power and communication resources of other planets. Without computers and power distribution systems that were found elsewhere, paper documents and books served as essential tools in education, dissemination of information and entertainment. There was a feeling of power, comfort, and safety that this room exuded; I decided almost instantly that this room would become my study. A huge desk was situated in front of the aquarium wall facing into the room. I sat down in my new favorite chair and took in the view of my surroundings. The scene looking into the aquarium behind me was calming. Sofas, settees and large chairs were situated around the room, some arranged around intimately sized tables and complemented with large, potted palm-like floor plants and ferns.

Just then, I received notification through the house computer system that Kala was attempting to reach me. I told the computer to connect me and her face instantly appeared in front of me on one of the many view screens located throughout the house. She immediately announced, "Tibby, Kerabac, the navigator that Lunnie and Reidecor recommended, is here for an interview."

"Bring him here, if you would, Kala, and notify Lunnie and Reidecor to join us," I replied, knowing that the house computer would guide them to where I was.

While I was waiting for them to arrive, I investigated the room further and discovered that some of the wall panels disguised accesses to a food synthesizer and a drink dispenser. I also located the controls to a sound system and an electronic music library. I sampled pieces of music and selected a grouping that played music much like the classical music of Earth. I was sitting in my desk chair, looking into the aquarium, when Kala and Kerabac arrived.

Kerabac was a man of average build and he had the darkest black skin I had ever seen. My community back on Earth was racially mixed and included a large black culture mixed with white and other races. I had served with a number of black sailors in the Navy, as well, and many of my closest friends were also black. But Kerabac was much darker in color than even the darkest of them. When he entered the room, I was impressed by his posture and gait, which was smooth and graceful. He wore a broad smile, accented by bright white teeth. He exuded an overall feeling of strength and good health.

Kala introduced us. I rose from my desk to greet Kerabac and indicated that we should be seated at a round table located further inside the room. I wanted both Lunnie and Reidecor present during the interview, so I decided to kill a bit of time with casual conversation before we began a more formal discussion.

"Would you care for anything to drink?" I asked both Kala and Kerabac. Kala indicated that she would like some foccee and Kerabac said he would like some also. Kala was about to issue an order to one of her assistants, when I gestured toward a panel and told her that I had discovered a drink dispenser in the room. Kala decided to serve us herself while I began talking to Kerabac.

"I understand that you have served with both Corporal Luinella and Lieutenant Reidecor in the past...?"

"Yes. I served with Lunnie right after she graduated from the academy. She was the assistant engineer on a frigate where I served in my first assignment as a navigator. We became good friends after winning a dance contest on our ship. The ship's weekly social included regular dance competitions; so, we became partners and ended up taking first place in one of the contests. We have been friends ever since. Whenever we find ourselves on the same ship or on the same planet, we try to get together for a meal or some dancing." He smiled fondly at the memories.

"It sounds like you know Lunnie quite well. Do you feel you would be comfortable serving on a patrol ship with her – possibly for months at a time?" I asked. By this time Kala had returned with three cups of foccee and placed them on the table in front of each of us. I made mental note as Kerabac thanked Kala for this foccee; and I did the same. It was important to me that people working together show small signs of appreciation and courtesy toward each other. I also noted that Kerabac's posture in his chair was relaxed in a way that displayed a sense of self-confidence and a warm, friendly nature.

Just then Reidecor, Marranalis and Lunnie entered. Lunnie exclaimed "WOW, now *this* is an office!" She then turned her attention to Kerabac, as he rose from his chair to greet Lunnie with a friendly hug. "Good to see you, Kerabac. I'm glad to see you're thinking about joining us."

"Good to see you again also, Lunnie. You never change," he replied with a warm tone and broad, affectionate smile.

"Nice to see you again, Kerabac," Reidecor said as they exchanged a head nod.

"It's always a pleasure to see you also," Kerabac answered. "After all, you saved my life."

"I haven't heard that story, would you mind sharing it?" I asked with piqued interest.

Kerabac's countenance reflected the memory he recalled as he began. "I was with a crew on a mission to Hugulsa after the uprising there, when our patrol ship was hit and we were forced to make a crash landing. I was injured and couldn't flee to safety. We were surrounded by rebel fighters. Everyone on my ship was dead – and I thought I was going to be shortly – when suddenly, Sergeant Reidecor came barging out of the jungle, running into my crashed patrol ship. He jumped in through the open hatch while shots were being fired at him. He didn't even have a gun to protect himself. His own ship had been shot down two days earlier and he'd been hiding in the jungle. He grabbed one of the guns from the ship's armory and began returning fire. I blacked out; and when I regained consciousness I was being carried by Reidecor through high grass to a rescue pod that had been dispatched to recover us. Before carrying me out, Reidecor had activated the beacon on my ship that hailed a rescue unit to respond. He had fought off the attackers for hours while I lay unconscious and then, again under fire, he carried me to the rescue pod and got us both out of there. That's how he received that long scar on his right arm, if you've ever noticed it." I had noticed, in fact, but never asked about it. "We became good friends and worked on the same patrol crew for a long time after that, until I was reassigned to base duty and he was assigned to the *DUSTEN*."

"So are you currently attached to the military? I notice you still wear the uniform," I asked.

"I am, but my tour of duty is finished at the end of this week," Kerabac replied. "I will either reenlist or I will sign up with you, if you decide to make me an offer – and if I like what I see and hear."

While we were talking, Kala had handed me a computer tablet displaying Kerabac's military personnel file. High praise had been given to him by all his commanding officers and he seemed to have performed well on all the assignments he'd had to date.

"Tell me one thing, Kerabac," I asked. "Why would you want to leave your military career to join this crew? Reidecor and Lunnie and the others still maintain their military ranks and status under an agreement I made with Admiral Regeny. However, that agreement won't cover any new people I hire. I can offer you a really good salary and benefits; but as far as your military career is concerned, it would be over."

"I've given that some thought," said Kerabac. "The fact is that I have been somewhat bored in the military. I have already seen you become a major part of the history of this Federation; and I have a feeling that you will continue to be. I would like to be a part of that – to be there – to see it happening. Plus, I need to stick to Reidecor. I still own him my life." He finished his reply with another sincere nod in Reidecor's direction.

"Hey, what about me," Lunnie chimed in. "You don't want to be around so we can win more dance contests?"

"That goes without saying, Lunnie," Kerabac said with a grin.

I looked at Kala. She gave me a small nod that expressed a big approval. Marranalis flipped his thumb up away from Kerabac's view so I knew he was in agreement. Both Lunnie and Reidecor had shared their feelings with me beforehand; so now the decision was up to me. I still had one question to ask – not just of Karabac, but all of them – and I wasn't sure how it would go over in the Federation culture.

"Just one more question – for everyone here... I don't know what things are like here in the Federation, but back on Earth where I'm from, there are many people who harbor racist beliefs – people who have prejudices against people of other cultures and races. Even now, though it is illegal to practice racist behaviors against others, some employers will not pay or give promotions to a person because of their race or culture, and some won't give those persons jobs at all. At one time on my planet persons of your color were kidnapped and held as slaves; and though that slavery ended hundreds of years ago, bitterness and prejudice still exist among them. I guess my question is, do such prejudices exist here in the Federation and, if so, I want to know what each of you here in this room think about it."

Suddenly the room went dead silent and every face took on a stone cold countenance.

"Kerabac, I would like to hear your thoughts first," I said plainly.

Kerabac had a hard look on his face and I could see that he was deliberating how to convey a very serious thought that communicated his convictions clearly.   He began slowly with controlled words.

"I will confess… that there exist such prejudices within the Federation… and I deeply regret that they do. I would hope that you not hold me personally responsible for the actions of my people, past or present. I do not harbor the feelings of superiority that many of my race do. I do not approve of or condone that they once enslaved millions of white people to toil their entire lives as forced labor on several planets. I deplore slavery of any sort and I would hope that I am judged on the basis of my personal character, as well as my conduct and accomplishments. I believe that all men are equal and should have equal opportunities, regardless of the laws and not because of them."

I was dumbstruck. It had not occurred to me that the converse scenario might have once prevailed in this galactic community, that a black race and culture would adopt an attitude of racial superiority and consequently practice the slavery of white peoples. Before I could say anything in reply, Reidecor burst out with, "I can attest to Kerabac's character and that he is not prejudiced in any way against any race. When I was on Ginet, which is a predominantly black planet, and I was being refused service in a bar, Kerabac boldly sat next to me as he bought drinks and, in defiance of others in the room, gave me one. The two of us drank together as equals – as comrades. If he was a prejudiced bastard, he would not have done that."

Lunnie likewise interjected. "Kerabac has never once indicated any discomfort, displeasure or embarrassment when being seen with me or when we have gone out dancing or to share dinner. You would never convince me that he's prejudiced."

I looked at Marranalis, fully expecting that he would speak strongly as well. "I've had some blacks that have looked down on me, but I don't have any hard feelings about them. I figure they just don't know any better and simply have grown up with attitudes and preconceptions that they never bothered to question."

I looked at Kala who seemed to have difficulty finding enough breath to speak. "Oh please, Tibby, tell me you don't have such thoughts…!"

I turned to look for a moment at Kerabac. "Okay, here's the deal. I'll pay you ten times what you are currently being paid by the military. You will be given accommodations here at the estate like the rest of my team. Reidecor is the chief officer on the *TRITYTE* and you will report directly to him. Marranalis is the gunner and is in charge of security, both on and off the ship. You will have a personal bodyguard at all times when you are off ship or away from the estate. When we acquire other ships, you will serve as navigation officer and in any other capacity that that I may decide to appoint. At all times Kala's orders or requests are to be treated as my own. If that's acceptable to you, you may move in here next week."

Karabac paused. "One question before I give you my answer – what would you have done, if someone here had given an answer implying that they felt differently?"

"I would have fired them immediately," I said with my voice full of conviction and my gaze fixed first on his eyes, and then on Kala's.

Kerabac's face widened into that familiar broad smile. "In that case, I accept."

I looked around the room to see everyone else relaxing and melting into smiles as well.

Lunnie and Reidecor left with Kerabac to show him around the estate and to find a suitable suite for him in the main house. Kala informed me that she had taken my advice and found an employment agency that placed ex-military people in jobs, which had resulted in an immediately available temporary staff for us. She was very hopeful that some may even become permanent.

Now that the estate purchase was finalized and staffing was nearly complete, I needed to see to fulfilling my promise to Admiral Regeny about training his people. I had to find some way to expedite the process. For this task I felt that perhaps Kala could put her staff to work.

"Kala, when I was on the *TRITYTE*, there a device that I put on my head that taught me your language. I need to find out who makes them, today if possible, and find out whether there has been any advancement in the technology over the past six hundred years since the one I used was made. When you find someone who can give me some answers, set up an appointment to meet with them. I may be looking to have one made that is somewhat specialized."

Just as I finished speaking, one of the staffers called me, advising that a person representing the shipyard on Nibaria wished to speak with me, claiming they had a wondrous opportunity that I must hear at once. Since receiving my first outpouring of cash from the Federation, I had received multiple such calls from just about everyone that had something to sell someplace in the galaxy; so this call came as no surprise. Kala started to tell the assistant to simply give this person the same reply that we gave all such parties so eager to partake of my wealth – that I was not interested in purchasing anything and that I did not accept solicitation calls (a reply that I remember giving to such callers back on Earth). But the assistant interrupted Kala, "But ma'am, the person calling on behalf of the shipyard is Senator Tonclin."

Kala froze in mid-speech. "Patch him through," she replied, as she looked at me and said, "It never pays to ignore a senator."

Tonclin was the first non-human sentient life form that I had a chance to observe close up, albeit via a view screen. There had been several non-humans at the Senate Dinner; but in the hustle of the crowd about me, none had been able to actually speak to me. With thousands of persons attending the event and non-humans sentient races representing less than 3% of the Federation, the non-human representation in the government didn't amount to very many. My first impression of Senator Tonclin was that he looked as though he was covered with rough tree bark; though there was a definite humanoid resemblance to him. He seemed somewhat short and squat and, from what I could tell, he appeared to have neither hair nor eyebrows. His eyes were round and a very dark shade of green – and I couldn't detect a pupil. From his appearance, I expected his voice to be a deep, gruff base; so I was rather surprised when instead I heard a high-pitched, rich soprano voice.

"Senator Tonclin," Kala began, "it's a pleasure to see you again. It's been three years since I was attached to your delegation on the *DUSTEN*. To what do we owe this honored call?"

"Major Kala, it is so nice of you to remember this humble one. I am most pleased to speak with you once again. I recall well the kind and professional manner with which you served our delegation. We were most appreciative.

"I am calling on a matter that we, the humble people of Nibaria, hope will be of interest to the Honored Citizen Tibby the Recoverer. We heard today of the Honored Citizen Tibby the Recoverer's acquisition of the estate of Galetils, the industrialist of Astamagota. He is to be congratulated on this wondrous purchase. I myself have been to this estate as a guest of Galetils and recall its grandeur. It is good to see that it has gone to one so deserving as the Honored Citizen Tibby the Recoverer.

"But as to the purpose of my contact with you today, I have been asked to inquire on behalf of the shipyard here on Nibaria as to whether the Honored Citizen Tibby the Recoverer would be interested in purchasing the space yacht that Galetils was having built at the time of his regrettable demise. As you are no doubt aware, this yacht it is the largest, the most luxurious and, though it is yet untested, the fastest space yacht ever built. The construction of this finely crafted airship was nearly complete when the unfortunate fate of Astamagota and regrettable demise Galetils occurred. May I add most humbly that Galetils still owed vast amounts of monies on the unfinished yacht, which was due to be paid in full upon its completion and delivery. After reconciling all of Galetils' debts with the wealth and remaining resources of his estates after liquidation, the Federation will still not have enough monies to pay in full the unpaid sums that remain after his regrettable departure. For the shipyard here on Nibaria and for many of the subcontractors and suppliers, this means *great* losses – so great that many of these otherwise prudent and prosperous tradesmen may be forced to close their businesses; and so it is that I come to the reason for my call. The shipyard is prepared to offer the Honored Citizen Tibby the Recoverer the space yacht of the late Galetils of Astamagota for a price equal to what remains as the outstanding sum. This yacht, two thirds value of which has already been paid and only one third of which would be required as the purchase price by the most Honored Citizen Tibby the Recoverer, is a wondrous ship that is now nearly ready to traverse the galaxy. If a qualified buyer interested in purchasing this extraordinary craft is not found very soon, the yacht will most regrettably have to be demolished and scrapped to pay the debts incurred by the shipyard during its construction. Such a result would be a terrible waste of resources and Nibarian craftsmanship. If the Honored Citizen Tibby the Recoverer were to express interest in acquiring this unique and remarkable product of Nibarian skill and ingenuity, the peoples of Nibaria would rejoice in knowing that this proud ship would be in the possession of one as great as the Honored Citizen Tibby the Recoverer."

From my position out of range of the camera, I motioned to Kala that I wished to talk to her and I mouthed the words, "I'm interested."

Without giving the appearance that I was in the vicinity, Kala replied, "Senator Tonclin, I am certain that Tibby the Recoverer will be most interested in hearing of this wonderful offer that you bring to him on behalf of the shipyard and the peoples of Nibaria. I shall personally inform him of your honored call and describe in full the offer that you have presented. Should Tibby the Recoverer be interested in acquiring this yacht, I am sure he would first like to visit and see for himself the wondrous workmanship of the peoples of Nibaria before making the purchase. We would, of course, be honored if we may respond to you personally and, should Tibby the Recoverer confirm his interest in seeing this ship for himself, we would be most pleased to meet with and greet the Honorable Senator Tonclin as well."

"You do me great honor, as always, Major Kalana," Senator Tonclin with a thinly veiled excitement in his lofty voice. "I shall be most honored to hear from you the decision of the Honored Citizen Tibby the Recoverer."

Kala waited politely for Senator Tonclin to disconnect the communication, after which she looked at me curiously. "What are you thinking, Tib?"

"Well, first of all, I am thinking that perhaps I should have paid full price for the estate after all. Second, I am hoping that I am not going to have to listen to that long spiel of the *Honored Citizen Tibby the Recoverer* every time we meet with some dignitary or government official."

Kala laughed and said with a bow, "Get used to it, Honored Citizen Tibby the Recoverer. It is the price you must pay for the glory and fortune that has been poured upon you. But on a more serious note, though I have not personally seen the yacht that Senator Tonclin speaks of, I have heard of it. It's been the talk of people for years. The craftsmen of Nibaria are considered the best in the galaxy; so I can't imagine the ship being anything less than the crown jewel of all ships in the Federation. Personally, I think you should at least go to Nibaria and look at it."

"Okay. Make the arrangements and we'll go, but we still have the matter of the dispositions for Corporal Lexmal's trial; so we'll have to wait for that to be behind us before we can go."

"You're right, though I may be able to arrange it so we need not attend the trial in person." Kala replied. "Perhaps we can give sworn depositions before the court prior to the trial that will suffice for the proceedings. After all, there are five credible witnesses, plus the testimonies of the Bunemnites that were on the freighter – and *they* have no reason to side with Lexmal – so the court martial is really going to be more or less a formality."

I grinned at this beautiful, brilliant woman before me. "Kala, what would I do without you?"

With a twinkle in her eye, she crossed over to where I stood, put her hands around my neck and kissed me. "Don't you ever dare try to find out!"

A week later, with our court martial depositions out of the way, we boarded the *TRITYTE* and headed for Nibaria. The trip was relatively short. Since Nibaria was the nearest adjacent planet in the same solar system as Megelleon, the duration to travel between the two was a matter of less than a day, using the *TRITYTE*. Reidecor, Lunnie and Kerabac were immensely excited about seeing the space yacht. It had been big news in the galaxy for years, since it was described as being the only one of its kind – a flying palace, complete with all the amenities of a luxury resort. Not only could it carry over 1,000 guests, but it required a crew of over a thousand. It had its own hangar bay suitable for housing smaller ships and shuttle craft, which were used regularly, since the ship itself was too large to land and needed to remain in orbit over its destinations.

Reidecor told me upfront that if I decided to purchase the ship, I would need to secure a more seasoned captain for it, as he was nowhere near qualified to captain such a craft. Lunnie and Kerabac, on the other hand, felt they would be able to fully serve on it with no restrictions. As Kerabac put it, mapping the route between stars is the same in a space liner as it is in a patrol ship. Lunnie was already familiar with the engineering systems of this unique craft and explained that, since solbidyum was restricted in its use to only powering planets (with the exception of the *TRITYTE*), the space yacht was powered by a fusion reactor – another highly efficient power source, though not nearly as powerful as the solbidyum.

According to the information we received from Senator Tonclin, the yacht was complete and ready to go, except for some final furnishings, general provisions and crew. The Nibarian shipyard was actually located on a lesser moon that orbited the planet.   The ship itself had been assembled in modules and constructed in an orbit near the moon.   Workers were shuttled from the planet to the worksite, many of whom stayed on the moon during the work week.   A work week on Nibaria consisted of ten working days followed by a four-day weekend.   The shipyard staggered the construction crews, so manufacturing and assembly operations could continue around the clock during the five-year duration of the construction schedule. When the orbiting ship came into view, I recalled how impressed I was by the size of the *DUSTEN* when it first approached the *TRITYTE*. The yacht was clearly smaller, but I was still overwhelmed at the sight of it. I had an inkling of the vast amount of wealth that Galetils must have amassed to have such a ship built, as well as the sprawling estate. We didn't go to the shipyard itself, but docked in one of the two hangar bays on the yacht. Though these hangar bays were not as large as that of the *DUSTEN*, they were still impressive and provided sufficient room for a few dozen ships of varying sizes in each bay.

The Nibarians stood at an average height of 1.4 meters tall, compared to my 1.83 meters. Senator Tonclin was among the group that had assembled for our arrival. I recognized him more because of his clothing than because of his physical appearance. Though I could see subtle differences between individuals, the Nibarians all looked pretty much alike to my untrained eye.

Senator Tonclin stepped forward and greeted me with what I assumed to be a smile. "Greetings, Honored Citizen Tibby the Recoverer. We are honored that you have chosen to accept our offer to view this magnificent ship. We trust that once you have seen it, you will recognize its unparalleled value and desire it for your own. It would be a great honor for the peoples of Nibaria to have the Honored Citizen Tibby the Recoverer become the owner of the finest ship ever built by Nibarian craftsmen."

"Greetings, honored representative of the people of Nibaria, Senator Tonclin," I said, just as Kala had instructed me. "Please, just call me Tibby; the titles make me feel uncomfortable."

"Ah, then it is true that you wish to only be called Tibby. As you wish, Tibby, and you may call me *Tonc*, if you wish. May I introduce Orcpipin, manager of the shipyard here at Nibaria."

Orcpipin gave a slight nod in my direction and I did the same in return. I introduced the members of my crew;

and without further delay Orcpipin began to lead us on a tour of the ship. I was amazed to find that the master suite on the ship was exactly as that in the estate house. There was also a replica study, complete with glass wall and aquarium, although in this case the aquarium was yet empty of water and fish. Many of the rooms that mimicked the ones at the estate had already been furnished but many more were not. I was astounded by the number of large dining rooms and the many galleys and kitchens. There was an onboard theater designed for live performances, several gyms, swimming pools and shooting galleries, and a huge central atrium that ran down the middle of the ship with arched windows spanning it. Massive trees and beautiful plants were interspersed along the walkways and streams meandered throughout the landscaping.

I think what amazed me most was the amount of detailed woodwork that seemed prevail in every space. The ship was truly amazing. I thought we would never get Lunnie out of the engine room; she was like a kid in a toy store, chattering and squealing about this and that. The look in Kala's eyes and the smile on her face told me how much she was enjoying Lunnie's glee, and I nearly bought the ship for that reason alone. All of this was truly extraordinary; but what made the greatest impact on me was the bridge of the ship. It was immense and decorated with the utmost of class and comfort. Throughout the ship the ornate and finely polished moldings, doors and archways constantly caught my eye, but the woodwork on the bridge was beyond anything else I had seen in the ship. The finishings were carved of a light pine-like wood worked into blended curves that complemented the contour of the hull where it joined the bridge. The room itself was accented by rich red carpeting and lit entirely with backlighting. Various stations were positioned strategically along the walls and customized with panels and screens around center consoles. Lush padded chairs stood at each station. Kerabac was drawn to one of these stations like a magnet. He commented on the quality and extent of navigational equipment that complimented the ship. I could see Reidecor taking it all in, equally impressed as he looked over all the stations carefully. Marranalis surveyed the room and the various stations very intently, when suddenly he became excited.

"This can't be what I think it is," he said in amazement. "This ship cannot *possibly* have an RMFF!" The blank look on most of our faces told him we didn't have a clue. "A *reverse mass force field*...the Federation military ships don't even have these, because there isn't enough power in a fusion reactor to sustain its operation."

Orcpipin stepped forth with a smile on his face and said, "That is indeed what you have found; and it is fully functional, except for the fact that, sadly, as you stated, a fusion reactor is not powerful enough to support its processes. Galetils had one of his companies on Astamagota working on the design for a new fusion reactor that was small, yet extremely efficient. It would have been capable of producing ten times the power output of conventional reactors. He had planned to install the new reactor in a space located just behind the forward hangar bay. Even today, all the ceramic power cabling and switchgear that provides power to the shields remains installed in the compartment. Galetils wanted to use this ship to demonstrate to the Federation the successful functionality of the shields when implemented in conjunction with his new reactors.   His ultimate objective, of course was to sell these reactors to the military for all the major Federation warships. However, with the loss of everything on Astamagota, including the designs of the reactors, it became useless."

"This ship might look like a luxury liner, but is equipped line a battle cruiser!" Marranalis exclaimed. "There are laser cannons, extreme long range gravity wave antimatter torpedoes, fission bombs, and a phalanx plasma gun system. This ship is armed to the max."

"Citizen Galetils was a bit paranoid, it seems. He feared that sooner or later war would break out again with the Bunemnites or one of the non-aligned systems and he wished to be prepared," Orcpipin explained. "But come, let us dine now. A meal has been laid out for us in the Starlight Hall."

The Starlight Hall was located in the uppermost deck of the ship, just under the arched window canopy. From this orbit we enjoyed a vista of the stars and the planet of Nibaria. Senator Tonclin sat at the end of the table as host and envoy; I was to his right with Kala seated beside me. To his left and straight across from me sat Orcpipin. The meal was just like the others I had experienced so far in the Federation – exquisite. As we dined, Senator Tonclin carried on a most pleasant conversation with Kala and me about our adventures after leaving the *DUSTEN* on the clandestine mission to return the solbidyum to Megelleon. Orcpipin and Senator Tonclin both tried to convince us to spend the night on the ship; but I declined, stating that there was much business that required our attention back at the estate. For a moment I sensed that both Orcpipin and Senator Tonclin took this as a sign that I was not interested in buying the ship, as that they were both downfallen by reply.

"So," I began, "how much are you asking for this ship?"

Immediately I saw Orcpipin's countenance brighten. Well, Honored – ahh – Tibby, the original price for the ship was 34 billion Federal credits, of which twenty-two billion has already been paid, leaving a balance of twelve billion

Federal credits, which is the amount we are willing to accept as the selling price."

I chewed on my lip a moment. "Hmm, I don't like that price," I said. I could see Orcpipin's countenance fall again. "No, no I don't, that price will not do. I think 18 billion Federal credits would be more to my liking."

Orcpipin and Senator Tonclin both sat wide eyed in frozen postures, trying to process my response and wondering if they had heard me correctly.

"But... but... that's more than we are asking," Orcpipin stammered in disbelief.

"Indeed," I said, "and I won't pay a cent less. Now do we have a deal or must I go someplace else to find a ship?"

And with that Orcpipin passed out.

As part of the closing deal on the yacht, I requested that I might have several minor modifications made to the ship. Orcpipin was more than happy to agree to my terms. I also asked that they provide a staff to assist in stocking supplies. Since, the ship had not yet been named, I insisted that it be christened the "*NEW ORLEANS*." At my request Orcpipin's crew painted the name across the bow and casted a brass plaquard be mounted on the wall inside the bridge. Naming this ship the *NEW ORLEANS* gave me another idea.

"Once a ship is named, is it possible to rename it?" I asked.

"But... we haven't put the name on the ship yet; so that would be no problem," Orcpipin responded, clearly perplexed at my question.

"I'm sorry," I said, "perhaps I should have made myself a bit clearer. I wasn't thinking of this ship; I was thinking of the *TRITYTE*. I was wondering if I could change *its* name."

Senator Tonclin looked at me as thought I had lost my mind. "But why would you want to do that? It's the most famous and recognized ship in the entire universe."

"That's precisely the reason why I would like to change its name," I said, "so it is *not* so easily recognized. The anonymity will make it easier for my crew and I to go unobserved, meaning overall reduced security risks. Besides that, I would personally prefer less fanfare when I travel." I could see heads turning, as people looked at each other in hopes that someone else would have a sensible answer.

Kala spoke up with a suggestion. "There are times when having the *TRITYTE* known by that name will have its advantages; but I can also see your point. I wonder... would it be possible for the ship to have two names on the ship's Federation registry? Perhaps there's a way of changing it from within the ship by means of a lit name on the hull that can be changed as we see fit."

"I like that idea. Does anyone know if it can be done?" I asked the group around us.

Senator Tonclin laughed. "For you Tibby, I think anything can be done. If you have problems reaching an accord with the Federation authorities on this matter, please feel free to contact me. I will go as far as bringing the issue to a vote in the next Senate session; however I do not think it will come to that."

"Reidecor, would you investigate this matter for me?" I asked.

"I'd be most happy to, Tibby," Reidecor responded. "Any idea as to the alternate name you would like to use?"

"I do indeed," I said.   "I'd like her to be called MOUND *ISLAND*."

"That's a most unusual name," Lunnie said with her typical impish tone and crooked smile.   "Any *special* significance to it?"

I laughed and shook my head at her mischief. "Yes, Lunnie, but I fear it's nothing as fascinating as whatever your sense of humor has dreamed up. Mound Island is the name of the location on Earth where I found the *TRITYTE*. I would like the ship to bear this name... so I never forget where I came from." For a moment everyone was silent, and I believed that each of them was trying to imagine themselves in my place.

"I do not understand this comment between Corporal Luinella and Tibby about a difference in significance of the name," said Senator Tonclin. "Perhaps you can explain it to me, Major Kalana, since you are an attaché and accustomed to explaining things not understood between cultures...?"

Lunnie started to snicker, but Kalana caught her off guard by replying, "I think perhaps Corporal Luinella would be better able to relate the significance, since she was the one who made the comment."

I could clearly hear Lunnie gulp. But then, in her typical brazen fashion and without so much as a hint of embarrassment, she explained to the senator, "At times and in certain context the human female genitalis is referred to as *the mound*," she said. "I thought that perhaps, since Tibby and Ka...."

Kala quickly interrupted, "THAT's more than sufficient information, Lunnie. I am sure that the senator and Orcpipin are now even more baffled, but at least they understand *your* reference."

"Most interesting. Is it customary for humans to name things after genitalia?" Senator Tonclin asked matter-of-factly, as though we had opened an area of human culture that might be of some importance in his senatorial duties.

"Usually in only derogatory slang references," Kala responded, while giving Lunnie a hard, cold stare.

"But then… I do not understand why she would think that Tibby would want to give a derogatory name to his ship," he said more to himself as he tried to sort out this bewildering topic.

"Senator Tonclin, I apologize for my sister's actions and comments. She has a rather twisted sense humor at times. It is better to ignore it than try to understand."

"Ah," the senator said with a polite smile, clearly not understanding, but willing to end the conversation. Lunnie hung her head and actually blushed – one of the few times when I saw her feel genuinely embarrassed by her actions. During the rest of the visit, she was noticeably quieter and more reserved, showing she clearly saw how far she had crossed the line of improper behavior in the presence of a foreign dignitary.

After the dinner with Orcpipin and the senator, I asked Lunnie to step aside with me for a moment. She obviously thought that I was about to lecture her on her behavior and immediately started to apologize before I had a chance to speak. She finished with a fervent promise to never again make any such comments or suggestions in front of others outside our immediate group – a promise I doubted she would be able to keep.

When she finished her capitulation, I said.

"Well, that's all very nice and I'm glad that you realize the embarrassment you have put us through, but that isn't why I wanted to talk to you."

"It isn't?" she said reverting to her old whimsical self.   "You mean I just made all those promises for nothing?"

"Oh, those were great promises, Lunnie, and I fully expect you to live up to them; but no, that's not what I wanted to discuss with you."

"Well, what do you want then?" she asked.

"Orcpipin mentioned that an area had been created near the hangar bay for the installation of that new fusion reactor that was supposed to power the defensive shields. He said that the area is already wired up to the shielding system and ready to go except for the reactor. I would like you to investigate to see if there is a way to adapt the wiring harness to connect to the *TRITYTE* when it's in the hangar bay. There's a power outlet on the hull of the *TRITYTE,* if I'm not mistaken; and if there isn't, I'd like to know what it would take to install one. If we can connect the *TRITYTE*'s solbidyum reactor to the –"

Lunnie's eyes widened, "Oh! I see where you're going with this! The solbidyum reactor can supply more than ample power to the shield anytime that it's aboard the *NEW ORLEANS*. All you need to do is to hook it into the power grid. I never would have thought of that, and I'll bet no one else has either."

"That's precisely what I am hoping for Lunnie, so I would really appreciate it if you kept this quiet and not share with anyone outside of our circle. Understand?"

"Tibby, I may like to joke and tease about personal relationships and often say things I shouldn't, but I never divulge secrets about my job – or about *anything* I have been asked to keep confidential."

"I know, Lunnie," I replied. "I've read your personnel files." And with that I turned and walked away, leaving her with a look of amazement on her face.

Orcpipin said it would take several days to fill my requests and ready the *NEW ORLEANS* for delivery, which was fine, as I didn't have a crew yet to man her. It would take a thousand people to fully staff this ship and at that point I had only five, four of whom were qualified to fill lead positions – Kala, Lunnie, Kerabac, and Marranalis. Reidecor, while a superb pilot for the *TRITYTE*, was by his own admission out of his league for serving as captain of the *NEW ORLEANS*.

We were on our way back to Megelleon when an urgent transmission came in. Corporal Lexmal had escaped from captivity. The court martial was held as planned and he was sentenced to death by release into the vacuum of space without a protective suit. This method was the standard corporal punishment for a Federation traitor. How Corporal Lexmal had escaped was unclear, but it was apparent that he had received help. While we were gone, the *DUSTEN* arrived at Megelleon. It was believed that his accomplice from the *DUSTEN*, whose identity Lexmal had never divulged, came to his aid, as several guards in the holding cell area had been rendered unconscious. Lexmal then made his way to the hangar and escaped in one of the patrol ships docked there.

Two additional messages came in as we continued our return trip to the estate. The first was from Captain Maxette, congratulating us on our success. He was hoping to meet with us while the *DUSTEN* was stationed in orbit around Megelleon for the coming month.

The next message was from Piesew Mecarta, also congratulating us and confirming that he had received our message regarding the offer of the position of house majordomo for the estate. He expressed concern that he was unsure whether he could handle the task, as he was more accustomed to an airship and its lifestyle. He believed, however, that he knew of someone who might be a perfect fit for the role and he hoped we could meet in person to discuss this candidate.

"Kala, contact Captain Maxette and schedule a dinner engagement for sometime early next week. Then make one with Piesew Mecarta for the following day, if you can. Tell both that we will pick them up with the *TRITYTE* early in the morning and that they should plan for the meeting to be an all-day event. Oh, and don't say anything to them about the *NEW ORELANS* just yet; I would like it to be a surprise." I thought for a moment. "One more thing – see if Admiral Regeny is available at the same time as the Captain. If he is, invite him also."

For those not involved in the actual flying of the ship, part of the day's return trip to Megelleon consisted of martial arts practice in the cargo hold, after which Kala and I spent some quality time together in our cabin. It was bothering me that, even though we were together most of the time, we really *weren't* together, at least not in the more personal way that we had been before my fame and fortune. Once we were back at the estate, I contacted one of the house staff and asked them to assemble a bouquet of the most beautiful flowers from the greenhouse and to deliver them to my suite. I also contacted one of the many chefs at the estate and had them prepare one of Kala's favorite meals. I dressed in one of my finest black dignitary uniforms and told Kala that there would be a special guest for dinner that night and to dress appropriately.

While she showered and dressed for the anticipated event, the staff arrived with the food and flowers and the table was set elegantly. I found some pleasant music similar to what we called *smooth jazz* on Earth to play over the audio system in the dining room.   Kala followed my instructions without asking who the special guest was; so when she emerged from the bedroom sharply dressed and ready to receive visitors and saw only two place settings at the table, she asked, "Who's the special guest... and why are there only two services set on the table?"

"Ah, my dear, everyone is here. *You* are the special guest." With that I pulled the bouquet out from behind my back and handed it to her. The look on her face was not what I expected. I had forgotten, and forget sometimes still, that simple customs from Earth are not necessarily understood in the same way within the Federation. Kala's questioning look at the flowers set me into a fit of laughter. This only increased her quizzical look and I had a hard time gaining my composure to explain.

"Kala, I never thought for a minute that things here might be different from Earth in this matter. On Earth, it is customary for a man, when he is enamored with a lady, to present her with a bouquet of lovely flowers. Flowers and bouquets are often given at other times as well, like for special events such as birthday celebrations and anniversaries.   Sometimes a gift of flowers can even accompany a gesture of apology or wishes for someone's well-being... and sometimes they're just meant to express love."

Kala tilted her head down and smelled the flowers; a slight blush glowed on her cheeks. "And which of these is *your* reason, Thibodaux James Renwalt?"

"Well, initially as an expression of love but, in reality, it should be all of the above. We've both been so busy of late that I haven't taken the opportunity to spend the time with you that I should; so I apologize for that. It is likely, too, that over the past month I've missed some significant event; so whatever it might be, I celebrate it tonight. But more than anything, I am – without a doubt – highly enamored with you; and this alone justifies the flowers."

Kala smiled coyly, "Nice choice of music. I like it. I'm assuming you have ordered something for us to drink as well...?"

"Indeed I have. It would appear that Galetils was a collector of rare wines from all over the galaxy, which I discovered in the cellar. I understand that, after his death, one of the house staff members went to great pains to protect the collection from being pilfered by others." I presented the bottle as if to advertise its rarity. "Tonight we are drinking a rare vintage from the third moon of Fiepur in the Loca System. It is said to have an aphrodisiac effect on its imbibers and a euphoric nature that enhances one's senses during lovemaking." I raised an eyebrow.

Kala laughed and said, "Well then, perhaps we should wait to drink it until after we eat. It would be a shame if the wine took hold too soon and we missed this lovely meal I see before me."

"I do believe that if we take just the smallest of sips now – *with* our meal – the wine will create in us such growing passions that the anticipation alone will be worthwhile," I said, hamming it up a bit.

Kala said, "All right, Tibby, at least I warned you."

We barely made it through the appetizer.

I want to tell you now that waking up next to Kala in the morning is without a doubt the greatest joy in my life. Never has anything pleased me more than opening my eyes to see her head on the pillow next to mine. She is worth far more to me than anything else I have gained from this experience and I would give it all up for her if I had to.

I watched her sleep for a while; and when she woke, we ate leftovers from the nearly untouched meal of the night before. Fortunately, none of the items had spoiled overnight and, though cold, every dish was still quite tasty. We both laughed, as we looked back at the trail of clothing leading from the dining room to the bed and remembered the haste with which we had left the table.

We had just finished eating, when a message came in for Kala from her staff advising that the company that produced the learning headbands had been identified. The company's scientists and production facilities were still in operation and located on Omalcron. Kala frowned and told me that Omalcron was at least a two-week trip across the galaxy from Megelleon. The aide went on to say that several of their top scientists and managers were scheduled to attend a week-long conference on Megelleon in three days. I gave instructions to Kala to invite the entire scientific team to the estate as my personal guests and to pay them whatever was necessary as a consulting fee, if it came to that, just to get them all to arrive together. I had a feeling, though, that it would not be necessary to pay them.

I had produced several vids of choreographed martial arts combat scenarios that Marranalis was using as training tools for development of our own security force. I would join the sessions for several hours a day to demonstrate moves, discuss concepts and philosophies of the art, and to critique the progress of the students as the expert or *Karateka*. The students addressed me as *Shihan Tibby*, as I was as close to a master as they were likely to ever get. Marranalis wasn't even close to achieving a true teacher status by Earth standards, but the students still called him *Sensei*, as he was definitely more advanced than them.

It was two days after our return from Nibaria that Kala came to my study to tell me that arrangements for the meetings with Captain Maxette and Piesew were confirmed. We would be able to entertain the captain the next day and Piesew the day after.

In the meantime, I received word from Orcpipin that a luxury passenger starship had collided in a glancing blow with an asteroid and was being towed into the shipyard at Nibaria for repairs. This ship would likely remain disabled for a year before being returned to service; and the starship line was forced to begin the process of dismissing most of the crew, as there were no available positions on other ships that would allow the employees to transfer. Orcpipin felt there was a good possibility that I could gain a relatively experienced crew from this situation – or at least partial crew that was accustomed to working together. He said the liner wouldn't arrive at the shipyard for another week; however, if I was interested, he would be able to communicate with the ship's captain before then and secure the required arrangements for me to interview these individuals as candidates for positions on the *NEW ORLEANS*. I thanked him and said I would be most appreciative if he would do so on my behalf and that I would gladly pay him a finder's fee, if things worked out favorably.

The unusually heavy stream of activity related to preparations at the estate and on the *NEW ORLEANS* meant that I was not having the personal contacts with my crew that I wanted. This team had become my family and I liked having them around; so I decided that every other day we would all gather together for the evening meal, which would give us a chance to stay briefed on everyone's progress and allow us to socialize a bit. We would generally keep the meals casual; most times eating around a simply set table in one of the dining rooms or sometimes outdoors on one of the patios or balconies, and we would take turns selecting the dishes. Our first dinner was a lot of fun and we all looked forward to the new tradition.

The following day Kala, Reidecor, Lunnie, Kerabac and I boarded the *TRITYTE* and headed to the orbiting *DUSTEN* to pick up Captain Maxette. Marranalis stayed behind to continue with the martial arts training. We arrived in the hangar, where a mass of troopers and dignitaries had gathered. On one wall a giant vid screen displayed scenes of Kala, Reidecor, Lunnie, Marranalis and me at the banquet with Admiral Regeny. The words "Heroes" and "Tibby the Recoverer" flowed across the screen, as we opened the door and walked onto the ramp, greeted by the cheers and applause of the crowd.

Captain Maxette came forward to greet us as the crowd cheered on. "Where is Sergeant Marranalis?" he said looking about.

"I regret we didn't bring him with us. He is overseeing the training of the security guards and Federation troopers at the estate. Had I known that this was going to happen, I would have made sure that he joined us. Perhaps we can bring him with us on our return tomorrow."

"I think those onboard the *DUSTEN* would appreciate that" the Captain said. For a few moments the Captain addressed the crowd, heaping praises on those of us who were present, saying that Sergeant Marranalis was regretfully unable to attend, due to other duties; but that upon his return the next day, the sergeant would also be there for those wishing to see him. Then he turned to enter the *TRITYTE* and we followed behind him. When we reached the control room, I let him take the command chair and situated myself in one of the chairs behind him next to Kala. It wasn't until after we had all settled in that I mentioned to him that he may want to contact the *DUSTEN* and let them know that we were flying to Nibaria and not back to the estate.

With a look of surprise the captain turned to me and exclaimed, "Don't tell me you bought the space yacht that Galetils was having built! I've been dying to see that beauty!"

"Okay, Captain," I replied with a grin. "I won't tell you, but we'll be there in time for lunch."

I was surprised at Captain Maxette's excitement as we approached the *NEW ORLEANS*. Since he was serving as the esteemed captain of one of the largest starships in the galaxy, I would have expected a lesser reaction. However, from the moment she came into view until we docked in her forward hangar bay, Captain Maxette was practically crawling into the view screen to get a better look.

"Incredible. She certainly is larger than any other yacht in the galaxy," Captain Maxette exclaimed. "You would have to shuttle people between her and the *DUSTEN*; there's no way she'd fit in the hangar bay. The hangar bays on her are pretty damn large for a private airship. Outside of military warships and transports I don't think I've ever seen bigger. You have two on her I understand – hangars that is…? Look at those lines! This ship is a real thing of beauty. What's that name glowing on the bow… *NEW ORLEANS*… what's that?"

"It's the name I gave the ship," I answered. "It's the name of a city near my home on Earth. I thought I would name her as a reminder of a place I loved."

"Ah, I see," said the Captain, clearly distracted by other vistas of the ship as they came into view.

After landing we were met by Orcpipin, who informed me that he had personally seen to all the arrangements related to my special requests, but he was still awaiting a GW pod message on the status of the passenger liner. He led us on the tour, making sure to point out a few of the minor modifications that my crew and I had requested. I told him that I had noticed the name *NEW ORLEANS* had been added to the hull per my request and that I was very pleased. With every bit of praise I gave Orcpipin he seemed to swell in stature a bit more; I was beginning to fear he soon would burst. The captain seemed to be in total glory, pointing from one thing to another, *oohing* and *ahhing* about everything he saw; but when we reached the bridge, I thought the man was going to have a coronary.

"This is unbelievable! It's like…like a luxury warship. And what's this? This *cannot* be what I think it is…an RMFF?! What's going to power it?" Orcpipin related the same explanation to the captain that he had offered us, after which the captain said, "Damn shame. What a huge leap forward that would have been. If the Federation space stations and major warships were protected by RMFF systems, the rebel worlds would be *crawling* back to the Federation, begging for re-admittance. As it stands now, you have a fully functional RMFF that has no power."

I made no mention to the captain of how I planned to get around that little problem.

The captain continued to survey the general information in the security database, amazed at the stock of munitions and the functionality of the weapons station. "Galetils had this ship built like a warship. It only *looks* like a luxury liner. I thought the *DUSTEN* was overly opulent, but this ship puts the *DUSTEN* to shame. Who did you pick for a captain?"

I laughed. "Well if *you're* available…," I began, knowing full well that he wasn't. "Seriously though, Captain, I was hoping you might be able to recommend someone."

"I'll tell you, Tibby, I would be seriously tempted, if I didn't have the *DUSTEN* running through my blood. This is a ship any captain would be proud to fly." He paused for a moment. "There is a man who I think would be good for the job – an excellent captain. He's ex-military, but he has a blemish on his record and was drummed out of the service – unjustly, in my opinion. He served gallantly in a number of run-ins with the rebel worlds, but his career went afoul with one of the higher brass at headquarters. There was an incident on his ship, an explosion and fire. At the time he was in his quarters sleeping. At his hearing he was accused of not responding to calls to the bridge when the accident happened and of failing to take appropriate actions, once he did finally awaken and take charge. The funny thing is that none of his crew supported the claims; nor was there any material evidence to support these very serious accusations. In the end, he opted to resign with honors rather than be dragged through the mud. It hurt a lot of us that he didn't fight it. Personally, I think he would have won in the end. He was well-liked by his crew and would have had their full support. I wouldn't be surprised in the least if he accepted an offer from you."

"I'd like to meet him, what is his name?" I asked.

"Stonbersa," said the captain. "Last I heard he was still on Megelleon looking for work on any large ship he could find. But most of the larger ships have lifetime captains; and until a new ship gets built or a captain dies or retires, which is rare, there are few openings. Even when an aging captain dies, the successor is usually his first officer. If you like, I will try to contact him on your behalf."

"I would be most appreciative, Captain," I said.

"I know of this one, this Captain Stonbersa," interjected Orcpipin. "He once brought the *DOEKO* here for repairs after the battle at Potaeria. He is a genuinely nice man... refused to leave the ship during repairs, like many captains do... conducted his own inspections, but was never harsh or rude, in the rare occasions that he found something amiss. Still, he was firm about getting things right. Even the workers here liked him."

Captain Maxette went to the communication console and turned to me, "Do you mind if I try to reach him now?"

A few minutes later a brown-skinned man with snow-white hair appeared on the screen. "Captain Maxette, WHAT a surprise! It's good to see you, you old Calagee. To what do I owe this call?"

"Captain Stonbersa, old friend, it's delightful to see you looking so well. The *DUSTEN* arrived in orbit a few days ago and I was hoping we might be able to meet during my visit."

"In orbit…?   Well, unless they did a bang up remodeling job on the bridge, I would have to say, looking at you here on the screen, that you are currently *not* on the *DUSTEN*," Stonbersa said with a grin.

"You are so right," Maxette replied, "but you will never guess just where I *am*."

"I'll grant you that, Captain," Stonbersa answered, "I can't think of a ship anywhere that has a bridge like *that*."

"I'm standing on the bridge of the *NEW ORLEANS* space yacht next to none other than Tibby the Recoverer… yes, the space yacht designed and built for the late Galetils of Astamagota."

"You lucky Calagee! I'd give my right foot to see the inside of that ship!" Stonbersa exclaimed.

"Really," Maxette baited, "and just what would you give to be *captain* of her?"

"Are you kidding?   I'd give both legs and ride around in motorized body scooter for a job like that."

Captain Maxette laughed, "Well, don't go planning any amputations just yet. Tibby is looking for a captain and I tossed your name into the pile. He would like to meet with you."

"Don't kid me with something like this! This is not some practical joke, is it? You could give me a heart attack if it is." Stonbersa's smile gave way to a look of shock as he steadied himself against a nearby table.

"Totally serious, my friend," Captain Maxette responded calmly. "Tibby, come here a minute so Captain Stonbersa can see that I'm not leading him on."

I walked up beside Captain Maxette and turned to face the screen. As I looked at Stonbersa's expression, I had a clear idea of how I must have looked more than once since my incredible adventure began. The shock and disbelief on his face said it all.

"Honored   Citizen   Tibby   the   Re-Recoverer," Stonbersa stammered, "I am deeply honored."

I laughed. "Don't be too honored yet, you haven't seen the ship and I haven't made you an offer. How soon can you be available for a trip to Nibaria to check out the hardware and join me for an interview?"

"Uh... well…I can be available any time that suits you."

"Good to hear, Captain. Pack an overnight bag. I'm having the *TRITYTE* fly back there immediately to pick you up. You should arrive here about the time that Captain Maxette is ready to leave this evening, unless…." I turned to Captain Maxette. "Would you be available to spend the night on the *NEW ORLEANS* and go back to the *DUSTEN* in the morning?"

"I think that can be arranged," replied Captain Maxette. "I'll just need to make a call to my First Officer."

"Okay then, Captain Stonbersa," I said,   "I'll have Lieutenant Reidecor provide you with instructions as to where to meet the *TRITYTE* and we'll have you here by dinner this evening. I look forward to meeting you, and I'm sure you and Captain Maxette will enjoy being able to see one and another as well."

I walked away from the view screen to speak to the crew. "Reidecor, contact Marranalis and tell him you're bringing him back here with you. Kerabac and Lunnie, your services are required aboard the *TRITYTE* for the trip. Kala and I will be staying here until your return."

Since a large number of the quarters on the ship had already been furnished, there was no problem finding one of the more luxurious suites for the captain. Unfortunately, we had no majordomo or serving staff, but Orcpipin was able to quickly gather a few persons to provide some limited services. Since Nibaria was a planet whose atmosphere was extremely rich in nitrogen, few humans ever went to the surface, much less lived or worked in the area on a regular basis; so the staffers that were rallied by Orcpipin that evening were all Nibarian. It was peculiar to see these short, tree-barked-skinned people scurrying around, trying to see to our needs on an unfamiliar ship. Nevertheless, they were a most pleasant people.

While we waited for the *TRITYTE* to make the several-hour trip to Megelleon and back, Kala and I took Captain Maxette to one of the nicer lounges on the *NEW ORLEANS* for some drinks and conversation. Now that his euphoria over the *NEW ORLEANS* was calming down, he was interested to hear the story of what happened after we left the *DUSTEN*. He said that, as I had predicted, a large portion of the Bunem fleet showed up on the long range scanners not long after we departed. As I suggested before leaving, the captain immediately sent off a message to the Bunem leadership, welcoming them to join in the hunt for the *TRITYTE*. The captain said that the Bunemnites were at first confused by the offer, but quickly put two and two together and came up with the exact conclusion we had hoped for. True to my prediction, they accepted Captain Maxette's offer to shuttle some of their officers to the *DUSTEN* for more efficient "coordination of efforts" and, also as expected, they brought a larger contingency than would normally be considered for such an operation. As the *DUSTEN* played host to the Bunem officers, their contingent of troops tried very hard to appear casual, while snooping about the ship in search of the solbidyum under the suspicion that it was secretly stashed onboard. Of course the search was fruitless; and by the time they realized the solbidyum would not be found, it was too late for them to go chasing after the *TRITYTE*.

In the meantime the other half of the Bunem fleet chased relentlessly after the GW pod signal, not knowing that it was a decoy. With no way for the Brunemnites to communicate with their pursuing patrol ships, those ships would continue their hunt until the GW pod ran out of fuel and they caught up to it or until their own supplies became so depleted that they had to turn around and come home. Either way they would have exhausted a lot of resources for nothing. Captain Maxette was still elated by the event and laughed heartily about it.

It was late afternoon when the *TRITYTE* returned with Captain Stonbersa. The man was so excited about the *NEW ORLEANS* that he could barely keep his composure. A meal was prepared, but Stonbersa barely ate, spending most of dinner asking one question after another about the ship. Meanwhile, Captain Maxette tried to relate to Stonbersa the details of what he was now calling the "Tibby Solbidyum Shuffle Event," and brag about how we'd gotten one over on the Bunemnites. Kala and I just sat quietly, watching and smiling as both chattered animatedly to the other – neither of them noticing that the other was paying no attention to what they were saying.

Finally, the meal finished and we took Captain Stonbersa to the bridge to start his tour. Captain Maxette accompanied us, even though he had previously seen this part of the ship, all the while continuing his one-way conversation from dinner as Stonbersa gasped and wondered at the features of the yacht on our way through the corridors.

However, when we arrived at the bridge and Captain Stonbersa set foot inside, all became quiet. Stonbersa actually started to weep as he walked about the bridge, looking at each station and touching each item as though it were the rarest and most precious collection in the universe. I knew right then – there could be no one else better suited to serve as Captain of the *NEW ORLEANS* than this man.

Stonbersa's reaction when he found out about the *reverse mass force field* was even more profound than Captain Maxette's. "Give us time," he said, "I'll bet we'll find a way to power her." I didn't tell him or Captain Maxette just yet about the idea to use the solbidyum power from the *TRITYTE* as an interface with the defense systems of the *NEW ORLEANS*.

We got as far as the engine rooms that evening before insisting that the rest of the tour would have to wait until morning. He was shown to the captain's suite, which had an almost Victorian look to it with the rich, woodworked interiors and large view ports framed in fine drapes and tapestries that looked out into the expanse of the galaxy. There was an air of propriety and humble wisdom about this space that made one feel both rejuvenated and relaxed. I think if I had offered Stonbersa the job right at that moment, he would have taken it for no pay at all, just to be on the ship.

The next morning Reidecor, Marranalis, and Lunnie left to return Captain Maxette to the *DUSTEN* and bring Piesew for his interview. Since the trip was within the same solar system, a navigator was not required; so Kerabac stayed aboard the *NEW ORLEANS* to assist with the remainder of Stonbersa's tour.

I was impressed with Stonbersa. It was clear why he was so endeared to so many; and I found it hard to believe that this man had been drummed out of the service for dereliction of duty.

Finally, around mid-afternoon I casually asked, "So, Captain, do you feel like you might be interested in serving on the New Orleans?"

"Oh my, yes," he said. "Serving as captain of this ship would be a dream come true. I would be a fool not to. This is probably the finest ship in the universe."

"Well, I am likewise interested in having you join my crew. What kind of salary are you looking for?" I asked.

I could see him struggling, trying to come up with a number.

"How about this... I'll pay you ten times what you were getting as a captain with the Federation, but not a penny more."

"You are joking with me," he said, wide-eyed with disbelief. "That's too much."

"Well that's my offer, take it or leave it."

"I'll take it!" he said, barely allowing me to finish my sentence and practically jumping up and down where he stood.

"Okay then, Captain," I said. "Welcome to the crew!

"Understand that I will need you to take command as soon as possible. With the exception of my own personal staff for my quarters, you will be responsible for acquiring the crew for the ship. Orcpipin may be able to give you some assistance; he knows a passenger liner that is dismissing its crew, due to a long interruption of service required to complete extensive repairs the damaged ship before it can be recommissioned. There should be a lot of people available that we can acquire quickly, but the choice is yours as to who is hired. I would like, however, that you consider giving priority to as many candidates as possible that have past military experience – especially when selecting individuals for bridge and engineering positions."

"I understand, Tibby, and as for when I can start, would now be too soon?" Stonbersa said. "I was temporarily renting a place on Megelleon while I contemplated what I was going to do next. I haven't even unpacked my possessions yet. I can send someone back to pick them up for me at a later time. I would much prefer to stay here now so I can begin to get things in order."

"You most certainly can do so, Captain," I replied. "There is one other thing I need to discuss with you soon – and this matter is to remain strictly confidential. The fewer people who know, the better. It has to do with the RMFF generator and the power requirements."

Later that evening the *TRITYTE* returned with Piesew and the rest of my crew. My original plan was for Piesew to be the house majordomo for the Megelleon estate; but when I made him the offer, he immediately stated again that he didn't feel anywhere close to being up to the task. However, he did mention that he would be interested in the job of majordomo for my quarters on the *NEW ORLEANS*, if I was willing to consider this alternative. As far as the estate, he knew of a qualified candidate, under whom he had worked and trained and who was, as Piesew stated, *the most honorable and honest man he had ever known.* Piesew also said the man would probably be willing to leave his current position. Even though his principles would not allow him to say anything negative about his employer, he was less than pleased in his present assignment. Piesew said that, if I was interested, he could arrange for me to talk to his former mentor within a few days.

I made Piesew my standard offer of employment, the same as I had made to those I had so far hired from the *DUSTEN*. He accepted immediately.

"Piesew, you will be responsible for hiring your own staff as soon as possible; and I would appreciate it if you would work in conjunction with Captain Stonbersa to acquire domestic staffs for the other suites on the *NEW ORLEANS*, as well."

"It would be a great honor," Piesew replied. "I know Captain Stonbersa well, having served on another ship with him in the past. He is a great man."

"That's good to know. I've heard nothing but good things about Stonbersa from the people I trust most. I also like knowing that my crewmen like and respect each other." I said.

Stonbersa came to me just a few hours after accepting my offer to advise that he had located a purser for the ship and that an account would need to be set up for them to draw funds for ship expenses. I asked Kala to find out what I needed to do and make the arrangements. I had barely finished talking to her when Kerabac approached me with a look of urgency and beckoned me to follow him.

"We just got word from the estate – there was an attack on the hangar. Two Federation ships were involved. Several of the Federation troopers guarding the hangar area were killed and three others were wounded. Of our own security force only two were wounded, but neither of them seriously. The attackers escaped, taking the two patrol ships with them. From the early reports we're getting, it seems they were looking for the *TRITYTE*. Security cameras at the landing field captured some images that Sergeant Marranalis thinks you need to see."

All the while that Kerabac was relating this information, we were headed towards the bridge at a running pace. We arrived to see Captain Stonbersa and Marranalis standing at the communications station. Marranalis was issuing orders to the security forces at the estate on one screen and had the commander of the estate's Federation security force on the other screen.

"Make sure the main house is totally secure before trying to do anything at the hangar and make sure guards at the lodge are all at the ready – they may try to attack there next. I want the patrol ship at the lodge landing pad sealed with the crew inside at the ready. Get them in the air as soon as possible, but they are not to engage *anyone* unless fired upon! None of our security crews are to pursue the stolen ships; the Federation already has a fleet deployed from the base to search for those. Just instruct them to continue in their duty to protect the estate and stay ready for anything that might happen. They should especially be prepared to defend the lodge or estate house." He turned to see us enter. "Kerabac, show Tibby the vids from the hangar attack please."   He then turned back to the screen, "Tell the Federation they need to set up some guns at the estate that can take out patrol ships, if necessary. If anyone gives you any resistance about it, tell them to check with Admiral Regeny!"

Kerabac led me to another vid screen and activated the playback. Images of about two dozen individuals attired like troopers suddenly appeared on the landing pad, firing weapons on the security guards and other troopers stationed there. Fire was returned both by the security guards and the Federation-supplied troopers. The skirmish didn't last long before the invading troops quickly boarded the two patrol ships on the landing strip. One of the men turned just before entering the ship and the camera caught his face full on. "Lexmal!" I exclaimed in fury.

"Notice anything strange about the raid, Tibby?" Marranalis asked.

"Yeah, they went straight for the patrol ships and nothing else. You don't think they expected one of them to be the *TRITYTE*, do you?" I said.

"That's exactly what I think," Marranalis responded, "and Lexmal was with them. He knows that the *TRITYTE* has a solbidyum reactor. I'll bet anything that was their target. Just one grain of solbidyum is worth a planets' wealth by itself. Lexmal no doubt has some confederates interested in getting their hands on that solbidyum. It's a good thing the *TRITYTE* was here at the time."

"Oh my god, where is Lunnie?!" I asked in a near panic.

"I don't know. She cut out of here right after seeing that vid. She said she had something to take care of right away," Marranalis answered. "She took Reidecor with her."

"Captain Stonbersa, seal off the ship and get ready for a fight," I said. "I fear we are about to receive company in the form of three fully-armed Federation patrol ships. I'm confident that by now they know where we are and are coming for the *TRITYTE*. We *must* not let them get either the *TRITYTE* or the *NEW ORLEANS*. If they were to find out about the RMFF on this ship... well, we can only imagine the damage they would do to the Federation."

"I already issued the order as soon as I heard of the attack on your estate," Marranalis reported. "This ship has good fire power, Tibby, but we lack trained people to handle the guns. I didn't think about the *TRITYTE* being the target – I thought it was you they were after. I'll get a message off to the Federation asking for backup."

"My guess is we have about an hour and a half before they show here. Pray that it's enough time for Lunnie to complete her task," I said.

"Lunnie?" Marranalis said questioningly. "What the hell can Lunnie do to help us?"

"You know about the RMFF on this ship…"

"Yes…but it's not functional. There's not power to – " Marranalis slapped himself on the head as realization hit him. "Of course! The solbidyum reactor on the *TRITYTE* – she's building an interface! When did you guys figure that one out?"

"Same day I bought the ship," I said. "I've had Lunnie working on a connection between the *TRITYTE*'s reactor and the existing *NEW ORLEANS* power grid through the hull power interface. I'm just hoping she has it completed and that everything else in the system is operational. Marranalis, you stay here with Captain Stonbersa to man the defense system. You can instruct the onboard security forces from here. Captain, take command. I'm headed to the hangar area to see if I can give Lunnie a hand. Let's hope we can get the RMFF running before the raiders get here."

When I arrived at the hangar I saw Lunnie, Kala and Reidecor using a small tractor to drag a massive cable assembly across the deck toward the *TRITYTE*. By the time I reached them, they had the cable in position under the power attachment point on the *TRITYTE*.

"About time you got here," Kala said. "We need some extra muscle." It was not until that moment that I realized that Kala had not been by my side as usual. She must have headed to the hangar as soon as she heard about the raid at the estate.

"Thank the stars you all took the initiative to get down here and get this thing hooked up! We don't have much time, maybe an hour at most. What do you need me to do?" I said.

"We need you to put your back under this thing with Reidecor," said Lunnie. "It weighs over 180 kilograms – and even as strong you both are, it's going to be a struggle to get this monster hooked, if we can at all."

Lunnie wasn't kidding when she said it would take all our strength. The cable was stiff and didn't want to cooperate as we lifted it into place. There were times I thought I was going to collapse under the strain of holding the assembly in position as Lunnie and Kala scrambled to engage the clamp that would seal the attachment. Finally, we heard the thud as the clamps locked. Lunnie gave it one final and careful assessment. "I think that'll do it."

Just then Captain Stonbersa's voice came over the com system. "I hope you have things hooked up, we have three incoming ships on the sensor screen right now and they're headed this way."

Kala, Lunnie, Reidecor and I ran into the *TRITYTE*. Lunnie headed to engineering and the rest of us went to the control room. I went directly to the com panel and brought up Captain Stonbersa on the main screen. "We just finished the hook up Captain. We're about to power her up, we hope."

"Tibby," Lunnie's voice came across the com, "I'm ready to initiate the toggle switch so the *NEW ORLEANS* can start drawing enough power to activate the RMFF."

Suddenly Marranalis yelled over the com system from the bridge of the *NEW ORLEANS*, "Captain! All three ships are firing on us!" and in response Captain Stonbersa urged, "Hit the button, Lunnie!"

There was a briefest moment of flickering lights in the control room of the *TRITYTE*... and then we waited. Seconds later we heard the whoops and yells of Marranalis, Kerabac, and Captain Stonbersa over the com system. "Did you see that?! Their shots were completely absorbed!"

Kala and I headed back to the *NEW ORLEANS* bridge, leaving Lunnie and Reidecor on the *TRITYTE* to monitor the stability of the power connection.

"Will you look at that," Marranalis was saying as we entered the bridge, "not even their plasma torpedoes can penetrate our defensive systems!"

We all watched in fascination as the torpedoes were launched right into the unseen RMFF. There was a burst of energy that sent lightning racing about on the surface of the RMFF shield, but that was all. Inside the *NEW ORLEANS* there wasn't even the slightest indication of an attack happening. On the screen we could see the rogue patrol ships circling around the *NEW ORLEANS*, firing with everything they had.

"Captain I am not very knowledgeable about the functions of an RMFF system. Nothing can get through it?" I asked.

"Not exactly," the captain replied," nothing can get *in* but things *can* get out. The RMFF is designed to project a force outward from the ship. If you were to throw a wrench out of the cargo hold, when it hit the field from the inside it would suddenly accelerate away from the ship and out into space at the speed of light."

"WOW," I responded. "So we can return fire on them with no ill effects to us?"

"In theory, yes," replied the captain.

"Let's try it. Use our weakest weapon and target one of the three patrol ships," I ordered.

The captain grinned and nodded to Marranalis, who immediately seated himself at the weapons console and began activating controls. Suddenly a beam of light shot out from the *NEW ORLEANS* and passed through the RMFF shield. Instantly the targeted ship exploded into a billion stars like a fireworks display. The other two ships immediately broke away from their attack and fled at top speed.

"What just happened?" Marranalis asked in amazement. "That shot should barely have made a mark on their hull!"

"I think the shield amplified the power of the shot," I said hesitantly, as I watched Captain Stonbersa, who was walking about the bridge with a beaming smile on his face, gently running his hand across the consoles. "Incredible," he whispered to himself. "Simply incredible."

"Captain," I said, "we need to keep this as secret as long as we can. We can tell people we have some new weapon, but we need to keep from mentioning the RMFF and the use of the *TRITYTE* as a power source in this operation."

"Yes, yes, I completely agree, Tibby," said the captain, still mesmerized. "I can also see where we are going to need to be extra careful in choosing the crew for the ship.   Sergeant Marranalis, I'm going to need the most highly trained security people you can get."

"Kala, is there a good way to quickly test people for loyalty?   Corporal Lexmal was supposed to have been screened before he was made part of our team, and yet he was a traitor. We can't afford even the slightest risk that this situation is repeated within our own security forces or crews," I said.

"I know, Tib," Kala responded. "That issue has bothered me since it happened. I brought it up with Captain Maxette when he was here. He said that, once they found out what had unfolded after the *TRITYTE* departed from the *DUSTEN*, they reviewed the events leading up to the treason. Corporal Lexmal was not among the originally selected crew members; but on the night before the operation one of the original crewmen took ill. Corporal Lexmal was picked to take his place. He was given the same psych test as the original crew member; however, the normal test operator who conducted the original tests of the crew had also taken ill and a replacement had to stand in to conduct the remainder of the tests. They have since discovered that the second operator, Lieutenant Loracie, used another person's test readings in place of Corporal Lexmal's. Of course, this went undetected at the time. By the time the investigators uncovered the truth, the *DUSTEN* was in orbit about Megelleon and Lieutenant Loracie had gone missing. It would appear that the crew members they replaced were given something to make them ill so the swap could take place. You will remember that Corporal Lexmal indicated to us when we were on the Bunem freighter that he had a confederate aboard the *DUSTEN*. We can only guess that she was the one; but there are certainly indications that there may be others, as well. Captain Maxette told me that nearly two dozen of the ship's crew, mostly troopers, have not returned from shore leave. This is *most* unusual. Occasionally an individual will go AWOL, but there's never been an absence of this scale before – and it certainly has *not* happened because working conditions on the *DUSTEN* are bad; it's one of the best and most sought after assignments for anyone in the service."

"We can only assume that Lexmal has more confederates on the *DUSTEN* that have not yet abandoned their duty," I said, "and that there may still be more on Megelleon. They stole three patrol ships, one during Lexmal's escape and two others from our estate. He seems to be trying to assemble a small force and it's clear that the *TRITYTE's* solbidyum reactor is their target. We're going to need to be extremely vigilant about keeping the *TRITYTE* safe at all times. At the moment I think the safest place is here in the *NEW ORLEANS*."

"Kala, do you know how to run one of the computerized psych tests?" I asked.

"Yes I do, why?" Kala responded.

"Because I want every member of the security staff to undergo the test – twice – once when we interview and hire them and once before they are assigned to duty. I want the second test done by someone I personally know and trust. I also want every crew member on this ship to be personally screened by you, Kala. I hope the testing process isn't too long or difficult."

"Actually," Kala responded, "it's very simple and lasts about one minute."

"Good, I want you start with the crew and security forces in place on this ship right now. I think there are less than two hundred people onboard.   You can skip Lunnie, Marranalis and Reidecor; but even thought I think Kerabac and Captain Stonbersa can be trusted, I want them tested as well. There's simply too much at stake to make even a single assumption or misstep.

It was about an hour later when a squadron of patrol ships arrived that were sent by the Federation.   Captain Stonbersa turned off the RMFF long enough to allow the pilot ships to land in the hangar bay so Federation troopers could complete necessary briefings and preparations prior to taking up security posts in vital areas of the *NEW ORLEANS*. I was surprised when Lieutenant Commander Wanoll from the *DUSTEN* walked down a ramp of one of the patrol ships and greeted me warmly. "Tibby, it's great to see you again. You never stop amazing me with your unique ways of overcoming obstacles. Major," he acknowledged Kala, who responded with "Lieutenant Commander."

"I understand Stonbersa has joined you as your captain now," Wanoll said. "Good man – one of the best. Admiral Regeny and Captain Maxette thought I should stop by and chat with you and Captain Stonbersa about security defenses. Captain Maxette seems to be of the opinion that you may have something in that bag of tricks of yours that might give the Federation an edge, if war should break out." The way Wanoll was wording his comments left no doubt in my mind that Captain Maxette had figured out that we had somehow gotten the RMFF to be functional. He was clearly hoping it would be something that could be employed successfully in larger Federation warships.

"There certainly are some things that we can discuss, but I fear they may not hold the promise for in Federation military application.   Let me get Piesew to make some arrangements for your quarters and those of your men. Once you've settled in, we can get together with Captain Stonbersa and discuss a few things."

"Piesew is here? I thought he was still employed aboard the *DUSTEN*?" Wanoll said with amazement.

"Well technically he is. I invited him here to make an offer to come to work for me and he has accepted. His tour of duty with the *DUSTEN* ends next week. He will be coming to work here for me directly thereafter; in the meantime, I'm a bit shorthanded on service staff and crew. I hope you don't mind the lack of amenities that you might normally be accustomed to receiving."

About two hours later, Lieutenant Commander Wanoll, Captain Stonbersa, Kala and I met in a small, yet elegant meeting room adjacent to the bridge. After briefing Wanoll on the attack at the estate and the earlier assault on the *NEW ORLEANS*, Captain Stonbersa and Marranalis summarized the crew's successful efforts to engage the RMFF using the power from the solbidyum reactor on the *TRITYTE*.

Wanoll sat back in his chair with a dejected sigh. "We were hoping that you had come to some breakthrough that enabled you to use a standard fusion reactor to operate the shields. There is no way we will ever be able to get the Senate to allow us even a small portion of the remaining solbidyum, after its distribution, to power reactors on our warships. I fear we will never be able to use RMFF shields to protect the fleet."

"Don't jump to that conclusion too soon," I said. "Galetils was on the verge of creating fusions reactors with ten times the power of conventional fusion reactors. If it was done once it can be done again. I have the resources, so I can privately fund the research; and I'd bet that there are remaining people somewhere out here from Galetils' enormous pool of expertise that can provide enough clues to make it possible. Let me see what I can find out. Orcpipin is the General Manager here at the Nibarian shipyard. He was supposed to install the reactor when it was finished. He may be able to direct us to Galetils' former associates... and he must have some sort of designs or plans in his records for the eventual installation of the reactor that may give us a clue where to start. You won't have RMFFs running by next week, but you will sometime in the future."

Kala spoke up, "What can you tell us about this rebel faction that seems to be trying to get the solbidyum? They seem to be just a bit too organized to have just sprung up since the recovery of the *TRITYTE*."

"You're right there, Major. The Federation Office of Investigation has discovered that Corporal Lexmal and Lieutenant Loracie were both members of an underground movement that's been around for over three hundred years. This group was founded as a secret society, but became little more than a drinking club until a few years ago, when it started to take on a new face for malcontents who believed that progress was being impeded by the Federation. Even so, their numbers remained relatively small up until about ten years ago.   At that time the group gained a new charismatic leader named *Eulshod Rendoid*. No one is sure of this man's background or origins and few have actually ever seen or talked to him directly. What we do know about him is that he is rich and paranoid. He espouses plans to make his followers rich and powerful, claiming that they will one day replace the Federation with a new government in which each of them will be leaders. Even with these developments, the FOI didn't foresee the organization as any kind of threat, as they appeared to be poorly organized and had no real hierarchy that could organize or achieve anything. Obviously the FOI profilers were wrong on that count; and it appears that Corporal Lexmal has enough sway within the organization to galvanize enough of its membership to support his efforts in hopes of getting rich. The FOI is trying to track down all the members now and identify which of them are involved in this plot."

"What of this Eulshod Rendoid," Kala asked, "Is he party with the raiders?"

"He doesn't appear to be. In fact, he seems to be more than willing to turn over the secret membership list to the FOI to aid in our investigation, so long as we leave him alone." Wanoll explained. "He may have been the catalyst that advanced the group's collective identity, but their current agenda is not one of his making or following – that much I know at the moment. Nevertheless, the FOI is keeping an eye on him."

"What can you tell us about this group?" I asked. "What do they call themselves? Do they have any special code names or secret passwords or maybe a means of recognition between members that might help us identify them?"

Wanoll sighed and said, "They call themselves the BROTHERHOOD OF LIGHT. They are said to carry a small coin-like medallion on their person; some wear it; some carry it in their pocket. On one side of the medallion is the symbol for *infinity*, which somehow seems to have evolved as a universal symbol, at least throughout the Federation territories and known fringe planets. On the other side is a mobius strip represented as a single half-twisted loop. To the group this symbol represents *Power Forever*.

Power Forever is their phrase of recognition as well. In a sense, solbidyum is the ultimate sign of their order, as it represents a very tangible manifestation of both *infinity* and *Power Forever*. One thing the FOI knows for sure is that they will attack again and probably on an even greater scale than we've seen thus far."

"That's not what I want to hear," I sighed and rubbed my head. "But for right now, if we can be sure of the loyalty of the crew and troopers on this ship, we are about as safe here as we can possibly be anywhere. Once the RMFF is turned on, nothing is getting in."

"I'm afraid that Admiral Regeny is going to be disappointed about the RMFF. He was really hoping you had found a way to power it using a standard fusion reactor," Wanoll said.

"Doesn't anyone have an idea where the rebels are hiding? I asked. Their base of operations has to be someplace close by."

"It a real mystery," Wanoll replied. "The FOI and the military have been using every available resource to track these people and we haven't a clue where they've been going. We're pretty sure they're hiding on Megelleon; but they have mastered clandestine travel, hugging the ground with their ships and using obscure routes that keep them from being observed. It's not easy to hide a patrol ship. We know they are not hiding them outdoors on the surface or we would be able to pick them up with satellites. Thus far we're getting nothing. All buildings and structures large enough to hide them are also being checked, but with no luck so far.

"Captain Maxette has asked me to provide you with one hundred fifty troopers for crew and security here on the *NEW ORLEANS* until you can get fully manned. The Federation can't have the *TRITYTE* falling into enemy hands. I'll also be staying here to help, though I have a feeling I will be learning more than I will be helping," he said with a chuckle. "You seem to be safe enough from *outside* attack with the RMFF up and running; however, you have little protection at the moment from *internal* attacks."

"I appreciate the offer of assistance, sir," I said. "However, I have one condition before I accept any Federation support; you – and everyone who will be stationed here with you – must undergo a mental probe to confirm loyalty."

"That's not a problem," Wanoll replied. "All the troopers sent here were tested back on the *DUSTEN* before being sent here."

"With all due respect, Corporal Lexmal was tested on the *DUSTEN*; and we all know how that turned out. We will be retesting everyone here again using our own processes. No one will remain aboard the *NEW ORLEANS* without being tested by Major Kalana. Furthermore, so long as it doesn't impact any of your primary orders from the Federation High Command, you and the troopers will answer to Captain Stonbersa's command while you are aboard the *NEW ORLEANS*."

Wanoll looked at me curiously for a moment and then laughed, "Tibby, I truly admire you, and you have every right to be cautious. I agree; you can start by testing me."

Kala began testing troopers shortly after, starting with Lieutenant Commander Wanoll. Wanoll passed, but out of one hundred fifty troopers assigned to the New Orleans for security, seven failed the test and were held for questioning. Five of the seven were found to have an affiliation with the BROTHERHOOD OF LIGHT. The other two were just mercenaries scheming independently in their desire to obtain solbidyum for themselves. Lieutenant

Commander Wanoll contacted Captain Maxette from the bridge of the *NEW ORLEANS* with these findings.

"Captain," Wanoll began, "we seem to have a bigger problem than we thought. Tibby, in his singular wisdom, insisted that everyone assigned to protect the *NEW ORLEANS* must be psychologically computer tested before being allowed to serve here, despite the fact that the troopers were previously tested onboard the *DUSTEN*. The troopers were all retested during the past several hours and the results are grim. Five percent of the previously tested troopers failed the second test. We have to conclude that we have persons operating the *DUSTEN*'s testing systems who are falsifying results in order to pass confederates. Our own ship could have more confederates and sympathizers aboard, sir. For the moment I am holding the troopers that didn't pass in order to keep word from leaking out. We believe that you need to immediately retest not only your troopers, but the test facilitators as well. It would appear that the rebels have been in place longer than we suspected. Now, with the return of the solbidyum, I fear we are on a collision course with problems that we have not seen in centuries."

Captain Maxette face took on an ominous cast as the news was delivered. He stared back at us through the screen. "Tibby, I don't suppose you have one of your magic tricks that can get us out of this mess, do you?"

"I'm afraid not, Captain," I said. "I wish I did."

"I will immediately start retesting everyone, starting with the test facilitators, but it's not going to be easy." Captain Maxette paused as he sorted through the possibilities. "And if anyone figures out what we're doing, I hate to think what might happen. There are thousands of people aboard the *DUSTEN*. If what you're saying is right, there's no telling what kind of trouble we could be in here."

He paused again, his mind working out the reality of his situation. "We must filter out the rebels swiftly. Of the ten thousand people on the *DUSTEN*, six thousands of them are troopers, most of whom are authorized to carry arms. If 5% of them are rebels, that's 300 that we have to worry about here. But it's the *TRITYTE* and the solbidyum they're after; and the *DUSTEN* has neither, so I suspect that we're safe until we can filter out and detain these rebels."

"I fear there is a much larger problem here than we are seeing, Captain, I just haven't figured out what it is yet." Wanoll said.

"Captain Stonbersa," Maxette said, "I'm glad to see you accepted Tibby's offer. I feel much better knowing that you're in charge of the *NEW ORLEANS*. Whatever happens, don't let the *TRITYTE* fall into the hands of the enemy – nor the *NEW ORLEANS*, for that matter."

"Rest assured, Captain," Stonbersa replied, "you have my word I will do all I can to protect both ships."

That evening Kala and I dined in our suite alone. Piesew ordered us some tasty dishes from the synthesizer and, after serving us, he retired to his quarters. We both ate quietly for awhile. Finally, Kala spoke, "Tib, what's bothering you? I can see it on your face and I know it's more than just the current situation with the rebels."

"I didn't think it showed, "I answered, "but yes something is bothering me. It is directly related to the rebels in a way. It's just that you and the rest – Lunnie, Reidecor, Marranalis, and to some extent Kerabac – well, you're all like family to me and I like having you near… I like talking and doing things with all of you. The past few days have been so busy and hectic, though, it seems we're all growing apart instead of being the team and… *family*… that I would like us to be. Right now Lunnie and Reidecor are aboard the *TRITYTE*, making sure the RMFF shields remain fully powered; Marranalis is working with Wanoll and the troopers, ensuring the integrity of the troops and confirming that the ship is guarded and maintained properly.   And Kerabac – what the hell is Kerabac doing, anyway?"

Kala chuckled. "He's been working with Orcpipin and the shipyard team on the navigation system.   Some portion of the system wasn't fully functional; and when we turned on the RMFF system, he discovered that it had stopped functioning all together. Orcpipin's engineers and Kerabac think they may have found a solution. They worked on it all day and continue to do so now, as far as I know."

Kala gazed at me for a moment, then got up from the table and came over to where I was sitting. She ran her fingers through my hair and sat down on my lap, looking into my eyes with a soft smile on her face. She wrapped her arms about my neck and said, "And what about me? Have you missed me being by your side all the time?"

"Kala, "I said as truthfully and sincerely as I knew how, "I have missed you most of all – every minute that you were not with me." Kala kissed me gently, then leaned back with a smile and said, "Good… and don't you ever forget it!" With that comment Kala stood up and, still holding my hand, led me to the bedroom.

In the morning I called my crew and Captain Stonbersa to a meeting in the galley of the *TRITYTE*. It was the first time that Captain Stonbersa had been able to board the *TRITYTE*. He was openly moved and teary-eyed about "this historic ship." He whispered, almost to himself, how he never thought for a moment that one day he would be standing inside of her. He talked about how, as a child, tales of the *TRITYTE* had intrigued him almost to the point of obsession.   It made me realize once again how truly significant this ship was to the peoples of the Federation. I began to formulate a new plan in my mind in this regard, but we had to survive the current situation before I could give it more thought.

After everyone assembled around the table and greeted each other, I began the meeting. "I called you all here today for several reasons. First and foremost, I want to see you all. The past few days have been very hectic and we haven't had any personal time together as a group in quite awhile. I hope none of you feel like I have forgotten you or that I am neglecting you. You've each done an incredible job, much of it without my asking, just like the team I hoped we would become and I am extremely proud of you. Reidecor and Lunnie, without your quick thinking and action when the raiders were on their way, we would probably all be dead and the *TRITYTE* and its solbidyum would be in enemy hands... and possibly the *NEW ORLEANS* as well. If the two of you had waited to receive orders from me to attach the power cable to the *TRITYTE* so we could use the RMFF, we would have been lost. I cannot thank you both enough. I know that Kerabac has been working feverishly to resolve a problem in the navigation system and Marranalis has been working with Lieutenant Commander Wanoll to shore up ship defenses and security. Kala has been busy retesting everyone that sets foot in the ship to protect us from potential threats. As for Captain Stonbersa, who barely set foot on the ship before having to take command during an attack, I thank you. Let's just say that everyone has gone above and beyond the call of duty in this situation and I will not forget it. I'm hoping that soon we can get on to more happy and relaxing pursuits."

"I for one have enjoyed every minute of this time," Lunnie interjected with what everyone could tell was going to be yet another of her glib remarks. "Having Reidecor all to myself here on the *TRITYTE* has been my dream come true," and with that she threw her arms around his neck and kissed his cheek. Reidecor blushed and grinned, but didn't try to disengage Lunnie's arms.

"Well, Lunnie, I was planning to ask for a progress report from all of you, but honestly, that was not the update I was looking for." Grins surrounded the table. Were there, or are there, any problems with the power feeds for the RMFF that we need to know about?"

"None that I can find," Lunnie reported.

"Captain Stonbersa and Kerabac, I understand that when the RMFF is operating, the navigation system is non-functional. What can you report on that?" I asked.

Captain Stonbersa smiled, "We have some interesting news for you on that one, Tibby. I'll let Kerabac tell you, though, since he was the one who made the discovery."

"Well I can't really take credit for it. I mean, it was just by accident that I discovered it," Kerabac began. "We all know that, up until yesterday, RMFF systems have never been operated except on the smallest scales in controlled laboratory test environments, mostly because of the incredible power requirements. So there are still many unknowns regarding this technology and the behavior of the fields. In our case, we found that the standard navigation system won't function when the RMFF system is active. We also learned that the RMFF system enhances the energy effect (kinetic and otherwise) of anything moving through it and outward from the ship. While probing the various parameters of the field generator, to get the navigation system back online, we tried at one point to piggyback the navigation signals onto a second magnetic beam and project it through the RMFF shield, when suddenly we received calls from Nibaria's space port, questioning what had happened to the *NEW ORLEANS*, as they could no longer see it or detect it on their sensors. When we turned off the magnetic beam that carried the navigation signal, the *NEW ORLEANS* reappeared. We tested it several times and found that the RMFF can operate as a cloaking device if we *inject* the field, so to speak, with a magnetic beam that carries a signal from the navigation system, a beam that is generated at a specific frequency. Oddly, it only works when the navigation beam is linked or "piggybacked" to the magnetic beam. It was pure luck that we figured this out."

"You mean, not only can we make the *NEW ORLEANS* invulnerable from outside attack, we can also make it invisible?!" I exclaimed.

"That's exactly what we mean," said Stonbersa, both he and Kerabac grinning ear to ear.

"What about the functionality of the navigation system itself?" I asked.

"That one had me stumped for awhile, until I realized that light from the stars was still passing through the RMFF shield; so I recalibrated the system to work on light instead of magnetic signatures of the stars and it works. Well, I should say it works as long as the RMFF field is up. As soon as it's dropped, the light signature system only works with nearby stars and not the more distant ones. So with the help of Orcpipin's crew working through the night and installing some new gear in the bridge, we now have a dual system that toggles automatically, depending on whether the RMFF is active. We also have a switch for the cloaking device as well," Kerabac concluded with a satisfied smile as he sat back in his chair.

"I've had them install a security mechanism on the system, so the cloaking device can only be activated by senior officers, meaning everyone here in this room," added Captain Stonbersa. "That way, if the ship ever falls into enemy hands, they can neither cloak the ship nor activate the RMFF. I can change that if you want, Tibby, but for the moment I thought you would prefer this arrangement."

"Well done, Captain," I said. "Though I do trust Lieutenant Commander Wanoll, for right now I feel it's important that he does not have access. More so, I do not want him – or anyone outside this room, for that matter – to know *at all* about the cloaking device."

"Marranalis, what can you tell me about the internal security at the moment?" I asked.

"The troopers sent by the *DUSTEN* are a huge step in the right direction. I know most of these troopers and they're all top of the line. All of them were shocked to find that there were insurgents in the *DUSTEN*'s crew and they're extremely embarrassed by it. I think they will all work extra hard to prove themselves, just because of that very fact. I talked to Orcpipin and he says his crew will be finishing up the last of the outfitting requirements in the next day and they will depart thereafter. The passenger liner coming in for repairs will arrive that same day, and I believe that Piesew, Kala, and Captain Stonbersa have already screened a number of applications received from the displaced crew. If they pass their interviews and loyalty tests, we should have a crew assembled, trained and ready to fly in about five days – assuming we are going to fly someplace," Marranalis said with a grin.

Finally, Kala reported that her assistant back at the estate advised that everything seemed to be restored to order and that the Federation sent extra troops to bolster security.

I suddenly had an idea.

"Kala, contact Admiral Regeny's office and tell him that I'm making rooms available free of charge to senior officers for up to a week at a time at the estate lodge as a gesture of my appreciation to the Federation for its protection. I doubt we will be using the lodge much, if at all, but it's a beautiful building with lovely accommodations and I am sure the senior officers will enjoy it."

"Yeah," Marranalis chuckled, "and you can be sure that if they are going to be using the grounds, the trooper security will be top drawer across the entire estate."

"Exactly!" I said, and everyone the room laughed.

The next few days went by rather quickly and, other than for routine business, the pace of things was less stressful. Between Kala's coordination meetings with her team of assistants at the estate she and I had a fair amount of free time and wandered about the ship. Our personal living quarters were identical to the ones we had back on the estate, right down to the study and the aquarium. I had a special fascination for this room and it became my personal working space. Between the day that I bought the ship and the final installation of finishings by Orcpipin's crews I had seen that the tank filled with water and quickly become populated with aquatic life. I discovered a large retractable view screen that, when opened, completely concealed the aquarium window. At times I would activate the screen and set the view to space. The image was so vivid that I felt like I could have stepped into it and drift off into the cosmos. The room's furniture included sofas crafted in a leather-like upholstery, large chairs covered in the same material and potted fern-like plants, all arranged into intimate gathering areas. Overall, the room had a very Victorian feeling about it, much like the captain's quarters. The only thing that was lacking was a fireplace.

Just like the estate the *NEW ORLEANS* was designed with multiple swimming pools, gyms and activity spaces. There were also a surprising number of food and drink dispensers situated about the ship including the garden-style atrium patio areas where people could gather informally to share a drink or a meal.

The further I investigated, the more I realized that the *NEW ORLEANS* was more like a floating town than a ship. I was amazed to find that the ship had its own hospital – not just a clinical facility, but an actual surgical center with an operating theater and several recovery rooms furnished with equipment and beds for the sick or injured. Kala said this was not uncommon on many of the larger ships and that our estate was equipped with a hospital as well. I wanted to ask her about doctors and nurses, only to discover that no word existed in Federation language for *doctor*. There were, however, words for *medic* and something like a nurse called a *medical aid*. Medics were basically persons trained to interpret or confirm the computer readings and to issue orders to the medical aides. The computer ultimately diagnosed the patient's condition and indicated the course of treatment and medication. The computer also carried out most of the treatments with various electronic instruments. The medic was responsible for issuing the orders for treatments that could not be provided by the computer and the medical aides saw to the basic care and needs of the patient. If surgery was required, the person was taken to an operating room, where a machine much like the one in the infirmary on the *TRITYTE* performed the necessary procedure.

I was told that some of the outbacks and primitive planets were staffed with fully trained medical personnel and limited resources for performing operations and the like, if need be; but essentially, every planet that held Federation membership was provided with at least one major medical center. If necessary, a patient would be flown to that facility from anywhere on the planet to receive care. All medical care in the Federation was free; no one was denied care or treatment, unlike the way medical programs were implemented on Earth.

It was two days after the docking of the disabled passenger liner at the Nibarian shipyard that we began formal interviews with the displaced crew members. Piesew remained aboard the *NEW ORLEANS*, as Lieutenant Commander Wanoll and Captain Maxette both believed it was prudent to suspend any travel until the situation on both ships was resolved. Piesew had only a few days left of his tour of duty with the *DUSTEN* anyway, so Captain Maxette said he could finish out his time on the New Orleans. With these arrangements in place Piesew conducted the interviews for service crews assigned to accommodations. Captain Stonbersa, Lunnie, Marranalis, and Kerabac all interviewed potential crew members for the ship's operations, security and engineering teams and Kala administered computerized psychological and loyalty tests. To our pleasant surprise only one person failed the loyalty test out of almost three hundred applicants. Equally remarkable was that every applicant was highly qualified. We ended up hiring everyone that passed the loyalty test.

For three days following the completion of interviews and tests the new crews were trained in their respective duties and briefed on the stringent security requirements. On the fourth day we decided to take the *NEW ORLEANS* back to Megelleon and place her in high orbit over the estate. Later that day Kala came to me.

"Tib, you asked me a few weeks ago to arrange a meeting with some of the scientists and manufactures of the learning headbands. With all that has been going on lately I sort of forgot about them; and I just got a call from my assistant at the estate that three of them just arrived. What do you want me to do?"

"Tell your assistant I want to commission their services starting today for, oh let's say a week. Tell her to stress to them that it's very important. They need only to name their price, after which she is to tell them that we will triple that amount. Let her know that we are on our way back to Megelleon and to put the scientists in a luxury suite with full accommodations and services and to see to their needs until we arrive later today. We'll need a shuttle to get down to the planet. I'm leaving the *TRITYTE* here hooked into the RMFF grid on the *NEW ORLEANS* for safe keeping."

While Kala carried out these instructions, I contacted Captain Stonbersa and instructed him to maintain the ship's position over Megelleon while some of us went to the surface. I told him to keep the RMFF shields up at all times and not to let anyone through the shield without clearing it through me or Kala. I also told him the *TRITYTE* would be staying on the *NEW ORLEANS*, as would Lunnie, Reidecor and Kerabac, but Marranalis would be going with Kala and me to the surface. I then contacted Piesew.

"Piesew," I began, "I would like you to contact a clothing designer and have them create uniforms for the crew, especially for Captain Stonbersa. I don't want anything over-stated or gaudy, rather something smart and recognizable. I would also like to see the designs before we commission any manufacturing."

"I know just the people to contact," Piesew said, "a couple on Megelleon that is noted throughout the galaxy for their designs of civilian, dignitary and military clothing. I will contact them immediately. When I tell them the uniforms are for your people, they will jump at the opportunity to design them simply for the fame it will bring them."

Next I spoke to Lieutenant Commander Wanoll, who was still in charge of the Federation troops on the ship. "Some of us are going down to the planet on business; I anticipate being there for a few days. Lunnie and Reidecor will be staying here and aboard the *TRITYTE* to maintain the connection for the RMFF. I think it would be a wise idea to have extra security in the hangar around the *TRITYTE.*"

"I agree, Tibby," Wanoll said. "It will be much easier to protect the *TRITYTE* from here."

I had one more task to take care of before leaving. I went to the hangar to talk to Lunnie.

"Hey, loverboy," Lunnie said with her typical sense of humor, "how are things going with you and my sister? She's keeping you happy, I hope."

"Lunnie, your sister does nothing *but* make me happy. I just wish I had more time to show her how happy she makes me." I said.

"Tib, don't worry about it. I can tell you that you have made my sister happier than I have ever seen her in my life. You're the best thing that has ever happened to her. But I don't imagine that you came here to talk about Kala, so what's up?" she said while she wiped her hands on a rag.

"I have a task for you to look into, but I need you to do it without anyone else knowing my intentions. I want to investigate what it would take to move the solbidyum reactor from the *TRITYTE* to the *NEW ORLEANS*."

"WHAT?!" Lunnie exclaimed. "If you do that you would have to gut the *TRITYTE* and install a new engine room. It would be cheaper to just buy another patrol ship."

"I don't want the *TRITYTE* gutted, but I don't expect it to fly after the solbidyum reactor is removed. I've decided is retire the *TRITYTE* and build a flying museum that will take the *TRITYTE* on tour around the Federation, so everyone can see it and appreciate it for what it is…or was. When I saw Captain Stonbersa reaction to the *TRITYTE* the other day, I realized just how important it is to the people of the Federation and I think everyone should have a chance to see it. But it's too huge a temptation for any one or any planet wanting to obtain its solbidyum heart; so we remove that, put it in the *NEW ORLEANS*, which is equipped to protect itself, and make the *TRITYTE* available for everyone to see and touch and walk through. We'll build a flying museum, complete with exhibits and the story of the solbidyum and the Great Wars, the rediscovery of the *TRITYTE,* everything right up to today, and fly it *to them* so everyone on every planet gets a change to see it." I looked at Lunnie and I saw tears in her eyes and she walked over to me and gave me a hug. "Kala is very lucky to have you, Tibby. You truly are a great and caring man – one of a kind, I would say. I'll look into it and let you know what I figure out."

The trip from the *NEW ORLEANS* to the surface went smoothly. I was surprised to see that the arriving shuttle displayed a *Galetils Industry* logo. "What's with the logo?" I asked Kala. "And where did it come from?"

Kala completed her communication with the shuttle pilot and returned to tell me, "The shuttle came with the estate. There's a fleet of about a dozen of them in the estate hangar and at the lodge complex. I suppose the logo is on there from Galetils prior ownership. You will probably want them removed."

"I just happened to be thinking that perhaps it wouldn't hurt if we had our own logo," I said, "something simple that people would quickly identify as being uniquely ours; but I have no idea what it should be or how it should look. We'll have to give it some thought."

After we landed and made our way to the estate house, I made my way to the comforts of my study and relaxed with Kala in front of the aquarium. Moments later, a young woman from Kala's staff announced the arrival of out three guests.

"Tibby, may I present Dakko of Tarola, Rivez of Koeis, and Cantolla from the University on Essen. Honored guests, may I present to you Tibby the Recoverer and Major Kalana of the Federation." Then she stepped back and waited by the door for further instructions.

Dakko was a rather short and squatty man with short stubby fingers and a hair style right out of the Wizard of OZ. Even his attire reminded me of the old Earth movie. He wore a bright yellow coat with a red vest, brown trousers, and shoes that looked way too large for his frame. Rivez was tall and thin, about 1.6 meters and maybe 81-82 kg. Unlike Dakko, he had long, thin fingers and had an air about him that made me think of Abraham Lincoln, including his dark, wavy hair and sad eyes. Cantolla, on the other hand was a strikingly beautiful woman about 1.75 meters tall. She had green eyes and long chestnut colored hair that caught the light and reminded me of the horses on a ranch next to my grandfather's home after they had just been currycombed and brushed. She was dressed in a rather form-fitting outfit that reminded me of brushed green suede and calf-high boots that accented the outfit perfectly. I could feel Kala tense up momentarily when she entered the room.

"Greetings to you all. Please be seated," I said, indicating the leather sofa and chairs at one side of the room. They seated themselves; Dakko and Rivez took the sofa, while Cantolla selected one of the plush leather-like chairs. Kala and I sat across from them in large easy chairs. Between us was a low table that could be raised and lowered if needed, but on this occasion it was kept low like a coffee table. "Would anyone care for something to drink?" I asked. Both Dakko and Rivez indicated they would appreciate some foccee, while Cantolla indicated she would take a "dayere," a drink I had never heard of before. Kala indicated to her aide that we would be having four foccee and one dayere. The aide retrieved the beverages from the dispenser, served them to everyone and then, at a nod from Kala, left the room.

"I trust each of you is comfortable and happy with your accommodations," I inquired, "and the compensation you will be receiving for your time?"

"Oh my, oh my yes," Dakko responded excitedly. "The accommodations are most exquisite, luxurious beyond belief, actually, and your generosity – oh my, oh my! What can I say?   It's more than ample, yes more than ample."

"I must agree with Dakko," Rivez said stoically. "My suite is larger than my house and certainly more lavish. The food has been divine."

"I'm satisfied with my rooms," Cantolla said coolly. "They are adequate for my needs, though perhaps a bit large for just *one* person; but then these suites are not designed for just *one* person, now, are they?"   There was a definitely emphasis on "one" that begged the question as to what her inference was, but I decided not to pursue it.

"I'm sure you're wondering why I've brought you here and, since I know you're all very busy people, I will get right to the point. My knowledge of the learning headband is very limited; so please bear with my ignorance and don't hesitate to correct me if I'm wrong. As I understand it, this device can transfer knowledge to a person on an intellectual level, but not the physical or kinesthetic level. Let me use art as an example – let's say painting. The headband can convey the facts related to mixing colors, types of brushes and brush strokes, the history and styles of painting, etcetera; but it cannot transfer the associated abilities or physical dexterities with which to do the painting? Am I correct?"

"Oh my, oh my, yes, you are ever so correct," Dakko blurted. "Basic knowledge can be implanted into the mind, but the physical components must be practiced and learned. These cannot be transferred."

"Yes, I agree with Dakko," Rivez said a bit less enthusiastically than Dakko. "We have been trying for years to find a way around that obstacle, but with no success."

I glanced at Cantolla, who was sitting in her chair, coolly staring at Kala and I while tracing her finger around the edge of her glass. She seemed to be lost in thought and then suddenly seemed to snap to the moment. "I've been doing some research along this area. I believe it can be accomplished, but it will be tricky. Unlike conventional information, movements and coordination rely on multiple senses – sound, vision, balance, touch, even smell, as dictated by many other factors in the brain. The body needs to access and integrate all of this information, in order to assimilate the intellectual knowledge with the appropriate muscular responses in the body. I think it can be done with more research, time, and above all, funding."

"I'm glad to hear you say that, Cantolla," I responded, "because that's exactly what I need you all to work on for me. Cost is of no concern, but time is. A laboratory will be set up for you here at the estate. Compile a register of any materials you need and they will be expedited to you. The sooner you can complete the task the better. Cantolla, how long do you think it will take you to accomplish this task, if you have all the resources you need and no interruptions?" Cantolla looked at me in a frozen gaze momentarily before responding. "I honestly don't know. A week, a month, a year, or maybe years. I honestly have no idea."

"Do it in a month and you each get one million credits as a bonus, three weeks and you get a two million credits bonus and, if you can accomplish it in two weeks, I will make it ten million credits each. Cantolla, I want you to head up the project, but all of you are assigned to this project and responsible for its success."

"Why are you putting Cantolla in charge?" Rivez asked in a slightly challenging tone. "Why not one of us?" Rivez was sitting forward in his chair in a challenging fashion, while Dakko was sitting back in his with his arms crossed in a somewhat pouting fashion.

"Because, of the three of you, she is the only one who said she thought it could be done and presented specific information that made sense to me. If you don't like the arrangement, you are free to leave; I will still pay you the agreed amount for your time when you accepted the offer to come here."

"What about the patent rights if we do succeed; who gets those?" Dakko wanted to know.

"Don't be stupid, Dakko," Rivez said, "You know as well as I do that, if we invent anything while in the employ of a company, the company retains the patent and you or I might receive a bonus check equal to a month's pay, if we were lucky. What Tibby is offering is way more than what we would see for compensation any other way."   As I watched this dialogue play out, I noticed Cantolla sitting back coolly in her chair, still tracing her finger on the edge of her glass, wearing a look of mild amusement at the volley of arguments between Dakko and Rivez.

"I for one," Rivez continued, "accept your offer."

"Oh yes, count me in too, oh yes. You're offering a much greater reward than I could ever hope for anyplace else, oh yes, most certainly!" Dakko said. "I will need to contact my company immediately to take an extended leave of absence. It should be no problem, as I have accumulated sufficient personal leave time and work is slack at the moment."

I looked at Cantolla, who had not shifted in position all the while and still bore the slight trace of a grin on her lips.   She sighed and then with all the grace of cat sat forward slightly and said, "Okay, I'll do it, and I agree that you retain the patent rights, if it works. Just one question, what do you want to teach with it?"

"Martial arts!" I responded, knowing that they would not be as familiar with it as my group had become. At most, they knew of it from the broadcasts of the demonstration that was recorded at Admiral Regeny's dinner gala. I noted both Dakko's and Rivez's eyes widen with curiosity, while Cantolla's seemed to squint in contemplation.

After the meeting, when everyone else had left, Kala and I relaxed on a small settee by the aquarium. I had my arm about her, holding her close, when she asked, "What did you think of Cantolla?"

"I think she is very shrewd and intelligent, controlled and methodical. I think she will do a good job trying to get the learning bands where we need them to be."

Kala seemed to interrupt herself as she tried to get her thought across to me. "That's not what I mean. I know you noted her... her movements and actions. Her body language – didn't her flirting *bother* you?"

"Bother me? Kala I have no interest in anyone but you. My interests in Cantolla are purely professional. You needn't worry. I have no interest in her sexual wiles."

Kala began laughing hysterically.

"What?" I said, "What's so funny?"

It took Kala a few minutes to regain her composure until finally, through smaller fits of laughter, she choked out, "I guess you didn't know... or realize it... but Cantolla was flirting with *me*! She's a lesbian. The University on Essen is a school for lesbians only."

"Well," I muttered, "In that case, we will have to see to it that your duties keep you far away from that research lab, I guess."

Kala laughed and put her arms around me. "Don't worry, my love," she whispered in my ear, "You fulfill all of my desires."

The next few days I spent working with Marranalis and the martial arts trainees, both our own and those of the

Federation. Progress was terribly slow and I was praying that Cantolla and her team would come through with a breakthrough in the learning device. Marranalis had been able to recruit nearly 100 ex-troopers for our security force; and we had an additional fifty trainees from the Federation that would eventually become instructors. Our classes were way too big to teach effectively, so we divided the group into three separate classes – one in the morning and two in the afternoon. Even with this change, the classes were still large, which meant that individual attention to each student was a fraction of what it should be.

On the third day I received a message from Cantolla saying I was needed in the lab. They needed to record my mental functions while performing various martial arts sequences. At first, I just went through various moves in a shadow boxing manner, announcing each move as it was performed while wearing headband device, only this device was set to record my mental signals rather than implant information.   After about an hour of these exercises, we called in Marranalis to assist with simulated hand-to-hand combat scenarios. When we finished, we called in a new recruit who had received no training at all. A data-loaded headband was then placed on his head in the teaching mode. After a period of "uploading" to the trainee's brain, he was asked to display certain moves that the headband had hopefully taught him.   The results were not terribly promising; while he knew and understood the moves, his reflexes and coordination were far from proficient. He went through the correct motions for each given scenario, but he did so clumsily and slowly, as he had to stop long enough to think of the correct sequence to apply to a given scenario. When Marranalis attacked him, he nearly flattened the poor guy and it was obvious that very little had been accomplished. On a whim, however, I asked that they place the band on Marranalis head to see if it resulted in any measurable improvement in his skills, since he had already mastered some fundamentals. Much to my pleasure, I saw major improvements in his abilities, leading me to believe that there would be at least *some* merit to using the headbands to teach the troopers.

Dakko and Rivez remained rather pessimistic about the lack of progress and lamented that it was next to impossible. Cantolla, however, seemed more optimistic; she felt that significant progress had been made in three days and that, by installing more receptors and transmitters into the headband, even greater improvements would be achievable very soon. I asked whether we could, in the meantime, utilize the current version of the device in a quick session with all the trainees, because it would greatly enhance the overall learning curve. Cantolla said she saw no problem with that idea and was confident that it would even help her to achieve a finer calibration of the bands.

I left the science team to make arrangements with Marranalis for the initial trial training and returned to my study. Shortly thereafter I heard from Piesew via vid com. He advised that he had managed to contact the clothing designers and had rather quickly received a file containing their prototypes for the *NEW ORLEANS* crew uniforms. He displayed the prototypes on screen.

I was impressed. For the most part the uniforms were similar in cut to those of the Federation. The primary difference was that the designers had assigned colors to correspond to each crew function. The ranking bands would also vary in color depending on rank and function and, instead of wrapping across the chest the bands were placed on the upper sleeve of both arms. Also, officer uniforms included a long sleeved jacket with a Nehru collar, similar to the diplomatic cut that I frequently wore, except the collars were designed in a contrasting color. Uniforms of the captain and first officer were designed in ivory and accented with gold piping and gold banding on the sleeves. The uniforms of other members of the bridge crew were of a royal blue shade with either gold or silver banding and piping. Most uniforms of the service crews of the ship were either green or a light yellow, with the exception of the engineering uniforms, which were in various shades of gray with silver accents.

I was very pleased with both the simple elegance and the logic applied to the designs. I asked Piesew how long it would take to get the uniforms made for everyone on the ship. He replied with an uncharacteristic laugh, "Sir Renwalt, the uniforms need not be *made*; the design parameters must simply be uploaded to the ship's computer and the clothing will be made for each individual according to their measurements by a mechanism installed within their own closets."

"I'm sorry, Piesew," I responded, "I still have much to learn. Please see to it that the program is installed on the ship's computer and immediately inform the officers and staff by way of broadcast they are to wear these uniforms while on duty, effective immediately. Also see to it that the ship's purser pays the designers double their fee with my compliments."

"As you wish, sir," Piesew answered, "I shall see to it at once." And with that he was gone. I was barely off the vid screen with him when a call came in from Lieutenant Commander Wanoll's quarters on the *NEW ORLEANS*.

"Greetings, Lieutenant Commander, to what do I owe this call?" I asked.

"I fear that I have some bad news, Tibby. With the discovery of the infiltration of the *DUSTEN*'s crew by rebels, the Federation has quietly begun a security sweep of everyone in the immediate area of Megelleon. There have been over a thousand Brotherhood rebels discovered so far and the sweep is nowhere near completion. It seems they have been operating covertly here for a very long time but lying low, quietly waiting for a reason to take action. And now, fueled by the potential that solbidyum could bring their organization, they have become a malignant body that we must deal with urgently. I understand you have swept all the personnel at your estate and on your ship and can be relatively certain of your security. I wish we could say the same for the Federation military. We're sitting on a time bomb that is ready to explode and, if it does, Captain Maxette isn't sure he can hang onto the *DUSTEN*, much less be able to provide aid to the *NEW ORLEANS*, if a situation arises here. Admiral Regeny is also concerned, as three rebels have been identified among his personal staff. He doesn't know what information they may have leaked to their greater organization."

"That sounds ominous indeed," I replied. "Is there anything I can do to help?"

"Tibby, I wish there were; but honestly, I'm not sure what anyone can do right now. We just have to hope the lid stays on everything for the moment. The first shipments of solbidyum were supposed to start going out this week to their respective planets, but right now we can't guarantee their safety… and if *just one* shipment doesn't make it… well, we'll be looking at the Great Wars all over again." We briefly discussed the security measures on the *NEW ORLEANS* and were just finishing up when a message appeared on the screen flagging an incoming call from Lunnie. I ended my conversation with Wanoll and toggled over to Lunnie.

"Hi, loverboy," Lunnie began. "I think I have some good news for you."

"You'll be the first one today, Lunnie, if you do," I said (which wasn't quite true, but uniforms don't count).

"I searched through the *TRITYTE* database for the ship's designs. I've located the complete plans for the solbidyum reactor. The reactor is not all that big, actually – less than a meter square. However, I'll need to replace the exotic metals, which we don't have here. But I'm sure I can get them shipped here quickly. Really, it would be much easier to build a new reactor and simply move the grain of solbidyum than to move the entire reactor; and I can build the entire assembly here in the onboard machine shop. If you can get me the metals I need, I can have your reactor built and in system in three to four days."

"Lunnie, you're a genius," I said. "Remind me to give you a bonus. Just requisition anything you need and put a rush on it. I have a feeling we are going to need that solbidyum moved very soon. Once you have the reactor installed in the *NEW ORLEANS* I want you to disguise it so no one knows what it is. Let them think the fusion reactor is the only power system on the ship. In fact, if you can construct it so the solbidyum reactor chamber is completely hidden behind a secret access, that would even be better."

Lunnie laughed. "Got you boss. I know exactly what to do. With luck I should have it operational in about four days."

After talking to Lunnie, I sent a signal to Kala asking where she was. As it turned out she had just finished up a briefing with her estate staff and was coming to look for me. I suggested she meet me at the private pool in our quarters for a swim. By the time I got to the pool, Kala had already stripped out of her clothing and was swimming laps.

I wasted no time getting my clothing off and jumping into the pool beside her. We swam side by side for several laps before stopping to say anything. When we did stop at the pool's edge, I asked Kala, "What was it like around here before I came along? I mean, it seems to me that since I arrived, it's just been one major event after another. Was it like this before I showed up with the *TRITYTE?*"

"No, it was quite different – much duller actually, but a lot less dangerous, too. The most exciting thing that happened before you was a heated exchange over trade agreements between planets – tariffs, taxes on goods, and the like. The most dangerous thing I had to worry about was a pet Oragnat that belonged to the mate of a diplomat that bit me on the ankle when I went to pick them up for a meeting.

"I must admit, I am working to the max since you arrived and at times I find it overwhelming; but I wouldn't give it up for anything." Kala came closer and touched my face softly. "In the end, Thibodaux James Renwalt, your presence has brought me something much greater than professional challenge. You have given me real love – the love that I feel inside me for you and love that you give me in return. I can't begin to tell you what you mean in my life."

Kala propped her chin and arms on edge of the pool and continued, "Before you came along, I believed that love was something that didn't really exist... I don't mean in a sense like a family, where kids love their parents and siblings and vice versa, but the love between a man and a woman – like the love that exists between us. I always thought it was just wishful thinking on the part of two people and that it really just amounted to nothing more than sexual attraction. But now," she tilted her head and looked at me,

"Now I know what it feels like, even though I can't put it into words."

"You don't need to," I said as I kissed her. We stayed in an embrace there in the pool for several minutes, just holding each other. It was the best moment of my day and I wished that I could hold her there like that forever.

Finally I said, "I got a call today from Lieutenant Commander Wanoll. He said that the double screening on the *DUSTEN* has turned up a number of rebels and that the Federation is now running scans on all their ships and troops. The problem is extensive; already more than thousand rebels have been exposed in the military and they have no idea how extensive the infiltration really is. Wanoll said that Admiral Regeny found three rebels on his own personal staff. Who knows what information they may have leaked out. The High Command is afraid to move forward with the scheduled deliveries of solbidyum, because they believe they will be intercepted en route to their destination planets, as it's likely that there are rebels on every ship in the fleet. They're holding up the shipments, which is only going to increase ill feelings and tensions from the planets; but they can't give the reason lest they force the rebels into acts of mutiny. They can't hold the shipments up too long though, or the planets will retaliate. The Federation is stuck in a no-win scenario."

"Tibby, I know you. You're planning something again, aren't you?" Kala asked, searching my face for the answer.

I sort of chuckled. "If you know me, what do you think I am planning to do?"

"Hmmm," Kala slowly leaned back into the cool water, making tiny circles with her arms. "Well, knowing you, it will involve the *NEW ORLEANS*... perhaps volunteering for a clandestine mission to deliver some of the solbidyum. The ship is invincible, as far as we know; but, Tibby, the Federation territory is way too vast for the *NEW ORLEANS* to deliver it all. It would take several lifetimes for us to make all the deliveries."

"Well, you're right, at least in part. I *am* thinking of using the *NEW ORLEANS* to make at least some of the deliveries. I also want to draw the raiders into attempts to attack and capture the *NEW ORLEANS*, while other less obvious ships slip out to deliver solbidyum to planets that are not *officially* being considered for receipt of shipments at that time. I think if we can complete several successful shipments, the Brotherhood's repeated failures to intercept will weaken the movement and they will lose some of their key members and support. As it stands now, the longer these shipments are held up, the more the rebels will be able to grow in strength."

Kala and I swam a few more laps, then showered and headed back to our quarters. We ate a light dinner and found our way into one of the rooms that we had previously not given much attention, but had passed through several times. It wasn't exactly a den or study, nor was it a living room; it was more of a sitting room furnished with large padded chairs and sofas around a real wood-burning fireplace. I started the fire quite easily and added a couple of logs. The wood was nothing like that on Earth. As the logs burned, they produced the most wondrous aroma of buttery spice, like that of the sweet baked goods we had on Earth called cinnamon buns. Kala and I chose the small settee and sat very still, wrapped in each other's arms, not speaking, just watching the flames flicker until we both fell asleep. We awoke there in the morning, the fire long out and our bodies stiff from sleeping awkwardly.

It was still early in the morning when I received another call from Cantolla, saying that her team needed me for another headband programming cycle. Once again, I performed the stances and, once again, poor Marranalis got tossed about the room. I must confess, though, he was getting better on his landings and seemed better able to get back on his feet unassisted after the throws. A new recruit was brought in and the headband fitted, only to achieve the same results as the first test. The recruit picked up the moves, but his body didn't know how to perform them smoothly. There appeared to be minor improvement from the day before, but certainly nothing significant.

Dakko and Rivez both shook their heads, bemoaning that it wasn't possible, while Cantolla looked at the headband with a sense of curiosity and confusion that said, "You should be working, why aren't you?"

On the other hand, the groups that Marranalis and I had been training after the application of the first generation headband showed a huge improvement in skills and ability. In this way the device had certainly moved the program forward by several months from the original course of training.

We received word that afternoon that another attempt had been made on the solbidyum at the Federation's main base where it was being kept under guard. A ship from Teahkins that had arrived days earlier to carry its grain of solbidyum back to their planet was redirected to stage at a waiting pad on the base, after being told there was a delay due to technical difficulties. They were not told that the reason had to do with the risk of rebel interception. Apparently the rebels didn't get the message about the delay, because they attacked the Teahkins ship, thinking it had received the solbidyum and was preparing to depart. Several rebel troopers suddenly appeared from various locations around the landing pad, attacking and killing guards on the ground as the ship tried to take off. The rebels successfully boarded and killed most of the crew, throwing them out of the open hatch as the craft lifted off.

An approaching patrol ship from the *DUSTEN* saw the fight erupt from the air and, upon orders from the *DUSTEN*, opened fire on the ship, blowing it up and killing all on board. Upon learning of the disaster, the senator serving on behalf of the Teahkins people demanded to know what was going on and why their ship had been attacked and destroyed. It was clear that soon the truth would be out and chaos would ensue. The *DUSTEN* was currently holding several hundred rebel prisoners in a makeshift brig, while at headquarters a plan was in action to nab as many of the rebels operating on the ground as possible.

Word of the attack and movement of confederate troops must have spread quickly, because rebels initiated a raid on a separate hangar only minutes later and successfully seized eight patrol ships. At the same time, mutiny broke out on the frigate *TASSAGORA*, which had been stationed in orbit around Megelleon. It was also taken over by the rebels. The loyal crew were all forced into escape pods and ejected from the frigate, their pods floating to the planet surface. It was estimated that nearly 200 rebels on the ground escaped by crowding into the holds of the stolen patrol ships and nearly two dozen more were on the *TASSAGORA*. With the addition of the confederates that escaped from Megelleon, there would be enough manpower to fully man the frigate as well as the stolen patrol ships, resulting in a growing fleet of armed craft in the hands of the rebel forces. Things looked very dark, indeed; and still the FOI had no idea as to where the rebels were vanishing with each successive assault.

It was about mid-afternoon when Kala and I were in my office study, discussing matters related to the estate, the

TRITYTE and the *NEW ORLEANS*, when we heard quick footsteps nearing the study. Suddenly the door opened – no knock – and Kala's assistant marched in at a near run right past Kala and me.

"Sorry to interrupt, but I think you both need to see what's happening." She gasped breathlessly and rushed to the vid screen. She stepped back with fear etched across her face as the screen activated.

Immediately we saw images of bodies strewn over the ground, along with the burning wreckage of several patrol ships. Troopers were scurrying amid the chaos and debris, as the commentator did her best to summarize the situation.

"…while Federation headquarters were attacked in an attempt to steal the solbidyum stores. We are being told that this is the second failed attempt to seize the heavily guarded solbidyum supply. An earlier attempt was kept quiet by the Federation, occurring only days after the arrival of the *TRITYTE* and solbidyum here on Megelleon. At this time it is unknown just how many troopers at the base have been injured or perhaps killed. Our sources inside the Federation headquarters tell us that the High Command became aware of this rebel group fairly recently and has been trying to quietly isolate its members before taking any overt action. The FOI has been aware of this group for some time, but believed them to be a benign organization, a subset of the BROTHERHOOD OF LIGHT, and gave them only a cursory review. We have gotten word that already a number of senators are calling for a formal Senate Inquiry to review the FOI and examine its inability to foresee and prevent this series of events.

"Hold on a minute. We're receiving a breaking news message from our associated reporter located on the

DUSTEN.   Cleainsta, can you hear me? You're live on planet-wide broadcast."

"Yes, Elige, I hear you.   This is Cleainsta reporting live from the *DUSTEN*, where moments ago fighting erupted near the bridge. It is not known with certainty at this time, but it is believed that the bridge has been taken – overrun by unknown assailants.   No one has been able to contact the bridge since the fighting started several minutes ago. There were earlier rumors of mutineers being held on the *DUSTEN* within the confines of its cargo holds, but there was no confirmation of this report until now. It appears that the detainees were part of an organized band of rebels, who have since escaped by some unknown means and have now gained control of the bridge and the forward hangar of the ship.   People on the observation deck behind me have reported seeing several patrol ships come into that hangar since then. It is believed that that these are more rebels that have arrived to –" The reporter was interrupted by a flurry of yelling voices.

"Wait a minute; the people back here are saying something... What? Elige, I am being told now that a frigate is approaching, and that there are a number of patrol ships leaving from the forward hangar of that ship to take up positions around the *DUSTEN*.   It looks like help has arrived.   Yes, the people behind me are saying that the frigate is the *TASSAGORA*. People are starting to chee...."

The screen suddenly went black, until Elige reappeared from his position on the Capitol grounds a few moments later.   "We seem to have lost contact with the *DUSTEN*, and it appears that communication was severed from that end. We didn't have an opportunity before losing communication to tell Cleainsta that the *TASSAGORA* had been captured by the rebels yesterday. It would appear now that the *DUSTEN* has also fallen into rebel hands. We can only pray that the nearly 10,000 people aboard her will be safe."

We sat quietly, watching the vid screen, silently horrified at the images we saw. The assistant had seated herself on a sofa and currently had her face buried in her hands, crying uncontrollably.

I felt Kala come to my side and put her arm around me, laying her head against my shoulder. "Oh, Tib, I hope the Captain is alright." While we watched further news reports, an incoming call cut in from the *NEW ORLEANS* and Lieutenant Commander Wanoll. The news images fell to the background as Wanoll filled the screen.

"Tibby, Major," I felt Kala straighten up next to me and listen, "I don't know if you have heard what is happening, but the *DUSTEN* has been taken by the rebels. Captain Maxette was able to get a message off to me just seconds before the bridge was taken. Commander Thimas is a member of the BROTHERHOOD OF LIGHT. He was never tested for loyalty. As first officer, the captain thought him to be safe and never pushed for him to be screened. Commander Thimas released the rebel prisoners from the cargo holds and coordinated the takeover of the ship. We don't know if the captain is alive at this time or not, but we suspect that he is. One thing is certain; if he *is* alive, he is most likely being held with other loyal troopers and officers that have been captured. Tibby, the last thing the captain was able to get out before the communication was cut short was to request your help. He said you and the *NEW ORLEANS* are the only hope the Federation has of stopping this rebellion." As Lieutenant Commander Wanoll spoke, a message began flashing on the screen that Admiral Regeny was trying to speak to us. "Hold on a minute, Lieutenant Commander, the admiral is trying to get through to us. Tell Captain Stonbersa to make the *NEW ORLEANS* ready, I will be coming up with about two hundred troopers and security shortly. I need to take this call from the admiral now. I'll get back to you later."

I switched the view to the admiral and no sooner established connection than he began speaking. "Tibby, have you heard? The Brotherhood has taken the *DUSTEN* and their forces are attacking in multiple locations at once here on Megelleon, as well."

"Yes Admiral, Lieutenant Commander Wanoll was just apprising me of the situation."

"The Lieutenant Commander is safe?" Regeny asked. "He's not aboard the *DUSTEN*?"

"No, sir, he's aboard the *NEW ORLEANS* and is quite safe. Captain Maxette was able to get a message to him just prior to the rebels breaching the bridge. Commander Thimas is a member of the BROTHERHOOD OF LIGHT. It was he who released the rebel prisoners and aided them in the takeover of the *DUSTEN*. They have since been joined by the other rebels and the *TASSAGORA.*"

"What the hell is going on?! Why are you getting this information before I am? Why in the blazes didn't Lieutenant Commander Wanoll contact me first? Hell man, you're not even Federation military and you've gotten info I haven't!" Regeny steamed.

"Lieutenant Commander Wanoll contacted me because Captain Maxette ordered him to do so. The Captain wanted the Lieutenant Commander to ask for my aid using the *NEW ORLEANS*," I answered.

"Harrumph," the Admiral steamed, "that at least makes sense. I was just contacting you to make the same request of you, along with all the men you have been training. You're the only ones we can count on. It has become clear that even my own staff has been infiltrated with traitors."

"I have one suggestion for you, Admiral," I interjected. "I would strongly recommend that you also come aboard the *NEW ORLEANS*. It's the most secure ship in the galaxy and the only one where everyone has been double-screened and cleared. Right now you don't know who around you can be trusted or even if you're secure in your own compound. You can run your operations from the *NEW ORLEANS* in safety and get up close and personal with the enemy, as well, if you catch my meaning."

"Hmmm," Regeny exhaled loudly, clearly overwhelmed by the recent events. "You have a good point there. I'd not thought about that, but I'll need some of my senior staff officers with me."

"Not a problem, Admiral," I said. "Just as long as everyone is aware that you will each be required undergo a mental screening when boarding the *NEW ORLEANS* – no exceptions."

"Everyone? Including me?" The admiral squawked.

"Yes, sir, even you," I responded earnestly. "No one – and I mean *no one* – boards the *NEW ORLEANS* until they've passed a thorough screening conducted personally by Major Kalana."

Admiral Regeny grinned, a twisted grin and said, "You're a tough piece o' meat, Tibby, a *smart*, tough piece o' meat… and I like the way you think. I agree. I'll get my officers and depart for the *NEW ORLEANS* immediately."

"Admiral, I would prefer that you fly here to the estate first, so Kala can screen you and your men here. I would like, for a number of reasons, to dock your ship on the *NEW ORLEANS*, but it'll have to drop its RMFF shield for you to get through. So we need to be absolutely certain that everyone on your ship is loyal, because I don't want us getting blown apart and scattered in pieces across space by a hidden traitor on your ship when we drop our shields."

"Agreed. We'll be at your estate in about an hour.

After talking to the admiral, I sent word to Marranalis to get all our security people and all the Federation troops at the estate quickly armed and standing ready at the hangar area for transfer to the *NEW ORLEANS*. He had already heard about the events on the news and didn't ask any questions. Pulling all the security and troops from the estate was clearly going to leave it vulnerable to attack; but I didn't think the rebels would try that tactic, as there was nothing on the grounds that they wanted.

I made a quick call to Cantolla and told them to pack whatever equipment they had and get it to the hangar area immediately; we were moving to the *NEW ORLEANS*. I was shocked when I arrived at the hangar area to find that the scientists were the first ones there. Cantolla, Dakko and Rivez all balked when they were told they would have to undergo screening before being cleared to go to the *NEW ORLEANS*; but when faced with the alternative of staying on the surface and facing a possible attack, they relented and submitted to the process.

The admiral and his staff, along with an entourage of troopers, arrived shortly after in a corvette called the *NIGHTBRIDGE*. I had not seen a corvette airship before. A corvette is smaller than a frigate, but larger than a patrol ship. At the time I didn't know what it was, until Marranalis explained it. Fortunately the hangar on the *NEW ORLEANS* was a large one, certainly big enough to hold the corvette and all the patrol ships we had assembled at the estate. Kala quickly screened all those who had not previously been screened. Ten patrol ships, the corvette and a small cargo ship all took flight in a rather sloppy formation and proceeded in the direction of the *NEW ORLEANS*.

Upon arrival, Admiral Regeny and his staff were quickly provided with accommodations more than adequate to meet their needs and a full crew that was trained to deal with the demands of an active environment; so the transition of High Command's operations to the *NEW ORLEANS* went relatively smoothly. Plenty of supplies were aboard and, with ample availability of synthesizers and beverage dispensers, we had sufficient food and other resources to maintain for the long term. One of the larger of the ship's conference rooms near the bridge was selected to serve as the war room. Galetils must have envisioned running some of his businesses from the ship, because many smaller rooms, suitable for use as private offices, were position around the perimeter of the conference room. The admiral was so pleased with the arrangements that I feared, when the time came, I was going to have a hard time getting him off the ship. We were just getting settled in for a meeting in the conference room, when an urgent message came in for Admiral Regeny. "Put it on the screen," Regeny ordered.

A rather disheveled looking major appeared on the screen. In the background was smoke and debris. "Admiral!" The major initiated communication without waiting for acknowledgement from the Admiral, which was a breach of protocol. "Thank the stars you are safe! The headquarters here at the base have been attacked. Your personal office and those of your aides were completely destroyed. A rather large raiding party hit the complex. They breached the vaults and got into the last one where the solbidyum was stored. Sir, it's gone. The solbidyum is gone! I fear the rebels have it!" The major was practically hysterical at this point and kept running his fingers through his disheveled hair. His eyes appeared bloodshot, like he hadn't slept in days or perhaps he had been crying moments before the communication.

"The solbidyum is gone you say? That *is* serious news," Admiral Regeny said just a bit too calmly over something so valuable to the Federation. He seemed only mildly interested, but let the major continue. "Yes sir, it looks like the rebels have it."

"And I'm assuming that the media has already been there and have filed their reports saying just that?" the admiral questioned.

"Yes, sir, I'm afraid they have. The news reports state that you and your staff are presumed to be dead and the solbidyum is gone."

"What's the situation there with the troops – how may wounded and how many killed?" Regeny asked.

"Casualty reports are still coming in, but it looks like we took a pretty hard hit. My guess is that we lost about 30% of the defensive forces here and at least another 20% are injured; so we have only about 50% fit for action. The rebels also got away with about a dozen more ships," the major replied.

"What's the situation at the Capitol? Are the leaders alright?"

"Yes, both are safe; but Leader Turaine is heading off world to Teahkins, in hopes of soothing the situation there. In case of another attack, the two leaders will be separated so they cannot both be killed. Both leaders sent word for you and the High Command to do as you see best, assuming that you had survived the attack.

"Alright, Major, get things back into shape there, we need fully functional intact units. Move people about, if you have to; but I need as many fully active units as we can get. So far as I know, all the action has been here at the main Federation base. None of the bases elsewhere on Megelleon have seen anything like this, nor have bases on the other planets suffered any hits so far that we know of. I'll personally contact them and order reinforcements to be sent to Megelleon immediately. Unfortunately, none of our other starships or frigates are in the immediate area; so it will be days before we can expect their support.

"I need to tell the other bases to only send troopers that have been given psychological scans a second time. I then want you to conduct another test upon their arrival. We'll also have the test facilitators scanned by three sources and have vetted observers scrutinizing every test. We need to seal up these leaks in security immediately."

"Yes, sir, but what about the solbidyum?!" the major exclaimed.

"Let me worry about the solbidyum; right now you have your orders," and with that the admiral, ended the transmission.

Everyone in the room was rather quiet and just a bit more as ease than I would have expected under these dire conditions. I could see that Kala was also totally mystified by their casual appearance. Her mouth was practically hanging open.

The admiral turned to me. "Tibby I want to thank you. If you hadn't suggested that we move our headquarters here to the *NEW ORLEANS*, every one of us would probably be dead by now. That was quick thinking on your part. We're going to have to prepare a statement for the news.

Lieutenant Commander Wabussie, could you see to having the Federation logo plaque removed from the staff room on the *NIGHTBRIDGE* and brought here.   I think this conference room provides an image of power and control that will help dispel many of the doubts and fears the public may have right now. We will display the Federation symbol prominently behind us to give the appearance of operating from some official headquarters rather than hiding in a bunker someplace."

"Yes, sir," Wabussie said as he left the room.

"One thing concerns me," I said. "The FOI doesn't seem to be supplying you with any sound information. Have you considered the possibility that the FOI has been compromised with individuals from the Brotherhood? Have any of the FOI people been tested?"

"Good question, Tibby," the admiral said. "I've been asking myself the same thing.   I don't like the conclusions I seem to repeatedly be reaching, that's for sure. For now I think it best that we leave the FOI out of the loop and assume they're compromised.

"Major Kalana, you seem to be concerned. What's troubling you?" Regeny asked.

Kala shook her head slightly as though to clear her thoughts and said, "Well, sir, it just that no one here seems to be concerned about the missing solbidyum. Shouldn't we be taking action to recover it?"

"Who said the solbidyum was missing?" Regeny asked.

"The Major at the base said... and you... well, you never did say much, now that I think of it." Kala responded. "Just *where is* the solbidyum, Admiral?"

"Why don't you ask Tibby? I think he's already figured out the answer to that question," Regeny replied with a slight grin.

Kala turned to me questioningly, eyebrows furrowed into a frown.

"It's here, Kala," I said soothingly, "on the *NIGHTBRIDGE* in the hangar. It will only be there until they can safely transfer it into a hold here on the *NEW ORLEANS*. This is the safest and most logical place to keep it."

"Right you are, Tibby," Admiral Regeny said. "When I heard about the *DUSTEN*'s fall and the series of attacks on Federation headquarters, I knew it was only a matter of time before the vaults would be penetrated and the solbidyum seized. It was obvious that there was little time remaining; and when Tibby offered the *NEW ORLEANS* as a safe base of operations for me and my staff, it dawned on me that this was also the safest place to hide the solbidyum. Right now the rebels have no idea where we are or where the solbidyum is. The longer we keep it that way, the more control we will have over the situation. And..." the Admiral continued with a deep sigh of deliberation, "...it buys us time to figure out what we're going to do to rescue the *DUSTEN*. The Brotherhood must know that we left headquarters in the *NIGHTBRIDGE* by now; but they'll have no idea where the *NIGHTBRIDGE* is. We're in hiding just like they are; but sooner or later, they will figure out that we're hiding in the *NEW ORLEANS*... and they *will* come for us. Luckily, this ship can outrun them and, from what Captain Maxette and Lieutenant Commander Wanoll have told me, the *NEW ORLEANS* is equipped with a working RMFF, rendering her impenetrable. They may be able to find us but they can't get in."

"Actually, sir," I cleared my throat as I began, "they may not be able to find us, either, even if we stay right here."

"I don't understand," Regeny retorted.

"We discovered that, when the RMFF was in use, our nav system didn't function. Kerabac believed this to be due to the warp of the magnetic field; so, as a possible solution, he tried using an optical navigation system – not as powerful, but adequate for short-range navigation. In the process of experimenting with his idea, he accidently discovered that, if an energy beam of a certain frequency is directed from the ship to the inside perimeter of the RMFF, the ship becomes cloaked – completely invisible. We've set up a control system that is keyed to senior crew members only, so the system can't be activated or deactivated by anyone but a senior officer of the *NEW ORLEANS*. Even if the ship were captured, an invading force would not be able to operate it, even if they knew what all it can do. The same holds true for the RMFF." Every member of Regeny's staff was now sitting forward in their chairs with looks of total amazement on their faces.

"But what of radar and other sensors, won't they still see the *NEW ORLEANS* other signatures?" Regeny asked.

"No, sir, the RMFF prevents that as well," I said. "In every way that they would observe, we simply would not be there."

"Impressive," Admiral Regeny said. "This certainly puts an entirely new perspective on things. We can sneak right up to the *DUSTEN*, and, and…."

"Yes, and what? An attack on the *DUSTEN* is not possible, yet, sir. There are too many innocent lives aboard that ship. More thought must go into a rescue plan," I insisted. "We can't fire on a ship that has 10,000 innocent people aboard. Beyond that, you can't leave this ship to get over there because we'd have to drop the RMFF to do so – and they would blow us to bits if we did. We could take out the patrol ships and the *TASSAGORA,* but how much would that accomplish? They would still have their main stronghold on the *DUSTEN* and would still be holding thousands of hostages."

"It seems like you have already given this some thought, Tibby, so what would you advise for an effective course of action?"

"First you make your announcement to the people of the Federation, confirming that you and the High Command are all safe. Inform them that your security team learned of the imminent attack shortly before it happened and that you and the High Command moved to a secured secret command center. Mention that, upon receiving intelligence of the imminent attacks, you also saw fit to relocate the solbidyum. None of this is a lie; but if you say it right, it will look as though you have counterintelligence sources in place that give you control of the situation. We must continue to give off the image that the Federation still has the upper hand. Once you have done that, I suggest we remain cloaked for protection and move into a position where we can view the *DUSTEN* and the *TASSAGORA* and monitor the movements of the surrounding patrol ships. I believe that, if we are patient, the rebels will unknowingly lead us to their headquarters. Because we are able to follow these ships without their knowledge, we can quickly and invisibly destroy their base. This scenario will automatically cause them to arrive at the conclusion that they have at least one Federation counterspy within the Brotherhood.

So, we have to force their hand and get them to lead us to the base. I suspect that will happen when the rebels see your initial broadcast. They will immediately suspect that the Federation has successfully planted spies in their midst, so they will be forced to turn their focus on themselves and begin a witch hunt to root out the perceived Federation infiltrators.   In the meantime, they will cease using their standard communications for fear that the Federation is monitoring them somehow; so they will subsequently begin using a shuttle or patrol ship to carry messages to and from their headquarters.   Once we find their headquarters, we destroy both the message ship and the base, make a vid of it, and broadcast it on the news with an announcement that Federation spies infiltrated the Brotherhood and successfully located their base, which has since been destroyed.   That should solidify a distrust among their own ranks; and some may even defect, hoping to get a reprieve by bargaining information for freedom or for their lives.   Once the Brotherhood's command is out of commission, we will move on the *DUSTEN* and the ships around it.

"Damn, Tibby, I think I should just retire and let you run the Federation military.   All right everyone, you heard what he said, let's make it happen!"

While the High Command and the admiral prepared his broadcast, Kala and I went looking for Lunnie and Reidecor on the *TRITYTE*.   I was taken aback when I found the *TRITYTE* dark and dead – no power at all.   Plus the cable used to power the RMFF from the *TRITYTE* was missing. Just as I was starting to panic, Lunnie and Reidecor came strolling toward the ship with their arms about each other.

"Hey, Tibby, sis, how you two doing?" Lunnie said smiling.

"What happened to the power on the *TRITYTE*?" I asked, choosing to ignore Lunnie's question.

"Oh, that?   You said to look into removing the solbidyum reactor from the *TRITYTE*, so after I found the reactor plans in the ship's computer and built one, I installed it in a hidden compartment, like you said.   Tibby, you couldn't find it if you had the whole crew searching for it. Anyway, I needed to test it; so, while we were in orbit over the estate, I moved the core into the new reactor and gave it a whirl.   It works like a charm.   But I've not had a chance to move it back, because of all the action that broke out shortly thereafter."

"So right now, as we speak, the RMFF is running off the new reactor you installed and not off the *TRITYTE*?"   I asked in amazement.

"Yep, guess you could say that."

"Lunnie, were I not madly in love with your sister, I would kiss you right now!"   I burst out in pure amazement, as I embraced her in a tight, almost bone-crushing hug. Then I felt my cheeks quickly turn red as the others laughed, and I quickly freed my grip and stepped back.

"Go ahead and kiss her, Tibby.   Maybe that will shut her up for a while," said Kala through a broad smile.   "I don't think you kissing her on this occasion counts for anything but a reward for a job well done."

So I took Lunnie in my arms and gave her a huge kiss.   When I stepped back, she said, "WOW, sis, you said he was a good kisser, but I didn't think he could be *this* good!   Say, does this mean that I can come and sleep with the two of you now?" to which Kala, Reidecor and I said in unison, "NO!"

"So just where is the reactor?" I asked Lunnie.

"Follow me," she said as she led us away from the hangar and down a short corridor to a small, inconspicuous looking storage room that had some pipes running through it and a pump sitting on the floor. "Here you are," she said.

"Where?" Kala and I asked in unison.

"You said you wanted it hidden, well there it is," as she pointed to the pump.

"You've got to be kidding," I said. "That's the reactor?"

With a huge satisfied grin on her face, Lunnie said, "Yeah! Pretty neat, isn't it? Hidden in plain sight. No one would ever think it was a reactor."

"What about radiation, heat, and all that stuff?" I asked.

"It doesn't work that way, Tibby," Lunnie said. "The reactor produces pure electricity. The cables are fed through the pipes, so they're concealed as well, and the reactor is actually inside the pump. I don't think anyone in a million years would suspect it of being a reactor."

"That's great, Lunnie" I said, "but what are we going to do with the *TRITYTE*? Now it's left with no power."

"Well, you said you wanted to use it as a museum piece and take it about the galaxy for people to see and touch." Lunnie said.

"You said that?" Kala looked at me with pleasant surprise.

"Lunnie, you weren't supposed to tell anyone about that," I said.

"I'm *not* telling anyone.   Kala and Reidecor don't count; they're family," Lunnie retorted.

I threw my hands up in exasperation, "Lunnie, when I say *no one*, I mean *no one!*"

I then turned toward Kala to make my confession. "Yes, I said that, Kala. When I saw how Captain Stonbersa reacted so passionately upon seeing the *TRITYTE*, I realized that this ship is something everyone in the Federation should be given a chance to see and touch. We obviously we can't allow that with a functioning solbidyum reactor in it; so I decided to have Lunnie move the reactor, or at least the solbidyum, into the *NEW ORLEANS*, so we could at some point in the future load the *TRITYTE* into a freighter and turn it into a flying museum. We can take it on tour around the Federation, so everyone has a chance to see the real thing at no cost."

"Tib, you are a wonderful guy, you really are." Kala said and hugged and kissed me.

"Okay," I said, "but now how do we get the *TRITYTE* out of here when we want or need to?"

"No problem, Tib," Lunnie said, "I can connect a small fusion battery into the ship that will provide sufficient power to operate and fly properly. It won't power the guns or anything, but it will fly – sub-light only…and no gravity wave."

I laughed. "Okay Lunnie, you did an amazing job. But get that battery hooked in to this thing as soon as possible. I don't want anyone knowing the solbidyum has been removed from the *TRITYTE* just yet. It may play out to our advantage for people to keep thinking the *TRITYTE* is fully functional.

"One more thing, I want you to find some empty cubby hole or recess big enough for the container of solbidyum that was on the *TRITYTE*. The admiral brought it with him and we need to hide it here for a bit. After securing it, I want the space plated over and painted to match the wall so no one, except us, will know where it is. If the *NEW ORLEANS* should get taken, they will not only be completely unaware that it's here, but they will also not find it by accident either. But please, keep it quiet... PLEASE!"

We all headed to the conference room and arrived just in time to see Admiral Regeny start his speech on the vid screen to the people of the Federation. The admiral's officers flanked his position at a podium and behind him on the elegant wood-paneled wall was displayed the Federation logo. While we were in the hangar, the room had also been rearranged to appear like that of an operational government facility.

"Greetings, people of the Federation territories, dignitaries and senators. I speak to you now from a highly secured Federation command facility to address the unfortunate events that unfolded earlier today. As most of you know by this time, the Federation military headquarters building was attack by mutinous factions in the Federation military, members of a group known as the BROTHERHOOD OF LIGHT. Rumors and news reports spread quickly that the High Command was taken out by the assault on the building and that the solbidyum stored there was seized by the raiders. Both of these accounts are false. Though the assaults have resulted in numerous casualties, you can see before you that none of the High Command were killed or injured.

"Moments before the attack took place we received word from a spy positioned within the raider's camp, warning of the imminent attack. Realizing that there was no time to fortify sufficiently against the level of attack aimed at our existing location, the High Command elected to move to a more secure secret site, where we can prepare and direct the assault against the traitors that have taken over the *DUSTEN* and the *TASSAGORA*.

"Today's attack on Federation headquarters was the third such attempt to steal the solbidyum. Recognizing that this unrelenting threat may eventually succeed in breaching the secured storage area, the High Command moved the entire supply to a secure and highly secret location. Let me assure you – not one grain of solbidyum has fallen into enemy hands. Our spies are working within the raider's camp as we speak; and we are receiving a reliable stream of information that will soon make it possible to end this nightmare that is blighting the Federation.

"We ask that you please be patient while this matter is resolved. If you have any information that is of use to the Federation's efforts, you may contact Federation headquarters, where we have re-established normal operating conditions.   Let me repeat, the rumors of death of *any* officers in the Federation High Command are false. You can see us all here – well and intact. Furthermore, rumors that the solbidyum has fallen into the hands of the raiders are also false. The solbidyum is secured safely in a new location and has been for some time. Rest assured that shipments to your planets will begin at the earliest and safest opportunity.

"Thank you."

With that the admiral's broadcast was terminated.

After activating the cloaking and RMFF shield, Kerabac and Captain Stonbersa maneuvered the *NEW ORLEANS* into a position near the *DUSTEN* and the *TASSAGORA* that allowed us to monitor all ships coming and going in the area. It wasn't long thereafter that we saw a small ship break away from the *TASSAGORA* and head for the planet's surface. We followed undetected, as the craft moved toward one of the planet's two expansive oceans and then suddenly dove into the water and vanished.

Admiral Regeny was on the bridge with several of his officers as this development unfolded. He exclaimed in amazement, "No wonder we couldn't find their base; they're hiding under water!"

Stonbersa said, "If memory serves me correctly, Admiral, back when Megelleon was patrolled by naval forces, there was an underwater submarine facility around this area. You don't think they may be using that as their headquarters, do you?"

Admiral Regeny didn't actually respond to his question, but he followed the captain's train of thought. "Captain Stonbersa, does the *NEW ORLEANS* have access to the Federation computers on Megelleon?"

"I'm afraid not," Stonbersa responded. "This is strictly a civilian ship; we don't have authorization codes to access the military databases."

"But your computers and communication gear are of the highest caliber and *could* successfully gain access, if the codes were available, I'm assuming...?" the admiral inquired.

"I believe so," Stonbersa replied.

"Wabussie, get the communications officer here immediately and provide them with the codes necessary for Priority One level access to all Federation computers and databases. We need some information from the archives," ordered Admiral Regeny, as he eyed the ocean's surface on the vid screen.

It took no more than fifteen minutes to secure the required connections and then another thirty minutes to searching the archives. An index was located, showing that a computer file and related data existed for the suboceanic base; however, when trying to access the file via the indicated path, the information was nowhere to be found. The admiral sunk back in his chair. "It looks like they've covered their tracks. We have no way of locating that base now."

"Don't be too sure, Admiral," I said. "Was the base location top secret at the time of its operation?"

Stonbersa spoke up. "I'm pretty sure it wasn't. I remember seeing vids about it when I was a teen. It fascinated me that they had developed this entire facility completely under water. As I remember, it was huge."

"Try referencing it through media archives – maybe press releases and such," I suggested. Once again, the media index was located but the applicable files were missing.

"It's useless," Regeny said. "They have removed any data pointing to its location."

"They had to have missed something." I thought for a moment. "I noticed some ships and other sailing craft down there. I'm willing to bet there are navigation maps that once showed this part of the ocean as a restricted area. See if you can find some old maps of that era – say, about ten years after the base was built. I have no doubt that every civilian map of that period indicates the area as off limits to civilian craft. There's no way that the Brotherhood could have sanitized every one of those records."

Once again, Lieutenant Commander Wabussie, assisted by Kerabac, sifted through the database and, minutes later, produced two navigation charts. One showed the area surrounding the base as restricted waters; the other not only showed the outline of the restricted area, but also the outline of the base and the submarine pens. The pens were clearly large enough to house patrol ships and possibly the *TASSAGORA*, as well.

"Looks like we found them, Tibby," the admiral beamed. "Would you like to do the honors of blowing them out of the water?" he asked, indicating the fire control panel.

"No, sir," I replied. "Captain Stonbersa is the commanding officer on this ship. The duty and honor should be first and foremost his own."

"Quite right, Tibby. I forget – this is *not* a Federation ship, nor am I in charge here. Captain Stonbersa, if you please." Again, the admiral gestured towards the control panel.

Stonbersa beamed. I could tell that he was extremely touched and honored. Up until this point he had been largely a bystander in all that was happening. Now he was going to be the one that fired the first shot in retaliation against a relentless enemy.

"The RMFF shield is going to amplify the power of this shot. I'm going to be using a GW plasma torpedo. Thankfully, there are no ships in the area, nor are there any nearby coastal villages at risk by the potential tidal wave that this shot may generate. Say goodbye to one rebel base." He targeted the base with the coordinates indicated on the map and pressed the fire button.

There was no delay. One second we were looking at the shining blue of the water and the next second our view of the entire ocean was obscured by a huge fireball and flash of light. When we regained a clear view of the area, we were looking at a gigantic water plume, a mushroom cloud of steam that reminded me of the films of atomic tests conducted in the Pacific Ocean that I had seen as a kid. This cloud, however, had to have been four times larger. Mammoth concentric waves of water spread outward in circles from the blast area. It very quickly became obvious that the impact of these waves at the coastlines would be more dramatic than we anticipated.

"What was that?!" Regeny exclaimed in amazement. "Did they have a huge underwater arsenal down there?"

"No, sir, I don't think so" I answered. "The RMFF shield seems to intensify anything we send through it – laser beam, GW torpedo, or probably anything else we direct into the shield from the inside. The result is some kind of exponential increase in kinetic energy or intensity of the weapon as it emerges on the outside edge of the field. I think what we just witnessed was the effect of the amplified impact. It's possible the torpedo itself never even exploded. We had a similar thing happen when we were encountered by three patrol ships at Nibaria. We directed a weak laser at one of the ships that should barely have grazed her hull, yet the ship was practically vaporized on impact."

We waited around for a couple of hours with our ship still cloaked, but nothing came up out of the water other than debris that could be seen floating on the surface, indicating that something had indeed been down there. Whatever it was, it wasn't there anymore.

"Did we get all that recorded?" Regeny asked. "I want an edited 20-second vid showing the patrol ship entering the water, our air strike and the explosion, and the rising debris floating on the surface. Nice shooting Captain Stonbersa. I'm glad to see that, while you no longer wear a Federation uniform, you're still a Federation man. Now, can you take us back to the vicinity of the *TASSAGORA* and the *DUSTEN*, please?"

"Admiral," Kerabac interrupted, "there is broadcast across all bandwidths from the *DUSTEN*. Would you like me to put it on the screen?"

"Yes, let's see what they have to say. I doubt they know about the destruction of their base yet."

The vid screen display shifted to the image of Commander Thimas standing on the bridge of the *DUSTEN*. Instead of his Federation uniform, he now wore a black uniform of similar cut with one white stripe about his chest and a white collar. Beside Commander Thimas stood Corporal Lexmal, also in a black uniform, but distinguished with two stripes.

"This is Captain Thimas of the BROTHERHOOD OF LIGHT aboard the ship *DUSTEN*," he announced. "The Federation is falling and our forces are here to bring the people of the galactic communities under the banner of our Brotherhood and bring new prosperity to those who follow us. Those who chose to resist or oppose us will find themselves cut off from all commerce, resources, and avenues of trade controlled by the worlds of the Brotherhood.

"Earlier today you saw and heard the Admiral Regeny claim that the Federation has spies within the

Brotherhood and that they were about to take action against us. This is a lie and will prove itself to be so.

"The starship *DUSTEN* and the frigate *TASSAGORA*, along with one small corvette, the *NIGHTBRIDGE*, are the only warships in this sector of the galaxy; and both the *DUSTEN* and *TASSAGORA* are now under Brotherhood control. Of the several hundred patrol ships in this sector, the Brotherhood now has over half of those under its control, leaving the Federation with next to nothing to stand against us. They cannot amass ships from other sectors to help them fast enough to stop us and, even if they did, there are members of our Brotherhood spread throughout the fleet in all sectors.

"We are calling for the Federation officers to stand down and surrender immediately. If they concede, their lives will be spared. We also demand that the Federation surrender the entire shipment of solbidyum, so that it may be used for the fortification and glory of the Brotherhood. If they fail to do so, the consequences will be swift and severe. The Federation has one hour to respond." The screen then went blank.

I looked at Admiral Regeny as he sat in the captain's chair, lips pursed and rubbing his chin. "Looks like they are calling our bluff. What would you do, Tibby?"

"As much as I would hate to lose one of my ships, Admiral, I would blow *TASSAGORA* out of the sky… and maybe even a few dozen patrol ships, too. We know there are only rebels on those patrol ships and that they removed all loyal Federation personnel to a detaining area when they took the *TASSAGORA*. I suggest you prepare and record your response beforehand. We can add the vid clips to the broadcast. Let the Brotherhood see that they are not as powerful as they think. I hate to see people die, Admiral, but

I would also hate to see tyrants come to power and take even more lives."

Admiral Regeny sighed and began to rise from the chair slowly. "You're right, Tibby, it's not an easy decision, but it's what I think we must resolve ourselves to act upon. Captain Stonbersa, can this ship fire both GW wave torpedoes and lasers at the same time?"

"We've never tried it, but I don't see why not," replied Captain Stonbersa.   "We can lock onto the coordinates of several small patrol ships with the lasers and the frigate with a GW torpedo. Having seen what happens when we fire through the shields, I expect there will be nothing left afterward but dust. How many patrol ships do you want us to target?"

The admiral looked at me and I shrugged my shoulders. "Your call."

He sighed again and said, "Make it swift, and target as many as you can. Just don't shoot the *DUSTEN*."

Captain Stonbersa brought the *NEW ORLEANS* around to a position where he could get a clear shot at the *TASSAGORA* as well as the patrol ships in the space between the *TASSAGORA* and the *DUSTEN*.   He and the crew entered the relative coordinates and a sequence of commands that enabled the computer to do all the firing with the single push of a button. Wisely, Captain Stonbersa programmed the weapons to fire with a delay of milliseconds between shots, as there was no telling what might happen if so much power were to be drawn from the solbidyum reactor or through the circuitry and switchgear all at once. Even in series the effect the rapid fire was an unknown factor; but by sequencing the shots, the risk was at least lowered. If all went as planned, in the blink of an eye most of the ships captured by the Brotherhood would be gone, leaving only the *DUSTEN* and a handful of patrol ships behind. Of course there were more patrol ships inside the *DUSTEN* – hundreds in fact – but there wouldn't be enough Brotherhood rebels left to fly them and also to guard the thousands of hostages. We were pretty sure they were stretched to the max with their forces inside the *DUSTEN*. We also doubted that any of them would want to come out after seeing the carnage that we were about to unleash upon them.

I had to grin once everything was in place. At Captain Stonbersa's announcement the Admiral and the officers returned to the bridge to witness the destruction of most of the Brotherhood fleet. Regeny had taken his seat in the captain's chair again; only this time Captain Stonbersa walked over and said, "Excuse me, Admiral, but I believe you are sitting in my chair."

The startled look on the admiral's face was one I will never forget. He froze for a moment and then laughed as he said, "Quite right, Captain, I apologize. I forgot again for a moment where I am," and stood up to allow Stonbersa his rightful chair.

At the weapons station stood Marranalis at the ready. By my side stood Kala, pale with anticipation, as we all watched intently.

Captain Stonbersa began the maneuver. "Kerabac, as soon as we fire, I want you to move the ship around to the other side the *DUSTEN* as quickly as you can without hitting anything. We don't want to allow any remaining ships to have even a moment to figure out that a cloaked ship is responsible and calculate any triangulations that reveal our position.

"Sergeant Marranalis, on my mark...." A heavy paused that filled the room. "FIRE!"

All at once the screen lit up in a blaze of fireworks as ships exploded in an inferno of flying shrapnel and burning vapor. We only had a few seconds to glance through the decimation, as Kerabac skillfully and swiftly negotiated the NEW ORLEANS through the debris to the other side the *DUSTEN*. Seconds later we saw shots fired from the *DUSTEN* in the direction of our former location. As anticipated by Captain Stonbersa, the *DUSTEN* had quickly triangulated the origin of the shots. We would not have been harmed had we stayed there, but the ship's shield would have been revealed as each strike dissipated in the webs of visible energy that would play around the RMFF shield. As it was, panic must have gripped the rebel forces at the sight of the mayhem before them. An invisible assailant had vanquished nearly all their ships in the blink of an eye... and retaliation was impossible.

"I think it's about time for our recorded broadcast," said the admiral, as he rubbed his hands together. Lieutenant Commander Wabussie worked quickly to edit and paste clips of this destruction into the Admiral's speech, along with clips from the annihilation of the Brotherhood's suboceanic base. Finally he turned to the admiral and said, "Sir, it's ready."

The admiral nodded for Lieutenant Commander Wabussie to cut into the interplanetary vid feed and begin playing the recorded broadcast, which would be received both on the planet and on the *DUSTEN*.

"People of the Federation territories and non-aligned systems, about an hour ago you heard the words of a villainous traitor of the Federation, Commander Thimas, who now calls himself Captain Thimas of the

BROTHERHOOD OF LIGHT. This Brotherhood, which has never built or produced anything and which has taken by force and violence the ships they now use in threats against you, are holding more than 1,000 Federation citizens as hostages for a ransom of all the solbidyum that is currently stored under the protection of Federation forces – a priceless resource that shall define the future stability and prosperity of every global community and one that is the rightful property of every citizen and planet that abides in peace within the membership of the Federation.

"The traitor, Commander Thimas, told you that the Brotherhood has prevailed and that they now possess all the firepower and strength and that we, the High Command of the Federation are liars and that we have no teeth left in our bite. At the time that the traitor Commander Thimas was making his announcement, he had no way of knowing that we had already attacked and destroyed the Brotherhood's underwater base in Megelleon's Western Ocean. We do not believe that he will see reinforcements responding from this base now or ever again."

Scenes of the strike at the ocean base played on the vid screen as the admiral's speech continued. "Just moments ago we delivered our answer to the evil traitor, Commander Thimas, in the form of the destruction of the *TASSAGORA*, as well as a major portion of the ships commandeered by the Brotherhood earlier today."

Scenes of the widespread destruction around the perimeter of the *DUSTEN* played out in slow motion on the vid screen. Even so, the images of each explosion unfolded in such rapid succession that it was hard to comprehend the speed at which so many ships met their end.

"In the event that the evil traitor, Commander Thimas, does not understand our answer, the answer is this:

We shall not be held to ransom and we shall not turn over to the Brotherhood so much as one grain of solbidyum. We are willing to discuss terms of surrender with the members of the Brotherhood, should they so desire to do so; but the Brotherhood is gravely mistaken, if they think the Federation is weak and unable to stand against them. The destruction you have witnessed against the Brotherhood only represents a small portion of the damage we are capable of inflicting. It is obvious that the Brotherhood's arrogance and belief of superiority is greatly misplaced.

People of the Federation, please be assured that the Federation still maintains power and that the traitors to the Federation will be brought to justice for their actions."

When the broadcast was over, the admiral said, "Doesn't anyone here ever eat? I'm starved." Everyone chuckled and Captain Stonbersa sent a message to the dining room to have a meal prepared. The admiral, his staff and many of the crew of the *NEW ORLEANS* that had participated in the events of the day all headed to the dining area in a roar of comments about the historic event that had just been witnessed. Members of *NEW ORLEANS* crew took over stations on the bridge under Reidecor's command while the rest of us dined.

As we ate, Kala asked me, "Tib, do you think the rebels will surrender?"

"No," I said. "They are too far into this now to surrender. If they do, most of them will be court-martialed and executed. If they are not executed, they'll have no chance of restored military service and will most certainly be imprisoned, after which they'll live out the rest of their lives in disgrace. If only out of desperation, they will still rather stay and fight for the slim chance that they might somehow win or escape, rather than face the alternative."

"It's all such a shame," Kala said with a heavy sadness in her voice. "I'm sure I know a lot of those people. Before the return of the solbidyum, they were my friends. When I was watching Commander Thimas on the vid earlier, I had a hard time thinking of him as the same man that the captain and I used to dine with on the *DUSTEN*. At one time I even considered him as a possible mate, though he never knew that."

"Really, you and the *evil traitor, Commander Thimas*?" I said, trying to do my best imitation of Admiral Regeny." Kala laughed and punched me on the arm.

Everyone had finished eating when a message came for the admiral from the bridge. It was Reidecor. "Sir, there is a new vid being broadcasted on the surface about the events of today; do you wish to see it on the vid screen in the dining room?"

"Yes, if you would please," Regeny responded.

The screen at the end of the table lit up and the image of Elige, the news correspondent, appeared on the screen in mid-sentence.

"…Federation had an hour to respond and, if they failed to do so, the consequences would be swift and severe. At the time, the rebels did not know that the Federation was taking action against their headquarters and, far from being the impotent group the rebels were claiming, the Federation backed up their earlier claims by blowing up the rebels' underwater base in the Western Ocean. The nature of the weapon used is unknown and of a magnitude that has our military experts thinking the Federation used some new secret weapon heretofore unknown to the public or that the rebel base had a huge stockpile of explosive materials that were detonated in the impact. The resulting tidal waves spread to all the shores of the Western Ocean and many small coastal towns were flooded and buildings destroyed. We have heard that there are thousands of civilian deaths and numerous injuries, though the precise numbers are yet unknown. While we cannot speak to the necessity of the action against the rebel base, many are questioning whether it required the magnitude of force used in the strike.

"Just minutes after these events unfolded in the Western Ocean the Federation again struck, wiping out nearly all of the rebels' captured fleet, save for the *DUSTEN*, which has close to ten thousand civilians and dignitaries aboard. Admiral Regeny offered the traitors an opportunity to surrender, but so far there has been no response from the rebels on the *DUSTEN*. At this time no information is available as to what ship or ships the Federation used in their actions against the rebels. Experts are mystified, as it was believed that all the Federation ships capable of assisting in this standoff are out of system and unable to respond to Megelleon for some weeks. Whatever the Federation is using in their defense against the confederate violence, they have demonstrated to the rebels that they still have the ability and strength to dominate the situation."

"What have I done?" I asked in horror. "Thousands injured and dead!"

Kala put her arms around me, but I stiffened.

"Tibby, it had to be done," Admiral Regeny said. "Don't blame yourself, this is war. It's nearly impossible not to have civilian casualties. I approved the action. I could have stopped it and taken other actions."

"It was my plan, and because of me people have lost homes and lives. When this is over I will see to it that everyone who has lost a home will get a new one worth twice as much and more than just that. I can't give back the lives, but I sure can make it easier for those who survived!"

Kala took hold of my hand and said, "Tib, I know you will. If you would like I'll call the estate and get my assistants started on preparations right now."

"I really would appreciate that Kala, thank you," I said, as I felt myself drowning in visions of loss and decimation.

"Tibby, don't let this weigh you down. First of all, you had no way of knowing what the effect was going to be when the base was destroyed; and secondly, it simply had to be done." Kala tried to reassure me, but my heart ruled my head on this matter and I was inconsolable.

"She's right, Tibby," Regeny said, "and before this is over we may have to make a lot of other difficult decisions on which many lives may depend. That, unfortunately, is the nature of war."

Just then Cantolla came into the dining room. "Tibby I think I may have it," she said with a thinly veiled excitement, "but we will need you to go through all your movements one more time."

"This could not come at a worse time – or a better time, either, I guess. I'll be there as soon as I can. I have no idea where you are set up on the ship, though."

Kala said, "I know where they are, Tib, I'll take you there when you're ready to go."

"She has what?" Regeny asked, clearly taken off-guard by the cryptic exchange between Tibby and Cantolla.

"I'll explain later, Admiral; but will tell you now that if she is right, it might help answer the problem of how we are going to rescue the *DUSTEN*."

Just then Reidecor's voice came over the intercom in the dining room saying, "Another broadcast is coming from the *DUSTEN*." Immediately the screen went to a view on the bridge of the *DUSTEN*, where Commander Thimas was there with a visibly less cocky attitude and a rather desperate look on his face.

"It is regrettable that the Federation has chosen the foolish course of action that they have demonstrated today. Unfortunately, they are forcing the Brotherhood to resort to more painful actions in order to convince them that we are not afraid to engage drastic means to prove our resolve. I call your attention to this vid which is broadcasting live from one of the cargo airlocks of the *DUSTEN*."

A view of one of the smaller cargo airlock areas appeared on the screen. Within the hold were about one hundred people – some dignitaries, some troopers and others simply civilian occupants and guests traveling on the *DUSTEN*. As Commander Thimas continued to speak, the red lights on the cargo airlock doors began flashing, indicating that the doors were about to be opened. People began screaming and panicking.

"Every hour that the Federation delays in meeting our demands, one hundred citizens of the Federation will be placed it an airlock and jettisoned into space." People began choking and gasping, as the air in the compartment was sucked out. Then with a sudden *whoosh*, the doors opened and the mass of bodies were ejected into the vacuum of space.

"It is not the wish of the Brotherhood to be unduly cruel, but we will not hesitate to use whatever force and method is required to attain our goals. The puny acts of defiance demonstrated by the Federation in its attack on our base in the Western Ocean means nothing. It is but one of many bases we have located on planets throughout the galaxy; hence, the Federation would be wise to give up its futile attempts to stop us. Rather, they should be looking to meet my demands and to surrender fully to my authority. Many lives, including their own, can be spared, if they follow my demands. I have brought their ex-Captain Maxette here to the bridge, so everyone can see what will happen to each and every one of the Federation officers who continue to defy me." Captain Maxette appeared, dragged into view on the bridge. He was bloodied and bruised but still able to walk and stand erect. From somewhere off screen, Commander Thimas produced a pair of shears, which he displayed clearly to his audience before walking toward Captain Maxette. "Now, tell everyone, ex-Captain Maxette, who is the captain of the *DUSTEN*?"

Captain Maxette responded defiantly, "I am!"

Thimas struck the captain full in the face as the two guards restrained him. Thimas forcefully bent the captain's wrist so he could not close his hand and then placed the shears over the captain's little finger. "Now, EX-Captain Maxette, who is the captain of the DUSTEN?" With every bit of resolve Maxette had, he said, "I AM!" There was a crunching sound heard as the shears severed the Captain's finger and he cried out in pain. Onboard the *NEW ORLEANS* I could hear the officers gasp and the Admiral say in horror, "By the stars, the man is insane."

"Tisk, tisk, EX-Captain," mocked Commander Thimas. "I fear that wrong answers will get you nowhere and will only result in the loss of body parts." Then he turned back to face the vid screen and address his audience. "The tribulations you are witnessing here shall become the rewards of every Federation officer who defies me." Then, turning back to Captain Maxette, he placed another finger in the shears and repeated, "Now, who is the captain of the *DUSTEN*?"

"I am!" said Captain Maxette through clenched teeth.

Commander Thimas was heard to emit a loud and melodramatic sigh before another crunch was heard and the captain cried out in pain. Blood could be seen spurting away from Commander Thimas, who blocked the view of the captain's hand.

"I fear that like the Federation High Command, EX-Captain Maxette has not yet endured enough loss to recognize the futility of their resistance," said Commander Thimas in an increasingly maniacal tone, as he turned slowly toward the vid screen to reveal the blood that had gushed over the front of his black uniform and his hands.

"You have one hour to turn over the solbidyum container – *one hour*... or more people go out the hatch. I want it delivered in the *TRITYTE* – NO ONE on board. We will take control of the craft remotely and bring it aboard the *DUSTEN*. In the meantime we shall have to see if we cannot get EX-Captain Maxette to recognize who the captain of the *DUSTEN* really is." The vid screen went blank.

Kala was hanging on my arm, her face buried in my shirt as she sobbing silently and deeply. The officers of the High Command all appeared to be paralyzed with shock.

Admiral Regeny said, "The man's gone mad. Did you notice how he has switched from talking about the demands of the Brotherhood to *his* demands, *his* wants, *his* authority? We might have been able to negotiate with the Brotherhood, but how do you deal with a madman? Every life on the *DUSTEN* is at stake as long as he is there, to say nothing of what he could do to the Capitol building and Megelleon itself.   There is enough firepower on the *DUSTEN* to turn all of Megelleon into a ball of fire. What can we do?"

"What he said, Admiral," I answered. "We give him the *TRITYTE* and the solbidyum container."

"Have you gone insane too?!" the Admiral said looking at me in disbelief. "Do you not yet understand the magnitude of the threat to the Federation and all its citizens that this *nut* poses if he should successfully gain that much power – let alone the Brotherhood, whose full intentions are not known?!"

"I didn't say we would give him the solbidyum," I replied with a dead calm, "only the solbidyum *container*. That's all he asked for. As for the *TRITYTE*, the solbidyum in its reactor has already been removed and Corporal Luinella is installing a small fusion battery that will permit travel for short distances under impulse power, but not enough power to support GW or light speed and certainly not enough to operate the weapons. Actually, I'm not really thinking of giving him the solbidyum container, but an exact replica of it – with me and seven others tightly crammed into it. I seriously doubt that anyone aboard the *DUSTEN* has the codes to open the real container – and I suspect it will take some time before they try – so we will be safe inside. We would need a means of opening it from within. They will most likely leave the container in the hold of the *TRITYTE* for the time being. Thimas won't want anyone but himself getting too close to it, so he'll have the guards posted off ship, probably around its perimeter.

"Once we know we are aboard the *DUSTEN*, we'll wait until we think things are clear. Then we'll exit the container, overcome the guards and immediately open the hangar's hatch. The *NEW ORLEANS* will be close by, cloaked; but as soon as we open the doors, the troops here will have to move quickly with the patrol ships and transfer into the *DUSTEN* as soon as the RMFF shield is dropped. They will have a minute or less to make it happen. The *NEW ORLEANS* will be too close for the *DUSTEN* to fire on it, but I doubt they will see it. I suspect that Thimas is going to want to make a speech, so while he is gloating and drawing all eyes on himself, no one will see us moving. We can get a hundred men aboard and take out as many of the Brotherhood as possible, while Thimas is making his speech. Hopefully, if the loyal troopers over there are still alive, we can free them and regain control of the ship before Thimas finishes. Taking the bridge will be the hardest part. Is there any way to disconnect the fire controls for the bridge from elsewhere in the ship?"

"Not easily," answered one of Regeny's staff. "The system was designed with redundancy. As soon as you interfere with one control mechanism, they will know on the bridge, because it will set off an alarm. You would have to disengage all redundant circuits simultaneously – and there is no margin for error."

"In that case," I redirected myself to the captain, "Captain Stonbersa, I suggest you place the *NEW ORLEANS* in harm's way between the *DUSTEN* and the planet so that the RMFF shields will take the hits, in case Thimas decides to retaliate and exact his revenge on the planet."

"I understand, Tibby," said Captain Stonbersa grimly.

"Well, Admiral?" I asked.

"I can't think of anything better; and unless someone else can, I think we need to get moving on it right away," Regeny said.

"We only have one problem," I said sadly. "We can't do it in the allotted hour; we will need more time than that. What I'm saying is… I don't think there's any way we can keep Thimas from pushing more people out of the airlock."

"Let me work on that issue. You just do whatever it is you need to do," replied the admiral.

"Tib, are you sure about this, you could get killed," Kala said as the distress in her face gave way to pure fear.

"Kala, if I don't do this and more people get killed I won't be able to live with myself. Right now I'm having a difficult enough time trying deal with all the lives that were lost as a result of actions taken in the Western Ocean. If I do nothing now, all of the lives lost in the tidal waves will be meaningless deaths. I can't live with that."

Kala hung her head. "I understand, Tib. Do what you have to do."

I would remember the foreboding in Kala's voice for the rest of my life.

The first thing I did was track down Lunnie. She was just about to seal the solbidyum container in a wall compartment when I stopped her. "Hold up, Lunnie, I have another task for you. I need you to build me an exact replica of this container – at least a replicated exterior. It needs to have a device that looks like the locking mechanism on the real thing and I need it to have a real lock that can only be controlled from the inside."

Lunnie looked at me like I had lost my mind. "What are you planning now?" I told her as quickly as I could and asked how long it would take. Lunnie considered what would need to be done as she thought out loud. "We have the materials in the shop... and with the cutting machines we have... in all I would say about three hours, and that's working like hell to get it done in that timeframe," Lunnie answered.

"Lunnie," I held her by the shoulders and looked directly into her kind, fiery eyes, "every hour on the hour Thimas is going to push 100 people out of the airlock on the *DUSTEN*. He's already killed a hundred that way; and he's torturing Captain Maxette by slowly cutting off his fingers – and who knows what else since then. Do what you can, Lunnie, but we need it NOW!"

Lunnie responded that she would, as she pulled some kind of device out of her pocket and began scanning the solbidyum container and recording its measurements. While she was doing that, I called Kala to give me directions to Cantolla and her team. Kala told me it was in one of the gyms that I was familiar with on the ship; I met Kala there moments later.

As we entered, Cantolla and her staff were gathered around a table with the headband and some instruments. Cantolla turned and noticed us on our entry and said, "Tibby, I think we have it. We decided to increase the number of input and output leads in the headband so that information is coordinated and synchronized between the areas of the brain that store factual input and portions of the brain that control muscular functions. We've tested it using ourselves to upload and transfer other physical skills and it seems to be working. All we need to do now is have you record the signals again."

Dakko added excitedly, "Oh my, oh my yes, Tibby, most assuredly we have it this time," while Rivez in his less enthusiastic manner nodded his head and grinned.

"Let's get to it then. If this works, it couldn't have happened at a better moment," I answered.

Once again I had to run through all the movements and sequences I could think of and once again poor Marranalis was pitched about as a test subject. By this time he had been sent flying through the air so often he knew what was coming; and now he either landed on his feet or in a reasonable position that would allowed him to quickly regain his balance and stance.

After nearly an hour we were interrupted by an announcement from Captain Stonbersa over the vid screen. "Another broadcast is going out from the *DUSTEN*." The image then shifted to the bridge of the *DUSTEN*, where a clearly demented and rambling Commander Thimas glared into the screen.

"It would seem that the Federation is not taking me seriously. Admiral Regeny and his staff wish to play games with me, begging for more time to retrieve the solbidyum and the *TRITYTE* from where ever they have them hidden and that I should be tolerant and not send any more people of out the airlock, but rather I should allow them the additional time to accomplish their tasks. They take me for a fool. I know full well they are devising some fiendish scheme to try and regain the *DUSTEN,* but I am *not* so foolish. It seems that it is necessary to remind the Federation just how strong I, Captain Thimas… and the Brotherhood…," he quickly added, "are. Our word is never to be questioned."

As he said this, the scene shifted to the airlock, which was now filled with more panicking people. Once again the red light began flashing and Thimas' voice was heard saying in a sickening tone, "Bye, bye people... say thank you to the Federation for your little trip!"

Behind me I heard someone get sick as the airlock was opened and the people were again sucked out into space. "Now, let us get back to business, shall we?" said Thimas, his malevolent image displayed on the screen once more. His mental state had obviously deteriorated in the past hour; the mad look of desperation and his erratic mannerisms becoming more pronounced with each sentence. The front of his uniform displayed more blood, obviously from Captain Maxette, who could be seen tied in a chair in the background, his uniform also covered in blood and his head hanging down, but still moving. We at least knew that he was still alive.

"Like ex-captain Maxette, who I am sure would gladly tell you, if he could speak, just who is Captain of the *DUSTEN* now and that it is not wise to resist my wishes." Thimas walked behind Captain Maxette and, grabbing hold of his hair, lifted his head so his bloodied mouth could clearly be seen on the vid screen." Behind me I heard Rivez voice exclaim, "My stars, he's cut out Captain Maxette's tongue. Then I heard a thunk, and looked to see that Dakko had passed out.

"One hour and 100 more people go out the airlock, unless I have the solbidyum and the *TRITYTE* here." With a maniacal sing-song pitch he added, "More will go every hour until I do. I hope that this little demonstration makes it clear to all that I am not to be disobeyed!" The screen went blank again.

Only a moment later Lunnie's voice came across my wrist communicator, "I saw, Tibby... working as fast as I can.   No promises, but I may have it in about forty-five minutes."

Her message had barely ended when Admiral Regeny's image appeared on the vid screen. "Tibby, I know we're under a lot of pressure here, but we need to do something to stop this madman as quickly as possible. Do you have anything at all that we might be able to do soon?"

"We're doing all we can. I need *all* the available troopers and my security people to get down here immediately for a three minute dose of mental input martial arts learning. We do not have time to test it out; and we can only hope and pray that it will work. I will need Marranalis, Reidecor and, if I can have him, Lieutenant Commander Wanoll, as well as four other troopers to go with me on this mission. Lunnie thinks she can have the fake solbidyum container ready in less than an hour. Also, we need to move the *NEW ORLEANS* out of visual range of the DUSTEN, so we can release the *TRITYTE* without revealing the ship. Then we need to direct the *TRITYTE* remotely from the *NEW ORLEANS* while remaining cloaked until it falls within range of the *DUSTEN* to take over remote control. We have no time to test anything, so I suggest that, if anyone has any gods that they pray to, do it now."

"Tib, you can't do this. Please, it's too risky, you could all get killed." Kala's pleas were heartbreaking, but I knew that we had to press forward.

"Kala, if we don't do it, in one hour more people will die. We can't *really* let Thimas have the solbidyum and the *TRITYTE*, so what other choice do we have? Sooner or later Thimas is going to decide to start blowing things up on the planet and thousands or even millions will die. That's a violent madman over there. There's no reasoning with him."

Troopers began arriving at the facility we had set up for Cantolla and her team and the learning downloads started. Each download took three minutes and I needed all seven of the people going into the container with me implanted first. Reidecor retrieved re-breather masks from the *NIGHTBRIDGE*, as the oxygen levels in the container wouldn't be sufficient to sustain us inside. Forty minutes later we were assembled in the hangar area, as Lunnie delivered the mock solbidyum container to the *TRITYTE* using an automated platform device that functioned both as palette and a forklift, only without the forks.

Behind us teams of troopers boarded and prepared the few patrol ships we had aboard the *NEW ORLEANS* as fast at Cantolla and her team could process them. Their orders were to deploy from the *NEW ORLEANS* to the *DUSTEN*'s hangar with as much speed and stealth as possible, once my team secured the hangar area. They would clear the ship room by room, taking out the Brotherhood guards and troopers as they advanced, ultimately closing in on the bridge, where everyone would regroup to take the bridge. As security officer of the *DUSTEN*, Lieutenant Commander Wanoll knew the codes for every secured area and item on the ship, assuming that Thimas hadn't changed them; and it was unlikely that he had, given his state of mind. Wanoll would be able to override the lockout on the bridge and get our people inside. It wasn't to be pretty, but it was necessary.

Admiral Regeny was in the conference room with the High Command transmitting a message to the *DUSTEN* saying that Federation would meet the demands, that the *TRITYTE* was on its way and that the *DUSTEN* should have it on its sensors at any moment. There was no response from the *DUSTEN*, but they must have gotten the message; shortly after the transmission two patrol ships left the *DUSTEN* and took up positions flanking the hangar bay doors. We hoped this was intended to be a security measure on Thimas's part and that once the *TRITYTE* was aboard the *DUSTEN*, they would enter the hangar again.   Regardless of how things unfolded from here forward, we were committed to our plan now, fail or succeed.

The mock solbidyum container that Lunnie had made was a perfect replica, right down to a deep scratch that scarred one side of the original. Unless the two containers were closely examined side by side, I doubt anyone would be able to tell the difference. Lunnie showed us how to open the container from the inside. The conditions were not going to comfortable once all of us were inside. We would barely have room to reach the latching mechanism that would let us out; but we could, and that was all that mattered.

Just before I entered the container Kala ran to me, throwing her arms around me with tearful kisses. We were running of time; and much as I wanted to hold her in my arms, I knew that I needed to go.

The team and I did our best to use the few remaining moments to mentally prepare for what came next. We hoped that we wouldn't have to be in the container longer than two hours; and it was going to be a guessing game, as far as when to come out. From inside we would be able to detect some muffled sounds, but that was about all. There would be no view out of or into the capsule at all.

The *NEW ORLEANS* reached its position just outside the DUSTEN's sensor range when we entered the container and sealed it.   We were jostled about a bit as Lunnie positioned the container in the *TRITYTE.*

Moments later we felt a slight movement as the *TRITYTE* departed from the hangar of the *NEW ORLEANS* into space. Then all was quiet. We had no way of talking with the re-breathers on, so all we could do was to wait. I still had my grandfather's watch which, while not very useful on the galactic time system, still gave me an indication of how much time was elapsing. Fortunately it had an illuminated dial and I was able to see it. I had worn it out of habit on my left wrist, while on my right wrist I wore the short-range communication band.

It seemed like we were in the container for an eternity.   One thing we had not anticipated was the accumulation of body heat. Between the mounting heat and the natural loss of water from perspiration, the inside of the container was quickly becoming a sauna and we were all soaked in perspiration. This only seemed to add to agony and length of the trip. At one point we felt a slight lurch and I hoped it was the *DUSTEN* taking over control of the *TRITYTE*. Then, what seemed an unbearably long period of time passed before we felt another lurch and a bump. Shortly thereafter was the sound of movement inside the *TRITYTE* and the sounds of muffled voices. There seemed to be some excitement and scuffling about, but there was no real way to discern what was happening from inside the container. Finally, all was quiet and again we waited. A few times we heard what sounded like people walking about outside the container and then, at last, there was only silence. We waited for a long period before we decided to move; and I hoped it was safe for us to make our exit.

I triggered the release and our container opened silently.   Immediately, Reidecor and Marranalis were out, guns in hand and ready for action. Fortunately, no one was in the cargo hold. The cool, dry air of the ship and chilling effect of our wet clothing was a relief after being in the box, as we began a sweep of the inside of the *TRITYTE*. Everyone was quiet, relying entirely on hand signals for communication.   Reidecor took a peek outside the hatch door, which was open.   Two guards stood at the base.

Surprisingly, there were no others that we could see moving about; but then, with a limited number of rebels and several thousand hostages to contain, they probably couldn't spare anymore guards.

Both guards stood with their backs to the ship. We were close enough for both Reidecor and Marranalis to leap from the threshold and dispatch them both in an instant. Moving forward quickly as a team, we headed to the hangar control room. This too was empty. Now was the part that was going to be tricky; we were hoping that Commander Thimas would feel the need to gloat over his triumph and that by now he would be broadcasting on the vid screen, but he wasn't – the vid screens were black. We had no way of knowing how many people were on the bridge or whether the sensor screens were being monitored. We had to assume that Thimas would be doing so, as any ship's rational first officer would do. I asked Lieutenant Commander Wanoll for his opinion, since he was most familiar with the *DUSTEN*.

"If the *NEW ORLEANS* is close enough to the *DUSTEN* when they switch off the RMFF, they may not be detected," Wanoll said quietly. "Normally the sensors are set for long-range detection. On the other hand, the *NEW ORLEANS* is so large that is almost impossible for it to not make *some* sort of signature on the sensors. It could set off the collusion sensors because of its close proximity. If that happens, well, I have no idea what will happen on the bridge."

I thought for a minute. "Do you have any idea where they may be holding the non-rebel troops?" I asked Wanoll.

"I have an idea," he said. "A few years ago we had to transport about 3,000 criminals from Megelleon to Nigan.

We used one of the large cargo holds that has only one access, because it was easy to guard. I would bet that is where Thimas would hold any prisoners.

"Marranalis, do you know the hold he is talking about?" I asked.

"Yes, sir, I do," he said.

"Take another man and see if you can get there quickly. Take out the guards and free the troopers. Well give you fifteen minutes and then I'm going to open the hatch. Hopefully they will have monitors on the hold where the prisoners are located; and when you break them out, attention will be drawn in that direction to try and contain the situation, while we then open the hangar – hopefully without being noticed."

"Wait, Marranalis, before you go," Wanoll said. "Thimas may have put lockouts on the weapons lockers and you'll need to arm the troopers when you break them out. There is an arms locker not far outside the hold where the prisoners should be. Let me give all of you my security access code; it should allow you to override anything Thimas may have locked to prevent access to the arms and other secured areas. Only Captain Maxette can block me and Thimas from being able to override the lockouts.

It was about ten minutes later when alarms started going off and Thimas's voice was heard screaming across the vid system. "The prisoner's in the hold are escaping! STOP THEM! Get down there and STOP them! Kill them if you have to but get them back into that hold!" While he was screaming, we opened the hangar's airlock from the control room. The *NEW ORLEANS* suddenly materialized and its hangar door also opened while a group of patrol ships quickly moved away from it and into the hold of the *DUSTEN*. The entire event transpired in less than a minute.

No sooner did the last ship clear the hangar door of the *DUSTEN* than the *NEW ORLEANS* vanished. Two seconds later we saw a light display, as energy beams played over the RMFF field of the NEW ORLEANS. She was under fire from the *DUSTEN*. Claxons sounded on the *DUSTEN* and the call to battle stations went out over the com system. Thimas voice started screaming again. "INVADERS IN THE FORWARD HANGAR BAY! INVADERS IN THE FORWARD HANGAR BAY! KILL ALL PRISONERS AND ATTACK THE HANGAR BAY!" As he shouted these orders, the hangar airlock closed and, before it was totally pressurized, troops were pouring out of the cargo holds of the pilot ships and headed toward the access doors to the *DUSTEN*'s interior.

Flashes of laser fire could be seen in the corridor as the troopers entered and men could be heard fighting. I tried to contact Marranalis on the wrist com, but got no response.

"There's a wiring trunk access at the end of the hangar that will get us up to the next level. It's probably not being guarded. We can get to the bridge from there," Wanoll said. We managed to pick up another four troopers coming off the last patrol ship and they fell in with us as we followed behind Wanoll. The access he told us about turned out to be a long trunk with a manway ladder in it. We ascended nearly ten meters before reaching an access door on the level above. We exited into a corridor of what appeared to be an accommodations section. No one was in sight and all was quiet. We all paused and Wanoll whispered, "My cabin is just down this corridor. If we can get into it, we should be safe for a few minutes while I pull up images from the remote security station in my cabin. I can also isolate certain sections to trap some of the rebels."

We followed Wanoll the short distance to his cabin and watched him apply his palm to the scanner plate. The panel lit green and we all entered, the door closing silently behind us as Wanoll palmed the switch plate inside.

His accommodation was much smaller than I had expected, after having seen the luxurious accommodations elsewhere on the ship. Though smaller, the several-room suite was still lavishly furnished but also conservatively and tastefully decorated. Wanoll immediately went to a small room, only big enough for a few persons to squeeze in. Inside were rows of view screens and a large control console with an array of buttons and lights on it. Without any explanation Wanoll began bring up view after view on the screens. Many sections of the ship appeared to be abandoned, especially the areas normally designated as crew spaces and zones for military people. In the civilian sections, however, some people, though not many, milled about anxiously. These people were civilians living on the ship in the non-crew areas. Wanoll indicated that the doors leading out of those areas had a red light overhead, indicating that these doors were sealed to prevent access to the engineering and military parts of the *DUSTEN*. Views from the opposite side of the doors revealed two rebel guards who were there to make sure no one got in or out.

"I think for now, the civilians are safest where they are. If they were able to get out they would only get in the way," Wanoll said, and I had to agree. He panned to the hold were several hundred troops were being held captive. They all appeared dead. We couldn't tell from the image whether Marranalis and his men were inside with them when Thimas ordered them killed. It appeared that they had likely died from suffocation; no doubt Thimas had the air evacuated from the hold, killing them all in a matter of a minute or two. While I hoped that Marranalis and his men survived, it didn't bode well that I was unable to get a response from him on my wrist communicator.

Other scenes of the battles involving the troopers we had brought from the *NEW ORLEANS* didn't look too good either. The troopers appeared sluggish as they tried to use the martial arts techniques against the rebels in hand-to-hand combat, perhaps posing more of a liability than an asset. Many of them were getting killed or severely wounded while trying to use their untested skills. Obviously the headband training was a failure. We were losing the battle rapidly and it seemed that only a miracle could save us.

Wanoll did manage to isolate a few rebel troops in one area and lock them in from his security console; but the bulk of them were in areas where there was little he could do. Suddenly, as he was moving from view to view, a room appeared where a man was obviously torturing a woman. Wanoll paused and then zoomed in closer on the woman.

It was Lunnie.

"What?!" I exclaimed. "How did they get Lunnie? What's she doing here? Where is she? We have to rescue her!" I exclaimed with absolute panic. Wanoll activated some controls and we were able to hear the conversation in the room. "TELL ME! WHY WERE YOU ON THE *TRITYTE*!" the voice of Corporal Lexmal demanded. I had not recognized him with his back to the view screen. "What is the Federation planning to do? TELL ME YOU DOESEE!"

Lunnie was tied with her arms stretched out and attached to the wall. She was naked from the waste up and it was clear that she had been slashed and stabbed numerous times in an attempt to get her to divulge information.

"Isn't it obvious to you, loverboy? I came all this way just to be with you," Lunnie said in her usual mocking way, only through a swollen mouth full of blood. Lexmal struck her across the face so hard that I was sure she would be unconscious; and I was surprised when she turned her head to him and spit blood in his face. "That the best you can do... loverboy?" Lexmal's body blocked the view as he obviously attacked Lunnie, slashing yet more cuts into her body. She didn't scream, though we could hear her grunt in pain.

"Now tell me, doesee," said Lexmal forcefully. "Why were you hiding on the *TRITYTE*? Why?!"

"I told you, you asshole. I was taking a nap in my bunk on the *TRITYTE* and don't know anything about the Federation's plans. When I woke up the ship was already being hauled into the *DUSTEN* hangar and I hid, hoping not to be found."

Lexmal hit her again, just as the compartment door opened and Reidecor's voice rang out. "GET AWAY FROM HER, YOU FILTHY BASTARD!"

Lexmal spun around to face him; but then two guards that had been out of view, appeared with guns firing in unison at Reidecor. He fell dead just inside the door, as Lunnie screamed, "NO! REIDECOR, NO!!!!" as the rest of us realized in horror that Reidecor was missing from our group. He had apparently slipped out as soon as he figured out where Lunnie was being tortured and had gone to rescue her.

"How do I get to that compartment?!" I asked Wanoll. Immediately he pulled up a chart on the screen that showed our location and the route to the compartment. Fortunately, it was a relatively simple route. I told Wanoll and the others to continue on without me – that I was going to save Lunnie. Then, without waiting for a reply, I was out the door and headed down the corridor at top speed. I found one raider lying dead in the corridor, who had obviously encountered Reidecor and come out the loser. A few steps further and around a bend I found yet another. I approached the door to the compartment where Lunnie was being held, quickly palmed the door and was prepared to enter the door low, while quickly firing left and right at the two guards that I now knew to be in the room. When the door opened, I found myself staring at two legs of a guard who was apparently about to exit the compartment from the other side.

I felt a sharp blow on back of my head and all went black.

When I regained consciousness, I found I that couldn't move my arms or legs. I was upright, but my head was hanging on my chest and it felt like the back of my skull had been ripped off. I slowly opened my eyes, my head still down, trying to remember what had happened. Nearby, I heard voices and tried to focus on them.

"You sorry, slime-eating doesee, you'd better talk soon or I'm going to have to start removing body parts." It was Lexmal's voice, still threatening Lunnie. "How'd you like that? We could start with a few fingers, like ex-Captain Maxette, or maybe with the nipples. How about that, doesee? Now are you going to tell me the Federation plans or not?"

"I hope they slow roast you in the lava pools on Rivalon," Lunnie said. I lifted my head and turned to look at Lunnie and Lexmal just as he reached out to strike her again. He must have caught view of my movement, because he stopped just short of striking her and turned to look at me.

"Well, if it isn't our mighty heroooOOOOOO AhhHH!...." Lexmal let out a scream as Lunnie moved her head quickly, catching her teeth in a solid bite around Lexmal's little finger, which he had left lingering close to her mouth. I could hear the crunch from where I was; and two guards from the back of the room sprang forward, as Lunnie spit half of Lexmal's little finger out of her mouth and across the room.

"YOU DAMN DOESEE, DAMN YOU, DAMN YOU, I'LL SHOW YOU, YOU DAMN DOESEE!" Lexmal screamed, as he raised the knife in his other hand, slashing and stabbing Lunnie over and over again. I struggled against my restraints, trying to get free to help her; but no matter how hard I tried, I couldn't move. "DAMN DOESEE! Someone find my finger and get it on ice so the med unit can reattach it!" Lexmal shouted at the guards, as he tried to curb the blood flowing from the severed stub.

Lexmal looked over at me, his face a twisted mask of pain and rage. "Well Mister *martial arts* man, I guess all your fancy dancing hasn't done the Federation any good, has it? That crew that you brought over here is all but wiped out; only a dozen or so remain. You'll tell us what we want to know about the Federation plans, or I promise you, there will be so many pieces of you that if and when they find you no one will ever be able to recognize what you are." He walked over to me and pushed the blade of his knife through the palm of my right hand and twisted it. I bit down hard with my teeth trying not to scream out in pain.

"Tough guy, huh?" Lexmal said with a sarcastic grin on his face. "Good. That will make it all the better when you finally do scream and spill your guts!" He pulled the knife out of my hand and then rammed it to the hilt into the fleshy part of my thigh, twisting as he pushed his red, sweaty face close to mine and said, "I'm going to really enjoy this.

Now how about you tell me the Federations plans, and how they got so close to us without being detected." He twisted the knife again, making me wince and fight against a rapidly growing roar in my ears. "…and where the hell did they come from so quickly?"

He pulled the knife from my thigh and stabbed it into my biceps, twisting it again. "What's the matter, something got your tongue?" he laughed. "Aww, don't worry, I won't cut your tongue out like Captain Thimas did with Maxette. It's too bad that Captain Thimas got impatient with Maxette's refusal to acknowledge him as captain before he could get the codes for the solbidyum container. We'll get that soon enough. Our brothers on Tenner have the codes. They're only a few weeks away. And what's a few weeks for all that wealth, eh Tibby old boy? Maybe you'd like to share some of your wealth with me in the meantime – you know, to make me stop hurting you?" he said as he stabbed me in the opposite thigh digging and twisting again. "Now how about you TALK!"

"Didn't mommy tell you never to play with knives?" I said between gritted teeth.

"You know, you're almost as funny as Corporal Luinella, but she isn't laughing anymore now is she?" he said, again shoving his face up close to mine. I watched his eyes and, just as I saw him begin to blink, I slammed my head into his face as hard as I could. I could hear the crunching of bone as his nose broke. "AAAAGGHHHH! YOU! YOU BROKE MY NOSE! YOU, YOU!" Lexmal screamed as blood and tears ran down his face. He raised his knife and stabbed me in the chest, then immediately raised his knife to stab me again. I was sure that at any moment I would be joining Lunnie, when Thimas' voice came from the view screen over the door. "*LEXMAL, WHAT DO YOU THINK YOU'RE DOING?! STOP THIS INSTANT!* We need Tibby alive, you fool!" Lexmal lowered his knife and turned toward the screen. "He broke my nose! That asshole broke my nose!" he stammered.

"I don't care if he cut the damn thing off," growled Thimas. "We need him alive. We must know what he knows; and for what he's worth, his fortune alone can keep the Brotherhood funded and supplied for centuries."

Thimas's eyes turned toward Lunnie's body, hanging limp and dead against the wall. "What happened to her? Did she talk?"

"The damn doesee bit off my finger," Lexmal said holding his hand up so Thimas could see the still bleeding stump.

"YOU KILLED HER?! You *stupid* fool! You killed her! We could have used her to make the others talk. You *idiot*! Did you even try to get Tibby to talk by threatening to kill her? By the stars, I should come down there and cut all your fingers off and make you eat them!" Thimas exploded at Lexmal from the screen, while behind him I could see Captain Maxette taking advantage of the distraction, working to free his bindings while everyone else's eyes were on Thimas.

"I can make him talk," Lexmal stammered. "He's alright. He'll talk!"

"He better," Thimas said, "or you'll be having your gonads for your next meal!"

I coughed and blood came out of my mouth, my head was roaring and I could feel my eyes wanting to close. I knew what was happening…and I fought with everything I had to keep them open.

"YOU FOOL, HE'S DYING!" Thimas shouted. "You bumbling fool! Just as we were gaining the upper hand, you blow it *again*!" As he ranted, the door under the vid screen opened and the blurred outline of some people stood framed by the incoming light. For a minute I couldn't focus my eyes; but as they slowly came into the room I saw Kala between two large rebel guards, each with a firm grip on her arms.

"Well, well, well. Look what we have here... and just in time for the party," Lexmal said. "I believe, Captain Thimas, that Tibby is about to tell us everything he knows. Bring her up here, boys. Put her where her sister was!"

I looked at Kala's eyes as she caught sight of her lifeless Lunnie. Shock, horror and anger filled them as she drew a single, unwavering breath. I watched her face twist in rage and then suddenly, she became a blur of motion.

Rising from the depths of her fury I saw her perform a martial arts move I had only seen once before and had never been able to duplicate. In an instant she broke free from the grips of both guards and had grabbed their knives from their scabbards, as she lunged forward with lightning speed, never taking her eyes off of Lexmal. Her arms first flung outward, cutting the throats of both guards. As she ran forward screaming, "YOU KILLED MY SISTER!" two other guards in the room moved forward to stop her. Without hesitation, her arms crossed over each other in an X and then back again, and both guards dropped to the floor with blood gushing from their throats. There was no pause in her motion. With eyes still fixed on Lexmal, who stood frozen at the sight before him, Kala arms crossed once more, slashing back like scissors and severing Lexmal's head from his body.

From the screen I heard Thimas shout into the screen, "NOOOOOO!" Behind him Captain Maxette had quietly freed himself, while everyone on the bridge had their eyes glued to the screen, gaping at the event that was unfolding in front of me when Lexmal's head hit the floor. I saw Maxette reach with his good hand to grab a gun from the holster of one of the guards.

As blackness washed over me, I saw him take aim and shoot Thimas in the back.

I instantly found myself standing in an open meadow in knee-high grass. To the right and left of me were hills covered with huge old trees. A breeze blew through the grasses; and ahead of me a little ways I could see Lunnie walking toward an embankment. I tried to call out to her but my voice wouldn't work. As she reached the crest of a small hill, she paused to look back at me with a smile and say, "Go back Tibby, it's not yet your time. You still have more to do. Go back to Kala. Take care of her, Tibby, she loves you."

I felt myself being pulled back as I reached out my arms toward her. My head was filled with the buzzing of bees as light and colors swirled around me and I heard a voice say, "We got a pulse. He's coming around." Then all was peaceful and quiet and dark.

When I opened my eyes I realized I was in a bed. I could feel someone holding my hand and turned my gaze to see Kala there, her face still splattered with blood and her hair matted against her forehead. I could see that she had been crying, but she looked at me and smiled. I tried to talk, but I was barely able to say, "Hi."

"Oh, Tib, thank the stars you're still alive," she sobbed. "I couldn't live if I lost you, too."

"Lunnie," I whispered with tears in my eyes. Kala nodded, tears running down her cheeks.

One of the medics came in, looked at some instruments and gave me a shot with a device and then left. The shot seemed to give me a bit more strength and I asked, "Did we win?"

Kala grinned through her tears but could only nod her head yes.

"Reidecor's dead," I said, and Kala nodded again.

I paused for the briefest moment to struggle for a breath. "Marranalis?"

"He's in the next room – a bit banged up he'll be ok," Kala answered while wiping away a tear.

"Captain Maxette?" I asked, half knowing what the answer would be.

Kala shook her head. "But he got that scum, Thimas. That's what ended it. Once Thimas was dead, everyone else just surrendered."

"Kala, what happened? I mean, how did you get aboard the *DUSTEN*? Those martial art moves… I've never done those, I've only seen them. And the learning band… it didn't work. How…?"

"It's not exactly true that the learning bands didn't work, Tib," Kala replied. "After you and the others left for the *DUSTEN* in the *TRITYTE*, Cantolla discovered a wire in the device that was not connected securely. But it was too late. There weren't many troopers left on the *NEW ORLEANS* – only ten, in fact. We all used the headband after Cantolla fixed it, but there were no patrol ships left.

Fortunately, we were able to maneuver the *NEW ORLEANS* close to the aft hold where Thimas had been dumping people into space. He had left the hatch open. We turned the RMFF off and, using spacesuits and rocket packs, we jetted into the hold. With all the fighting onboard the *DUSTEN,* no one noticed us. Fortunately, the door switches on the *DUSTEN* were still keyed to my commands and I was able to activate the airlock door and get us inside. From there it was simply a matter of fighting our way forward. One of the prisoners we took was a person I knew on the *DUSTEN.* I think he was sick of what he was seeing unfold with the Brotherhood and with Thimas. He told me that Lunnie and you had been detained and were being tortured. The quickest way to find you was to get captured, so that's what I allowed to happen and, fortunately, they brought me to where you were before Lexmal could deliver a final blow and kill you. But I was too late for Lunnie," she sobbed; and I let her continue sobbing as long as she needed.

"Once Thimas and Lexmal were dead, the rebels simply surrendered and it was over. Tib, over 5,000 loyal Federation troopers died… and more than 300 diplomats and civilians that Thimas released into the vacuum of space."

I closed my eyes as I grasped for something good amid all the bloodshed. "Kala, I was there when Lunnie was killed. You would have been so proud of her. She is a true hero. She never broke under Lexmal's torture. She even bit off his finger in defiance. But what I don't know is how she got aboard the *DUSTEN* or how she got captured."

"I can answer that," Lieutenant Commander Wanoll's voice came from the doorway.

I looked over to see him enter the room and stand at the foot of my bed. "Glad to see you made it, Lieutenant Commander," I said.

"Actually, it's now Commander Wanoll," came another voice from the corridor. I looked again to see Admiral Regeny standing there. "He's temporary acting captain of the *DUSTEN*, until we find a new captain to replace Maxette."

"Admiral, it's good to see you." I choked back my grief and guilt. "I'm sorry. I'm sorry my plan was such a disaster... so many lives lost."

"Tibby, it wasn't your fault. From what we can see, your plan would have worked perfectly, if the learning device hadn't been compromised by the loose wire. As it was in the end, it did the job. As for the lives that were lost, well, Tibby, they are the casualties of war. Your actions were sound; and in the end it was your plan that kept the Brotherhood from winning. The Admiralty takes full responsibility for your actions, as we asked for and accepted your plans. Don't go shouldering the entire burden for these lives, Tib. We could have stopped you by saying no at any time. The fact of the matter is that we have not had any serious wars in the past two hundred years and we really don't know how to plan battles anymore. We have minor policing actions on planets from time to time and have quelled them with brute force – not with brilliant strategies. I fear that without your help we would have ended up blowing up the *DUSTEN* with all its passengers –civilians, military, diplomats, and rebels alike – to prevent the solbidyum from falling into the hands of the Brotherhood."

Kala interrupted, "You said you can explain how Lunnie got onto the *DUSTEN* and got captured."

"Yes," Commander Wanoll answered, as he walked to the view screen at the foot of the bed and placed a small chip in a slot along the side. "Corporal Luinella left a message on the computer of the *TRITYTE* for you. We just found it about an hour ago." Wanoll activated the screen and Lunnie's image appeared.

"Hi, sis. If you're seeing this vid, it's because I didn't make it back and I know that you and Tibby and a dozen others are wondering how and why I was on the *TRITYTE*. I had told Tibby that I could power the *TRITYTE* with a small fusion battery, which was true; but I didn't have time to make a solid connection and someone was going to have to be onboard to maintain the connection manually or it would have failed before the *TRITYTE* ever made it to the *DUSTEN*. I couldn't let Tibby know that... and I couldn't let the mission be delayed after seeing what that asshole Thimas had done to Captain Maxette, as well as all those other poor people on the *DUSTEN*.

I've never been one to try to be a hero; I only joined the service to be like you, Kala." Lunnie tilted her head and flashed her usual mischievous smile as she continued, "...and because there were lots of cute men in the service." But then her smile gave way to a more serious countenance. "I'm not trying to be a hero now, either, Kala, but I can't stand by and let more people die because, well, you know.

"Anyway, sis, I want you to know I love you, I always have. I am extremely glad that Tibby came into your life. I know he is not the man you dreamed of, because he is way *more* than you ever dreamed of... I can see it in your eyes every time you look at him. I know he loves you and I hope the two of you stay together, cuz if you don't, I will come back and haunt you both! Oh and one thing more, sis, if you and Tib have a baby girl – and I know you will – name her after me. I never believed in reincarnation; but if it exists, I can't think of two people I would want more for parents.

"I've got to go hide now. The *DUSTEN* has taken over controls of the *TRITYTE* and we'll soon be brought into their hangar. I was going to say wish me luck, but I guess you already know how that turned out."

Kala dropped her head against my chest, fortunately not where I was stabbed, and I put my bandaged arms and hands around her as we both sobbed. Lunnie had been a true hero in every sense of the word. Kala and I stayed like that for a long time; and when we finally looked up, the admiral and Commander Wanoll were gone, leaving us alone to share our grief and console each other in the wake of the tremendous loss.

Over the next few days I recovered quickly. I was able to see Sergeant Marranalis the next day. During the conflict at the cargo hold where the troopers were being held, he had managed to get into an adjacent compartment while under fire. When Wanoll sealed off some of the compartments to trap the rebels and prevent their movement in the ship, he also sealed in Marranalis with five of them. Marranalis took them on and single-handedly killed them all, but ended up with the broken leg and a concussion in the process – besides managing to break his communicator.

Three days later Marranalis, Kala and I left the *DUSTEN* and returned to the *NEW ORLEANS*. The *NIGHTBRIDGE* had been removed from our hangar and, other than for the patrol ships belonging to the troopers assigned to me by the Federation, and the just barely functional *TRITYTE,* the hangar bay looked pretty empty. Captain Stonbersa, Kerabac and Piesew welcomed us back. We rejoiced to see each other; and together we mourned the loss of Lunnie and Reidecor.

We would need a new ship's engineer, that was a certainty; but a pilot was another matter. With the

TRITYTE's future planned to become part of a flying museum exhibit, there was no need for a pilot – at least not at the moment. We would be spending our time either on the ground or on the *NEW ORLEANS*. Once we got back to Megelleon, I intended to have Captain Stonbersa acquire several shuttle craft for the *NEW ORLEANS*. Some of these would, of course, require pilots, but of a much lower caliber than Reidecor had been.

We had been back on Megelleon about three days when word came to us that the Federation was planning a special event to honor those who had fought for the Federation in what was now being called, oddly enough, the *Battle of the NEW ORLEANS and the DUSTEN*. Kala and I really didn't want to attend, the loss of Lunnie and Reidecor still aching wounds for us; but Admiral Regeny pointed out that Kala was still military and that he could make it an order. If Kala was going, I felt that I needed to be there as well; and so it was that Kala, Sergeant Marranalis, Kerabac, Captain Stonbersa, and I all dressed in our best formal whites and appeared at the event. Kala and I – and I imagine the rest of the crew – were of a pretty somber mood as we strode the carpeted walk from the shuttle to the Senate Hall where the event was to take place. This was the same hall where, just a few months earlier, I had been named *Tibby the Recoverer* and was given a vast fortune as the finder's reward for the recovery of the solbidyum. Back then I was filled with excitement and wonder at all that was happening. Last time I had walked briskly, but today I walked with a limp from the still healing wounds I received at the hands of Lexmal and the heaviness of the even greater wounds inflicted by grief and unshakable guilt. Once again, when we reached the two tall doors that went into the great hall, we paused as our escort lined us up; Kala and I entered first, side by side, followed by Marranalis, Kerabac and Captain Stonbersa, who were to walk three abreast. When we were all lined up, we entered the great hall and, unlike last time, the tables had been removed and chairs now crammed the space on every deck of the auditorium. We were told that over 100,000 people were in attendance.

Large screens around the hall displayed our images as we entered and all drew quiet as the escort moved forward to announce, "It is my honor to present Citizen Thibodaux James Renwalt, also known as Tibby the Recoverer, Major Kalana, Sergeant Marranalis, Captain Stonbersa and Kerabac. Citizens of the Federation, I present to you our heroes."

At this announcement everyone rose to their feet and loud cheers and applause rang throughout the hall, as we were led to a circular revolving stage in the middle of the Great Hall. Only one small table stood near the center of the arena bearing several objects. On each side of the table stood two cloth-covered pillars. Chairs circled the edge of the platform facing inward. All but five seats were filled and we were seated at the remaining chairs in the order in which our names had been announced. I was seated to the right of Leader Rieam. Leader Turaine was still off planet, as was Leader Maragon. Kala was seated to my right, and so on down the line until Kerabac was seated as the last of our group.

To Leader Rieam's left was Admiral Regeny; and it was he who first rose to speak. "Citizens of the Federation, we are gathered here today to pay respect and honor those who have shown outstanding performance and heroism on behalf of the Federation and without whose sacrifices this very planet may not be here today.

"By now all of you have heard the stories of how a group called the BROTHERHOOD OF LIGHT rose to mutiny within the Federation military forces, not only to steal the Federation's supply of solbidyum, but to overthrow the Federation military and government and place all its planets under their domination. In a few well-planned and daring actions, this rebel faction managed to quickly capture two large warships, the *TASSAGORA,* and the *DUSTEN.*

"With no other large warships within five days of the Megelleon system to come to the defenses of the capital, the Brotherhood also managed to capture over 80% of all patrol ships in the immediate area, leaving only one corvette, the *NIGHTSHADE*, and the remaining 20% of the patrol ships to protect all of Megelleon. The Brotherhood attacked and bombed the Federation High Command headquarters; and only by the foresight of Tibby the Recoverer was the High Command spared. Fortunately, the High Command prudently took the solbidyum away from the Federation base where it was being stored and secreted it away to a place known only to the officers of the High Command.

"Let me pause to say here and now that the dispensing of the solbidyum will occur as promised and that not one grain of it has been lost.

"When the *DUSTEN* and the *TASSAGORA* fell to enemy hands, the Brotherhood was controlling and running operations from a secret underwater base. It was Tibby who devised the plan that got the Brotherhood to lead us to their headquarters and it was Captain Stonbersa who provided us the information needed to find the hidden base. It was from the Tibby's yacht, the *NEW ORLEANS*, that the Federation High Command gave the orders for the base to be destroyed. No one could foresee the extent of explosive force that would be generated by the destruction of the base and we can only conclude that a large arsenal of explosives existed within its confines.

"It is through Tibby's generosity that a special fund has been set up to see that all persons suffering damage from the giant waves created by the blast will receive full compensation for their losses and that each family who lost a loved one shall receive one million Federation credits." Applause and cheering broke out once again.

"It was Tibby who devised the plan," Regeny continued, "to destroy the *TASSAGORA* and a large portion of the patrol ships that had fallen to the Brotherhood rebels. I am not at liberty to tell you how this was accomplished, as it is classified information that is vital to planetary defense. I can only tell you that it is because of Tibby that this victory was possible. It was Tibby, again, who came up with the means for us to enter the enemy-held *DUSTEN* and bring an end to the tyrannical occupation and threat posed by its captors. Though many lives were lost, thousands more lives on the ship and possibly millions of lives here on Megelleon would have been lost, had it not been for his plan and his actions. It was Tibby who personally led the raid on the *DUSTEN,* where he was captured, tortured, and nearly killed in the effort to free the hostages and reclaim the ship and to keep the Federation's solbidyum out of the hands of the enemy.

"Tibby did not act alone. Many others who were involved paid the supreme sacrifice to preserve our freedom and to keep the solbidyum out of the hands of the Brotherhood. Many of you have heard and seen demonstrations of Tibby's fantastic skills in hand-to-hand combat, a technique that he calls *martial arts*. It was hoped that special units could be trained with these techniques in order to fortify our ranks against the increasing violence of the Brotherhood. Unfortunately, time didn't permit for this to fully happen and desperate measures were used to try to bring about a more rapid training. This process didn't happen soon enough for the troopers going into battle against the enemy; hence, most of them died trying to reclaim the *DUSTEN* from the armed traitors. Though vastly outnumbered, records indicate that these troopers still managed to take out three rebels for every one of their lives that were lost. There were, however, a few individuals trained in these skills who *did* ultimately bring about the downfall of the Brotherhood rebels. We will address this more later.

"In recognition of his actions and sacrifices that have done more to save the united peoples of the Federation than any other person in the history of the Federation territories, the Federation Military High Command wishes to acknowledge Tibby the Recoverer's outstanding service to the Federation forces by bestowing on him the honorary title of Vice Admiral and proclaims that he shall be shown all the respect, recognition and benefits that the rank of Vice Admiral in the Space Fleet affords."

This pronouncement was followed by yet another round of applause, while an aide handed a leather-bound document to the Admiral, who in turn handed it to me. "Now, I believe that Leader Rieam has something to say."

Leader Rieam rose and moved to the podium. "Vice Admiral Tibby, for your selfless service to the Federation; and for placing yourself in harm's way to prevent the solbidyum from falling into the hands of the enemy; and for your planning and leadership in a raid to prevent the loss of more lives and possibly the loss of the Federation itself; it is the will of the Senate that we bestow on you the highest honor the Federation has reserved for a citizen. From this day forward you shall be known as First Citizen Tibby the Recoverer. The title of First Citizen has only been given out three times in the past six hundred years. We are proud to bestow this title upon you."

Applause rang out through the hall. Leader Rieam went back to her seat and once more Admiral Regeny took the podium.

Admiral Regeny continued, "As stated before, Tibby did not do all of this alone. Kerabac performed dangerous and complicated navigation procedures that made it possible for all of these things to happen. I regret that, once again, I cannot reveal details, as most of this information is classified. Captain Stonbersa, who, I regret to say, is recently retired from the Federation Space Force, but is now Captain of Tibby's space yacht, the *NEW ORLEANS*, also played an enormous and dramatic role not only in delivering the blow to the Brotherhood's headquarters, but in the successful transport of troopers to the *DUSTEN* and the recovery of this Federation ship. His outstanding skills as a captain made it possible for recovery operations to succeed.

"Sergeant Marranalis, a trooper of the Federation Space Force on special assignment to the now Vice Admiral and First Citizen Tibby, trained diligently under Tibby in the martial arts and led a team in an attempt to rescue the loyal troopers held captive in *DUSTEN*. During the skirmish he was trapped in a compartment with five rebel troopers, whom he was able to overcome utilizing hand-to-hand combat methods taught to him by Tibby. It was Marranalis who trained and led both the troopers of the Federation fleet and Tibby's personal security team in the taking of the *DUSTEN*. Sergeant Marranalis is, as of today, officially elevated to the rank of lieutenant. Congratulations, Lieutenant Marranalis.

"During the actions taken to recover the *DUSTEN,* two individuals showed the ultimate acts of courage and heroism. Without the bravery and conviction of these two individuals, the mission would have failed. The first of these two individuals was Corporal Luinella, affectionately known to her crew members and friends as Lunnie.   Corporal Luinella was an Engineer with the Federation Space Force and was assigned to permanent duty under First Citizen Tibby. During one of the critical phases of the operation to retake the *DUSTEN*, Corporal Luinella discovered that a critical component on one of the crafts used in the operation was faulty and that only by placing herself at risk of being captured would the ship be able to perform its crucial function. Rather than allow the mission to fail because of this one piece of equipment, Corporal Luinella stayed with the craft, unbeknownst to her fellow crewmates, so that the recovery operation could unfold with the strongest possible force. Had she not done so, additional lives would have been lost. Corporal Luinella was captured by the enemy and brutally tortured and mutilated without ever revealing a single detail of the operation that was taking place. She was able to inflict injury to her torturer, none other than the traitor and fugitive, Corporal Lexmal, by biting off his finger even though she was physically restrained. She was then brutally stabbed multiple times. Corporal Luinella died as a result of the injuries and torture inflicted upon her.

"Likewise, Captain Maxette, Captain of the *DUSTEN* who, after being captured, mutilated by having his fingers cut off and his tongue cut out, managed to free himself from his restraints, steal a gun from a rebel guard and kill the Federation traitor and rebel leader, Commander Thimas, before dying himself at the hands of his remaining captors.

"I now turn the podium over to Leader Rieam for the next portion of the ceremony."

Leader Rieam took the podium and began, "For their unselfish sacrifice and dedication to the Federation above and beyond the call of duty and in recognition of their courageous actions by which the Federation was saved from possible defeat and annihilation, the Federation bestows posthumously on Captain Maxette and Corporal Luinella the Honor of First Citizens of the Federation and, so that the memory of their ultimate sacrifice will not be forgotten and that all shall remember them for ages to come, the Federation has commissioned these statues in their honor…" There was a brief pause while the coverings over the pillars were withdrawn to reveal two perfectly detailed statues of Captain Maxette and Lunnie, twice their actual size, carved from a magnificent, opalescent stone.   Leader Rieam continued, "…that shall stand in the main plaza of the Capitol building for all to see and remember." Kala turned and grabbed hold of me and we both wept openly, as Leader Rieam said, "I now return the podium to Admiral Regeny."

Regeny took the podium once more and began, "There is one more who must be recognized, without whose actions none of this would be celebrated at all. Without this person, Tibby would have died, Corporal Luinella's death would have been in vain, Captain Maxette never would have been able to reach the gun and shoot Commander Thimas, and the BROTHERHOOD OF LIGHT would have prevailed. What you are about to witness on the vid screens about the hall is gruesome, I must warn you, but it is necessary for you to see and understand the full gravity of the situation and the importance of this single individual in all that has happened."

On the vid screen appeared in split-screen view the scenes that unfolded on the bridge of the *DUSTEN* and in the hold where Lexmal had killed Lunnie and tortured me. The scene started at the point where Thimas shouted, "You fool! He's dying, you bumbling fool! Just as we were gaining the upper hand, you blow it *again*!" Within the scene taking place in the compartment where I was held Lunnie's body could be seen in the background, hanging lifeless against the wall, and me, also hanging from restraints with blood streaming from my wounds, while in the foreground stood Lexmal looking back at the vid screen over the door from which Thimas's image yelled.

Suddenly, light streamed in from the opening door, and the shadows of three people stretched across the floor as they moved into the room. Kala is seen clearly, her arms gripped by two goonish rebel troopers. Lexmal can be heard saying, "Well, well, well. Look what we have here, and just in time for the party. I believe, Captain Thimas, that Tibby is about to tell us everything he knows! Bring her up here, boys. Put her where her sister was!"

Kala stiffens and suddenly becomes a blur of motion as she performs a martial arts movement so swiftly that it is almost indiscernible in all its detail. In an instant she breaks free from the guards and is suddenly seen holding the knives from their scabbards; and, while moving in on Lexmal, her ultimate target, she flashes her arms across the throats of her captors and two additional guards who rush in to subdue her. The swift crossing of her arms unfolds in a single blur of metal and blood, her gaze never leaving Lexmal, who stood frozen in fear before her. As Kala arms cross once more, Lexmal's head is severed and the enemy is defeated.

At the same time, the scene at the bridge is displayed on the other half of the split screen as Thimas shouts, "NOOOOOO!" while behind him Captain Maxette frees himself from his bonds and reaches with his good hand to grab a gun from the holster of one of the guards and shoot Thimas in the back.

The audience let out a collective gasp as the vid screen went blank. Kala once more buried her face in my sleeve, sobbing and weeping.

Admiral Regeny continued, "In order for Major Kalana to get to Lexmal and rescue her crewmates, she had to deliberately allow herself to be captured. She did so knowing that she would likely be killed, but she triumphed by killing the escaped traitor, Corporal Lexmal, and, in doing so, put into motion the events that lead to the death of the traitor and rebel ring leader, Commander Thimas. In recognition of her demonstration of skill and dedication to duty, the Federation Space Force elevates Major Kalana to the rank of Lieutenant Commander.   Congratulations Lieutenant Commander Kalana. I believe that Leader Rieam has something to say also."

Leader Rieam rose and moved to the podium. "Lieutenant Commander Kalana, for your selfless service to the Federation and for placing yourself in harm's way to prevent the solbidyum from falling into the hands of the enemy and to bring an end to the tyranny of Lexmal and aiding in the defeat of the tyrant, Thimas, the Federation is proud to bestow upon you the Title of First Citizen and the Title of Kalana the Avenger. Never before in the history of the Federation have there been two living persons holding the title of First Citizen at the same time; however, we cannot conceive that of one of these two individuals is less deserving than the other. So it was the will of the Senate that both be so named. There can be no persons more deserving of the title than you, First Citizen and Kala the Avenger, and you, Honored First Citizen Tibby the Recover." Concluding her announcement, she walked to Kala and kissed her on the forehead, then to me, also kissing me on the forehead for the second time in just weeks. Kala and I turned to each other and, in front of thousands of people, embraced and kissed, as all in attendance cheered and applauded.

And that, my children is how I came to be known as First Citizen Tibby the Recoverer and how your mother came to be known as First Citizen Kalana the Avenger.

THE END

of

BOOK 1 – BATTLE OF THE NEW ORLEANS

SOLBIDYUM WARS SAGA – BOOK 2
SWEET HOME ALLE BAMMA

Having barely recovered from injuries that nearly took his life in the battle with the Brotherhood of Light to reclaim the Federation star ship DUSTEN, Tibby must fight again in a struggle of a different kind when both he and Kalana are poisoned by enemy operatives. Tibby's Earth DNA proves to be stronger than the deadly poison; Kalana, however, is rapidly succumbing and must be placed into stasis. One antidote exists against this toxin and it can only be found on the remote planet of Alle Bamma, a non-aligned jungle world on the fringe of the Federation territories. Tibby abandons Admiral Regeny in the Federation's plan to ambush the Brotherhood at the planet Prolaxen, in order to race to the jungle planet with his crew aboard the space yacht, NEW ORLEANS, in search of the rare Rugian eggs that are required to make the antidote. Tibby arrives at Alle Bamma only to discover that the Brotherhood has established bases and drug labs on the planet for processing the illicit drug called God's Sweat and that they have enslaved the indigenous natives to harvest and process the drug. In order to save Kalana, Tibby and crew must defeat the Brotherhood, free the natives, find the Rugian eggs, and deal with a mysterious god entity called Thumumba.

About the Author

Dale Musser was born in 1944 in a small rural community of Pennsylvania. From 1967 until 2012 he was employed as a structural and piping designer in the industries of marine and offshore resources, cogeneration power and hard rock mining. His work at three shipyards and assignments with several  engineering and naval architectural firms during his careers in Virginia, Texas, and Maine, took him to such places as London, U.K., Abu Dhabi, U.A.E., Scotland and Mexico. During this time, he was responsible for the design of reactor compartments for nuclear aircraft carriers and submarines for the U.S. Navy and the structural designs of numerous offshore semi-submersible oil rigs, tanker ships, supply boats, and other vessels and equipment used in the offshore industry. After the death of his wife in 1999, Mr. Musser changed careers and went to work in Arizona and Utah in the hard rock mining industry. He retired in Fall of 2012 and currently resides in Mesa, Arizona; however, his plans for the near future involve a move to New Mexico.

Dale enjoys rock hunting and lapidary work, gourmet cooking, writing, poetry, art, music, religions and philosophy in small doses, astronomy and the sciences in general, hiking, camping, the outdoors and the gifts that nature provides. Mr. Musser is a member of Mensa and remains an avid reader, having lost count of all the books he has read after 3,000.

The greatest joy in his life is his daughter, Heather. Affectionately they call each other "BUBBY."

Contact Information:

Those wishing to write to Mr. Musser may do so at
dalemusser1944@yahoo.com.   Although he attempts to
answer all correspondence, heavy emails may prevent him
from responding to everyone.